A KIND OF IMMORTALITY

Margaret Thomson Davis has lived in Glasgow from the age of three, except when evacuated during the war. She is the author of eighteen previous novels, an autobiography and over two hundred short stories.

Also by Margaret Thomson Davis

The Breadmakers
A Baby Might Be Crying
A Sort of Peace
The Prisoner
The Prince and the Tobacco Lords
Roots of Bondage
Scorpion in the Fire
The Dark Side of Pleasure
The Making of a Novelist (Autobiography)
A Very Civilised Man
Light and Dark
Rag Woman, Rich Woman
Daughters and Mothers
Wounds of War
A Woman of Property
A Sense of Belonging
Hold me Forever
Kiss Me No More

A Kind of Immortality

Margaret Thomson Davis

ARROW

Published by Arrow Books in 1997

1 3 5 7 9 10 8 6 4 2

© Margaret Thomson Davis 1996

The right of Margaret Thomson Davis to be identified as the author
of this work has been asserted by her in accordance
with the Copyright, Designs and Patents Act, 1988

First published in the United Kingdom by
Century in 1996

Arrow Books Limited
Random House UK Limited
20 Vauxhall Bridge Road, London SW1V 2SA

Random House Australia (Pty) Limited
20 Alfred Street, Milsons Point, Sydney
New South Wales 2061, Australia

Random House New Zealand Limited
18 Poland Road, Glenfield, Auckland 10, New Zealand

Random House South Africa (Pty) Limited
Endulini, 5a Jubilee Road, Parktown 2193, South Africa

Random House UK Limited Reg. No. 954009

A CIP catalogue record for this book
is available from the British Library

Papers used by Random House UK Limited
are natural, recyclable products made from wood grown in
sustainable forests. The manufacturing processes conform to
the environmental regulations of the country of origin

ISBN 0 09 935361 X

Printed and bound in Great Britain by
Cox & Wyman Ltd, Reading, Berkshire

To my son and my adopted son,
the two men I most admire

The loneliness which we rightly dread is not the absence of human forces or voices – it is the absence of love ... Our wisdom therefore must lie in learning not to shrink from anything that may lie in store for us, but so to grasp the master key of life as to be able to turn everything to good and fruitful account.

Caroline E. Stephen, *Christian faith and practice in the experience of the Society of Friends*

Art was given for that;
God uses us to help each other so,
Lending our minds out ...

Fra Lippo Lippi
Robert Browning

LOVE

Love endures through all our years, and ties
Us fast together, though with silken ropes;
Love need not shout, nor look with jealous eyes,
But seals in quiet trust our faiths and hopes,
And when surrounded by our darkest shades
Love is the guiding light that never fades.

But more than this, when we are gone
Our love will live in memoried care,
And others in their loving dawn
May feel its presence in the air.

James Muir

I

BESSIE ALEXANDER KNEW she was a disgrace. She sat in the Quaker Meeting House with head lowered, listening to the reverent tick of the clock on the wall high above her. To all outward appearances she was a decent, pious woman of forty years, loyal wife of Peter, devoted mother of Daisy. Instead of praying, however, she was thinking randy thoughts about Gregory Seymour. The awful thing was, he was married as well. Her thoughts became so lewd and indecent that her cheeks began to burn and she surreptitiously glanced around, afraid that some of her fellow worshippers could see into her heart. But everyone except her seemed perfectly at peace in the deep silence in the Meeting House.

It was a spartan place of plain painted walls, with no curtains at the window. Everyone sat on wooden benches arranged in a three-sided square with a table at the fourth side. At the table two elders, a man and a woman, sat, sometimes with closed eyes, sometimes just staring blankly out at their fellow Quakers. Their inward eye, Bessie felt sure, was concentrating on higher things. On the table lay a copy of the Bible, a copy of *Christian faith and practice in the experience of the Society of Friends*, and a copy of *Advices and Queries*. The latter was the nearest thing Quakers, or members of the Society of Friends, to give it its proper name, had to dogma. Except it was nothing like dogma. It didn't lay down any law. It didn't answer any questions.

Her question at the moment was: should she or shouldn't she? Gregory was doing everything he could to persuade her. She didn't need any persuading, really. She wanted to. Indeed, in her mind, she'd had wild, passionate sex with him a thousand times. She was doing it again!

Hastily she picked up her copy of *Advices and Queries* and opened it at random.

'Are you patient and considerate,' she read, 'even towards those whom you find it hard to like and those who seem to you unloving and ungrateful?'

Sometimes she felt she'd been too damned patient and considerate with Peter. That was half her trouble. And he was certainly unloving and ungrateful. Not that she wanted any gratitude. But a little loving now and again wouldn't have gone amiss. Of course it could be argued that it was all her own fault right from the beginning.

She began to sweat again. Fool! Fool! And a wicked one at that. She stole a glance at the person sitting next to her. It was Mary Harvey, looking serene in a khaki anorak and striped woolly hat and apparently unaware of the proximity of such wickedness. Of course what had happened when she'd first met Peter was before she'd joined the Society of Friends. Peter had been, and still was, her father's accountant. He 'did' her father's books. Or at least one set of them. She knew perfectly well that her father kept two sets of books for the shop: one for Peter and the taxman, another truer account for himself. Mother and Father were devout members of the Church of Jesus and worshipped in that imposing building with its spire reaching high into the heavens. But it was the stained-glass windows that had fascinated her when she was a child.

Oh dear, oh dear. Bessie mentally shook her head. The hypocrisy of it all. It surely wasn't necessary to defraud the income tax in order to succeed in business. There were many Quaker firms to prove that honesty could be the best policy. Cadbury's, Fry's, Rowntree, Horniman's Tea, Clark's Shoes, to mention but a few. Indeed, she sometimes thought that Quakers seemed to have an embarrassing knack of making a great deal of money if they went into business.

She'd met Peter when he'd come to the house to see her father.

It had happened one New Year's Eve when her sister Moira was spending New Year with a colleague in Dundee. Mother and Father were away at a friend's ruby wedding party which coincided with New Year. They were staying in a hotel and couldn't take the dog, so she was detailed to be dog-sitter. She had been surprised when they'd trusted her with old Towzer. They had never believed she was good enough for anything else. Of course they were probably quite right. Peter, not knowing they were away (or so he said), had arrived on the doorstep on Hogmanay to 'first foot' them. He had brought the traditional bottle of whisky and piece of coal for good luck. Some good luck he'd brought her!

But then she shouldn't have drunk so much. Well, she didn't really. Not that much. She just wasn't used to the stuff. She didn't even like the taste of whisky.

But there you are. The next thing was she'd woken up feeling hung over and awful cramped in bed. Then, swivelling a bloodshot gaze sideways, she'd been astounded to see this baldy-headed wee man lying in bed beside her. Shock! Horror! He wasn't quite old enough to be her father. But almost. She'd never liked him. Then the guilt set in. She could almost see her mother rearing up at the foot of the bed pointing an accusing finger.

'You have sinned!' Again! Bessie was always doing something wrong. Admittedly this was a new low.

Even yet, after twenty years of marriage, she still squirmed. She still suffered mental anguish at the thought.

She should never have married him. Especially when it meant taking on his old devil of a father as well. But there it was. Her mother, her father, the Sunday School, her sister Moira, the Bible class, the Church, God Himself, had all seemed to gang up against her at the time and force her to assuage her guilt and make an honest woman of herself by entering holy matrimony.

How could she have done such a thing? Of course, this was an all too familiar cry about everything. Every member of her family flung the question at her at some time or other.

Not only about marrying Peter. As if it wasn't enough that she had never fitted into her parents' home. Now she didn't fit into her husband's. Nor had she ever fitted into their church. On the occasions when her father was in a jolly mood, like in the shop on a good day, he'd say, 'I think there's been a

3

mistake with Bessie. Either there was a mix-up in the maternity hospital, or she's a changeling.'

She'd grown up with their reluctance to lay claim to her. Even her granny, when she'd been alive, and a kinder woman you couldn't meet, often used to say, 'I don't know where she's come from.'

It wasn't her appearance. Or maybe it was? She could never be sure about anything. Nowadays she tended to slouch about in trousers, baggy tops and comfortable sandals. And she was always getting her clothes and her hair smudged with paint. Her mother and Peter and even Daisy were always lecturing her about what she ought to wear. And why she should give up this filthy hobby she had of painting awful pictures. Her mother, in a gentle way; Peter with his own almost permanent sneer. It infuriated Peter how she spent so much of his 'good money' on canvases and paints and 'all that rubbish'. He had tried every way he could to cure her of this 'ridiculous habit' down through the years. All to no avail. She could be too soft and easily put down in other ways but as far as fighting to keep on painting was concerned, she was like a tiger.

'It's an obsession with you,' Peter accused. 'It's not natural.'

There was a floored loft area in the flat with a ceiling that sloped almost down to the floor at one side. It had big dormer windows that let in lots of light. Bessie had immediately commandeered it as her studio and kept her easel and all her canvases up there. She had spotlights fixed up so that she could, if necessary, work late at night. Often that was her only chance, because during the day Granda always needed so much attention. And of course there was all the cooking, housework and shopping to do. Often when Peter commanded her to come down from her loft retreat she responded by desperate singing to drown out his voice, or shouted out, 'I'm not listening. I'm not listening.' Sometimes she took the radio up and turned it on full blast to drown him out. Or she'd belt out Beethoven's Ninth Symphony on the record player.

Daisy was embarrassed and ashamed of her. Daisy was a younger version of her Aunt Moira, whereas Bessie was as different from them both as chalk and cheese. Old photos showed her with a riot of fair curly hair. Her mother said it

4

was a terrible job to keep that hair tidy. She had serious eyes and a gentle, timid expression, almost as if she was expecting someone to hit her. Nobody did, of course. At least, not at home. She'd got the belt a few times at school but then, who hadn't?

Moira had straight, dark hair like in youthful photos of their mother and father. Right from an early age Moira had to wear glasses (also like Mother and Father). Moira had always been the favourite. Moira had been brainy, of course, and always correct and conventional, even as a child. Now she was a senior librarian. She had never married and was still at home in Bearsden with Mother and Father.

Bessie couldn't imagine Moira getting drunk and sinning with a man. Or being dreamy and forgetting things she'd been asked to do. Or not being able to hold down a 'decent' job. Or – horror of horrors – wanting to go to Art School and mix with all the hippie riff-raff in the country.

The 'decent' job had been helping Dad in his small but select menswear shop in Bearsden. She was never allowed to measure an inside leg, although once she had while Dad had slipped through to the back shop to the lavatory. She'd protested later in her own defence that he'd never told her that that particular part of the job, or the anatomy, was taboo.

'If you'd any common sense or decency you wouldn't need to be told,' her father had said. 'You just can't be trusted for a minute on your own.' The later incident at New Year proved this to be only too true.

Now her senses were in danger of deserting her again. Mother and Father had always tried to stop her 'wasting time' with drawing or painting pictures. It had been all right at first when she'd been small. Well, not *perfectly* all right, because they never understood her pictures. Nobody did. Least of all Peter who made such a fool of them. Peter's old father, who was the Neil Alexander half of the accounting firm, Alexander & Son, was the same. She was sure he had Alzheimer's disease but Peter wouldn't hear of it. Peter's talent was to close his mind and shut his eye to anything he didn't want to acknowledge, and he had become a hundred times worse since the time not so long ago when she'd put one of her pictures into the Shawlands church bazaar. Gregory Seymour, who had come along with the people he'd been visiting, had not only bought it but had tracked her down to tell her how original and talented she was.

He was an art dealer and owned a couple of art galleries. Surely he must know what he was talking about. He certainly seemed a very intelligent and knowledgeable man. Oh joy of joys! Oh warm glow of gratitude! Oh golden mesh of delight! She would have done anything for him: fallen at his feet, kissed the ground he walked on.

When he asked to see more of her work she dug out canvases from under the stairs, from up in the loft, from under the bed. He was astonished and undeniably impressed. He stood, stroking his beard and staring at her pictures. He'd suggested an exhibition of her works at one of his galleries. It was a very small gallery and the exhibition had only been on for a few days, so no more than a handful of people had seen the paintings. Nevertheless, Peter had been furious as well as shocked. So had her parents. Admittedly some of the pictures contained nude, rude parts. That reminded her of one of her earliest sins. Her mother and father had never to this day got over it. She had been hardly more than a child herself when she'd persuaded a boy to strip off so that she could make an accurate drawing of his body. Such a thing had never happened in the history of Bearsden.

She could defend herself in one thought – if only to herself. After all, they hadn't allowed her access to books on anatomy, and had subsequently forbidden her to go to Art School. They had threatened God's wrath and her rapid descent into hell if she went to evening classes on the subject. They had heard that there were nude models there as well as in the Art School. They sincerely believed, because they were fundamentally sincere, good people, that this strange side of her nature, this peculiarity, was something that, for her own sake, her own protection, had to be rooted out, purged and purified.

It wasn't as if she drew nice flowers or fruit and just as a wee hobby. She seemed to have this shameful obsession with naked bodies. There was something, it seemed to them, unnatural and obscene about her pictures that truly upset them. She was really sorry. Over and over again she tried to stop, tried to please them, but failed. Now her thoughts were scattered by the sudden creak of the bench as someone got up to speak – or 'give ministry', as they called it in the Society of Friends. It was Penelope Braithwaite (a right old Quaker name, that). She had chosen to read from the *Advices and Queries*. What was said in ministry often spoke to someone's 'condition', to use another Quaker phrase. In this case it was Bessie's.

'Do any of your interests, important though they may appear to you, unduly absorb your time and energy to the hindrance of your growth in grace and of your service to God?'

Could this mean her interest in art? Or the art gallery owner, Bessie wondered. Probably both. Remembering Gregory – big, barrel-chested, very masculine Gregory – started her thinking of sex again. And could anyone blame her? She'd never had any for about fifteen years. Not since Peter had become impotent. Or, as he said, 'gone off' her. He'd only married her in the first place because he had to, he said. Out of respect for her parents, not her. She'd missed a period. Fancy, just after that one time at New Year.

But there you are. Everyone would blame her. She blamed herself. Especially for what she was thinking right now. She lowered her head again.

She wished there was music at Meeting for Worship. It would have been a welcome diversion. However, although there were other occasions devoted to music, Meeting for Worship concentrated on just that. No music, no clergy, no rituals – nothing was supposed to come between each individual and their direct communication with God. Normally she enjoyed the silence and the idea of communication, but today she was too busy tussling with herself.

'Oh to hell!' she thought eventually, knowing at the same time that that was exactly where she was heading.

II

WHEN JENNIFER ANDERSON was small she absolutely
adored Andrina. She had never looked like anyone else's
mother, with her beautiful turquoise eyes, her warm ruby-
coloured hair and her curvaceous body. Jennifer remembered
desperately wanting to stay with her when the marriage broke
up and her father walked out. As a little girl at primary school,
it had been Robert she'd hated for taking her away from
Andrina. Her hatred had been a powerful force that could
visibly shake her whole body. Yet she still loved him. It was
funny how such strong emotions could alternate or even exist
side by side at the same time.

No one had explained why the marriage had come to an
end. Her mother had been bitter and said that Daddy had left
them because he didn't love them any more. Every time she'd
had access to Jennifer, Andrina had bitterly complained about
Robert. After he remarried, Jennifer had been sent back to
her mother.

Now, at sixteen years of age, Jennifer had grown to resent
her mother for many reasons, but most of all for putting her
against her father. As a young child she had been insecure
enough without being devastated, utterly destroyed, by her
mother's bitterness. In one way, her mother telling her about
all the things she'd suffered with Robert and what a bore he'd
been seemed to bring them closer together. After all, Andrina
had never spoken much to her before and she'd always longed
for her mother's attention. So often she'd been ignored by her,
told to go away and be quiet, banished to her granny's, been
forgotten and left at school. She'd learned to come home on
her own, despite the intimidation of the busy roads between
school and the flat. Then if her mother wasn't there, she'd

either sit on the stone steps outside the building, or she'd go across to Glasgow Green. Their building was practically *in* the Green, it was so close. She'd wander about the Green for a while trying not to feel hungry. Or worse – frightened. Not because of the tramps and old winos who sometimes hung about the place. Her terrors were always that her mother would not return. She always did return, though. Usually looking flushed and out of breath and looking more beautiful than ever. She'd hug Jennifer and hurry her inside saying, 'Don't tell Daddy I was late, will you, darling? It wasn't Mummy's fault. Mummy needed to do so much shopping in town and the traffic was horrendous on the way back.'

Jennifer had always been so relieved and happy to see her again, so surrounded by the warm glow of the hug that she'd never noticed the lack of shopping. Never one package or parcel. Never one shopping bag. Now she remembered with a bitter twist of her mouth the glamorous dresses, the tight skirts and sweaters, the sheer stockings, the high-heeled shoes.

She'd been with a lover. Jennifer wondered who the man had been. Or men. Knowing her mother now, there would have been more than one. Oh yes, there had been quite a string of 'uncles'. Sometimes, instead of being sent to her granny's, she would be cajoled into going to bed early. She'd lie and listen to her current uncle's throaty laughter and her mother's giggles. Then there would be other, stranger sounds that would make her cover her ears with the blankets, or burrow deep underneath them and weep helpless tears.

Her father had tried to keep in touch after his marriage to Laura. Every week he'd collect her and take her to the zoo or the cinema or to a toy shop to buy her a dolly or a teddy. Whatever she wanted, in fact. Later, he'd tried to interest her in clothes.

'How would you like Daddy to buy you a new dress?' he'd say.

She'd thought it pathetic. She'd hung back, moody, resentful and depressed. It was him and his love she'd wanted. Her father and her mother together, an ordinary family, like the families of the other children she knew. Mothers used to come to the school gate every playtime with flasks of Bovril or juice for their children in case they became cold or thirsty. Never once had her mother been among that eager, loving group. Nor had she ever turned up at open days when the pupils' work was proudly displayed. She remembered a picture she'd drawn that had been pinned up on the class wall. It was of her mother and father holding hands. Sheer imagination. She'd never seen them holding hands. Or kissing. As far as she could remember they either ignored one another or argued.

She remembered how furious her father had been when he'd discovered Andrina had not gone to the teacher-parents' night at the school. She'd told him she had gone and had made up a pack of lies about Jennifer's progress.

The primary school teacher had eventually got in touch with Robert at the secondary school where he taught and told him how worried she was about his daughter. How withdrawn she was. How she wasn't able to concentrate on her lessons. How she seemed unable or unwilling to mix freely with the other children, even in the playground. Always hanging back on her own in some corner or other, watching but never taking part.

'I had a headache and couldn't go,' her mother protested. 'Why should it always be me, anyway? Why can't you take some responsibility for your own daughter?'

'You know perfectly well why I couldn't go,' her father shouted back. 'I had to be at Sinnieglen talking to the parents of my pupils on the same night. As head of the Art Department, it's my job to organise everything and to show a good example. I *had* to be there.'

'Show a good example?' her mother echoed sarcastically. 'That'll be the day . . .'

And so it went on.

Headache, was it? Jennifer remembered being alone in the house. Walking with fast beating heart through the heavy silence of each room, then standing in the windowless hall, paralysed.

She didn't know what she felt about her father now but she knew what she felt about her mother. Her father's new wife was also a teacher. They had no children and were obviously devoted to one another. There was no place for her there. Oh,

Laura was always nice to her when she went to visit. A lovely tea was provided. Polite conversation was maintained. Her father pushed plates of sandwiches and cakes towards her. Then before she left to return to her Granny Sophie's house along the road, he'd slip a pound into her pocket.

Once a week she visited her granny just along the road from where her father now lived. She stayed overnight at her Granny's house. Grandpa McPherson was dead now and Granny was always glad of her company. Granny gave Andrina short shrift. For years she hadn't even spoken to her daughter. Granny was a very enthusiastic churchwoman. Even now in her late sixties, she was still on innumerable committees and was always doing something for either the Church of Jesus to which she belonged, or for some charity or other. Sophie had kept on speaking terms with her son-in-law after the break-up of the marriage, but not with her daughter. Jennifer had often wondered why. Now she knew.

Her mother's present lover was called Paul Fisher. He was married and that was why, her mother explained, they couldn't become man and wife at the moment. He was going to get a divorce, however, and as soon as it came through, they planned to marry. He was a slim man with cream-coloured hair, pale eyes and a neat blond moustache. He always wore bow-ties and immaculately pressed clothes. He frightened Jennifer. Not, of course, that her mother noticed. Her mother was up on cloud nine, all sparkly-eyed and ridiculously flirtatious for a woman of forty-two years of age. She ought to be ashamed, but Jennifer had long since come to the conclusion that her mother was incapable of such an emotion.

Paul Fisher appeared to have plenty of money, which figured. That's why Andrina never had any respect or time for Robert Anderson, a dedicated teacher with next to nothing as a wage and apparently quite satisfied to continue in such an unrewarding profession. As far as her mother could see, that is.

Jennifer suspected that Andrina had married Robert in the first place to please Granny McPherson. Or that she'd been under pressure from her. Sophie McPherson was still a very strong character. In the many long conversations Jennifer had had over the years with her granny, Sophie had confided in her. Especially since she'd been a teenager and almost a grown-up. Although, as her granny said, there had always been a serious part about her that was far beyond her years.

Granny said that her mother had this boyfriend – oh, from way back.

'From your age. Can you imagine? A hard-faced, wicked young man. I just knew by the look of him. But of course he came from a rough family. A Catholic family too. Unfortunately, your poor grandpa wasn't such a good judge of character. Your grandpa thought he was all right. But that was before we found out.'

'Found out what?' Jennifer asked although, knowing her mother only too well by this time, there was really no need to ask.

Her granny sadly shook her head. 'I always knew in my heart of hearts she was up to something. But I tried my best, my very best, Jennifer, to keep her on the straight and narrow. To protect her. I gave her, your grandpa and I gave her, a good Christian upbringing. But it was all to no avail. I'm sorry to say this, Jennifer, but Andrina has bad blood in her.'

She shook her head again.

'Oh, the awful deceit of her. When I think of all the lies . . . Anyway, we found out eventually when that awful man actually came to my door to tell me. When I wouldn't let him in – to be honest Jennifer I was afraid of the man – when I slammed the door in his face he shouted through the door what they'd been doing for years behind our backs. Your grandpa, me, Robert's mother, God rest her soul, and of course poor Robert. Oh, and what vulgar, obscene language that man used, Jennifer. I couldn't repeat it. *And* he accused me of preventing him from marrying Andrina in the first place. I was the one who was to blame for everything, according to him. Do you know, Jennifer, I thought he was going to kill me. I really was petrified of that man. I remember at the time the papers had been full of the murders of respectable women of my age. And of course I got it into my head – I know it sounds daft now but there were other reasons for me thinking that he was the murderer.'

Jennifer found these stories fascinating. She had seen the cuttings her granny kept in a leatherbound scrapbook all about the 'Glasgow murderer' and how her granny had been attacked one dark night as she walked home from her flower-arranging class. How she'd fought her attacker, scratched his face and neck and had finally been rescued by Robert, who had been babysitting at her granny's house while her grandpa was away in England on some council business or other. It was after the break-up of her parents' marriage, and God alone knew where her mother was that night. Probably with another lover.

Anyway, when her granny hadn't returned as early as she'd promised, Robert had got a neighbour in and gone to look for her. That was when he'd rescued Granny. The murderer hadn't been the man Granny had thought at all.

Jennifer loved her granny more than anyone else in the world. Her granny was always the same, and always there for her. It was her granny who'd said, 'Bring any of your friends home here and I'll give them a really good tea. Or you could both stay overnight. You know how I enjoy your company. And I know what your mother's like. Your friends would get scant attention from her.'

She didn't tell Granny that she would be ashamed to take any friend home. And she had a special friend now. A best friend. Her very first. She loved her almost as much as Granny. When she did take Daisy Alexander for tea to Granny's, Granny really liked her – which was a great relief. Granny could be very strong in her beliefs and opinions. But then Daisy looked very serious and respectable with her straight hair and horn-rimmed glasses. She had an Aunty Moira who worked in the library, which was also a help. Nevertheless, Granny had checked all Daisy's credentials.

'What church do your folks belong to?' Granny asked and Jennifer had been worried about that because Daisy's mum was not a member of the Church of Jesus. Worse, she was a Quaker, which seemed odd. But of course, Daisy's mum was a very odd person altogether.

Surprisingly, Granny had been intrigued, even impressed.

'Quakers? They're very good-living people, I've heard. I'd like to meet your mother some time.'

Afterwards Daisy and Jennifer discussed how they could

manage to persuade Daisy's mother to clean herself up and at least *look* respectable.

'All that stinky paint!' Daisy rolled her eyes. 'If I don't do something, she's liable to turn up with green and purple hands. She even gets the stuff in her hair.'

Daisy suffered terribly with her mother.

III

SUNSHINE FILTERED THROUGH the window of the cottage, Sambered the dark red flagstones of the kitchen floor and cast a lazy haze over everything else.

'I've baked an apple pie.' Caroline squeezed her plump body past her husband to admire the table and straighten the cutlery and serviettes. 'It's one of Bernard's favourites, isn't it?'

Michael O'Maley rolled his one eye ceilingwards. His other eye had been put out during a boxing match. For years he'd worn a black eyepatch. What with that and his flattened nose he was 'no beauty', as Big Martha, his mother-in-law, never tired of telling him. He was Bernard's twin brother but as Martha also observed more than once, 'You're as different to look at as chalk and cheese. He's a handsome big fella, our Bernard.' He noted the *our* with a secret sarcasm that bordered on bitterness. Both his mother-in-law and his wife made such a goddam fuss of his brother.

OK, Bernard had done them all a big favour by letting them rent this cottage and at next to nothing. He had saved them from a rotten miserable life in a high flat in Castlemilk. That damp hell-hole had been slowly killing the kids with asthma, and Martha with arthritis.

The cottage had originally been Bernard's love nest. He'd seen Bernard with a woman in a car one day when he was working on a country building site. Then on another occasion, just a day or two after the first, he saw him going into the cottage with the same woman. In a rash moment he'd mentioned it to Caroline, and later she confessed to him that she'd let it slip to Bernard's wife. That was something she now felt guilty about. In those days Caroline had never liked Bernard. Bernard had refused to help him out with money and called him a drunken bum. Caroline couldn't forgive him for that. At least not then – even though he'd told her a thousand times after the incident that Bernard had been quite right not to give him a handout. He'd only have spent it on booze. He was an alcoholic and Bernard knew it, but he was off the drink now, thank God. And Alcoholics Anonymous. He still went to the meetings as often as he could.

Neither Jane, Bernard's wife, nor anyone else, had discovered who Bernard's fancy woman was, but Jane had flung Bernard out and the marriage had broken up. He'd bought a flat in the city because, he said, he needed to be nearer his office. Then he'd offered them the cottage.

Since then, Bernard could do no wrong as far as Big Martha and Caroline were concerned. Michael was grateful too but there was a limit to anything.

After all, he'd always worked hard to provide for Caroline and the family. In his boxing days, he'd made a fair bit of money. Immediately, he felt guilty. He always did when he remembered that time in his life. He was only kidding himself when he said he had always provided for his family. When he'd been drinking he spent every penny he had. Often there had been no food in the house. But that was a long time ago. Since he'd been working on the building sites he'd done OK by the family. More than OK. He'd done his damndest to make up for all the bad times. He'd even put up with Caroline's old harridan of a mother for years. Not that Big Martha had been quite so bad since coming to live at the cottage. She'd mellowed a bit, but not much.

Of the four O'Maley brothers it could be said that Michael O'Maley was at the bottom of the pile. Bernard employed God knew how many men now in his security business and he travelled all over the world. He regularly bodyguarded famous film stars and pop stars and organised crowd control at big events. He moved in a different world from the rest of his family now, but as Caroline said, 'He's still the same old Bernard.'

He had to agree. Bernard had always been cool and laid back yet with a subtle swagger of self-confidence. His iron-hard muscular body certainly hadn't softened now that he was in his forty-sixth year. If anything, he looked tougher. Caroline said it was something to do with his eyes. Always had been.

'Those dark eyes of his are so sexy,' Caroline enthused. 'I know there's an awful hard glitter there at times as well. But a kinder man no one could meet. Look how good he's always been with the children. And with Mammy.'

That really got to Michael. He was the one that had been saddled with 'Mammy' for donkey's years. He was the one who'd been daft enough to buy her a wheelchair and condemn himself to pushing her about in it every day. After a hard slog at work he had to heave the mountainous ould sod around and listen to her rabbiting on non-stop. He even had the job of cutting her hair and her toenails. Once she'd got stuck in the bath and Caroline had to shout for his help to heave her out. Christ, what a sight! It was enough to put a man off women for the rest of his life. Fortunately, Caroline was nothing like her mother – except in her adoration of Bernard. To her credit, though, Caroline never compared him to Bernard, never pointed out how Bernard had done so much better financially. Or Frank. Even Tony had gone up in the world. Martha often said, 'I don't know what the world's coming to when that idiot brother of yours can make so much money. All he does is bang away like a madman at those drums of his. At least you do a decent day's work for what you earn.'

It wasn't often that his mother-in-law paid him a compliment, and he appreciated it. It wasn't easy to cope with three successful brothers. Frank was famous as a television playwright. Michael could never quite get over that. He'd never believed for a minute that Frank would come to anything. None of them had. Many a time he or Bernard, or even Tony, had rescued Frank from some playground bully. Later there had been street corner thugs. The O'Maley family had been brought up in Blackhill, real gangster land. You had to be tough to survive that place. Frank had been a skinny sensitive child and a lanky, dreamy young man. The only thing he'd shown any toughness about was in his determination to become a writer. There never had been any budging him from that. They'd all had a go at him about the daft wee poems he used to scribble in his Woolworth's jotters. Many a clip on the ear he'd got from their da, God rest his soul. But Frank had stuck to his guns, and look at him now. At least he had more brains than Tony.

'Are you going to get yourself washed and changed?' Martha said now. 'Or are you going to look like a one-eyed down-and-out when Bernard arrives?'

'Aye, OK. OK.'

'Put on your good navy suit, dear,' Caroline urged.

'What?' he cried out in protest. 'It's a Sunday forenoon in the height of summer and I'm going to do a bit of gardening.'

'No, you're not, dear.' Caroline dropped a kiss on the top of his head. 'At least not until after Bernard's visit.'

'He'll not be wearing a bloody suit. I'll just look ridiculous.'

'Yes, he will,' Caroline said, 'Bernard is always perfectly turned out.'

Martha shouted from the other side of the room, 'You'll look ridiculous anyway, you ugly one-eyed monster.'

'Mammy!' Caroline chided, and then to him, 'You know fine how smart Bernard always is. But you can put on as good a show if you try.'

'I don't want to put on a show. I just want to relax in my own house.'

That was a mistake, and Big Martha of the big mouth, as well as the big bulk, immediately pounced on it.

'It's not your house. It's his house and don't you forget it. If it wasn't for our Bernard we'd still be living in misery in that dump in Castlemilk.'

'Aye, OK. OK. I'll go and get ready to receive Saint Bernard.'

'I'd probably be dead by now,' Martha said, 'if it wasn't for him.'

Curses on his head, Michael thought, but managed to keep his mouth shut. Through in the bedroom he shared with Caroline he could hear Maureen on the garden swing. It creaked lazily backwards and forwards. He didn't need to peer out of the small bedroom window in its perfumed frame of roses. He made a mental note to cut back the wild profusion of green and pink before it completely darkened the whole room. He could see clearly in his mind's eye his youngest child outside in the garden, kicking up her heels. At fifteen and a half Maureen, their youngest, alternated between resentful, rebellious adult and loving, vulnerable child, depending on her mood of the day. The twins, eighteen-year-old Sean and Sally, were in their rooms dolling themselves up for Bernard's visit. Annoyance needled Michael again. Sean seemed to think more of his Uncle Bernard than his own dad. Sally had actually begun to flirt with him.

Caroline had laughed when he'd told her this.

'You're just jealous.'

'What? Of Bernard?'

'You know fine all the children adore you. It's just that Bernard is so glamorous . . .'

'Glamorous?' he'd echoed incredulously although he knew exactly what she meant. They didn't see Bernard all that often and when they did he could tell them all sorts of tales about glamorous places and famous stars. Then there was the danger element that the children found so exciting. This had become a real worry. Sean wanted Bernard to give him a job.

'After all the sacrifices we've made to keep you and Sally at school, you'd throw away all that good education to be a glorified bouncer!' he'd roared at them. 'Over my dead body!'

It was this aspect of the job that worried Michael the most. Bernard had been shot at more than once and nearly killed when he'd been bodyguarding some politician or industrialist or other.

But Bernard always survived. He had the luck of the Irish. Sean might not be so fortunate. Now even Sally was thinking of asking Bernard if he could take her on.

'After all,' she'd pointed out, 'Uncle Bernard has lots of women as well as men working for him.'

She, like Sean, had been taking lessons in karate and God knew how many keep-fit classes to toughen themselves up and impress their uncle. Both of them were forever jogging about in their T-shirts and shorts, up hill and down dale. They had weights that they trained conscientiously with, sometimes in their rooms, sometimes out in the garden.

Michael loved his children and was already losing sleep worrying about their safety. It seemed to him that Bernard, who had once been the family's saviour, was about to be the cause of their destruction. He tried to keep a sensible balance in his mind but despite his struggle, he'd never been nearer to hating his brother.

'Here's his car. Here he is!' The excited cry rang out.

Michael remained rooted in front of the wardrobe mirror staring, unable to go and look at his handsome brother's face.

IV

AFTERNOON TEA IN Bearsden. Bessie sighed. For Daisy's sake she had agreed to put in an appearance. Not only that, she had promised to have a bath beforehand, wash her hair and wear something that had never been anywhere near her loft studio. She had to be absolutely paint-free, in other words. There was something funny about the invitation because it was not from Jennifer, or Daisy's best friend's mum, but her granny. Jennifer's mum lived beside (almost inside) Glasgow Green, a much more interesting place, in Bessie's opinion, than Bearsden. Glasgow Green was the most important historic site in the country. It was one of the great battlefields of Scotland and a place of meetings and demonstrations. The fight for political freedom – one man one vote, then one woman one vote – had been fought there, for instance. From her reading of its history and from her imagination, Bessie had painted many of the turbulent scenes that had taken place there. She still had an ambition to paint James Watt as he strolled on the Green one Sunday afternoon in 1765 and thought of the idea of a separate condenser. The application of this idea in the development of the steam engine had changed the whole course of industrial and human history. The mere thought of the place excited her.

Bearsden didn't excite her at all.

'Jennifer's granny's awful nice, Mum,' Daisy assured her for the sixth or seventh time, which made Bessie suspicious. Daisy had already warned her not to mention her painting but added, 'She's interested in you being a Quaker so that's all right.'

Bessie had set off with her daughter from their flat at Shawlands Cross, in the southern part of the city, with a heavy heart. Although she'd been brought up there herself, and her parents before her, Bearsden was not her scene. It was, she had come to believe, death to an artist. It was too conventional, too comfortable.

Peter had wanted to buy a house there when they'd got married. It was the one thing she'd fought against. Well, not fought exactly. She'd pointed out how much more expensive it would be and enthused at how beautiful the warm, red sandstone building was at Shawlands Cross, how classy the tiled close and the stained-glass windows on the landings. How reasonably priced the flat was, how handy it would be for Peter to get to his office in the centre of town. It was all perfectly true, of course. It was just she hadn't mentioned how wonderful she thought the loft would be as a studio. Nor had she realised the power of the financial side of her argument. She'd learned over the years how mean Peter was. He was practically a miser. It was soul destroying. According to him, if she treated herself to a cup of tea in town, she was a lunatic spendthrift whose reckless extravagance would be the death of him yet. At first he'd tried to teach her how to keep housekeeping books in which she had to detail every penny she spent, down to the last toilet roll. He had questioned the amount she spent on that, even asking her how many pieces of paper she was in the habit of using. Two pieces was quite sufficient, he'd said; any more was sheer extravagance. And the money she spent on sketchbooks and the like nearly drove him to distraction. But Bessie had made such a mess of the accounts he had been forced to give up in the end. Or, as he said, go mad. She forgot to record purchases, or she lied verbally and on paper about the price of things. Especially things for herself. She always knocked a few pounds off everything. If Peter had his way, she would be going about minus make-up and knickers. All in the cause of saving money. In fact, she would rather have gone without make-up and knickers than paints and canvases.

He was more indulgent with Daisy, but not that much. Peter liked the good things in life, like tasty food washed down with a glass or two of wine. He enjoyed his evening tipple of whisky as well. He needed it to relax him and help him to sleep, he said. Where did he think she could get the money to pay for luxuries like that?

He didn't want to know. She was supposed to work some kind of miracle: to be frugal and save him money yet make it possible for him to live the life of Riley. At first she'd done it by getting into debt. Then robbing Peter to pay Paul, as the saying went. Only she'd never robbed the real Peter. Far from it. If anyone robbed anyone it was the other way around. As often as not, she borrowed money from her mother. Occasionally she sold a painting; if in desperation for money she was able to force herself to copy a photo of some friend of her mother's or customer of her father's.

Not that she minded putting any money she earned into the kitty. If only Peter would at least recognise that she did her best to contribute to the home and its occupants. The fact was he did his best to stop her painting.

Peter hated Gregory yet any time they'd met he'd been perfectly nice and polite to him. It really sickened Bessie. She'd come to the sad conclusion that Peter was a weak man as well as a two-faced one. Probably he was two-faced *because* he was weak. He bullied and browbeat and made a fool of her in the privacy of their home. In public, or to outsiders, he was a right little charmer.

The address she and Daisy were going to was one of the terraced houses along from the shops in Drymen Road. The end terrace, it turned out, a big corner site with a lane running along the back. This part of Bearsden had always been known as 'the village'. Drymen Road, although a main thoroughfare, rustled with trees and in summer the sun dappled through the branches and made intricate patterns on the clean warm pavements. Most of the houses were large villas set back from the road fronted by velvety lawns and silvery grey stone walls.

Bessie's mother and father lived at the other end, the not nearly so posh part, of Bearsden. Their flat was above another line of shops, which included the menswear shop. Her father had recently retired and his place of business, as he called it, had been taken over by a Pakistani who sold papers and groceries, and everything else on earth by the look of the place.

'They take no pride in their windows,' her father complained. 'Everything's just stuffed in there any old way. It really lowers the tone of the place.'

As far as Bessie knew, Mr Akhtar was the first Pakistani to scale the heights of Bearsden. He seemed a nice friendly man of about her father's age. He and his wife and their daughter and a son lived in Great Western Road in Glasgow. Of course, mother and father would be polite to the Akhtars. Father was a bit like Peter in the two-faced stakes but Mother was generally kindly and would never have the heart to snub anybody. Still, she often sighed and shook her grey head in the privacy of her home or the home of one of her friends, and wondered what the world, and Bearsden in particular, was coming to.

'McPherson?' Bessie peered at the nameplate as they waited for Jennifer's granny to open the door. 'That name sounds familiar.'

'It's a common enough Scottish name,' Daisy said.

'I know but . . .'

Just then an elderly woman as thin as a greyhound, with steely grey hair and eyes to match, opened the door. Her welcome was warm and enthusiastic.

'Come away in, come away in. Jennifer has told me so much about you. I feel I know you already.'

She had a tea trolley set with the most mouth-watering home-baked cakes Bessie had ever seen – fairy cakes with cream bulging up between sponge wings. Tiny iced cakes topped with a scarlet cherry. Wicked-looking chocolate gâteau. Crisp fingers of sugar-dusted shortbread. Sandwiches, too: cucumber, tomato, date and banana, chicken mayonnaise.

Bessie tucked in with great enjoyment. She was so accustomed to serving other people, indeed being at everyone's beck and call, that it was enormously enjoyable a treat to be made a fuss of by someone else.

'Just call me Sophie,' Mrs McPherson urged as she poured out Bessie's third cup of tea. The older woman seemed to be genuinely happy to make a fuss of her and the girls. Bessie was having an unexpectedly lovely time.

'Here,' she suddenly cried out, 'are you the woman who once fought off the Glasgow murderer?'

Sophie laughed.

'Goodness me, that was a long time ago.'

'I knew the name McPherson rang a bell. But when you said Sophie, it all came back to me. My mother and father are members of your church. I know it's a big congregation and you probably won't have met them . . .'

Sophie looked thoughtful.

'Alexander . . .'

'No, that's my married name.'

'Oh, of course.'

'McVinney. Mamie and Guy McVinney.'

'No,' Sophie shook her head. 'I can't say I know the name. But as you say, it is a big congregation. I'd maybe know them by sight. Do they belong to Bearsden?'

'Down Emerston Road.'

'That's where a Pakistani family have moved in.'

'Well, they've opened a grocer's shop where my father's menswear place used to be.'

Sophie shook her head again.

'Isn't it awful. I haven't anything personally against coloured people, you understand,' she added hastily, 'but they're not Christian. We must remember that.'

Bessie wanted to say 'Why?' She was tempted to recite number 22 of the *Advices and Queries* out loud: 'Do you behave with brotherly love to all men, whatever their race, background or opinion? Do you try to make the stranger feel at home among you?'

For Sophie's sake as well as for Daisy's, she managed to keep her mouth shut. After all, according to Daisy, Sophie was very highly strung and on medication for her blood pressure.

'You're a member of the Society of Friends, I hear,' Sophie said, her stiff, lean frame tipping forward with interest and curiosity. 'That's a very narrow sect, I believe. Very strict.'

'Oh no,' Bessie laughed. 'Not at all.'

'But I heard that even music isn't allowed.'

'That's just at Meeting for Worship. Other than that we believe that music, and drama, and painting and sculpture and books all help develop our perception and enjoyment of life and the search for truth and fulfilment.'

'Oh.' Sophie didn't look too sure about all that. A glint of suspicion entered her eyes. Maybe it was the word enjoyment. Bessie thought it wiser to change the subject.

'Fancy you being the woman in all the papers. You were headline news at the time, I remember. Very courageous, they said you were, and no wonder. I'm sure I would have died of fright.'

'My son-in-law was the brave one. I'd never have survived had it not been for him coming to my rescue. He's married again and lives just along the road in the bungalows. I'm always encouraging Jennifer to visit him when she comes to see me but she's not keen on his wife. I don't know why. Laura is a very nice woman.'

Bessie decided not to pursue this subject in case she put her foot in it, but it seemed an interesting situation. Several times Sophie mentioned her son-in-law and even his wife with affection, but never a word about her daughter. Jennifer didn't mention her mother either.

Later when they were back home, Bessie remarked on this to Daisy.

'Oh, Andrina's awful.' Daisy screwed up her face. 'Jennifer hates her.'

'Oh dear, surely not? Her own mother?'

'There's this man comes to the house and Jennifer says he's not the first one. She hates him as well. She tries to keep out of the house when he's around.'

'Oh dear,' Bessie repeated. 'The poor girl doesn't appear very happy, right enough. She's got a kind of haunted look about her.'

'Mum!' Daisy groaned. 'You're beginning to sound like your pictures look.'

Bessie laughed at this but in an absent-minded way. A feeling of unease hung about at the back of her mind. It wasn't just about Jennifer either.

She'd enjoyed the visit to Bearsden yet now, looking back and thinking of Sophie, she felt worried. There was something disconcerting about the woman. She tried to pinpoint exactly what it was. She kept wishing she could have the opportunity to capture the strong essence of Sophie on canvas. There was certainly an unusual intensity about her. It seemed to be burning somewhere within her outer shell. No matter what perfectly ordinary comment Sophie had made or question she had asked, the intensity flamed in her eyes.

She's like two people, Bessie decided. The outside person is the middle-class, conventional grandmother with her etiquette book and her immaculate house. No doubt every house in the terrace served afternoon tea on a trolley, used bone china and offered crustless sandwiches and dainty home-made cakes.

The inside person was the one who intrigued Bessie. Inside Sophie she suspected there hid a can of worms. She had a sudden colourful vision of a can of worms but immediately banished it. No wonder the family thought her paintings so weird. She did get some awful ideas that too often she transposed on to canvas.

'How about Sophie and Jennifer's mother, then?' she asked Daisy.

'Oh, Sophie thinks Andrina's awful as well. She's disowned her.'

'Surely this Andrina can't be as bad as all that. And even if she is, it's very sad to think of so much hatred in a family.'

Daisy shrugged. 'I suppose. But that's how it is.'

It occurred to Bessie that that's how it was with her as well. She hated Peter and Granda. She felt so guilty and ashamed of this sudden insight she made a special effort to cook them a really good dinner.

V

USUALLY BERNARD HAD no problem concentrating one hundred per cent on his principal, as the person being looked after was called. What distracted him in this case – and it was very dangerous to be distracted – was the fact that the pop singer, Eve Page, reminded him so much of Andrina McPherson, or Anderson as she'd become. He hadn't thought of her for years. Not seriously. Now, his mind kept sinking in a morass of lust and anger. No woman he'd known since could match her for uninhibited passion and sexual fulfilment. He'd lived for her then; but later he had realised what a bitch she was. She'd kept him dangling for years – half a lifetime – in the hope that she'd leave her husband and marry him. He groaned every time he thought of all the deceit the affair involved. Her husband, Robert, had taught him at school, then coached him in karate. Robert Anderson had been his mentor, the man who had saved him and so many other youngsters from the streets and a life of crime. Robert had trusted him, but he had been so obsessed with Andrina that he'd betrayed his best friend.

He'd betrayed his wife too. Jane had had everything – beauty, and fitness that would have rivalled any of the women security officers he now employed. She had also inherited that huge villa in the Pollokshields from her father, not to mention a very large sum of money. They'd had fitness training in common: every day they'd worked out together in the gym she'd had installed in the villa, and he'd started giving her karate lessons. Many a good laugh they'd had as well. The truth was, Jane had much more in common with him than Andrina. He was glad that, during the past ten or eleven years since the divorce, she seemed to have lost most of her anger and bitterness. They'd at least become friends.

Why had he never felt for her as he had for Andrina? Why had Jane's lean body never excited him, drowned him in passion, like Andrina's soft voluptuous curves? He told himself that Andrina would now, in her early forties, look fat and matronly compared with Jane.

Even after all these years his anger could still flare up. It was anger directed at himself as well as Andrina. He, as much as Andrina, had been the cause of her marriage to Robert breaking up, and his own marriage to Jane.

He succeeded in banishing Andrina from his mind at last. At first he managed this feat of willpower by throwing himself into his work. In a way, his obsession with Andrina had taught him a lesson connected with his work. Or rather, reinforced something he'd always known. In his job, to do it properly, he needed to focus completely on what he was doing. He could never afford to be seen to be too close to anyone, because they would become his Achilles' heel. It was for that reason that he never employed any of his family. They might have distracted his attention when he was looking after a principal.

That was why he was angry now for allowing himself to think of Andrina. Eve Page was so like the Andrina he remembered. She had the same coppery glints in her hair, the same creamy skin, the same curvaceous shape. Only the eyes were different. Andrina had such unusual aquamarine-coloured eyes. Those eyes could change from childish innocence to impish mischief, to smouldering passion. He remembered her in every mood. They had both revelled in the danger and the excitement of their lovemaking. They'd had sex on many crazy occasions practically under the noses of Robert and Jane. They'd made love while Andrina and Robert were visiting the villa. Or while he and Jane were visiting Andrina and Robert's place at Glasgow Green. Every moment they found themselves alone in a room, they had these crazy hurried sessions. At other times they had long indulgent hours in Robert's bed while he was at work. Or in Jane's bed while she was out at one of her yoga or keep-fit classes. Robert had found out eventually that Bernard was Andrina's lover but Jane had never found out. Jane often spoke about Andrina: they were still the best of friends. It was obvious from these conversations that Andrina was not only the deceitful bitch she always had been, but that she was still after sexual excitement. Apparently she was now involved with another married man. God knew what was happening to that daughter of hers. He recalled Jennifer as a serious, gawky child, anything but happy looking. He'd been perfectly willing to accept Jennifer along with her mother. If they'd just been able to get married it would all have worked out happily enough, he'd thought at the time. At least he'd no children of his own to worry about.

He had been the one who had finished the affair. Enough was enough. His life was being ruined. He was being made a fool of by her – and he was making a fool of himself. He'd told her to fuck off, and that was that.

He was taken by surprise at how quickly the old wound opened up again when he'd met Eve Page. It wasn't, strangely enough, that he felt any attraction towards her. Maybe because he had been a professional too long to allow himself to become in the slightest involved in any personal way with a principal. His reputation was high in the business. The highest, in fact. He prided himself on that. He always kept things under control. He didn't have to make an effort to prove anything. His reputation, and people's perception of him, was enough.

His next job was to organise Eve's visit, along with her backing group, to America. She and the group were performing in a film that Paramount Pictures were making. She was only in a few scenes, so her stay in Hollywood wouldn't be for long. But she and the others would no doubt want to visit restaurants or clubs in Los Angeles and God knew what else. All the work it entailed for him and his men was onerous, even for a short visit.

He'd to fly over to the States in a couple of weeks. First he'd promised to visit Michael and the family at the cottage. This time he wasn't looking forward to his visit as much as usual. The cottage had been the love nest he'd shared with Andrina on so many passionate occasions. Now, with memories of her stirred up, it was painful to see the place. Again the pain took him by surprise. The cottage was sparkling white in the sun with its small windows glinting like diamonds. It sat back from the road in a colourful profusion of flowers. Close behind it rose a velvety green hill.

As usual, Caroline, Big Martha and the children made him almost embarrassingly welcome. Michael, when he finally appeared, was slightly more restrained in his greeting. No wonder, with everybody making such a fuss. Poor old Michael, slogging away as a brickie, still lumbered with his monstrous mother-in-law. He couldn't offer him a job. What use would a one-eyed ex-alcoholic boxer be in his business? Anyway, Caroline had long ago made it plain that she couldn't stand the thought of Michael being in such a risky occupation. She'd suffered enough worry when he'd been boxing. In the past he'd tried to slip Michael a few pounds but Michael had been adamant that he didn't need handouts. 'You've done more than enough letting us have this cottage,' he insisted.

Bernard was taken aback – indeed they all were – when, after a good lunch in the kitchen with its low oak-beamed ceiling, the twins said they wanted a job in the business. He'd always been fond of Sean and Sally. They were the nearest he had to children of his own. He'd always spoiled them, bringing them gifts, indulging their eagerness to hear all about his adventures.

Now his stories were coming home to roost. He was horrified, although he managed to keep his usual cool on the outside. Before he could say anything, Caroline cried out,

'Are you mad, the pair of you? Your Uncle Bernard has a very dangerous job but he's used to it. You two would get yourselves killed.'

'No, we've been training.' The twins were starry-eyed with enthusiasm. 'We've both got our black belts in karate. We're fighting fit and ready to go.'

Michael looked across at Bernard. 'Thanks very much,' he said.

'Look,' Bernard protested, 'I started them in karate as a sport, something for them to enjoy and to keep them fit. That was all.'

He realised for the first time, admitted it to himself, that he'd enjoyed the love and admiration of his niece and nephew and had done everything in his power to encourage it. Even now he couldn't bring himself to disappoint them or to risk losing any of that affection.

'Oh please, Uncle Bernard.' Sally was fluttering her eyelashes at him. She moved nearer and looked as if she might even slip on to his knee and entwine her arm around his neck as she'd done so often when she was small. For the first time it occurred to him that she was no longer a little girl. Yet at the same time she was so innocent. Especially as far as the security business was concerned. She hadn't a clue.

'Sally, Sean,' he managed, 'you might think you're trained but you're not. I have to be honest with you about that. There's a lot more to it than a black belt in karate.'

They had been brought up in this gently idyllic place. Could they learn what being streetwise meant for a start? He had learned it from the moment he could walk: his training had been in the streets of Blackhill, Glasgow's gangster land. There he had developed an instinct for survival that they'd never have.

But they were pleading now and ignoring their mother and father and grandmother's objections. Eventually he said, 'I'll make a bargain with you. I'll see that you get the training you do need. If the pair of you survive that, and still want a job, you'll get one.'

On the face of it, it seemed a risky line to take. But he hadn't known ex-SAS men for nothing.

VI

BESSIE STRUGGLED ALONG Kilmarnock Road towards Shawlands Cross, arms gorilla-length with the weight of two shopping bags. She was developing round shoulders with being such a beast of burden. Peter didn't believe it was manly to go shopping. 'It's a woman's job,' he maintained. Daisy was usually either at school or away somewhere with her friend, Jennifer. The two girls had become like Siamese twins. Granda was too old to help, even if she'd wanted his help – which she didn't. He always put a price on everything and she knew only too well what kind of repayment he'd try to elicit from her. Dirty old codger. He'd once offered to help her by paying the gas bill when she hadn't known how she was going to pay it. She'd been sitting staring at it in horror and despair when he made the offer. Thankfully, she had accepted. What a load off her mind it had been and, after all, Granda used most of the gas. He had that big gas fire of his going full blast morning, noon and night.

As soon as she'd accepted his kind offer, he had made a pass at her. Immediately she'd shrunk away from him, her horror returning a thousandfold at the feel of the gnarled old hands trying to grope her. He looked huffed and disappointed.

'Old-fashioned type, are you?' he'd sneered.

'I obviously must be.' She'd got up and was backing away from him, nearly knocking the chair over in her agitation.

He flung the gas bill back at her.

'You can forget that then.'

Meaning his offer to pay. She should have let her anger rip then.

Dirty, rotten old swine! she'd wanted to shout. You're as mean as your miserable pig of a son.

She didn't, though. She'd long since found that losing her head or arguing with Peter or Granda didn't get her anywhere except into a state of exhaustion and depression. It was usually Peter she argued with. Granda tried to argue with her but nowadays she just agreed with him, tried to pacify him no matter what crazy thing he said. He was always accusing her of not giving him his meals, for instance. Sometimes she gave him two breakfasts or dinners or teas rather than get into a pointless argument. She often wondered how he'd been as a husband when his wife was alive. He was a right whining, complaining, argumentative old sod as a father-in-law. He was also far from clean in either his person or his habits. It was a devil of a job to force him to have a bath. He had a dirty mind as well. She was sure he was angling for her to give him his bath. But she'd get a nurse in first, even if it meant going round the doors trying to sell her paintings to get enough money. Or maybe she'd get a man. That would maybe stop the dirty old devil.

He'd made several advances and propositions over the years. The first time she'd been really shocked and upset. She had told Peter as soon as he'd arrived home, but Peter had just laughed and said at first she must be imagining things. Then when, still trembling with distress, she'd insisted, he'd become impatient and dismissive and said: 'For God's sake stop making such a stupid fuss about nothing.' He'd said that the old man must be in his second childhood, and in one way he certainly had returned to childhood. He regularly peed the bed. Bessie was sick, sick, oh so sick, of stripping his stinking bed and washing his stinking sheets. Sometimes she wondered if he did it on purpose. He wasn't that daft. He could appear perfectly sane and sensible, usually when Peter was around. It was when Peter wasn't there, or during the night when Peter was dead to the world, that the old man went to pieces. She'd smell burning and hurry out of bed to see what he was doing. Sometimes she'd find he'd tried to light a paper at the fire in his bedroom and let it drop on to the carpet. Sometimes he'd dropped his pipe and it lay smouldering. She'd never dared to take a sleeping tablet but remained apprehensively awake for long hours every night.

Sometimes he raved a lot of nonsense at her in the wee small hours. She could see then that the poor man was senile. She had tried to get the doctor but Peter insisted that there was nothing wrong with his father. The old man, in his lucid times when Peter was there, would insist exactly the same thing.

'You're not going to get me put away,' he'd say. 'I'm not daft.'

She'd feel sorry for him then. It was understandable he didn't want to end up in some institution. Not that she had any intention of banishing him to one, even if she'd been allowed to. Although she had once, on the point of collapse, pleaded with Peter to arrange – or allow her to arrange – for his father to go somewhere, anywhere, for just a week or two to give her a break.

'What?' Peter had been outraged. 'Turf my father out on to the street . . .?'

'No, of course not. That's not what I said.'

'I'll see you on the street first!'

She'd hidden herself away upstairs in her loft studio as soon as she could after that. She clambered up the ladder and crashed the hatch down. She scrabbled the bolt into its catch, effectively imprisoning herself. The back of her mind registered the ranting shouts from below as a background buzzing as she looked round for sanctuary. The pungent smells of turps and linseed oil wafted over her. She picked up her palate and a handful of brushes and attacked her canvas with savage brushstrokes. She worked furiously, stabbing and sweeping her brush over the large surface. New marks and splashes spattered the old timber flooring, mingling with the layers of dust. She kept working till the pale slanting sunlight that filtered in through the dormer window cast a massive and gloomy shadow across her canvas. Then she slowly sank to her knees, rocking to and fro, her hands, smeared with paint, clasped round her legs as she quietly wept. Gregory later said that painting was an astonishing statement of passion and anger. She had never sold it, though. People couldn't face it on their walls. Too disturbing, apparently. Her brushstrokes had slashed at the canvas. Glaring purples and throbbing reds streaked across it, sombre greys and blacks oppressively crushing, overwhelming anyone who looked at it. Her anguish was a tangible thing pulsating over the surfaces of every picture. Especially this one.

'You appear such a gentle little soul,' Gregory said. 'It just goes to show that one can't go by appearances. No one has any idea what goes on inside someone's head.'

True. True.

She remembered the incident with Granda and the gas bill for another reason which was even more shameful. In desperation she'd sneaked into the old man's room that night when he was in the bathroom and pinched ten pounds out of the Oxo tin he kept stashed with notes under the bed. She could never justify that act of dishonesty to herself. Although often and often she'd tried. She always ended up cringing with guilt and thinking: Some Quaker!

Over and over again since, in an effort to prevent a repeat of the crime, because it had to be said she was tempted, she read *Advices and Queries*.

'Are you honest and truthful in word and deed? Do you maintain strict integrity in your business transactions and in your relations with individuals and organisations? Are you personally scrupulous and responsible in the use of money entrusted to you, and are you careful not to defraud the public revenue?'

It was really dreadfully difficult being a Quaker and she often wondered why on earth they had accepted her into the fold. She lived in constant expectation of being drummed out in disgrace. Or at least for being totally inadequate. All the others in meeting seemed so morally and spiritually strong. They all took their turn at sharing in the responsibility of running the meeting and the meeting house. There were elders and members of committees that did good works, in 'Meetings for Sufferings', 'Meetings for Church Affairs', 'Eldership and Oversight', and 'The Peace Testament'.

All she'd ever done was scrub the floors in Meeting House when it had been decided to convert the basement into a multi-racial nursery. They had praised her for doing that as if the menial task had been important. Her heart had warmed towards them and she'd felt like scrubbing the whole building from top to bottom in gratitude. After that she'd eagerly volunteered for any cleaning jobs or for dish-washing or any shopping that was necessary. Shopping was something she had years of experience at, but carrying heavy loads so often didn't do her back any favours.

She was having such a struggle getting along Kilmarnock Road with her two shopping bags that she hadn't even enough spare energy to think of Gregory Seymour.

'Just another few yards,' she kept urging herself onwards. Dammit, she wasn't going to let half a stone of potatoes, a few vegetables and a dozen assorted tins of beans, spaghetti and processed peas get the better of her. She gritted her teeth and staggered on until it seemed that the shopping bags were dragging her along on her knees. But, as usual, she made it to the close. It was cool there, a dark tunnel out of the sun where she was able to rest for a few minutes leaning against one of the maroon-tiled walls. There, she could gaze up the well of the stairs and gain some comfort from the beauty of the stained-glass windows. The dancing pattern of coloured light shimmered like a spiritual being encouraging her on. Then there was the next leg of the endurance test: the stairs to the flat.

'Daisy,' she called out once she'd unlocked and pushed open the front door. The long empty corridor stretched dark and gloomy.

No reply. It was the school holidays. Daisy would be away somewhere with Jennifer. Peter would be at work. She didn't want to know where Granda was. She dumped the bags on the kitchen table, filled the kettle and lit the gas. A cup of tea would soon put her right. She slumped into a chair.

It was then, half comatose with fatigue, that thoughts of Gregory came drifting back into her mind. What a fine-looking big man he was – maybe a bit on the hefty side but she'd always thought a man should be bigger and stronger than a woman. In her romantic dreams her perfect man had been big and strong, but gentle and tender at the same time. Did such a paragon exist? In her dreams now Gregory was like that. He was gentle and tender and promised to protect and look after her and keep her safe.

In reality he had asked to have sex. Did that mean love? He'd never said he loved her. Neither had Peter. Neither had Mother. Neither had Father. None of them were demonstrative people. They shrank from any display of emotion as if it was a sin. It occurred to her that Sophie McPherson was like that. All tight and held in. Sophie hadn't even shaken hands with her. Instead she'd given a brief nod when introduced. It was the same when she and Daisy had left after that afternoon tea in Bearsden. Sophie had visibly shrunk back. A brief nod again and, a minute or two later, a wave from her window. She'd been very kind and hospitable all the same. Bessie still nursed happy memories of those home-baked cakes. Sophie had invited her to return and Bessie had every intention of returning.

We're all victims of victims, she often thought. A child shows love innocently, generously. But so often that expression of love is rejected, ridiculed, betrayed, until it becomes a source of vulnerability, even danger, that has to be hidden or hardened away. She had been rejected and betrayed in a thousand ways she could not bear to think about.

Probably so had Sophie. But Sophie McPherson had created a hard shell with which to protect herself. Bessie Alexander had not yet managed it.

'Have you not got the tea made yet?' Granda came shuffling into the kitchen. 'What are you lazing about there for? Peter'll be in in a minute.'

He was a small man like Peter and age had shrunk him even further. His long cardigan hung over a bundle of bones. So did his trousers. Both, especially the trousers, were disgustingly stained. Peter was always going on about how she neglected his father.

'I got you a washing machine,' he'd say although in fact she'd got it for herself from the sale of a painting of an old man. 'There's absolutely no excuse for neglecting Granda and not keeping his clothes clean.'

She was always washing the bloody things. It was impossible to keep up with the dirty old devil.

'OK. OK, Granda.' She got up and started putting the shopping away in cupboards. 'I was just going to make it.' Bang goes my quiet cup of tea, she thought, as Granda settled down at the table.

'I bet you've forgotten my paper.'

She had.

'I'll run back out and get it.'

Anything to escape the catalogue of moans and endless lists of her faults and foibles that would inevitably follow.

'Oh don't bother for my sake.' The old man's mouth drooped and slavered. 'I'm just a poor old man. No use to anyone. Just a nuisance, a burden . . .'

It was self-pity day.

'Won't be long,' she called out, already flying along the lobby.

Peter was slowly climbing the stairs as she was descending. He had the same drooping, bitter mouth as his father.

'Where do you think you're going?'

'I forgot Granda's paper.'

'Trust you.'

Oh, if only someone would.

'The kettle's boiling and I won't be a minute.'

The kettle could boil its head off. It would never occur to Peter or Granda, or even Daisy, to make the tea. She must have spoiled them, done something wrong. Everything, probably.

She phoned Gregory while she was out. He might have been somewhat fierce-looking with his thick mane of hair and bushy beard, had it not been for his soft brown eyes. He had a gentle voice too. Very serious, though. He was an earnest man.

'How could I possibly get away,' she spoke half to herself. 'I mean, what excuse could I have? I'm losing sleep over this, Gregory. I can't just . . . not just for that. In the first place, I'm a hopeless liar.'

Silence for a long minute. Then Gregory said, 'I tell you what. There's a summer school down south. I'm going to be talking at it. I'm also going to see what potential talent there is.'

'Talent?'

'New talent.'

'Oh . . .' For a minute she'd taken the wrong meaning of the word. Sometimes she thought she had a one-track mind.

'Work to display in one of the galleries. I like to encourage young people. Why don't you come along?'

'I'm not young.'

Unfortunately.

'You know what I mean. Tell Peter you feel you've a lot to learn.'

Hadn't she just!

'Tell him this summer school is just what you need. Bring your paints and canvases. There'll be plenty of easels there.'

'They'd never manage on their own.'

'It's time they learned.'

She supposed it was, really.

'Peter would never let me go.'

Gregory sighed.

'Bessie, you're a mature woman living in a free country. You're not his slave. It's time you had a life of your own. Just say you're going, that's all.'

Only, that wouldn't be all.

VII

'ARE YOU GOING to be in this evening, darling?' Andrina asked.

'You mean, get out of the way because Mr Fisher's coming,' Jennifer said.

Andrina rolled her eyes. Eyes made even more vivid and sparkling with a dusting of green shadow, and mascara separating each long curly lash. She was elegant in a beige dress and high-heeled sandals. She never wore slippers or anything unglamorous, even when alone in the house.

'I meant no such thing. You're always snapping my head off these days. I only wondered if you were going to visit Granny. And it's Uncle Paul, Jennifer. We both want you to call him Uncle or at least Paul, if it makes you feel more grown-up.' She pouted full, rosy lips. 'Mr Fisher sounds so formal and unfriendly.'

'He's not my uncle. And I don't want to be friendly with him. He's a creep. I hate him.'

Andrina sighed and turned away, glancing appreciatively at her reflection in the glass door of the kitchen cupboard. Already her cheeks were showing the first flush of excitement. She wondered if she had been so extreme and emotional when she was sixteen. She had not been in love with Robert. It seemed ridiculous now but she'd actually married him to please her mother; also, of course, to escape from her. She remembered how eagerly she'd looked forward to queening it in a house of her own. Doing what she liked, dressing in whatever way she fancied. She had always to dress so primly to suit her mother while all the time she longed for low-cut dresses, high heels, dangly earrings, bracelets. Robert had scarcely featured at all in her hopes and dreams. To be fair, though, she had

41

kept the house shining clean, his clothes were always laundered and pressed and no one could fault her cooking.

As it turned out, she hadn't escaped from her mother. Far from it. Even now her blood boiled at the memory of how Sophie had pestered her with phone calls and unexpected visits in order to spy on her and check on her every move.

If it hadn't been for her mother laying down the law, she would have married Bernard right at the start. But Bernard had committed three unforgiveable sins. First, he was too 'physical'. By that her mother meant sexy but could never bring herself to utter the word. Secondly, he was a Catholic. And thirdly, he not only came from a Catholic family but a 'tough crowd' from Blackhill. Blackhill was another name for hell. His father and his brother Tony had been in Barlinnie Prison. As far as Andrina remembered, their crime had been nothing more serious than breach of the peace. They'd been drunk at the time. That carried no weight whatsoever with her mother. Indeed her mother had always had such a passionate hatred for Bernard, Andrina often wondered if there was some other deeper reason for the emotion that even the mention of Bernard's name could trigger off. Andrina suspected that, even more than his religion and his rough background, it was Bernard's strong aura of sexuality that upset Sophie so much. Her mother had a phobia about sex: she was terrified at the mere mention of the word. Now she had dangerously high blood pressure, so Jennifer said. No wonder, the way she carried on. She'd always had a neurotic need to fit in, to keep up with the Bearsden Joneses. Most importantly, a spotless Christian reputation was the be-all and end-all of her life. Her daughter had to be a clone of her, reflect even more glory in her direction. She had always enjoyed it when her church friends called her daughter a 'little angel' when, dressed in virgin white, Andrina used to sing solo in the choir.

Andrina realised what a shock it must have been to her mother to discover the affair with Bernard. She had been shocked to the core herself by Bernard's betrayal of her and had strenuously fought to deny any intimacy with him. All to no avail. She could now at last look back on their passionate lovemaking with erotic pleasure. She had enjoyed other lovers since. How wonderful it felt to be herself, to know herself. She had no false modesty. She was a beautiful, sensual and loving woman and could see nothing but good in loving a man. She still stood up and sang with heartfelt sincerity in the choir of the Church of Jesus. Only now she never visited the church in Bearsden. The Rose Street church in town was the one she attended. She went regularly, although not three times every Sunday, as she had been forced to do as a child.

Paul laughed the first time he saw her pray. She was so surprised and upset that he'd apologised and never laughed at her again. Often now, he accompanied her to church. He lived in Edinburgh but stayed with her when he worked late at his Glasgow casino. No one at the Rose Street church knew that he was married. They thought he was her fiancé, and so he was. As soon as his divorce was through, they were going to be married.

Paul was not a wonderful lover like Bernard, but he had infected her with his own brand of excitement. He had introduced her to the world of gambling and many a thrill she'd experienced standing by his side in the plush glamour of casinos.

Paul was different. He was a dapper man, fastidious about his appearance. He kept his fair hair slicked back with haircream and his moustache was always neatly trimmed. He went for a regular manicure. He was not as tall or as well made or as handsome as Bernard. But Paul was wealthy, which could make up for a bit. He owned a large casino in Glasgow. Not only could he give her a good and secure life, but he could shower her with whatever her heart desired. That's what he wanted to do. Already he'd offered to buy her a decent house.

'I don't like you living so near the Green on your own,' he'd said. 'It's becoming very seedy and run down.'

'I won't be alone once we're married,' she told him. She was determined that they should set up house respectably together. She had no intention of being shuttled into the position of a mistress; Paul could become satisfied with that. As it was, she could still keep him guessing. She was the one who called the shots. If she so wished, she could invite someone else to her own home, and sometimes she did. She could refuse Paul sex. She had never been able to refuse Bernard. Sometimes she even fantasised that it was Bernard she was having sex with while Paul was making love to her. Nevertheless she and Paul had some great times together, especially at casinos. One of these days he was going to take her to Las Vegas. As it was, he'd flown her to Paris for the weekend. Another time to Amsterdam. Always he took her to the best hotels and restaurants. And of course they visited all the casinos and gambling clubs everywhere they went. Paul often laughed at the keenness of her appreciation.

'You almost purr with pleasure,' he told her. 'Like a cat enjoying a bowl of cream.'

His wife was a semi-invalid, crippled with arthritis. That was the problem. It wouldn't be easy to walk out on her. Then of course he had three grown-up children. Andrina had pointed out to him that it wasn't as if he'd be leaving his wife on her own with no one to care for her. Not when there were three daughters. She was sorry for Linda of course but, after all, arthritis wasn't a life-threatening disease. Lots of people had it. Money was a great comforter too and Paul would not leave Linda penniless.

He was putting his daughters through university. 'I want them to have the chance that I never had,' he told her.

She had laughed at him then, 'Darling, you've done very well without a university education and I'm sure they could too.'

But he had a real 'thing' about education and his lack of it. Come what may, his daughters were going to get the best education money could buy. He'd even offered to pay for Jennifer to go to university as well. He was very generous. She loved him for that – although she doubted that Jennifer would thank Paul for anything.

VIII

As it happened, Jennifer had planned to go to Daisy's anyway. First she washed and brushed her hair, glad its glossy brown colour had none of her mother's red in it. Daisy's hair was straight like Jennifer's but black, and without Jennifer's fringe. In fact, Daisy was a younger-looking version of her Aunty Moira. Glasses and all. She wasn't as prim and proper, though. Daisy had bought tickets for the Who Dunnits' open-air concert in the Kelvingrove Park. The Who Dunnits weren't her favourite group but they were all right. They had originated from Glasgow – Old Garngad of all places. Hardly the stuff that excitement was made of yet Jennifer was soon caught up in the tide of emotion all around her. She was jumping up and down and screaming with everybody else. Only her screams were more an expression of despair than appreciation. She was adding her racket to the huge tide of hysteria careering out of control as a kind of release as the Who Dunnits belted out their hit numbers in a determined fight to be heard. At the end of the concert when they tried to leave, the crowd swelled forward. Daisy and Jennifer, near the front, were swept along, their feet hardly touching the ground. A row of security men and women formed a barrier round the stage. Two or three of them leapt up on to the platform and hustled the performers bodily and none too gently away out of sight. The other security men and women held their ground and kept roaring out that it was all over. Time to go home.

Jennifer thought of her mother in bed with Paul Fisher and felt sick at heart. She longed for her own bed, her own room, her own home. But no chance. Not while *he* was there. Tears came near to welling up. At the same time she felt angry at the way she was being knocked and pushed about – behind by others in the audience, in front by one of the security women. More of a girl she looked, hardly much older than herself. Suddenly the woman put a hand on her shoulder – barely touched it, it seemed, yet the pain was excruciating. It brought Jennifer to her knees, screaming in agony.

'Hey you!' Daisy was struggling towards her and shouting at the woman. 'What the hell do you think you're doing?'

But before Daisy could reach her Daisy was brought down as well. Then a bunch of security men closed in – huge gorilla-like guys. Suddenly the crowd caught a glimpse of the Who Dunnits' limousine bumping across the grass towards the road. The yell arose: 'There they are!' – and everyone sped after the vehicle.

Daisy and Jennifer were helped to their feet. The physical pain had been the last straw for Jennifer and the tears were spilling out, blurring her vision. All she could see was a vague shimmer of a face bending over her. It belonged to one of the security men.

'Here, take this.' He offered her his handkerchief. After she mopped at her eyes, she was able to get a better look at him. He seemed familiar. He grinned at her. 'Come on, cheer up. It's not the end of the world. I'll tell you what. I'll arrange for you to meet the Who Dunnits. That should cure the pain, eh?'

Daisy let out a squeal of delight.

'Me too? She hurt me too.'

'Yeah, yeah. You too.'

It was the wink that brought it all back to Jennifer. He was one of her earliest 'uncles'. One that she'd really liked. Her Uncle Bernard. He used to visit the house when her dad was there. He was a friend of her dad's. So he must be different. He was all right.

'Uncle Bernard,' she said, unexpectedly pleased and happy.

He stared at her, puzzlement darkening his eyes. Then in astonishment, he said, 'Jennifer?'

'Yes.'

'My God, you've changed!'

'Well, I should hope so. I was only about six or seven the last time you saw me.'

'Yet in a way you haven't,' he mused. 'I should have recognised you.' He smiled down at her. 'You were always a very serious little girl.'

'You once brought me a teddy with a bow-tie round its neck and looking very smart in a tartan waistcoat.'

'Did I?'

'You don't remember? I've still got that teddy. I've always loved it. I used to sit on your knee when you came to visit.'

'Oh yes, I remember that.' He gave another wink. 'We must do it again some time.'

Daisy piped up then, 'Excuse me if I interrupt your stroll down memory lane, but when are we going to meet the Who Dunnits?'

'You know the Central Hotel?'

'Of course.'

'Well, be there tomorrow morning around 10.30, 11a.m. I'll arrange for you to have a cup of coffee with them and get their autograph.'

'Oh great,' Daisy enthused. 'Come on, Jennifer. We'd better get our beauty sleep tonight and look our best for tomorrow.'

'You're sure you're all right?' Bernard asked Jennifer.

'Yes, fine, thanks. I've forgotten about the pain in my shoulder with the surprise of seeing you.'

'I still have to attend to some things here but I could arrange for a taxi to take you home.'

Daisy answered for her.

'That would be great. Thanks a million.'

Later, in the darkness of Daisy's bedroom, Daisy still couldn't stop talking about the night's events and the wonderful, incredible date they had the next day.

'I'm glad the holidays are nearly over. I can't wait to get back to school and tell everyone. Can you imagine how jealous they'll all be? And we'll have the autograph to prove what we're saying is true.'

'I don't want to go back to school. In fact, I've made up my mind. I'm not going.'

'You're kidding,' Daisy squealed in astonishment.

'No, I'm not.'

'But what about university?'

47

'I don't care about university.'

'But you must.'

'You're beginning to sound like my mother. I can just imagine my father being the very same when I tell him.'

'But . . . but . . . what else can you do?'

'Get a job of course. I'm sixteen, not six.'

'But surely you'd get a far better job if you had a uni degree?'

'I just can't wait that long, Daisy. I've got to get away from home. I've been thinking – if I got a job, any kind of job, I don't care as long as I make some money. Then I could get a place of my own – even just a room in digs.'

'Is it that awful?'

'I can't stand it any longer. Not with that man there, and he's there every week now.'

'Gosh. I don't know what to say. My mum has her faults. She can be real dippy. You should see some of her crazy paintings. But at least she's not a tart. She'd never cheat on Dad. Do you think your mum takes money for it?'

'She's not a prostitute,' Jennifer shouted.

'OK. OK. Keep your voice down. There's no need to fly off the handle or blame me. It was you who told me your mother kept bringing guys to the house. What am I supposed to think?'

Jennifer was glad of the cover of darkness. She was trembling violently with distress.

'I'm sorry,' she managed, 'it's just all the excitement of tonight. And thinking about tomorrow . . .'

'I know. It's driving me bananas as well . . .' Daisy was off again but Jennifer was no longer listening. She wanted to weep but didn't know why. One moment she felt grown-up, determined to find a job and make a life for herself on her own. The next minute she was afraid and wanted to cling to her mother and feel safe. But safety, like love, was an illusion. She was on her own, always had been and always would be. Her aloneness was deeply rooted inside her.

Her fear increased a thousandfold. Lying in the now silent darkness in one of the single beds in Daisy's room, she wished with all her heart she'd remembered to bring her teddy. Thinking of it brought Bernard into her mind. She remembered the dark eyes, the tight jaw, the bulky muscles. She'd touched his upper arm as she'd passed him to climb into the taxi. It had been a spontaneous gesture of affection and thanks for his kindness. She was surprised at how iron-hard his muscles were. His eyes had smiled into hers as the taxi moved away.

He had been a friend of her father's. She supposed he must be old enough to be her father. She recalled the affection she'd always had for him.

Uncle Bernard. Bernard. A new confusion added to all the others in her life that she was trying to cope with.

She closed her eyes. But Bernard's face was still there.

IX

'AYE OK, SALLY. So you're tougher than I thought. But listen to me. In my outfit you avoid violence as much as you can. Whether it's a karate strike or a head butt, you don't use it unless as a last resort. Violence is mainly used – when you have to – to defend a principal. Are you taking this in?'

Her eyes were bright stars in a round baby face.

'Yes, yes. But did you see how easy I brought those two girls down, Uncle Bernard? And I could have done the same with a man.'

Bernard pinned her with one of his hard stares.

'If that's what you're in the job for, if that's all you can be proud of, you can chuck it right now.'

Her joy wilted with uncertainty.

'I thought you'd be pleased.'

'You've hardly been in the job thirty minutes and you use a pressure point on two schoolkids. I've been in the job for the best part of thirty years and I've only used that particular one on a single occasion. That was on a man who kept challenging me to a fight. A huge gorilla he was. An aggressive and determined guy too. There was no other way to stop him. Five times I had to put him down before he called it a day.'

There was admiration in Sean's voice.

'I can just see you do that, Uncle Bernard. Cool as a cucumber you'd be. I don't believe you've an ounce of fear in your body.'

'Don't be stupid. It's important to feel fear in dangerous situations because it's natural. It helps the adrenalin flow, and channelled into the right places, that's what makes you tick.'

'I felt the adrenalin tonight. I really felt *alive*,' said Sally.

Sean enthusiastically agreed.

Bernard sighed.

'And here was me thinking after a few jobs you'd go off the idea.'

'No way!' Sean said. 'Just you tell us what the next job is and we'll be there.'

'No, you won't. I'm going over to Hollywood with Eve Page and the Page Boys.'

'Hollywood!' the twins yelled in unison. 'Oh please, *please*, Uncle Bernard.'

'No way. It's a close protection job — bodyguarding — and that's very different from crowd control at a pop concert. You put your life on the line with bodyguarding.'

Sally was bouncing up and down on her chair with enthusiasm. She was so childish in her eagerness it was ridiculous.

'You've seen how tough I can be, Uncle Bernard. I could stand and fight. I could fight any man who tried to attack — '

'Sally, have you not heard a word I said?'

He regretted allowing Sean and Sally to have had any training, or allowed them to come on a job.

'If you're a bodyguard, the *last* thing you want to do is stand and fight. You want to extract your principal from the area. If someone pulls a gun, all you can do is block the bullet, and if you've got a gun yourself, fire back.' He had a sudden horrible vision of Sally being in such a situation. It made him experience a deeper fear than he'd ever felt before. He forced himself to continue in a calm, even tone. 'If it's someone with a knife, what you aim to do is disarm that person, or keep the person at length, away from the principal. It's not easy.'

'We could learn, Uncle Bernard,' Sally assured him. 'Couldn't we, Sean?'

'Definitely,' Sean agreed. 'No problem.'

'No problem?' Bernard echoed. 'Christ, Sean, you don't know what you're talking about. There's problems all right and plenty of them. If you're a bodyguard, you have to defend because that's your job — you're defending the principal, and yourself second. You have to think of the principal first at all times.'

'Be fair, Uncle Bernard. You've admitted you've been doing

all this a long time. You've learned by experience. We have to learn by experience as well. You've got to give us a chance to get that experience.'

Sally joined in.

'And you *promised*, Uncle Bernard. And we *trusted* you. We took you at your word. The job would be ours if we survived the training, you said. We'd be on the permanent staff of your firm.'

'Hang on. I didn't go as far as that.'

'Oh, Uncle Bernard.' Sally moved closer to him. '*Hollywood*! It would be a dream come true. Oh please! *Please*!'

'Sally, you're forgetting something. You're only eighteen. I'd feel responsible if anything happened to either of you. Your mother and your granny'd be worried sick. Your dad's mad at me already and I don't blame him.'

Christ, he thought. Jennifer was even younger than eighteen. Just a schoolkid. And some of these pop stars could be bastards. He'd better check that everything was all right. He'd never forgive himself if anything had happened to her.

'Oh, please, please, Uncle Bernard.'

He really was distracted now.

'Oh all right,' he said impulsively. His immediate concern had shifted to Jennifer. 'But crowd control, remember. You just deal with the fans.'

His thoughts turned to Jennifer again. He couldn't get her serious, vulnerable little face out of his head. The Who Dunnits would be well away from Glasgow by this time, otherwise he would have gone to the hotel and had a word with them. He decided, for his own peace of mind, to go to Monteith Row and check with Jennifer.

It was years since he'd been near Glasgow Green. The sight of Monteith Row and Andrina's close brought memories crowding back. He'd come here on visits with his first wife and his second. He'd also come alone. He'd fucked Andrina in every part of the house, including on top of the kitchen table. He'd never been with such a passionate, such a sex-hungry woman, before or since.

His blood began to heat at the thought of seeing her again and he fought to control the spasms of excitement he felt as he entered the familiar building. By the time he'd reached her door, he was breathless with sexual tension.

'Damn the woman,' he kept thinking. 'Damn her!'

He rattled noisily at the letterbox.

Jennifer answered the door. It was as if a light switched on inside her head at the sight of him. Her eyes brightened.

'Bernard!'

'Just came to see how you got on at the hotel the other day.'

'Come in. Mum's out just now but she won't be long. She said she'd be home in time to make the evening meal.'

He followed her into the kitchen and watched as she began filling the kettle at the tap.

'Meantime I'll make you a cup of tea.' Her eyes filled with anxiety. 'Or maybe you'd prefer something stronger?'

'No, tea'll be fine. So, tell me. What happened? How did you get on?'

'It was great. Daisy went on about it for hours. She's the fan, you see. Their music's all right but I don't go overboard for them like Daisy does. Still, it was quite an experience meeting them like that and getting their autographs. They gave us lovely chocolate gâteau with the coffee. I really enjoyed that.'

Bernard laughed, more with relief than anything else.

'I'm glad it went well. I know quite a few celebrities. Maybe I can arrange for you to meet someone you really admire.' Although not a male someone, he told himself.

She was a nice kid. He was drinking the tea and chatting to her when the kitchen door opened and Andrina came in. For a moment she looked as if she was going to faint. Bernard rose, surprised that Jennifer had obviously not told her mother about meeting him. Yet not surprised. It was then that he noticed the man behind her.

'Well, this is a turn-up for the book,' the man guffawed. 'Our Jennifer caught entertaining a secret lover.'

What a fool the man was. Bernard stared him down and his laughter petered away foolishly.

'Paul,' Andrina said, recovering. 'This is Bernard O'Maley, an old friend of my ex-husband. Bernard, this is my fiancé, Paul Fisher.'

'Pleased to meet you,' Fisher said.

She was as beautiful and as sexy as ever. Amazing woman. All the time since he'd last been with her melted away. The chemistry between them sparked across the room.

Jennifer looked sullen and withdrawn now. Obviously there was no love lost between her and Fisher. He didn't blame the child. He didn't like the look of the man himself. A right shifty-eyed git.

'I bumped into Jennifer the other day and arranged for her and her friend to meet some pop stars I know. I called to see if she'd enjoyed herself.' He glanced at his watch. 'But I'd better be going. I've an American tour coming up and still some organising to do.'

'I'll see you to the door,' Jennifer said.

He looked at Andrina as he passed her. Looked into her eyes and recognised the same hungry passion he'd known so long ago.

They didn't say a word to each other, never touched, but he had an erection before he reached the darkness of the street outside.

X

BESSIE MIGHT AS well have announced 'I plan to commit a gruesome murder and cause my whole family as much pain and scandal as possible.' Everyone could not have been more shocked and against the idea.

'Anyone would think,' she tried to laugh, 'that I'd announced I was going to commit some heinous crime. I only said I was going away for a week's course in watercolours.'

'To England!' Peter said. As if that compounded the crime.

Peter had always gone to Millport every year as a child, then as an adult. He had Millport on the brain. Not that she had anything against the place. It was a lovely little island. But as far as she was concerned, once was enough. There were so many lovely places to see – in Scotland, in England, all over the world. Each year she'd tried to persuade Peter to go somewhere else but he had the solid and enthusiastic support of his dad and his daughter. She was always howled down. She'd hoped – no, felt sure – that once Daisy had reached her teen years she would be an ally and rebel at such boring repetition: year after year, the same place. But not a bit of it. Daisy was building up her own precious stores of fond and happy memories of dear old Millport. Just like her old dad and granda.

'Live adventurously' had been one of the *Advices and Queries* that had most attracted Bessie to join. She daren't, of course, mention Quakers to Daisy. 'Trust you, Mum. It's just the kind of thing you *would* go for.'

In every other way Daisy seemed a normal teenager. She went ga-ga over the most repulsive-looking pop groups and played their music loudly on her record player.

The fact that she rebelled against her mother and everything her mother stood for didn't worry Bessie. Or, at least, she suffered it as best she could. It was very hard at times, though. Especially when Daisy criticised the clothes she wore, and the way she did, or didn't do, her unruly hair. And of course the heinous crime of getting paint under her fingernails. Obviously what Daisy wanted was a normal middle-class, middle-aged mum. She was always lecturing her about looking her age and dressing her age and behaving like a woman of her age should.

'You really embarrass me, Mum,' was Daisy's usual heartfelt cry. As if denim trousers, Indian shirts and curly hair was somehow the sole and sacred prerogative of the young.

But apart from how she looked and her love of painting, had she done anything so terrible? OK, she did disappear up to the loft at every opportunity. Nevertheless, she had been their 'normal' skivvy – no, absolute slave – for years. Lifting and laying for them, cooking and scrubbing for them, always being at their beck and call. All right, she didn't wear hats and carry handbags. So what? Thank God nobody bothered about such things at Quaker meetings. She had immediately felt at home among the motley crowd in the Meeting House. No fashion plates, no fashion rules and regulations there.

'Trust you,' Daisy cried, 'to get in with a crowd of cranks and eccentrics.'

'They're no such thing.' Bessie tried to defend the faith and the faithful but her words fell on deaf ears. (There were one or two eccentrics of course but what was the harm in that?) Daisy, she often thought rather sadly, was far more Peter's daughter than hers. She always echoed what Peter said, even what Granda said. They all backed each other up, a solid, impenetrable wall against her. Always had been.

But this time, although they didn't know it, she had Gregory on her side.

'Don't ask them,' he'd advised. 'Just tell them you're going and no argument about it. You're entitled to your own time.'

She'd known that there *would* be an argument. And that wasn't the worst of it. It was the continuous carping that always got to her. The way she was mocked and made a fool of and undermined. It had become like a Chinese torture. Often it confused her to such a degree she didn't know who she was any more. It depressed her so much she became paralysed. Hidden away in her bedroom she'd feel too weighed down to do anything but stare at the walls. At other times she'd feel like committing murder and then the only pleasure she got out of her existence was thoughts of murdering Granda. Granda had met a horrible death in all sorts of ingenious ways. Only Granda didn't die. In despair, she believed he never would. At other times, she felt full of guilt and remorse at having such wicked thoughts. She'd even on occasion harboured them in the peaceful silence of Meeting. To make up for her thoughts she'd cook Granda one of his favourite meals and let him beat her at dominoes. Then she had to struggle valiantly against a resurgence of murderous plans when he gloated over his victory, or laughed at how stupid she'd been. Or when he gleefully suggested a game of strip-poker.   •   •

Peter always thought this hilarious.

'Granda's a right card.'

Often she nursed murderous thoughts against Peter as well. But she seldom if ever spoke up, certainly never argued. Oh, once she had, long, long ago. And even then, she had been far too reasonable. She'd always tried to see the other point of view.

Gregory said, 'You know your problem?'

'No.'

'You're such a gentle soul.'

'Me?' She enjoyed a genuine laugh at that. Her with the murderous intentions?

'Yes, you. Try to be firmer with them. Harder, Bessie. Speak up clearly. Tell them what you want to do and then just *do* it.'

So she'd stood up in front of Granda and Peter and Daisy and said, 'I've booked to go on a week's course for watercolours at a college in York. I leave on Saturday. I've bought my train ticket and everything's organised. I'm really looking forward to it.'

'What?' they'd screeched in unison.

'Don't be silly, Mum,' Daisy said. 'College at your age? You're just making a fool of yourself again.'

Peter and Granda said, 'What about us? Who's going to look after us? Who's going to cook our meals?'

'I told you,' she said, 'I've everything organised. The fridge and freezer are packed with things I've already cooked. All you have to do is defrost them as you need them, and heat them up.'

She'd worked herself nearly into the ground with shopping and cooking and getting everything ready for them in advance. She felt absolutely knackered. It would be a miracle if she'd enough energy left to pack her case. It was always the same. Even when they went to Millport. She never had any time to herself for seeing to other people. It was just as well on this occasion that she'd been too busy to think, otherwise she would never have got as far as buying the train ticket. Now, with the house hoovered, the kitchen scrubbed and even the meals made for them, there was just her bag to pack. Now, she was beginning to worry. Not about Granda and Peter and Daisy. She was beginning to worry – no, panic – about having an affair with Gregory. That's what it would be, wouldn't it? Her heart swelled up to her throat with the fearful, sinful enormity of what she was planning to do. After all, whether you were the Church of Jesus, the Society of Friends or the Salvation Army, it said quite categorically in the Bible: 'Thou shalt not commit adultery.'

She hadn't been able to face going to Meeting the previous Sunday, as if God would be there in person to accuse her. It was bad enough to think of facing other Quakers. She felt she was letting the side down. That was the least of it, though. She was panicking on a far more urgent and practical level. She kept examining herself naked in the long mirror on the back of the bathroom door. What a humbling sight! She was pear-shaped. Boobs too small, hips too big. Her ankles weren't as slim as she'd like them to be either. She stood on tiptoe to simulate high heels. That helped, but she seldom if ever wore high heels.

She was about to get herself into a vulnerable situation where all her faults and weaknesses would be on public display. That's what it felt like. She'd known Gregory for only a few weeks. He was a stranger. How could she do it? If she had the appearance of a Marilyn Monroe it would have been entirely different. But look at her! She even had stretch marks on her belly.

In desperation she covered herself in Johnson's baby oil. Then she didn't have time to massage it in before Granda started banging on the bathroom door. He took these terrible urgencies to get to the lavatory pan and always, it seemed, while she was in the bathroom. She had to slither rapidly into her clothes. She was lucky to have been able to snatch the time to have a bath.

Usually she wore tights and white cotton panties and bra, and in the winter found comfort in her thermals. For the York trip she'd bought a black lacy bra, a narrow strip of frilly lace that purported to be a suspender belt, and black stockings. Feeling like a cross between a thief and a Jezebel, she'd secreted them at the bottom of her case inside a pair of bed-socks. (She had awful poor circulation and was afraid a strange bed would be too cold.) At the last minute she'd splashed out on a new nightie and négligé. Black too, both flimsy and free flowing from the wickedly low-cut neck. Not that she believed that she and Gregory would actually sleep together. The college brochure had contained pictures of small, spartan-looking single rooms with narrow single-sized beds. Anyway, she'd never sleep a wink in such nerve-racking circumstances. She had a vision of him perhaps visiting her on a respectable business pretext. She hadn't imagined the details of what exactly that might be. She would let him into the room, in all the glamorous glory of the black nightie and négligé. Her riot of fair curls would be a shining frame to her modestly blushing face and he would tell her how beautiful, how gorgeous, how desirable she looked.

The vision crumpled and dissolved into dust. In her heart of hearts, she couldn't believe it. Brainwashed into thinking the exact opposite for too long, she was left wishing she could dissolve into dust as well. Disappear into nothing. How could she have ever thought for one moment that she could put herself into such a vulnerable position – *again*? That's what had happened with Peter and she was still suffering the trauma and degradation of it. She couldn't possibly take any more. She'd rather die.

Yet she'd bought the ticket to York. She'd told the family. She'd packed her case and now it was Saturday and she was setting off despite the heavy gloom behind her. She had left the family sitting as if in mourning at a wake. Not her wake, though. The way things were they'd be more likely to cheer if anything happened to her. Cries of 'Serves you right. Good riddance to bad rubbish' would follow her to the grave.

Nobody had helped her to carry her case to the waiting taxi and it weighed like an elephant. What on earth had she crammed in there? Her packing had been done so quickly she couldn't remember. She hurried down the stone stairs jerking awkwardly from one side to the other like a man with a wooden leg. Inside she was in terrible turmoil. It was as if she was leaving her family for ever, shamefully deserting them, letting them down. She wished with all her heart that she wasn't going. She wished she'd never heard of York, or Gregory Seymour.

The devil, along with the crowd at the station, jostled her onwards and before she knew it, she was aboard the train and it was hastening her on to perdition.

XI

JENNIFER TURNED HER key in the door as quietly as possible. She had returned early from another overnight visit to Daisy's house. It hadn't been much fun at Daisy's this time. There was a terrible atmosphere in the house. Daisy's mother was away somewhere enjoying herself on her own, without a thought for Daisy and her family, it seemed. This surprised Jennifer, as it had astonished and outraged Daisy. Jennifer envied Daisy for having such a calm, motherly kind of woman who was always there to look after everybody and listen sympathetically to their problems. But to Daisy her mother was a source of constant irritation.

'All right,' she'd argued with Daisy more than once, 'your mum's hair is a bit wild, and she buys her clothes secondhand from Oxfam, but at least she doesn't grudge you anything and she doesn't put every horrible Tom, Dick and Harry before you. You come first with your mum. You really *matter* to her.'

Admittedly she couldn't at this moment add her usual 'Your mum's always *there* for you.' But after all, Daisy's mum had only gone for a week's painting holiday. It was the first time in Bessie Alexander's whole life she'd been away anywhere on her own. She'd said that in Jennifer's hearing. Bessie had never even gone anywhere on her own before she was married. Surely she deserved a break.

'I don't know what you're moaning about,' Jennifer had told Daisy. 'My mum's always disappearing. And not just to do something harmless like painting a picture either. You should think yourself lucky, Daisy.'

But Daisy didn't. It occurred to Jennifer that Daisy was a bit spoiled. More than a bit, really. She'd been glad to escape from Daisy's selfish, self-pitying complaints. The house at

Shawlands Cross was horrible and depressing. For the first time, Jennifer realised that its warm and welcoming atmosphere had been solely generated by Bessie Alexander.

The door opened with a creak and Jennifer tiptoed into the silent hall. She couldn't be sure if she was alone in an empty house or if her mother was still asleep. Her mother had never been an early riser. Then she was startled by the appearance in the bedroom doorway of Paul Fisher, clad only in a pair of Y-fronts. Jennifer averted her eyes and went into the kitchen. She'd left Daisy's place before they'd got breakfast organised and hadn't even had a cup of tea.

To her apprehension, Paul Fisher appeared behind her. He looked obscene. She fixed her attention on the kettle.

'I'll make Mummy's tea,' she said. 'There's no need for you to do it.'

'Mummy has run out to the grocer's to buy some milk.' His sneery tone of voice frightened her.

'Then I'll just leave her to do it herself.'

Jennifer's priority now was to reach her own room. Head lowered, she hurried past him. Sensing as well as hearing the pad of his steps following her, terror spiked her. She reached her bedroom and tried to shut the door but his foot was in it. Then he was in the room.

'Get out of my room.'

Her voice sounded childish and trembling. 'I'm going to tell Mum on you.'

He mimicked her. 'I'm going to tell Mum on you. Yes, you like trying to come between your mother and me, don't you? Always putting me down. I'll give you something to complain about, my girl.'

The speed with which he roughly grabbed her and knocked her on to the bed made her gasp and choke. Before she could scream his hand clamped over her mouth. Beads of sweat suddenly glistened on his forehead. His other hand fumbled with her clothes. She punched and kicked and struggled with all her strength but couldn't get free of him: she remained pinned underneath his body. The horrible hard thing he began bumping between her legs sickened her beyond all sickness.

Suddenly, he scrabbled away from her and rushed from the room. Her mother's voice now, calling from the hall:

'Sorry I've taken so long, darling. The man in the grocer's had slept in, would you believe? He was at a friend's "stag do" last night. I got some rolls as well. Would you like one with bacon and eggs?'

Fisher's voice. Calm. As if nothing had happened.

'Wonderful, darling. I'll come through and make a cup of tea while you're seeing to the fry-up. Won't be a tick. Just getting dressed. By the way, have I ever told you that I love you?'

Soon Jennifer could hear giggling. Then she caught the sound of her mother's little moans of pleasure. She felt ill. She was shivering violently.

'Mummy,' she called out. 'Mummy, please . . .' She could hardly talk for nausea, and the way her body was jerking and shaking.

'I didn't know you were home, dear.' Her mother came smiling into the room. The smile vanished at the sight of Jennifer and she rushed over to take her daughter in her arms. Jennifer clung gratefully to the soft, perfumed flesh.

'Jennifer, what's the matter, dear? Have you caught a chill or something? Shall I send for the doctor?'

From the corner of her tear-filled eye, Jennifer saw Fisher standing in the doorway. Dapper in flannel trousers, pinstriped shirt, and bow-tie.

'Don't let him come near me, Mummy,' she wept. 'Please keep him away.'

'Ssh, ssh, darling. You've just been having one of your nasty dreams. Mummy's here now. Everything's all right.'

Jennifer's sobs sharpened with anger and frustration. 'I haven't been dreaming. I've been over at Daisy's. I've just come in. How could I have been dreaming? It's him. He tried to have sex with me.'

'Who, dear?'

'You're the dreamer. Who do you think?'

For a moment her mother looked genuinely puzzled and Jennifer felt that, despite her warm perfumed nearness, Andrina was as far away and as alien to her as she'd always been.

Her mother turned her gaze towards Fisher.

'God.' He shook his head. 'I've always known that she hated me, Andrina.' He sounded as if he too was about to weep. 'But this is too much. I can't cope with lies like this.'

Andrina swivelled her attention back to Jennifer, at the same time shrinking away from her.

'This is what comes of you going over to my mother's so often. It's her that's put you against me. She did the same with your daddy. She's always hated me and tried to prevent me from having a little happiness. You're not to go over there again, do you hear?'

Jennifer fumbled for a handkerchief and rubbed at her eyes. 'That's so typical of you,' she said. 'You're incapable of thinking of anyone but yourself. You've never cared about me!'

'What nonsense. I've not only given you a good home and provided for you all these years, I've been the one to put up with your moods and your troublemaking and your constant criticism of me. You get more like your father every day.'

As usual, at the mention of Robert her voice acquired a bitterness tinged with petulance.

Fisher said, 'Well, you might have to put up with her, Andrina, but I don't. I'm not going to stay here and have her make accusations like that against me. For whatever reason, she's always been hell bent on ruining our relationship. Well, this time she's succeeded. I'm off and I won't be back.'

'No, wait!' Andrina cried out. 'Darling, don't go. She's young. I'll speak to her. It'll be all right. She won't act like this again. I promise.' She got up and followed him hastily out of the room, turning at the door for a brief moment with anger flashing in her eyes.

'How could you do this to me, you wicked, ungrateful girl. You'd better apologise to Paul, do you hear?'

Jennifer heard the kitchen door shutting. The shivering and shaking was now deep inside her. There was no way she could defend herself, no way she could cope. She grabbed the backpack containing the overnight things she'd had at Daisy's. She crept from the bedroom and house, hardly daring to breathe until she reached the street. Then she began to run and didn't stop until her legs gave way. She had to hide in a close in one of the streets: she collapsed and crouched there, hugging her knees, rocking backwards and forwards, staring at the large billowing masses of cloud in the sky. Seeking comfort but finding none.

Eventually she gathered enough thoughts together to decide to go to Bearsden to Laura's house. She could never think of it as her daddy's place because it had always been Laura's house. Her daddy had just gone there to be with Laura.

At first Jennifer thought of going to her father as a solution. Once she got off the Bearsden bus, however, and was only a few yards away from Laura's bungalow, she began to tremble with uncertainty. Her father was happy and settled with Laura. They were perfect partners with everything in common. Both were art teachers, both liked the same kind of music and theatre. A runaway daughter suddenly turning up on their doorstep would surely upset their happy lifestyle, and cause unwelcome problems. She would be a nuisance here with her father just as she'd been a nuisance at home with her mother. Still in a state of shock, however, and the need for her father's protection outweighing every other consideration, she knocked at Laura's door. No one came to open it. She knocked again. And again. Still no reply. Then, like a physical blow to her heart, Jennifer suddenly remembered that her father and Laura had gone off to Florence with a group of their pupils. She had been too distraught to remember. She was still distraught, and thirsty and hungry too, as well as needing the toilet. Helplessly she looked around. She wandered back to Drymen Road. It was then that she saw her granny's house just along the road. Of course, she would go there. She almost wept with relief. She didn't know why she'd thought of her daddy first. Except that he was the one who had protected and comforted her when she was a little girl. He had always put her first and had been on her side then. But that, of course, was before his marriage to Laura. Laura was his first love now. Jennifer hurried across the road and along to the end terrace house. Her granny didn't have anyone else to be loyal to or put first. Her granny would protect her and look after her.

'Jennifer!' Sophie stood aside to let her in. The hall was spotless as usual. There was always a strong smell of lavender wax polish and every surface had a hard gleam of reflected light. It was the same in the kitchen. Only, in the kitchen, the pungent smell was of pine disinfectant.

'What a nice surprise,' Sophie was saying as she plugged in the electric kettle. 'That's right, take off your haversack, or whatever you call it. I take it that means you're going to stay the night. I wasn't expecting you but of course I'm delighted. Absolutely delighted! You know you're welcome at any time, Jennifer. You're just in time for morning coffee and I've got – '

'Oh, Granny, it was terrible and I was so frightened.' Jennifer burst into sobs punctuated by loud moaning sounds as if she was in a panic of pain.

'Jennifer!' Sophie hastened towards her, caught her by the arm and led her to one of the kitchen chairs. Sophie had never been a demonstrative woman, never had cuddled her grandchild, had never given anything but the most fleeting kisses. She was a taut, held-in woman who was incapable of showing love and affection. But Jennifer knew she loved her in her own way. It was the one thing she'd always been certain of. Her granny was the one sure, safe rock in Jennifer's life.

'Now just you sit there and try to calm yourself,' Sophie said. 'As you know I'd normally never give someone as young as you any strong drink. But I do believe at the moment a little whisky might be the best thing to strengthen you and calm you down. All right?'

Jennifer nodded, still sobbing and making little animal noises.

The whisky made her cough and burned her lips and throat but it gave her a warm feeling that brought a comfort of sorts.

'Now,' Sophie sat opposite her at the table, 'tell me what all this is about. What was terrible? What were you so frightened about?'

Jennifer hesitated. She had been so shaken by her mother's disbelief she was now afraid that her granny might not believe her.

'It was that man.'

Colour began to drain from Sophie's face.

'What man?'

'Mr Fisher. He did awful things to me. Dirty things, and Mummy didn't care.' Her sobs grew louder at the sight of her granny's grey, horrified expression. 'I'm sorry, Granny, don't be angry with me, oh please don't. It wasn't my fault. And I'm not telling lies. I would never tell lies to you. Please believe me.'

'I'm not angry with you, child. How could I be angry with you? It's that filthy pair of perverts I'm angry with. I've always been afraid of this happening again. It's been a recurring nightmare all my life . . .'

Jennifer's sobbing hiccupped to a stop. She started in perplexity at the older woman.

'Again?' She wiped at her eyes with the back of her sleeve. 'It didn't happen to me before, Granny. I've never felt safe since he's been around but it never . . .'

Her granny was no longer listening. There was a haunted faraway look in her eyes.

'I hated them, the dirty perverts. I was glad when they died. After what they'd put me through. They committed suicide, you know. Older than I am now, they were. And they'd long since ruined me and my whole life . . .'

The words were babbling out as if the older woman had completely taken leave of her senses.

'Granny, please, I don't understand . . .'

'No, nor did I at first. I was only a child. Younger than you. Much younger. When they died they left a note saying "Sophie, we're sorry." Sorry? Not as sorry as I am that they'd just taken sleeping pills. I'd wanted them to die a painful death. I wanted to watch them die in agony. That's what I wanted . . .'

'Granny, please don't. You're frightening me.'

'Everyone thought I was grieving but I was secretly rejoicing . . .'

Jennifer couldn't cope with this new horror. The shock of hearing what Paul Fisher had done had obviously been too much for the old woman. She had taken ill. She looked demented. Her talk as well as her appearance were becoming wilder and wilder. Then suddenly it stopped. Her face twisted, drooped down at one side. There was tragic appeal in her eyes. Jennifer began to weep.

'I'm so sorry, Granny. Oh, I'm so sorry . . .'

XII

HIS WIFE. HIS *wife*? Bessie couldn't believe it. Gregory had actually brought his wife with him to the college. It defied understanding. She knew he was a cool customer, but this was ridiculous.

'Pleased to meet you,' she said, smiling uncertainly at the woman with the tired-looking skin, a mole on her left cheek and a short uneven haircut. Her hair looked as if it had been chewed by the dog.

'Nice to meet you too, Bessie,' Isa said. 'So you're the new genius of a painter Gregory has discovered.'

'Yes. I mean, no. I'm no genius.' Her laughter sounded false. 'For goodness sake!'

'Gregory says you have a very original and striking talent. He's very proud of you.'

They were chatting while Gregory stood calmly by, his head tilted slightly back, for all the world looking proud of both of them. He must be mad. Or was a situation like this normal in the outside world? She had been dreaming, and worrying, about a secret love affair. Later at the college, when she'd managed to get speaking to him alone, she said, 'You brought your wife?'

'Oh yes, she always comes with me when I have a lecture engagement.'

'But . . . I thought . . . You did ask me to sleep with you, didn't you?'

'To have sex with me, yes.'

'Not to sleep with you?' She was confused and had to get things straight in her head.

He smiled patiently. He looked like some Sultan from one

of the books of fairy tales from her childhood with his noble head, warm eyes and great bush of a beard.

'We'll arrange that for a later date. There will be plenty of opportunities for us to enjoy each other here. Isa doesn't attend the lectures or the painting sessions. She's just come for her own kind of holiday. She'll be perfectly happy exploring York.'

'I see.' She didn't really. *Enjoy* each other? Did people enjoy quick sex as a change of entertainment from going to the theatre or a concert nowadays? Was she so out of touch with modern trends? Had she spent too long in the Co-op, cloistered in the aisles of fruit and veg, soap powder and detergents?

To add to her confusion, she *liked* Isa. They sat beside each other at mealtimes and chatted happily. She discovered that Isa was going to the theatre with a couple of American ladies she'd met in York. Isa was a very friendly easy-to-get-on-with person in her Jesus sandals and shapeless cotton dress. Bessie couldn't understand how Gregory could contemplate cheating on her. Or even why he'd *want* to. Isa Seymour wasn't catwalk material. But then, neither was Bessie Alexander. Even after knowing Isa a couple of days, *Bessie* couldn't contemplate cheating on her. That evening, the evening Isa was going off with her American tourists, Bessie avoided Gregory, avoided everybody in fact by shutting herself away in her room directly after dinner. She decided to go to bed early and read the book she'd started on the train. Abandoning now all thoughts of a Mills and Boon romance in real life, she gave only a passing regretful glance at the black see-through nightie. With a sigh, she donned the cotton pyjamas she'd bought in a sale at a cut-price store. How low can you get? Peter had been with her and suggested the purchase. He loved a bargain, especially if it meant saving money on her. She propped herself up in bed and had just got to a romantic part of her book when she was startled by a gentle tapping on the bedroom door. Before she could call out, 'Who is it?', the door opened and Gregory entered, closing it quietly behind him. For a moment, Bessie's mouth literally hung open in shock. Then, panic coming to her rescue, she clutched the blankets up to her chin – a quite unnecessary act of modesty as her pyjamas were nearly throttling her.

'You can't come in here,' she said. But of course he already was in. His big body dwarfed the narrow room. He was towering over her, his bulk casting a giant shadow.

'It's all right,' he said gently. 'Isa is away to York.'

'It's not all right.' Her voice sounded high and strident. 'She might come back at any minute and your room is just across the corridor.'

'What are you getting into such a panic about?'

To hear him speak it was as if he'd just dropped by for an innocent cup of tea. His voice had a slightly puzzled, faintly injured tone.

'Go away!' She aimed a whispered shout at him. 'I want you to go away.'

He sighed.

'Very well.'

He looked really huffed. Her distress of course had been partly due to the shame and embarrassment of the thick winceyette pyjamas. At least she hadn't been caught wearing rollers.

She watched him leave and shut the door behind him. Only then did relief set in. It was wonderful to think she had nothing to worry about now, no guilt to torment herself with. She could relax with a clear conscience and appreciate the holiday. No anxiety about what she was going to give the family for their next meal, no cooking, no shopping, no hoovering, no washing, no scrubbing. *No Granda!*

What ecstasy! She cuddled down in bed, hardly able to wait until next day when she would be able to paint to her heart's content.

It only took another couple of days to send her into raptures of happiness. The freedom to sit at her easel out of doors was indescribable. It was a freedom of spirit Bessie had never experienced before. So happy was she, and so full of gratitude, that her heart overflowed with the need to share everything with Peter and Daisy – and even Granda if he wanted to listen. She longed to tell them all about the college with its big bright art department and the campus with the colourful flowerbeds and the lake and the way the pale green leaves of the trees glistened like silver in the sunshine. And how when she was painting outdoors she'd heard, through the open windows of the music room, someone playing Mozart. She had been, still was, on a high of happiness.

Her fingers fumbled impatiently as she dialled her home number.

'Peter!' she shouted with excitement. 'Peter, is that you?'

'Who did you think it was – Prince Philip?'

The sound of the sneering voice immediately chipped the keen edge off her blissful state. She had forgotten what it sounded like. But she still had an eagerness to tell him about the college and some of the friends she'd made. Before she could launch into all the details, however, his voice pushed on:

'You never left enough milk and we'd to take our tea black. It made Granda feel sick. Everything takes far too long to defrost and I had to go out for fish suppers last night and they were nearly the death of me. I've been suffering purgatory with indigestion ever since.' He belched to prove the point. 'You know how greasy stuff gives me the bile.'

All her enthusiasm, all her happiness, seeped down and down until it trickled out of her toes and disappeared. After she replaced the receiver, it took a minute or two before she could rouse herself to move away. She suddenly saw, with frightening clarity, what her life was like at home. It was too terrible for tears. She felt dazed with the thought of it. But after a good night's sleep, and waking up in the college bedroom with the sun beaming in, Bessie's gratitude rushed back. She bounced from the bed and sang as she dressed. She could hardly wait to get to her easel.

First there was the delight of joining all the others in the canteen where the noise of enthusiastic chatter filled the room. Bessie enjoyed a good breakfast – she never had much of an appetite at home – and added to the racket of talk and laughter.

Gregory still looked huffed. She detected it in the increase of dignity about him, the slight tilt of his head, and the accusatory note of his cool politeness. She felt a pang of guilt, but was able to distance herself from him by sitting at the far end of the table between two women from London. She successfully avoided him for the rest of the week by sticking like a limpet to whoever she could. Including Isa. She didn't feel a bit jealous, nor it seemed did Isa when it became obvious that two of the younger students were trying their best to flirt with Gregory.

She didn't risk phoning home again. Didn't have time, really. There was a last-night party which was great fun. She hadn't laughed so much in years. Gregory didn't attend. Probably he was away somewhere with one of the admiring girls who had been in the audience when he'd given his last lecture. Bessie didn't care. She was as free as fresh air to enjoy herself.

On the way home she could hardly wait to tell Peter and the family all about her adventure. A born optimist, she always forgot the bad. The moment she entered the house, it all came back to her. It was like stepping into a funeral parlour. Or a tomb. She'd even forgotten that the flat – especially the kitchen at the back – was so dark and oppressive. The sun didn't seem able to penetrate the gloom. The only place it reached was her studio. Granda and Peter were sitting side by side waiting for her like judge and jury. Their sour faces proclaimed an unmistakable verdict of guilty.

Beside Alexander, you are found guilty of cruelly neglecting your poor old husband and his poor old dad and you are sentenced to long-drawn-out reminders of your selfish behaviour ad infinitum.

She dumped her case down and went over to the sink to fill the kettle. Four rheumy eyes, full of bitterness, bored into her back.

Now she wished that she *had* enjoyed a bit of loving from Gregory. She began thinking about him again, in the romantic terms she'd done before she'd gone to York. She needed any straw to hang on to, any vestige of hope. Oh, how stupid she'd been. She'd spoiled the one chance she had of loving and being loved. Could she never do anything right?

She put cups and saucers on the kitchen table. Peter and Granda still sat like two accusations set in stone. Shadows gathered around them. Through the bitter silence, the kitchen clock slowly tick-tocked her life away.

XIII

'MRS PEMBERTON?' ANDRINA repeated into the phone. 'Mrs Pemberton, did you say?'

'Yes, dear, your mother's neighbour. Poor Sophie is in hospital. Jennifer was in a dreadful state when she came to my door. The poor child didn't know what to do. I could see at a glance that poor Sophie had taken a stroke and so I immediately returned to my own house and told Mr Pemberton to phone for the doctor. There was really nothing else I could do.'

'A stroke?'

'She's always been so highly strung. It came as no surprise to me, really. It's only a wonder she didn't take a stroke or a heart attack years ago. I said at the time when her poor husband died – and everyone in the terrace agreed with me – that I'd always thought – '

'What hospital?' Andrina interrupted, and when Mrs Pemberton replied, she asked, 'Did Jennifer go with her?'

'No, the doctor gave her a tranquilliser or a sedative or something, and told her to rest. There was nothing she could do either. She'd just be in the way, the doctor said. She could visit her grandmother later. The poor child was in such a state. Quite hysterical – but of course she's always adored her grandmother. Sophie has been so good to her. I always said – '

'I'd better go to the hospital right away,' Andrina interrupted again. 'Will you excuse me?'

'Of course, my dear . . .'

Andrina hung up.

'What's wrong,' Fisher asked, strolling into the hall.

'My mother's taken a stroke. I'll have to go to the hospital.'

'She's getting her just desserts at last, is she?'

'Paul! That's a terrible thing to say.'

'Be honest, darling. You hate her guts!'

Andrina avoided his eyes. 'She's always been a difficult woman,' she said. 'But she's still my mother. I can't just ignore her when she needs my help.'

'She ignored you when you needed her help.'

Andrina lit a cigarette. It occurred to her as she did so how horrified her mother would be if she saw her smoking. Anyone would think, to hear her mother talk, that 'Thou shalt not smoke if thou art a woman' was one of the Ten Commandments. For a long time now Andrina had taken perverse pleasure in smoking, even at times using a long, fancy holder. She enjoyed imagining each cigarette as cocking a rebellious snook at her mother. Even though her mother didn't know it. For so many years she had been intimidated by Sophie, dominated by her, been fearful of her. Not any more.

'I'm her only child.'

'She still treated you like a child, and a wicked child at that, even after you were married and a mother yourself. Bullying you, spying on you, you told me.'

'I know, I know. But apart from anything else – what would people think if I didn't go?'

'Ah!'

'Don't "ah" me! It's not only how it would look. I do have some feelings for her, despite all she's done. You don't need to come with me. I can phone for a taxi.'

'No, I'll drive you there if that's what you really want to do.'

'I'll just fetch my handbag.'

They didn't talk on the journey to the hospital. Andrina's mind was in turmoil. One minute she had slipped back to when she had been a baby and had been neglected and abandoned by Sophie. The next minute she remembered how, after her mother had been 'saved', she had gone to the opposite extreme and tried to stamp out every natural expression of Andrina's passionate personality, her taste in clothes, in jewellery, in make-up, in men. Her mother had forced her into a life of deceit for years.

Did she really want to see her mother? They had successfully avoided each other for years. She'd almost forgotten in her busy, happy life how her mother used to make her feel. Now, it was all tumbling back to her: the fear, the self-consciousness. She became aware of her low-necked emerald dress. Green, according to her mother, was a Catholic colour as well as an unlucky one. Her expensive gold choker and earrings would not meet with approval either. Nor would her high-heeled shoes. Her make-up, of course, had always been a bone of contention. Now the black mascara and eyeliner that dramatically framed her eyes would shock her mother. As would her full lips, their sensual pout accentuated by lipstick. Another thought struck her. Maybe her mother would be unable to say anything because of her stroke.

Andrina felt bitter laughter swell up like a lump in her throat. Her nagging, neurotic mother, who never stopped talking, being struck silent by God. She liked that idea.

She would see of course that her mother received every medical care and attention. *She* would not disown or neglect her. She was a true Christian as well as a good daughter.

She liked that idea too.

Paul sat at one side of her mother's bed and she sat at the other. Strange how shrunken and grey Sophie looked. Not frightening at all. And she really couldn't speak. Andrina felt a surge of elation and self-confidence.

'Now, don't worry, Mummy,' she told the tragic-eyed figure in the bed, 'you're going to be all right. I'll see to everything.' If there was any fear present, it was in her mother's eyes. 'You're not going to stay in a public ward like this. I'll have you transferred to a little private room on your own. We don't care what it costs.' She fluttered her dark screen of lashes across the bed at Fisher. 'Do we, darling?'

'Whatever you say, sweetheart.'

'After we leave here today, I'll go over to your house, Mummy, and see what Jennifer is up to. She just disappeared from home, you know. We were terribly upset, weren't we, darling?'

'Appalled, more like.'

'At the lies she was telling, Mummy. She really is a very difficult child.'

Her mother was struggling to move her head.

75

'Forgive me for saying so, Mummy, but the trouble is you've always spoiled Jennifer. It's time she learned not to keep running to you every time she takes a tantrum.'

She was enjoying herself. Never before had she been able to express herself like this. She fancied a cigarette but automatically suppressed the craving. Then she thought: why should I deny myself the pleasure? There never had been any pleasure she denied herself – except, that is, in her mother's presence. She had always been far too afraid to be her natural self with her mother. But now, right now, the fear had gone. She made quite a sensual performance of taking her gold cigarette case from her handbag, selecting a cigarette, tapping it on the case, then lighting up with the gold lighter. She inhaled deeply, pleasurably, like she did after enjoying sex. Then, blowing a leisurely stream of smoke across the still figure in the bed, she observed the horror in the dark sunken eyes, and was glad she had come.

'I know you love her, Mummy, and you mean well, but she's got to realise that her home is with me.'

XIV

BERNARD WAS GLAD that the Boeing 747 was steadily piling up the miles between him and Andrina. It had shaken him to discover how strong the chemistry was between them. No way was he going to dance to her tune again, but it took all his self-discipline to banish her from his mind and concentrate on the job in hand. He had already been over to LA to make sure that the arrangements were right for the arrival of the principal. His priority was the female singer. He had detailed his men to bodyguard the three Page Boys. Although the Page Boys shared in Eve's worldwide popularity, it was Eve who was the main focus of the fans.

He'd walked the route. He'd also met the owner of the company who was going to provide the stretch limos, talked with the drivers, and had a look around the cars. Right now, Rod McGowan, his number two, would be going through the whole checking process yet again. He'd made sure the cars were fully equipped, that the drivers were competent and the company had back-up should one of the cars suddenly break down.

He'd met the hotel manager of the Beverly Wilshire and the hotel security manager had gone over all the plans. He'd arranged for his security people to protect the floor where the principal's room was situated – day and night. He'd also cleared it with the police that he and his men should carry guns.

The plane swooped downwards. There was a judder as the undercarriage hit the tarmac. Then the race along the runway until the speed was brought under control and the plane stopped. Eve was stretching and yawning, catlike, Andrina-like. He wanted to avert his eyes, to blot Andrina from his mind.

But Eve's life might depend on him doing no such thing. He must keep his attention riveted on her.

He'd warned the twins, Sean and Sally, to stay clear of him. He didn't want to see them or speak to them if it could be avoided until the job was over and they were all off duty and back home in Scotland. They were working on the crowd control side with some of his best and most experienced men. He could now only trust that they would be all right and put any worries about them out of his mind as determinedly as he was trying to banish Andrina.

He got Eve into the limo and he sat in front with the chauffeur. In front was another limo carrying three of his security men. Behind was a back-up car, another limousine with the band's manager and the three Page Boy musicians, Joe, Billy and Dave.

Later, alone in this hotel room, Bernard sank once more into sensual dreams of Andrina. He felt himself drowning. He closed his eyes and smelled her perfume.

XV

'COME IN.' BESSIE stood aside to let Andrina enter the lobby. 'I'm afraid Jennifer isn't here but maybe Daisy will know where she is.'

Bessie led Andrina into the kitchen where Daisy was doing her homework at the table.

'Darling, do you know where Jennifer is? Here's her mum looking for her. Do sit down, Andrina. I've a pot of tea made. I'll pour you a cup.'

Andrina smiled.

'Thank you.'

Bessie thought – what a beautiful woman! If only I looked like that the world would be my oyster. She had a sudden vision of herself in a slinky dress with a low-cut top and a slit skirt with a shapely leg teasing out, and men whistling at her. It only lasted a second.

Andrina was about the same age as herself but with full upturned breasts and straight back. No rounded shoulders there.

Daisy said, 'I thought Jennifer was at her granny's.'

'She was. Then her granny took ill. My fiancé and I have been at the hospital. But when we went out to Bearsden to collect Jennifer, she'd gone.'

Bessie poured the tea. 'She probably went home to Monteith Row.'

'No. Paul and I have been home. I've left him there in case she turns up. He said he'd phone here immediately to let me know. Can you think of anywhere else she might be, Daisy?'

Daisy shook her head. Andrina continued: 'It's really too bad of her, worrying Paul and me like this. She's always been difficult, of course. Her father's away on holiday so he can't be of any help. Not that he ever was. He was never there when I needed him.'

Bessie had a sudden urge to paint her. It was something about the full pouting lips and the unusual coloured eyes. Those eyes could be wide and childlike one minute and dark with emotion the next. She could see the smouldering background to the painting – ominous clouds with streaks of fiery red building up.

She pulled herself together and said, 'Daisy, are you sure you don't know of any place or any other friends she might be with?'

Daisy flashed her a dark look. She was still clinging to the sulk she was using to punish Bessie for going away to York and neglecting her.

'She hasn't got any other friends.'

'Has she done anything like this before?' Bessie asked Andrina.

'Oh yes. She's always disappearing off without as much as a by-your-leave. But it's usually to her granny's. What worries me is that Mrs Pemberton, my mother's neighbour, told me the last she'd seen of Jennifer was walking down Drymen Road wearing a backpack. When she wasn't home, I was sure she must be here. Apart from my mother's, this is the only place she's ever stayed overnight.'

'Oh dear.' Bessie was now worried as well. She liked Jennifer and had tried to mother the child because she always looked so lost and vulnerable and in need of a reassuring cuddle.

'Maybe you should contact the police.'

Daisy cast her a look of disgust.

'For goodness sake, Mum.'

'Well, if she's been missing all night.'

'And all day,' Andrina added.

'Oh dear. Yes, definitely, phone the police, Andrina. Poor wee Jennifer!'

'For goodness sake, Mum. She's sixteen. If she wants to go off on her own, why not?'

Bessie nearly said, 'I'm forty and you don't think I should go off on my own', but she was too distracted by visions of

Jennifer's pale unhappy face to get into an argument with Daisy. She addressed Andrina instead.

'I'll go with you to the police station.'

'I don't like to bother you.'

'It's no bother, Andrina. Honestly.'

Just then Granda came shuffling into the kitchen.

'Is my tea not ready yet? I'm sitting through there starving. I could be dead for all you care. No wonder I'm down to skin and bone . . .'

'Oh, I'd better go,' Andrina said, already backing towards the door. 'You've enough to do without me bothering you.'

'No, really, it's no — '

'I'll get Paul to take me. I should have thought of that in the first place. He'd want to go with me.'

Bessie saw her to the front door nursing murderous thoughts of Granda. There were times when she really hated the selfish old sod and this was one of them.

'I'm sorry, Andrina. If there's anything I can do to help, please don't hesitate to ask.'

Impulsively she gave Andrina a hug and she was rewarded by a smile and a wide-eyed gaze shimmering like a rainbow. Bessie felt moved by such beauty. One day, she determined, I'm going to paint her.

She'd hardly had time to return to the kitchen when Peter arrived. Peter of the sallow skin with the deep lines down each cheek into which the corners of his eyes and mouth sank down. She was sure he had ulcers because he really did suffer with his stomach at times. But would he eat the special light dishes she tried to make for him? Once in a blue moon, if she was lucky. She was so fed up trying to coax him to eat a poached egg or milky porridge for breakfast instead of the big fry-up he favoured.

'Your tea won't be a minute,' she told him. They still did things the old-fashioned Scottish way with dinner in the middle of the day and 'high tea' in the late afternoon. Usually it was a fry-up. Or fish and chips. Scones and cakes, too, and plenty of butter and jam. Occasionally during the summer she tried to get away with cold meat and salad but it always meant a hue and cry of 'Where's my chips?'

'You must have passed Andrina, Jennifer's mum, on the stairs. She was up here looking for Jennifer. The child seems to have gone missing. Isn't it awful?'

'Where's my chips?' Peter had got his eye on the cold meat and salad.

'I haven't had time to make chips. I just told you – Andrina was here. I had to stop to talk to her.'

'Your tongue never stops. And when you're not wasting your time gossiping, you're acting like a schoolkid splashing colour on bits of paper.'

She took a deep breath. Memories of the happy hours at the college flooded over her and nearly brought tears to her eyes. Only she'd never been a crying kind of person. At the college there had been such stimulating, intelligent conversation. She had never been used to such talk. Indeed she had long since had any suspicion of it mocked out of her. For years, she'd never visited an art gallery, never been caught reading anything serious. Her mind had atrophied. Her capacity for loving had shrunk back, given up, lost hope.

No, not quite. There was a stubborn bit about her. She never gave up hope altogether. As she chewed absently at her salad and chips, as Granda's and Peter's and Daisy's voices moaned on like a Greek chorus, she remembered York. She remembered Gregory, who could talk about so many interesting things with such authority. More than that he listened to her as if what she was saying was of riveting interest. Gregory looked at her with such serious concentration, it was as if she was the only person in the world.

She determined to phone him.

XVI

JENNIFER TOOK THE train to London. No one knew her there. The tannoy at Euston Station had a ghostly ring. She couldn't make out what it was saying. Allowing herself to be carried along with the people from the train, she found herself in the vast forecourt. Sound echoed hollowly round her head in a meaningless buzz. For a few minutes, she stood wondering what she'd do next, where she'd go. People brushed by, two-dimensional images flowing round her. Panic made her heart pound in her ears as the enormity of all that had happened and what she had done became a reality.

The attack by Fisher was horrific enough. Her granny's illness was horrific enough. But then her granny had been taken to hospital and Mrs Pemberton had said, 'I've phoned your mother, dear. She and her fiancé are going straight to the hospital. Then after they see your granny, they'll come and collect you and take you home.'

She couldn't go home. Not with Fisher there. She just couldn't. Sweat broke out all down her spine and she shuddered involuntarily. She had no choice but to run away. But how could she with no money? That was when the most awful thing happened. At least the thing that was causing her most anguish and guilt. She had stolen all granny's money. Granny's handbag had been lying on the kitchen chair. She'd opened it and taken all the notes from the wallet, and all the coins from the purse. About fifty pounds in all. It was like stealing from the dead. No, worse than that, because her granny had been the one person who'd loved her and been good to her for as far back as she could remember. Then, another even worse anguish made her bend forward and screw up her face with the physical pain of it.

She had been the cause of her granny taking ill. It was because her granny loved her so much that she had been shocked and distressed at what Fisher had done. Over and over again, Jennifer flayed herself for telling her granny. It had been so selfish and thoughtless. After all, Granny was an old woman. How could she have done this to her? She might even die. Mrs Pemberton had warned her to prepare for the worst. There was no doubt in Jennifer's mind that this awful stroke had been her fault. Granny had been perfectly healthy and happy until she'd arrived.

'Are you all right?'

Jennifer looked up. A man was bending over her.

Like a startled fawn she took to her heels and didn't stop running until she reached Euston Road. Heart pounding and gasping for breath, her throat raw and painful with the undue exertion, she leaned against the wall of a building across the road from the station. After a minute she glanced back and was relieved to see no sign of the man. She tried to be sensible. The fact that Fisher had attacked her didn't mean that every man was a potential attacker. Her mind told her that. Her emotions, however, were no longer governed by logical thought. She now found she was afraid of men. There was no use denying it. But then, she told herself, it had only been a day or two since the attack. Given time, she'd get over it. Yet despite how she struggled to reassure herself, she believed the fear had gone too deep. No matter how she might appear to recover, she could not imagine deep down ever being free of such terror. Even her trust in Uncle Bernard had been spoiled. He had been the first person she'd thought of going to for help. He was clever and strong and it was his job to look after people, and to protect them. She'd even got as far as his office. Then she'd begun to tremble so much she had to retreat out to the street again. She had remembered his maleness and his dark sexual eyes, and she'd become afraid. Safely away from the office, she told herself not to be so stupid and melodramatic. But it was no use.

At least she had money and could get away, pay for somewhere to stay, buy something to eat. How she got the money smashed in her skull again and she wanted to die. She found herself hitching up her backpack and starting to walk along Euston Road. She hadn't gone very far when she saw a building with a noticeboard on the wall. The word QUAKER caught her eye and she stopped to read it. Daisy's mother was a Quaker. She'd wanted to go to Daisy's house but that would be the first place her mother and Fisher would look for her. She read: 'Once we have said "Our Father" in the morning, we can treat no one as a stranger for the rest of the day.'

Jennifer felt like weeping, it meant so little to her. Behind her on the pavement hurried innumerable strangers. On the road, endless traffic thundered past. At the side of the building which proclaimed itself 'Friends House' there was a garden: on the gate it indicated that any members of the public were welcome to rest there. Jennifer went in. There were a few seats among the greenery and thankfully she took off her backpack and sat down. The garden was an oasis of peace. She must have dozed off, because all at once, it seemed, it was dark. Her wristwatch told her it wasn't all that late but she remembered her daddy telling her that it got dark quicker down south in England. The traffic had thinned out and there weren't as many people around. She wished there were more: the noise and bustle seemed safer. Despite having rested, she still felt tired. The air had a chill in it and she shivered. It occurred to her that she'd had nothing to eat for a long time so she put on her backpack and returned to the station. She bought a sandwich and a paper cup filled to the brim with boiling hot tea. It was so hot it was difficult to hold the cup. It tasted good, though. She enjoyed the sandwich too and began to feel better.

Now she needed somewhere to stay until she found a job. Fifty pounds wouldn't last for ever. She felt reluctant to leave the station. At least she could find her way around there and wouldn't get lost. Everything was signposted. It wasn't so cold as outside either, and it was dry. It had begun to rain just before she'd come in. She couldn't bring herself to venture back out into the darkness to look for a hotel or some sort of lodgings. It seemed a much more sensible idea to wait until morning. Nothing seemed so scary when it was light and there were ordinary, normal people going to their work in offices and shops. She hunkered down with her backpack clutched in front of her. At least she wouldn't look suspicious if any police-man saw her. She could be waiting for a train. Nevertheless, a policeman did eventually move her out of the station. 'Come on, you can't stay here all night,' he'd said but in quite a kindly tone. She sat outside then, in the covered area where the buses stopped during the day.

Sleep didn't come easily. She kept dozing off and waking with either a police siren screaming past, or an ambulance, or the shouts and laughter of drunken revellers. Finally there were the early deliveries to the station shops and restaurants. English accents echoed all around her, emphasising the fact that she was alone in a strange country, among strangers. Half the time she didn't understand what anyone was saying.

She floated in and out of a world in which the border between nightmare and reality had become blurred. Her physi-cal discomfort became so acute that she was forced to move. Her thigh bones felt bruised as if the flesh had been rubbed away and there was nothing left to cushion them. Every part of her had stiffened and she cried out with the pain of straight-ening up. The station had come to life again. The first place she made for was the Ladies, where she relieved her bladder and washed her face and neck. As she tugged a comb through her hair, then secured it with an elastic band, she stared at herself in the mirror. Her fringe was plastered wetly to her forehead. Her eyes were dark-rimmed and brimming with apprehension. She hoped her appearance wouldn't make it difficult for her to find a job. Her unmade-up face and dusting of freckles had the look of a ten-year-old. She decided that she must buy make-up. That would make her look older.

The first thing, though, was to find a place to stay. Still reluctant to leave the station, she lingered over a cup of tea, a bowl of cornflakes and a slice of toast in the buffet. But at last she had to venture outside. The throng was even greater than the day before. She stood helplessly watching, completely over-whelmed by it, sometimes jostled by hurrying passers-by. Not long ago she'd thought Glasgow was a busy metropolis. It had been the centre of her earth, but it could not compare with this. The mere thought of Glasgow made her homesick. Only now did she begin to realise that she loved the place. She prayed that she would be able to return there one day.

Too nervous now to cross the traffic-crowded road, Jennifer kept to the side she was on. She began walking away past the station frontage and then round a corner. It didn't take her long to spot a B&B sign on a run-down-looking building. The windows were dirt-stained and covered by drooping lace curtains. Above the door it said 'Guest House'. Obviously the bin men hadn't yet been round. Boxes overflowing with refuse and piled on either side with black bin bags waited to be cleared.

Jennifer would have preferred a decent hotel in a nicer area but she suspected that a single night in a decent hotel in London could swallow up what money she had left in one go.

She rang the bell and a hard-faced woman appeared. Her blonde hair had an orangy tint and was dark and greasy at the roots. Her make-up ended in a brown line under her jaw and her neck was a mouse grey.

- 'I am looking for a room.' Jennifer controlled the urge to turn and run.

'Got any money?'

'Yes.'

The woman gave a jerk of her head and stood aside to allow Jennifer to enter.

Inside the shoebox of a hall there was a smell of cats and stale sweat. There were a couple of doors on the right side. On one door, a piece of cardboard indicated that it was the dining room. The other had a bell on the tinted glass and a notice that said 'Private. Ring for proprietor. In an emergency out of hours ring . . .' with a telephone number. It wasn't until later that Jennifer realised that Mrs Phillpot, the landlady, did not live on the premises. Payment was asked in advance before Jennifer was even shown the room. Not knowing if this was normal practice or not, she didn't argue. Her heart sank when she saw where the woman led her. It was a tiny attic, three flights up with a sloping ceiling. The floor was covered with brown linoleum, much worn and holed in places. The only other articles in the room apart from the bed were a small chest of drawers and one spar-backed chair. Still, it was a roof over her head and the bed looked clean.

The problem that really worried her was that she did not have enough money for more than perhaps a couple of nights. It was now a matter of urgency that she find a job. She asked Mrs Phillpot if it would be all right to leave her backpack in the room while she went to look for a job and Mrs Phillpot agreed. Despite her hard eyes, she seemed a very easygoing sort of person.

Back outside Jennifer took special note of the street so that she would be able to find it again. Its proximity to the station would help, of course. There could be no better landmark. She began wandering from street to street. Every time she came across a café or restaurant she plucked up the courage to go in and ask for work. Waitressing, washing dishes, scrubbing floors. Anything. They just took one look at her and shook their heads. One woman said, 'Run away from home, have you?'

Jennifer blushed guiltily and the woman said, 'Take my advice, love. Get on the next train back to Scotland.'

But apart from anything else she no longer had enough money to get back to Scotland. It was frightening how quickly money disappeared. All she'd had was a couple of cups of tea and a pizza all day, and she had taken a bus at one point. Her feet were killing her. In Oxford Street she asked for work in innumerable shops, again without any luck. One of the problems was that she had neither training nor experience. She spent money on some cheap make-up in an effort to make herself look older. All to no avail. By the time she returned to the guest-house, she was exhausted and sick with worry.

'No luck?' Mrs Phillpot asked.

Miserably Jennifer shook her head.

'Have you been to the DHSS?'

'No.'

'You'd better.' The landlady scribbled an address on a piece of paper and handed it to Jennifer.

Jennifer was profuse in her thanks. It really was very kind of the woman. She felt cheered and went to bed thinking that tomorrow was another day. Everything would be OK tomorrow. Before she could get to sleep, however, she lay listening to the night noises of the house, the creaks and groans, the muttered voices, the padding feet.

Outside distant traffic rumbled and every now and again the siren of a police car or an ambulance wailed louder and louder, then receded. She was just dropping off to sleep when she heard footsteps outside her door. Suddenly remembering that there was no lock, she sprang out of bed, grabbed the chair and wedged it underneath the door handle. She could hardly breathe, her heart was beating so fast in her chest and throat. She remained standing, tightly gripping the chair, shivering in her pyjamas, bare feet sticking to the linoleum. She could hear breathing at the other side of the door.

No more sleep.

XVII

HISTORICALLY, BETWEEN LOS Angeles law enforcement and private security, there existed a snob element. Police officers looked down their noses at security people. They regarded them as not very bright, people who couldn't do anything in life. John Hudson, chief of security at Paramount Studios, had more of an open mind although he was an ex-police officer. A calm, intelligent-looking man, with sandy brown hair and thoughtful grey eyes, he could sit perfectly relaxed behind his desk, hands loosely clasped in front of him, and make you feel he was listening with keen interest to every word you uttered. He gave the impression of a man who had all the time in the world to devote to you. He was, as it happened, extremely busy but he was well organised. Everybody from outside the studios, and often inside too, who came to see him was given the length of time for the interview beforehand from his secretary. After the allocated time span had passed, one of his security men or his secretary would come and remind him of another appointment. Or he would glance at his watch, rise, stick out his big hand and say, with what anyone would swear to be totally sincerity, how he'd enjoyed the meeting.

Like most men in his profession he was fit and had a good physique, although he was not young. He had been with the LA police department for twenty-seven years and retired as captain in charge of training for the department.

The boss at Paramount Pictures liked his police connection, especially as Paramount was in the middle of LA police department. This was why the president of Paramount had offered Hudson the job. There had been no regrets on either side.

'I make all private security people check their guns,' he told

Bernard. 'The exception was when we had the President here. Secret Service came then and I allowed one or two of their guys to carry a gun.'

Bernard wasn't thrilled with the idea of him and his men being unarmed and he said so. 'Look, I don't need to tell you that there's some crazy people around, John. Miss Page has already had a couple of phone calls and letters from some nutcase.'

'I don't want guns on the lot,' Hudson repeated patiently. 'My people are not armed. Look, Bernard, I want her safety as much as you. I don't want anything to happen at Paramount. But if I didn't lay down ground rules here, there would be bodyguards coming in with Uzis. Some guys tend to see an assassin behind every bush and they get trigger happy.'

Bernard grinned.

'No Uzis. I promise.'

'OK, OK. You can carry a gun, but only you. Not any of your men.'

'Fair enough.'

'And don't worry. I'll have plenty of my uniformed guys around. As I said – I don't want anything to happen any more than you do.'

Afterwards they went to the cafeteria, where Bernard met some of Hudson's men. One of them, with a neck like a tree trunk and shoulders a couple of monkeys could have perched on, came swaggering up to Bernard and said, 'I hear you're *the* karate expert in your country.'

Bernard laughed.

'I wouldn't go as far as that.'

'That's what I heard. And you're *the* expert in Atemi.'

There was a challenge in the man's tone and Bernard thought, You're thick in the head as well as on the neck. But he kept a smile on his face and said, 'So?'

'So try me.'

'Try you?'

'Try to put me down with a pressure point. Any one of them. You won't be able to. I've had a Japanese master try with me and fail.'

'Great,' Bernard said, 'but I'd rather just get on with my beefburger.'

'Leave it, Earl,' Hudson told the man. 'You don't need to prove yourself. We all know how good you are. Let the guy get on with his meal.'

'I just want him to try me. It won't take a second.'

'Forget it,' Bernard said, already eating the beefburger. Earl seemed to take his enjoyment as a personal slight.

'So you're not so tough, eh?'

'That's right,' Bernard said, helping himself to more tomato sauce.

'All I'm asking you to do is try one pressure point, for Christ's sake.'

Bernard looked over at Hudson, who gave him a barely perceptible nod and a wink.

'OK.' Bernard rose. 'Grab my right wrist as hard as you can.'

Earl got a grip of Bernard's wrist.

'Hard as you can,' Bernard repeated and Earl grimaced with concentration.

'OK now,' Bernard said. 'Shut your eyes.'

Earl squeezed his eyes shut and no sooner had he done so than Bernard's left fist belted round and smashed into the side of Earl's chin. Earl went down like a log and lay prostrate beside the table.

Hudson laughed.

'Yeah, there's nothing to beat that pressure point on the chin. I've used it many a time myself.'

In a moment or two Earl regained consciousness and struggled to his feet.

'Christ, that was great,' he said. 'How did you do that? I don't know what happened, but I've got to give it to you.' He stuck out his hand. 'Put it there, buddy.'

They gave each other a hearty handshake.

'Great,' Earl repeated before swaggering off.

'Sorry about that,' Hudson said. 'Earl's a good guy. One hundred per cent conscientious. He lives for the job and keeping himself one hundred per cent fit for it. If he's around the movie lot where your principal's working, you can rest easy.'

Bernard didn't feel so sure.

XVIII

'I KNOW WHAT she's like and yes, I know the trouble and worry she's caused us but she's still my child.' Andrina gazed appealingly across at Paul Fisher, who was intent on donning his tailored jacket, straightening his bow-tie and smoothing back his hair. 'Try to understand, darling. Something terrible might have happened to her.'

'There's people go missing every day. They usually turn up sooner or later.'

'Usually, but not always. If I just knew where she was. If I just could be sure she was all right. My mother keeps asking. Every time I go in to see her she goes on and on. It's beginning to get me down. It's not easy to look at Mummy's face all twisted like that either.'

Fisher made a close-up check of his moustache in the mirror.

'It would have been better if the stroke had killed her.'

'Don't say that, Paul. Sometimes you can be so cruel.'

'Not cruel, just honest. You've thought that yourself, I'm sure. Especially the state she's in now.'

'She's my mother.'

Satisfied with his appearance, he turned to Andrina.

'I know she's your mother but as far as I've heard – from you, don't forget – she's the one who's been cruel.'

'Oh, that was long ago. When I was a child. Before she was "saved". Now, poor soul, she's like a child herself and it's not doing her any good pining for Jennifer. My first loyalty is to you, darling. But you of all people should understand.'

'I do understand.'

'I'm talking about your loyalty and devotion to your wife.'

'Andrina, I'm here living with you now, three or four days out of every seven.'

'Have you told her yet?'

'She must know. She's not stupid.'

'But have you *told* her, Paul?'

'Not in so many words.'

'What on earth does she think you are doing through in Glasgow so much?'

'The casino. She knows I work till all hours. It's more sensible that I stay here. I used to try to persuade her to come to live in Glasgow. I offered to buy her the best house I could find in the best district. I've never spared her anything. But she's Edinburgh born and bred and all her relatives are through there. The climate's not so damp on the east coast. Glasgow makes her arthritis a hundred times worse, she says.'

'I don't know why you worry so. If the pair of you were divorced, she wouldn't be on her own. She'd have her children and all her relatives to comfort and help her. In my mother's case, I'm all she's got.'

'And she's damn lucky she's got you after the way she's treated you.'

She rewarded him with another kiss. She loved to see him in the casino. Someone obviously in charge, in his smart dinner suit, his expensive haircut, his neatly manicured hands. Once they were married she would be sure of his devotion and loyalty.

She would make sure too that he never strayed again. He swore that he had never been unfaithful to his wife before he'd met Andrina, and Andrina believed him. That was the kind of man she wanted for a husband. Robert had been so unglamorous and such a bore. Bernard was far too randy to be trusted. Any glamour that had surrounded Bernard had been dangerous, even life-threatening. It had never been the kind of life she'd wanted anything to do with. He'd mixed in a terrifying world of gangsters and criminals in the clubs and pubs of the city.

No, she was far better with Paul. At her age especially. She wasn't a teenager any more. She slid on to Paul's knee and kissed him more deeply. She felt him begin to tremble. But as he caressed her, and they had sex, she kept thinking of Bernard.

Then she remembered Jennifer again. Her mind strained, trying to imagine where she might have gone. Then, with images and sensations of Bernard still fresh in her mind, she recalled that he'd had contact with Jennifer not that long ago. Hadn't he been getting her involved with some pop group or another?

Her heart began to race with anger and concern. She'd kill him if she discovered that he was the cause of all this upset and worry. Or if he'd done the child any harm. Her first impulse was to tell Paul. Then she thought better of it. Paul had only met Bernard for a few fleeting seconds but he hadn't liked him.

He'd better not have had anything to do with Jennifer's disappearance. How dare he upset me and worry me like this? she thought angrily.

As soon as Paul had gone she dressed, hurried from the house and took a taxi to Bernard's office. It was only after she'd climbed the stairs and opened the door marked CPS – Close Protection & Security – that her courage began to desert her.

One man was perched on the edge of the nearest desk. Big and broad-shouldered, he had a cropped head and wore a black patch over one eye. The way he was staring at her made Andrina feel nervous.

The bespectacled young woman at the desk said, 'Can I help you?'

'I'd like to speak to Mr O'Maley, please.'

'Bernard O'Maley?'

How many O'Maleys were there? Andrina thought irritably. Bernard had three brothers, but as far as she knew, none of them were in the security business.

'Yes, Bernard O'Maley.'

'I'm afraid he's in America at the moment. He won't be back in Glasgow for another few weeks. But perhaps I can help . . .'

'No, I don't think so.' On second thoughts – just in case – she said, 'Actually it's about my daughter, Jennifer. I'm terribly worried about her. She's gone missing. I know Bernard saw her not that long ago . . .'

'Oh yes, it was me who arranged for her to meet the

Who Dunnits. Jennifer and her friend Daisy. Nice girls. Daisy especially was in seventh heaven about meeting the group.'

'Have you seen her since? Jennifer, I mean?'

'No. I'm sorry. Have you reported her missing to the police?'

'Yes, of course, but they haven't been very helpful. Oh, I suppose they do their best but apparently there's so many missing persons on their books.'

'I could give you the name and number of a good detective agency. We don't do that kind of work as a rule. Although if Bernard was here he might do something because Jennifer's a relation. She called him uncle, I remember.'

'No, he's not a relation. He was a friend of Robert, my ex-husband . . .'

The man with the eye-patch spoke up.

'You must be Andrina Anderson.'

'Yes.' Andrina gave him a puzzled look. He put out a hand.

'I'm Michael, Bernard's twin brother.'

'Gosh.' Andrina couldn't contain her astonishment. He looked so unlike Bernard, except perhaps for the build.

He laughed.

'I know. I know. He's the one with all the good looks. I'm the ugly one.'

'No, I . . .' Andrina flushed with embarrassment. 'You'll have to forgive me, Michael. I'm so worried about my daughter I hardly know what I'm saying or doing.'

'I know exactly how you feel.' His broken-nosed face became serious.

'What do you mean?'

'My son and daughter have joined Bernard's firm. They're only eighteen, just kids, and they're over in America just now getting into all sorts of dangerous situations for all I know. I came up here to find out if there was any news of them. The wife and I have had no letters, nothing, not even a postcard to let us know if they arrived safely. The twins didn't leave us an address. You'd think it was the secret service they'd joined.'

The woman said, 'Trust me, Michael. Bernard and the twins are OK.'

'I know Bernard'll be OK. He's got the luck of the Irish

and he's an old hand at this. But my children . . . Bernard's my brother and I love him but I feel like killing him at times.'

Andrina's attention had returned to the girl at the desk.

'He didn't take Jennifer with him, did he? Surely he couldn't have . . .'

'Of course not,' the girl said. 'Bernard was reluctant enough to allow the twins to go. He thought *they* were too young. No, no, Mrs Anderson. You can definitely put that out of your mind.'

Andrina sighed.

'I'm sorry to have troubled you.'

'As I said earlier, I could . . .' the girl began but Andrina was already opening the door on her way out.

Michael followed her.

'Can I give you a lift home?' he asked. 'My car's outside.'

Andrina smiled and fluttered her eyelashes at him.

'Thank you. That would be very kind. My own car's out of commission at the moment.'

XIX

'HERE, YOU'LL NEVER guess who I've been with!' Michael burst into the cottage. Caroline and Big Martha were sitting in front of a crackling log fire. A shaggy red rug accentuated the warmth and the firelight flickered across the varnished wood floor and cast dancing shadows up to the beamed ceiling. It was still September but the weather had turned chilly and Big Martha's blood had become thin.

'The twins?' Caroline and her mother cried out eagerly. He hated to disappoint them. Some of his excitement siphoned off.

'No, of course not. They're miles away, worse luck.'

Caroline's attention returned to her knitting. 'So they couldn't help at the office?' she asked.

'It's maddening. Because neither Bernard nor the twins gave us an address or phone number, the office are afraid to give one. I told them what harm could it do knowing where they were, for God's sake. But at least they've promised to get in touch and tell the twins to phone us.'

'Thank goodness for small mercies. Now maybe I'll get the chance to ask them about everything, including exactly when they'll get back.'

'Yes, they're fine. The girl assured me of that. We've to stop worrying, she said.'

Martha was dozing in her rocking chair but listening at the same time. At seventy-three she wasn't nearly such a thorn in Michael's flesh as she used to be. He had grown quite fond of her despite the fact that she was like a mountain to push around in her wheelchair and she still had an awful tongue in her head. He called her his sparring partner and she called him a flat-faced, one-eyed monster. 'Well, who have you been with?' the old woman asked. Trust her not to miss a thing.

'Andrina Anderson.'

Caroline looked puzzled.

'Who's Andrina Anderson?'

'Does Robert Anderson ring a bell?' Michael asked.

Silence for a long moment. Then Martha said, 'Is he the one who used to be Bernard's teacher?' She turned to Caroline: 'Bernard's talked about him. Remember when the twins asked him how he learned karate, he told them about his old teacher who ran a karate club. You don't, do you? You're only a girl and your mind's like a sieve.'

Caroline laughed and rested her knitting on her lap.

'Hardly a girl, Mammy.'

'Anyway,' Michael pressed on, 'Andrina is – or rather was – Robert's wife.'

'So?' Martha asked.

'Remember Bernard was married to Doris, then Jane.' Suddenly it came back to him. Years ago he'd made the mistake of mentioning to Caroline he'd seen Bernard with a woman, first in a car, then going into a cottage. This very cottage had been their love nest. Caroline had told Jane. The result was that Jane had thrown Bernard out and eventually divorced him. He'd regretted telling Caroline and already he was regretting saying anything now. The trouble was that he and Caroline were so close they just naturally told each other everything. But still . . .

'Well then . . .' both Martha and Caroline urged impatiently, 'what about it?'

'Listen, Caroline, and you too, Ma' – although he realised that old Martha wasn't that daft – 'you must promise to keep this strictly between ourselves.'

'What, for Christ's sake?' Martha shouted at him. 'Will you spit it out?'

'Mammy! What have I always told you about using bad language!'

'Oh, shut up,' her mother said.

Michael raised a conciliatory hand.

'OK. OK. Remember why both Doris and Jane got a divorce?'

'Now look, Michael,' Caroline said gently, 'I know Bernard has his faults. I know he's a bit too popular with women at times but he can't help being such a good-looking man. It's not his fault that women chase after him.'

'My God!' Michael groaned, 'if Bernard committed murder, you'd try and make out it was the bloody victim's fault.'

'Now, don't you start . . .'

'Well, you'd make anybody swear the way you go on about him.'

Martha hooted derisively.

'He's jealous, and no wonder when he's stuck with an ugly mug like that.'

'You're no raving beauty yourself, Ma.'

Caroline tutted.

'Stop it, you two. And just you remember, Michael. Bernard has been good to us.'

'How could I ever forget it?'

'All right,' Martha said, 'we remember how Bernard had a fancy woman. Here . . .' A light dawned in Martha's rheumy eyes. She never missed a trick, that ould woman. 'Are you trying to tell us it was that Andrina Anderson?'

'The very one,' Michael said. 'She came into the office while I was there. I knew right away she looked familiar.'

'It must be more than ten years ago.' Caroline sounded doubtful.

'Listen, pet, if you'd seen her, you'd know why I remembered. She's an absolute stunner.'

'Here,' Martha was wide awake now, 'she was friendly with his second wife. Don't tell me she was pals with his first as well.'

'Must have been. He and Doris used to visit her and Robert. Then, after he married Jane, he and Jane used to visit them. Best of buddies they all were.'

'And neither of the two wives ever twigged?'

'Oh!' Caroline gasped, 'what a wicked, deceitful woman. I've never heard the like of it!'

'I could hardly credit it myself. He must have known And-rina for years – off and on. More on than off, I'd say.'

'That woman must have cast a spell on Bernard. There's a soft bit about him.'

'What?' Michael's voice screeched up two octaves. 'Bernard? Caroline, now you're being ridiculous.'

'With women, I mean. He must be, to get himself entangled like that.'

Michael remembered how, long before Bernard had got himself married, his brother had been indifferent to girls who tried their damnedest to entangle him. He had some sort of charisma – probably sexual – that females went for. If he knew Bernard, it would have been him that took the initiative with Andrina. If Bernard wanted something he never gave up until he got it, and Andrina Anderson was a very desirable woman.

Caroline said: 'Fancy causing all that unhappiness, breaking up two marriages. It's really wicked. A woman like that ought to be punished. She shouldn't be allowed to get away with it.'

'Now, Caroline, I warned you. All that's in the past and it's none of our business. It never does any good to meddle in other people's affairs.'

He hoped she'd take the hint and remember her part in causing Bernard's divorce. Admittedly she'd had a couple of glasses of whisky at his other sister-in-law's funeral at the time. He accepted Caroline's story that it had been the whisky and the upset at poor Theresa's death that had loosened her tongue. But telling Jane, for whatever reason, had certainly not done Bernard's marriage any good.

'I'm only saying . . .'

'As long as you don't say it to either Doris or Jane.'

Martha piped up then.

'What are you blethering about? Do you think either of them are likely to drop in here while they're passing on their way to a climb up the Campsies?'

'Aye, OK, Ma. I'm just saying.'

What he didn't say was that Bernard had become friendly with Jane again over the years. Perhaps he'd already told Caroline that, or Bernard had. He couldn't remember. But surely even Bernard would never have the gall, the brass neck, to bring Jane to the cottage where he'd had his fling with Andrina. No, definitely not, Michael assured himself. And there was no other way that either Doris or Jane was likely to meet up with Caroline. Not that Caroline would purposely . . .

'They'd batter the shit out of her if they found out, and serve her right,' Martha said.

'Mammy!'

'Well, wouldn't they?'

'Yes, they would,' Michael agreed. 'I wouldn't be surprised if they resorted to murder. That's why I hope to God they never do find out.'

'Are they still friendly with her?' Caroline was obviously intrigued.

'Yes. Bernard's said that Jane was still the best of friends with Robert's ex-wife. It was one of the times he was telling me how sorry he was that he'd lost touch with Robert. I'm not sure about Doris but I wouldn't be a bit surprised if she's still pals with Andrina as well. Could you beat it?'

They couldn't.

XX

To Bessie the quiet backwater of the small gallery in Parnie Street had the hushed atmosphere of a church with its deep pile carpet and oak panelling half-way up the walls. Only a few minutes' walk away and parallel to the street was the busy Glasgow Cross, the oldest part of Glasgow. In Parnie Street, more traditional paintings were exhibited. In Gregory's equally small but brighter West Campbell Street gallery, modern works had pride of place. Here the walls were painted a stark white and the floors were uncovered wood that made feet clang and echo. Bessie had gone to West Campbell Street in the hope of seeing Gregory. She regularly dreamed of him now, as the only water in the desert of her life. Even if the water was only a mirage, it was better than nothing. A sparkle of hope.

He had been his usual charming self since the York débâcle, yet she detected a subtle coolness about him. Well, not so subtle really. Before York, he'd flirted with her at every opportunity. He'd come up behind her while she was admiring a picture and slip an arm around her waist. Or he'd tickle her ribs and make her giggle and squirm away. Sometimes he touched her hair and told her how pretty it looked, so soft, so honey-coloured. She giggled and blushed as if she was sweet sixteen.

Now he was polite. He even offered her a cup of coffee. But he was not in the least flirtatious. He seemed shut into himself, although he still paid her the compliment of listening intently to every word she uttered. She thought him a true gentleman in every sense of the word, and with such an impressive appearance. Gregory would always stand out in a crowd and have admiring glances from every woman, married or unmarried, stealing towards him. He said it was nice to see her again and invited her to call in any time.

She starting taking the flirting initiative. Only in the mildest, most tentative way. An occasional flutter of the old lashes, a gazing up with widened eyes, a sidling nearer than was necessary when she spoke to Gregory. Anyone seeing her would think either he'd gone deaf, or she'd gone daft. The latter, of course, she was forever telling herself, was the truth. What on earth did she think she was doing? Alone in her saner moments she'd try to think things through. If he responded, then what? Could she – as the saying went – go the whole hog? And him a married man to boot. To boot? In the middle of her other wonderings, she wondered what these expressions actually meant. Where and how had they originated? Anyway, she knew what she meant.

Every time she imagined going the whole hog she took fright. In one way she wanted to. In another – well, actually, in two other ways – she didn't know how she could. One of the two negatives – three actually, when she counted Isa – was how she would look to Gregory, stripped of her Wonderbra and her panties that concealed the stretch marks. She lived through and suffered this scenario a thousand humiliating times, as she bent over the sink peeling potatoes or washing dishes. Or while she cooked the meals, or did the ironing, or scrubbed the kitchen floor. Scrubbing the floor made her knees dark red, not a pretty sight either. Even struggling along the street weighed down with bags of shopping she could still see Gregory's disgusted expression at the sight of her naked body. In the middle of Sauchiehall Street she would groan, sometimes out loud, at the shame of him turning away from her. She couldn't imagine herself ever being able to face such a dreadful situation. She'd had to face so many humiliations in reality, she'd run right out of courage.

The other stumbling block was her membership of the Society of Friends. That didn't cover being *too* friendly. She went through every word of the *Advices and Queries*, and even the *Christian Faith and Practice*, searching for a loophole.

'. . . are you sufficiently conversant with our Christian discipline,' she read, 'to be able, when difficult questions arise, to consider them with an informed mind as well as a loving and tender spirit?'

Well, she was considering the question all right, and trying her best to do so with an informed mind. And she was loving. The trouble, she decided, came from the fact that she was loving in the wrong kind of way.

But there it was. There *she* was. In her desert and with such a thirst in her. It was fortunate in a way that she had other even more urgent matters to take up her time and attention. Granda was really going beyond the score. There was another one. Beyond the score? Life was full of questions. Granda was worrying her to death. Sometimes he acted so crazy she had quite a struggle to hang on to her own sanity.

He would keep speaking to people who weren't there. Weren't alive. She'd hear him chatting away, or shouting angrily, at his long-dead mother or father. He was a bit deaf and always shouted even when he was just asking what time it was. He'd talk to a customer about his account. At times she could swear there really *was* somebody in the bedroom with him. She'd knock on the door and go in, and there Granda would be, propped up in bed or sitting on his saggy armchair by the bedroom fire talking to himself. It could be quite eerie, especially in the middle of the night when the rest of the house, the rest of the world it seemed, was dark and silent. Sometimes it was as if she and Granda were alone in the universe. She was so tired at times she too became disorientated. She would go into the kitchen for something, and for the life of her couldn't think what she'd come for. She'd find herself in the kitchen, or any place for that matter, and have no memory of *how* she got there, never mind why. She was getting depressed more often too. After a terrible night with Granda, and only an hour or two's sleep, she'd stagger from bed and just stand in the middle of the room – like an idiot, Peter said – with a completely blank mind. She's stand for ages like that unable to puzzle out what to wear, even *how* to get dressed. It took all her willpower and determination – and she'd decided she had an incredible amount of willpower and determination – to get started, and to plod her way through another day.

Peter insisted that, as far as Granda was concerned, it was just old age. Peter of course slept the whole night through without moving a muscle. So deeply still and peaceful did he look that sometimes she thought he was dead. Occasionally she shook him awake to make sure he was all right. A couple of times it was because she was so desperate for help with Granda. He'd been furious. Admittedly by the time he'd stomped through to Granda's bedroom, Granda was sound asleep and snoring. It wasn't the only time she'd wished them both dead. Only for a second, and she didn't really mean it. That's what she told God anyway.

Peter said it was her that was going off her head. Even though he'd seen Granda behaving very strangely during the day. Only occasionally though, and at weekends. Peter was at the office every day during the week.

'You'll be old yourself some day, don't forget,' Peter told her.

She felt ancient already.

It had become too much of an effort to go to the gallery. Still, tired or not, she always managed to climb up to the loft and cling to the altar of her easel.

Life was funny. Funny meaning queer, odd, contrary. Just when she'd given up all thoughts, even dreams about Gregory, he contacted her. Phoned her out of the blue. And not with his cool, dignified, huffy voice either. He sounded sad, rather pathetic really. He had missed her. Dreadfully.

They were on the phone for a long time. At last he persuaded her to come to the West Campbell Street gallery next morning for a cup of coffee.

'It would do my heart good to see you again,' he said.

It didn't do her heart any good. She suddenly realised she'd been letting herself go. She'd never shampooed her hair for nearly a fortnight. Her make-up purse was empty. Not that she ever wore much make-up at the best of times. She used to think she'd quite a good skin until Peter said a ghost would look brighter. She did have a somewhat drained appearance. With an effort she stirred herself and plodded out to the shops again. This time to buy an expensive Estée Lauder face powder, lipstick, rouge and even mascara. She felt she'd 'gone the whole hog'. Excitement gave a bounce to her step.

XXI

No luck at the DHSS. For a start they asked too many questions and that made Jennifer nervous. She couldn't give the address of the guest-house. She was too frightened to stay there another night. She told the DHSS woman that she had just arrived and hadn't booked into any place yet. The woman asked where she came from. She said Glasgow but gave no specific area. Even having mentioned Glasgow was worrying. What if her mother had reported her missing and the police traced her? Then Fisher would come for her. The DHSS woman asked why she'd left home. She couldn't bring herself to tell the truth. Who would believe her? Her mother hadn't. Already the DHSS woman's eyes were hard with suspicion and disbelief. She looked that way at everybody but Jennifer didn't know that. She made up a story about her mother not wanting her at home any more. Which was true up to a point. Since Fisher had come on the scene she was just in the way.

The woman said to come back with her address so that the DHSS could get in touch to let her know if she was entitled to anything. It could take several weeks, she warned, before any decision was made.

Jennifer left the DHSS office without hope. She trailed the streets again looking for work, again without the slightest success. There were too many people after too few jobs, and she didn't look nearly as clean and as well turned out as most other applicants. She longed for a hot bath and a change of clothes, especially underwear. This morning she'd changed into the spare panties and bra she'd been carrying in her backpack. Now they felt sticky and dusty.

Utterly worn out, she decided she'd simply have to book in

at one of the many small hotels she'd seen, even if it took her last penny. She ended up in one near the British Museum, in a street of Georgian terraced houses. Nearly all of them had been converted into hotels, mostly of two houses made into one while preserving the elegant outside façade. It was sheer bliss to get into a decent room with a bathroom attached. There were even tea-making facilities, including sachets not only of tea, but of coffee and drinking chocolate and sugar and miniature tubs of milk, and even some biscuits. After washing her hair and soaking for ages in a hot bath, she drank two cups of chocolate and ate all the biscuits. Her feet still throbbed but apart from that she felt wonderful. At the back of her mind, though, and at the pit of her stomach, fear and apprehension still wisped about. She tried not to think of what would happen next day. She'd seen the hotel tariff and calculated that bed and breakfast would take all but fifty-six pence of her money.

Fifty-six pence would probably not even buy her a fish supper. A couple of cups of coffee if she was lucky and that would be it. And nowhere to sleep. Her heart fluttered at the thought. She must banish it from her mind, she told herself. She must concentrate on appreciating this blissful night in this beautiful warm room. It even had a television set. She undressed, washed her underwear and her T-shirt, and hung everything over the radiator to dry. Then she lay in bed feeling clean and cosy and safe. She enjoyed watching television programmes as if she'd never watched them before. She could have stayed in that room for ever.

Morning came too soon. She had another bath. She dressed slowly, then sat at the dressing-table mirror combing her hair and trimming her fringe with her nail scissors. She was ravenously hungry and looked forward to eating a good breakfast downstairs in the dining room. But she wanted to delay the time when she would have to leave the sanctuary of the hotel. It seemed incredible that she would have to walk the streets again.

She ate as much as she could at breakfast and lingered as long as possible over a cup of tea. Eventually there was nothing for it but to pay her bill and leave. Once outside she berated herself for spending so much money. It had been a crazy thing to do. Now what? She no longer believed there was any chance of finding a job. Oh, she tried. And kept trying. For several long hours, she wandered this way and that. It had already dawned on her how enormous London was. She'd never given the capital city much thought in the past. If she had, she'd vaguely taken for granted it was something like Glasgow. Bigger, of course, but not *that* much bigger. There seemed no end to it. And no one seemed in the least friendly. No one smiled at you. No one chatted at bus stops and exchanged comments about the weather or the latest news. No one launched into their life's history. No one cared.

She'd tried to ask a woman for directions to the nearest railway station and all she got was a dirty look.

She'd been hoping to go to the toilet there, and shelter from the rain. If you'd asked a woman in Glasgow to direct you to any place at all, she would have directed you. The chances were she might have *taken* you to the place,

If Jennifer had never known homesickness before, she knew it now. She could have wept. London was too big for her. Far too big. It was getting dark and it had begun to rain. Water straggled her hair and trickled down her face and neck. She didn't know where she was. Too weary now to go any further, she sat down in a shop doorway and hugged her backpack in front of her. She laid her head down on it and allowed the tears to flow. Completely drained, she sank into sleep.

'Shove along, hen!'

Jennifer awoke in confusion. She thought she heard a Glasgow voice. Sure enough, a woman was bending over her.

'This is ma skipper, hen, but ah don't mind sharing. Just shove along a bit.'

'You're from Glasgow.' Jennifer uttered the words like a hallelujah.

'Aye. You as well?'

'Yes.'

'A posher bit, ah'll bet.'

'Not really. Monteith Row.'

'Oh aye. At the Green. It used to be posh but it's gone right downhill. What's your name, hen?'

'Jennifer.' She was wide awake now and wondering if it had been wise to give her address. But the woman was obviously homeless like herself. What harm could she do?

'I'm from Anderson, the other side of the Clyde,' the woman said. 'Here, that sounds like the line of a song.' She burst into a parody of a drunk's slurred singing, 'the other side of the Clyde.'

Jennifer began to feel nervous, wondering if she was drunk.

'Bev's the name,' the woman said. 'Short for Beverley but I've never been called that. Just Bev.'

Bev had two plastic carrier bags and from one of them she was pulling a ragged blanket, a pair of men's socks and a headsquare. She tugged the socks on over her shoes. Then she produced a piece of cardboard and slid it underneath her bottom.

'Aren't you going to take your shoes off?' Jennifer asked.

'Not on your nelly. I've had a good pair of shoes pinched off my feet as I slept. Pinched off my bloody feet. Now I make it as difficult as I can for the thieving bastards. I tie a piece of string round my feet as well.' This she proceeded to do.

'The place is hotching with thieves. Present company excepted, of course. You look a decent wee lassie. Run away from home, have you?'

Jennifer nodded.

'Let me guess,' Bev said, settling down beside Jennifer and tucking the blanket around her thin legs. 'What they call a broken home. Meaning your mammy's got a new man and he's a fucker? Could be the other way around, of course. I've known folk that their daddy's brought a girlfriend and she's made him choose. Her or me. Sometimes it's young lads who've been chucked out. There's plenty of young lads around who've been abused. Lads or lassies, the problem's usually a fucker.'

'He tried to have sex with me and my mother didn't believe it.'

'What did I tell you? Even if your mammy did believe you, she'd think it was your fault. Funny that, isn't it.'

'I'm frightened to go back home. But I wish I was back in Glasgow all the same.'

'That makes two of us, hen.'

'Why did you leave?'

Bev fished a packet of cigarettes and a box of matches from her other carrier bag and offered Jennifer a cigarette. Jennifer shook her head.

'Huh! You'll be glad of a smoke yet, hen. It takes the edge off of your hunger. You'll see. Anyway . . .' Bev lit up and inhaled deeply. 'I came here to escape a man – more than one. I'm hell of an unlucky with boyfriends. One after the other, they just take one look at me and think I'm a punchbag. Maybe it's my big boobs.'

'They hit you?' Jennifer sounded incredulous.

'Battered the living daylights out of me, hen.'

'That's terrible!'

'Usually when they were drunk, right enough. But what the hell, drunk or sober, it doesn't hurt any less. By God, when I think of it . . .' She took another long drag at her cigarette.

'I couldn't stay with anyone like that. Once would be enough for me.'

'All very well to talk, hen, but where do you go with a black eye and a burst mouth? No cash either. And you're loath to give up your nice wee house. It was rented but it was in his name, you see. You talk about being frightened? Well, I was frightened all right. Frightened for him coming in drunk. That was Jimmy Rossy, the one before last. I started taking a drink myself to try and give myself a wee bit courage.'

'Had you no family to help you?'

'Naw. They're dead and gone donkey's years ago.' She laughed. 'I might not look it, but I'm a year or two older than you, hen.'

In fact she looked old enough to be Jennifer's mother. In her late thirties, Jennifer guessed, but still a good-looking woman with her corn-coloured hair and blue eyes. Despite her too big sweater and faded denims it was obvious that she had a shapely figure.

'The trouble was,' she went on, 'that wee drink grew into quite a few wee drinks. Then one day he threw me down the stairs and I broke my arm and after I came out of hospital I was far too terrified to go back so I slept in the park.'

'Glasgow Green?'

'Hell, no. I haven't sunk that low yet. No, I always slept under the bushes in Kelvingrove Park in the West End. You met a really good crowd there.'

'Under the bushes?' Jennifer echoed incredulously.

'There was a bit of the park called Skid Row. OK, we were all drunks but we helped one another.'

'But why did you leave Glasgow?'

'I'm telling you. I thought Jimmy Rossy was bad. But that was before I met Gus McCabe. I'd pulled myself together, got a job as a waitress, hadn't touched a drink for months and then I met Gus. The perfect gent he was. Or so daftie here thought. He'd come to my table and order a meal, nice as you like, and leave me a great tip. Eventually he asked me out and soon I'd moved in with him. I'm telling you, hen, I thought my ship had come in. He came from a good family, that man, and he'd this lovely flat in Byres Road.'

'Don't tell me he started hitting you?' Jennifer was so horrified and fascinated with Bev's life story that she had forgotten how soaked she was and how miserable and shivery she felt.

'Hen, you couldn't imagine what this guy was like. He was evil. Do you know what finished me off with him?'

'What?'

'He poured hot oil down me.'

'Oh no!' Jennifer screwed up her face in sympathy.

'Aye. All down my chest. I was in agony. There I was in the hospital again. I was on first-name terms with all the doctors and nurses in Casualty by this time. I'm telling you, I had to get *right* away, *far* away from that nutcase. I'd started drinking again, of course, and I knew I'd never get off the bottle if I stayed with him. He had me crying, hen, and I don't cry easily. Oh, see that man. A real nutcase, so he was.'

They were both silent for a few minutes. Then Jennifer said, 'How do you manage to live down here? Even just to get enough money to eat? I've spent all my money already. I've been to the DHSS. They said they'd let me know what they decide about my case.'

Bev laughed.

'Want to know what they'll decide? They'll decide you're not entitled to a penny because you've made yourself homeless. You left your home voluntarily. That's what they told me. Of course, I gave them a false name and address. I was that scared of Gus McCabe finding me. I'm still scared of that. He'll never give up trying to find me. Once he gets an idea into that twisted brain of his . . .'

'He'll probably have forgotten all about you and be living with somebody else.'

'I keep trying to tell myself that and oh, I'd love to believe it. For my own peace of mind. Anyway, I tried to get work just like I bet you have. But nobody wanted to know.'

'But how are we supposed to live?'

'We beg, hen. All day and every day. Even then most folk don't want to know. They hurry past you looking the other way. Sometimes I only make enough for a sandwich. And that's my lot.'

Jennifer shrank inside. She felt herself growing smaller.

'I couldn't beg. Oh, no, I just *couldn't*.'

'Listen,' Bev confided, 'if you're hungry enough, you'll stoop to anything. If begging's the worst you have to do, you'll be lucky.'

XXII

'How do you find this job compares with your work as a police officer?' Bernard asked. He and Hudson were walking towards one of the many gates.

Hudson said, 'Well, mostly as a police officer, I was dealing with strangers, out in the city of LA. Here, most of the people I deal with are known to me. And it's not a democracy in a studio like out in the streets.'

'How come?'

'It's how much money you're making and did your last picture do well. You don't treat every case the same in here. There's a lot of politicking. You have to be a public relations person, hold people's hands, make them feel safe, make them feel loved.'

Bernard grinned.

'That doesn't sound like such a bad deal. There's some beautiful women around here.'

'Oh, I don't mind looking after the women, but when it comes to holding hands with the men . . .'

Bernard was still laughing after they'd said goodbye. He hailed a cab to take him back to the hotel. Eve Page was sleeping until lunchtime after partying most of the night. He had been at the party with her and had been bored out of his skull with all the chattering and false laughter and even false 'kiss, kiss' bonhomie. All the 'look at me' posers, ready and willing to do anything to get a decent part in a picture. He had left a security woman in the suite with Eve, a man outside the door and one at each end of the corridor. The Page Boys were staying with a songwriter friend at one of the Beverly Hills hotel bungalows. Their friend had pretty good security arrangements there already. It was Eve Page he was worried about. Some guy kept phoning and writing and trying to bring her gifts.

On one occasion, Sally and Sean had stopped him in the hotel foyer. That worried Bernard too. He could hardly say, 'You shouldn't have done that. You're only supposed to be on crowd control.' However, the man could have pulled a gun on them. It made him sweat to think about it. He wished to God he'd never allowed the twins to get into the business and he determined to find a way of getting them out of it. The trouble was, not only did they love the job, they were damn good at it.

He'd no sooner entered the hotel suite than the bedroom door opened, and Eve Page appeared. Every time he saw her, Andrina came to him like a tug at his gut. He would be glad when this job was over.

'Ready?' he asked.

'The last thing I feel like doing is playing a love scene, far less singing right now. Hours and hours of filming.' She rolled her eyes. 'It wouldn't be so bad if it was only one take. It's going over the same thing again and again that gets me.'

'Just keep thinking of the money,' Bernard said, going to the door and checking outside before ushering her from the room.

They went down in the lift and he preceded her into the foyer, his big bulk all but hiding her from view. Everything seemed OK and they continued side by side, not talking any more. One of his men joined them, as hard-eyed and as watchful as Bernard. There were a few hopeful fans outside. Eve Page stopped to sign some autographs, then it was into the limo and away. As usual, Bernard sat in the front beside the driver. Able to relax a little now, his thoughts returned to Andrina. What was it about the damned woman? He'd known many other beautiful women in the ten years or more since he had been with Andrina. He'd even been tempted to marry again. Third time lucky, he'd thought. There was a lovely woman he'd met in Edinburgh. He and Helen had been seeing each other for nearly a year now. Not all that often because he was away so much. Helen was a widow in her thirties with three children, a girl almost Jennifer's age and a younger boy and girl. All of them were still at school. Helen was in no hurry to get married again and neither was he. They understood each other. He felt wonderfully relaxed in her company. She had a peaceful, calming effect on him.

Andrina always had exactly the opposite effect: she had excited him to the point of madness. God, he didn't want that any more.

The limo was stopped at the gate of Paramount and their credentials were checked. The guards already knew each of them in the limo but Bernard admired their conscientiousness. John Hudson had trained his men well. Several of his uniformed guards were on the movie lot.

'You'll stay here?' Eve Page asked. She was nervous and jumpy.

'Relax.' He smiled at her. 'Everything's going to be OK.'

'That man phoned again.'

'Don't let a nutter like that spoil your performance. Trust me. You're perfectly safe.'

She smiled in return.

'I should, shouldn't I? You've a very good reputation.'

He winked at her.

'The best.'

'And modest with it?'

'If you've got it, flaunt it!'

She walked on to the set, laughing now.

He watched her sashaying along in her skin-tight dress. She had a figure like Marilyn Monroe. So had Andrina. And they could flaunt it, all right.

He longed for a cold shower.

XXIII

SHE AND GREGORY had been flirting again. Bessie bowed her head at Meeting for Worship. She knew perfectly well where her behaviour was leading and so would God. God wasn't daft, any more than she was. She'd got into the habit of speaking to God in her head, trying to explain to Him, trying to justify herself.

I've been having such a terrible time with Granda. He's getting worse. He soiled his bed the other night. I could have died. I know he can't help anything any more and I don't get angry with him, I mean, what good does getting angry do? Anyway I haven't the energy nowadays. But, oh, it's terrible. I feel I'm sinking deeper and deeper into a black pit. The times I'm with Gregory are the only bright moments of my life. They're like stars shining in my darkness.

Her conversation with God was interrupted by a man getting up and talking about international responsibilities, reconciliation and cooperation.

'We call upon people everywhere . . . to behave as nations with the same decency as they would behave as men and brothers . . .'

It didn't 'speak to her condition' at all. Except of course that she was teetering once more on the verge of behaving indecently.

Did You really mean that commandment — Thou shalt not commit adultery? Was it really You who wrote it? Or was it just Moses who made it up to get a bit of publicity for himself? Maybe he fancied himself as a creative writer. There's a lot of them around. Tell me, please. Give me a sign.

She closed her eyes tightly and waited. But there was nothing but an occasional shuffle of Quaker feet and a creaking of hard benches.

God obviously didn't believe in making it easier for anybody. Why should He send her a sign? Her, of all people. A mere speck in His universe. Why should He listen to her?

I'm sorry for 'the stars shining in my darkness' bit. I must try not to be hypocritical and hide from the truth. The truth is Gregory Seymour – that's him who owns the two art galleries – wants me to meet him in London and share a hotel bedroom with him there. In other words, commit adultery. He'd made up a whole tale about organising an exhibition of my work in London and I must be there with him to meet the gallery owner and sort out what paintings will be most appropriate to include in the exhibition. There's no exhibition, of course. I only wish there was. Gregory plans to take me to a couple of theatre shows. It sounds so wonderful, like a beautiful dream. Just to get away from home and Peter and Granda. Even Daisy is a trial at times.

She waited, but God didn't answer. At the same time the peace of the Meeting did help. Maybe that was God speaking to her. In the lovely soothing silence. Thankfully she relaxed into it, and felt better. After Meeting she enjoyed the warm handshake with everyone and the usual cup of tea and biscuits. She hung around, eager to join in the chat.

But, eventually, she had to leave. The other Friends at Meeting weren't any help to her although she admired them enormously and loved them dearly. But they all seemed so clever and so strong – mentally and spiritually, if not physically.

They didn't fuss, or boast, or talk about what they did at all unless in an official and practical way. They never tried to tell anyone what they should do, or criticise or condemn or try to convert anybody. You could turn up at Meeting for years and even take part in the business side and never be asked to join the Society. There were all sorts of folk really, some with very strong views and sometimes opposing opinions. But most of them tried to live up to the *Advices and Queries*, especially when it said 'In your relations with others, exercise imagination, understanding and sympathy. Listen patiently, and seek whatever truth other people's opinions may contain for you. Think it possible that you may be mistaken . . .'

Mistaken or not, she went to London. Gregory was arriving on a later train. She slunk into the hotel like a Russian spy. It was as if everyone in the city knew what she was up to. Gregory had booked her in as Mrs Seymour. Trembling, she accepted the key from reception and took her overnight bag up to the room. She'd already had several dry Martinis on the train and bought two miniatures for her handbag. She'd swallowed more than one Valium. Yet she was still in an anguish of nerves. She was in physical agony as well, because she wasn't used to wearing a suspender belt, and the silly wisp of a thing she'd bought in Glasgow was sawing into her belly like a razor blade. The suspenders weren't what she'd call comfy either. In fact, she discovered that she was allergic to nickel. A furtive inspection revealed strawberry red patches, one on the front and back of each thigh. She gave the patches a quick scratch. But scratching only made them more itchy than ever.

She decided to go down to the bar for another drink. It wouldn't look so eager if she met Gregory in the lounge rather than the bedroom. In truth, she was not in the least eager. She simply could not believe she was doing this. She had another drink. She took another Valium. Her head began to whirl. She became so light she seemed to be bouncing, unable to keep her feet on terra firma and not in the least caring. When Gregory arrived, she grabbed his hand and dragged him into the lift. Before he could recover his surprise, she hustled him into the bedroom and cried out, 'Alone at last.' Gregory's eyes bulged and his mouth gaped like a goldfish. He watched aghast as she started to fling off her clothes and dance around the room.

'Don't you want a drink or something first?' he managed. He was normally a dignified, well-organised man who did things properly. In reply Bessie startled him by belting out a striptease tune as she whipped off her cardigan (the pink cardy her good-living Christian mother had knitted for her last year).

'Da-da-da-de, da-da-da . . .'

Off came her skirt and was kicked high into the air. Then her blouse and her bra.

Gregory was plastered against the door somehow looking astonished, stunned and dignified at the same time. Gregory never lost his dignity. However, as she was happily rolling off her stockings and twirling them over her head, he came to life and began to divest himself of his jacket and trousers. In the unaccustomed haste, his feet became entangled and he stumbled wildly about for a few seconds until he managed to steady himself against the bed. As he was tearing off his Y-fronts, he tripped and fell but scrambled quickly to his feet again. Bessie had already removed every stitch. She bounced on to the bed and lay on her back, still being musical. He lay on top of her and began talking incessantly as he plunged in and out of her. Somehow he still kept his dignity and his head held high. It was her turn to be astonished. He twittered on like a bearded budgie.

'You're nice and moist for me. Yes, grip your legs around me. Yes, that's nice. Yes, that's right. Yes . . .'

They bounced up and down and sideways and rolled about until, before either of them realised it, they had tumbled off the bed and landed on the floor. Gregory hardly lost his bouncy rhythm but as he'd landed his elbow jabbed into her ribcage. It was then she heard (and felt) one of her ribs crack. She tried to keep a stiff upper lip but he was a heavy man and she had never been robust.

From then on it was downhill all the way.

God had spoken.

Go to Hell, He'd said, and when God said Hell, He meant it.

XXIV

'How like you to suggest it was my fault,' Andrina complained. 'You've always been the same. Always blaming me. It was one of the happiest days of my life when our divorce came through.'

'That makes two of us,' Robert said. 'But if you can tear your thoughts away from yourself for a moment to think about our daughter and try to answer my questions about her . . .'

'I don't need to talk to you at all. Why should I have to put up with you grilling me like a criminal?'

'I'm not grilling you like a criminal. I just want as much information as possible so that I can try to find Jennifer.'

'The police are trying to find her.'

'Her and a million others. I must do something. I can't just sit around wondering what might have happened to her.'

'What can you do? You're at work every day.'

'I can search for her after school and at weekends.'

'Anyway, Paul and I have already searched everywhere.'

'I must do something,' he repeated.

He felt guilty as well as distressed. He wondered, in his heart of hearts, if he'd failed the child, shut her out since his marriage to Laura. Not consciously. He'd told Jennifer she was always welcome to visit. Both he and Laura had genuinely tried to make her welcome when she did arrive at the door. Laura made a special meal. He always slipped Jennifer a generous amount of pocket money. But now he remembered the times he'd gone into the kitchen to give Laura a hand and left Jennifer sitting alone in the lounge. Perhaps she'd wanted and needed to talk to him.

Scenes rolled before his mind's eye. He laughed and chatted happily with Laura as she stood at the cooker while he set the kitchen table. They missed each other with being out all day teaching at different schools. There was always so much to tell each other after work. Funny stories to share about the children's antics. He remembered returning to the lounge and being stopped in his tracks by the sight of Jennifer's drooping, tragic figure.

'Jennifer, are you all right, dear?' he'd asked.

She straightened up and a mask of brightness clamped over her face.

'Fine, Daddy. I'm fine, thank you.'

'Are you sure?'

'Perfectly.'

He was about to say that he was sorry to have left her sitting on her own but just then Laura called:

'Come on now, before it gets cold.'

He put his arm around Jennifer as they went through to the kitchen. He was extra attentive to her, or so he thought at the time, urging her to eat plenty. He also made a point of asking her how she was getting on at school. All the same, now, when his tortured mind picked over that and other scenes, he realised that his admiring glances at Laura, their secret loving smiles, could have made his child feel lonely and shut out.

'Had there been a quarrel or anything?' he asked Andrina now. 'There must have been some specific trigger, surely.'

'Nothing at all.' Andrina's eyes slid away from him. She went over to the sink to fill the kettle. 'Would you like a cup of coffee?'

He knew she was lying. He'd experienced her evasive tactics so often in the past.

'I'd prefer if you told me the truth.'

She turned to stare at him, eyes round, childish, brimming with innocence.

'But I have told you the truth.'

Once he would never have doubted her. Now he knew there was no limit to the deviousness of which she was capable.

'Not any more, Andrina.'

'What do you mean?'

'I know you too well. There's something you're not telling

me. Has it anything to do with that tailor's dummy you're sleeping with at the moment?'

'How dare you insult me and my fiancé . . .'

'Fiancé is it, this time? Well, that's a new one for you. What does his wife say to that? Of course, he's an Edinburgh man, isn't he? So at least there's a few miles between you and the present Mrs Fisher?' His voice acquired a threatening tone. 'But you listen to me, Andrina. If it *has* something to do with that creep, he won't know what hit him . . .'

She gave a burst of sarcastic laughter, spiced with triumph.

'Oh, I think if it's the person I suspect who has had something to do with Jennifer's disappearance, you'll not find him so easy to deal with.'

Robert was taken aback.

'What are you getting at now?'

'I came home here one day and Bernard O'Maley was here with Jennifer. I nearly fainted from shock.' Her beautiful face contorted with bitterness. 'I'd never seen him for years and didn't want to after the wicked way he treated me. But there he was, cool as a cucumber, and with Jennifer.'

'It must have been you he came to see.'

'Oh no, it wasn't. Apparently he'd met Jennifer at one of these pop concerts and then he'd arranged for her to meet the stars and get their autographs. Naturally, she was thrilled and I remember him saying that he'd arrange for her to meet somebody even better.'

Robert felt sick.

'I don't believe you.'

'A lot of good you'll be at finding her. A lot of good you've ever been to her. At least I went to his office and tried to find out. He's away in America just now bodyguarding Eve Page and the Page Boys. They're in Hollywood making a film. They admitted at the office that Jennifer and her friend Daisy had been to a hotel to meet a group of men. They swore blind though that Bernard hadn't taken Jennifer to America. But I don't know. How can I be sure?'

Robert sank down on to a chair.

'But . . . he's old enough to be her father.'

'Bernard pursued me since I was fifteen – younger than Jennifer is now.'

'He would have been nineteen then. Only a few years older than you were. Nobody knows better than me that he's no angel but I still can't believe what you're suggesting . . . not with a child . . . and certainly not with Jennifer.'

'Trust you to defend him. Your long-lost buddy.'

Andrina sat down opposite him. 'I went to see Daisy too. Daisy Alexander. But she said she didn't know anything.'

'The artist woman's daughter?'

'Yes. Bessie Alexander was very nice and wanted to help but there was nothing she could do. Despite what you obviously think of me, Robert, I've been extremely worried. If I just knew for certain where she was and that she was all right . . .'

There was a tense silence for a moment. Then Robert said, 'I'm sorry. Of course you must be worried. Could you give me Daisy Alexander's address? I'll have a word with her and her mother. I've met them a couple of times at Sophie's and I know they come from the south side, but . . . By the way, I was very sorry to hear about Sophie's illness. I must try to get in to the hospital to see her.'

'I've got the address and phone number here.' Andrina reached for her handbag and found her address book. She opened it and handed it across to Robert.

'Thank you.' He jotted the address down and passed the book back to her. 'I might be more successful than you. I don't mean that as a criticism,' he added. 'It's just I've had some experience of this sort of thing at the school. Young girls confiding in their best friend and swearing them to secrecy. That's probably what's happened.'

He sounded so matter of fact. So formal. So calm. Inside he felt ill with worry and confusion. He believed, as he'd always done, that Andrina had neglected Jennifer. She'd put her lover first when Jennifer had been a baby and he'd no doubt that she still put her lover and her own gratification first. Nor would she, he suspected, be capable of experiencing any guilty conscience about her behaviour. She'd certainly never showed any conscience in the past. Hatred of her surged up inside him when he remembered some of the things she'd done. He controlled the emotion and continued to speak calmly.

'It could be that she's persuaded Bernard to take her with him to meet the stars. The chance to go to Hollywood would be every young girl's dream and to her, he was always Uncle Bernard, remember.'

'What difference would that make?' Andrina asked.

None to you, he thought bitterly. You would sleep with anyone if they took your fancy.

'Bernard mixes with all these glamorous women. Why should he want to seduce a little freckly-faced girl?' A sudden picture of Jennifer nearly brought tears to his eyes. The hair she used to wear in pigtails now held tightly back with an elastic band except for a fringe covering her brow. Her face with its vulnerable expression, its dusting of freckles across her nose and cheeks, and her wide, sensitive mouth. He couldn't bear the thought that someone, anyone, might have hurt her. Or that she could be in danger.

Andrina said, 'I'd believe anything of him, after the way he treated me and the wicked lies he told about me.'

She really was incredible. A masterpiece of self-deception. If anyone deserved first prize for lying, it was her.

'I'll pursue that line of enquiry, of course,' he said. She laughed. She actually laughed.

'Oh Robert, you haven't changed. You were always so terribly *serious*.'

His daughter was missing, for Christ's sake. How was he supposed to be? He felt like slapping the stupid laugh from her face. He had better things to do with his time and energy, however. He rose.

'I'd better go. I'll be in touch if I make any progress.'

She rose gracefully from her chair. There was an awareness in every movement, every sensual curve, as she preceded him to the front door. There she favoured him with one of her pseudo-shy sideways glances and provocative smiles.

He went down the stairs and out on to the street thanking God for Laura.

XXV

THEY WERE HUNCHED in a deep bowl of blackness. The only light was from the fire in the centre which was fed with old cardboard boxes, bits of wood, newspapers, anything anyone could find. The rank odour of stale sweat, rotting food and cats' urine hung like a fetid blanket over everything. Against the inky blackness, the silhouette of derelict buildings quivered through the flames. A motley crew hunkered and squatted and sprawled around the fire. Most were men; they looked old but could have been any age. Most were glassy-eyed and loose-mouthed with drunkenness. Bev had made extra at the begging and had bought a bottle of William & Humbert Walnut Brown sherry. Jennifer had pleaded with her to stay off the drink but Bev had been in a strange, reckless kind of mood and wouldn't listen.

'Listen, hen, we deserve a wee bit of comfort now and again. And after the day I've had . . .'

They had separated earlier and agreed to meet up outside the National Gallery at five o'clock. Bev was going to work Trafalgar Square. If they were lucky and had made enough, they would go for something to eat at five.

'The National is usually a good pitch. You try working that today,' Bev advised. 'Although of course it's well past the height of the tourist season now. Tourists would have been your best bet.'

'What do I do?' Jennifer felt really miserable but she was ravenously hungry and neither she nor Bev had any money, not even for a cup of tea between them or to get past the turnstile in the station lavatory. They'd had to find a bit of wall to hide behind and each took a turn as a lookout while the other squatted down for a quick pee. Then they hadn't been able to have a wash. There was nothing for it but to beg.

'You just hold out your hand if you haven't a hat or a box or anything else. And you say something like, "could you spare some change so that I can get a cup of tea, please?" Or if you can find a bit of cardboard and a pencil or a pen, you could write on it, "I'm homeless and hungry. Please help me".'

'Must we separate?' Jennifer was terrified to be alone again.

'There's no chance at all of making anything if two of us are hanging about the same spot,' Bev told her.

Jennifer thought she'd never felt more ashamed in her life when she'd had to relieve herself in a public place. However, hanging about in front of the National Gallery with her hand held out and murmuring, 'Could you help me please? Have you any spare change please?' came a close second. She couldn't raise her head to look people in the eye. Most didn't look at her either. One or two who did were rude and made her feel a thousand times worse. 'Why don't you get a job and do a decent day's work,' one woman said in disgust. Another said, 'I'm not giving you any money to go and spend on drugs.' Some people were embarrassed and apologetic. They dropped a few coins into her hand and said, 'Sorry, that's all I've got' before hurrying away. At the end of a long stint, when she counted what she had, it only amounted to a few pence over two pounds. She'd had nothing but a cup of tea and a bun all day because she didn't begin to get decent money until later in the afternoon. Now she was frozen stiff, as well as famished. Bev hadn't arrived by five o'clock. Or even by half-past. By a quarter to six Jennifer was nearly fainting with a heady mixture of thirst, hunger and panic. More panic than anything else. She could see Trafalgar Square from the steps of the Gallery but it was dark now and she realised with mounting panic that, despite the glittering array of lights, it wasn't going to be easy to find Bev. She would have stood her ground – she had to sit eventually – for longer at the Gallery but a couple of youths began to pester her. She suspected they were drunk but that did not make them any less frightening. She ran into the square, then stopped abruptly. The place was milling with people. Jennifer's throat tightened with fear. To her immense relief, she spotted Bev sitting near the foot of Nelson's column.

'Bev!' She flew over to her. 'Oh, I'm so glad I've found you. I thought you said you'd meet me at five o'clock. I waited and waited.'

'Did you, hen?' Bev laughed. 'I must have taken longer than I meant to at my ablutions. Ah wis havin' a wee paddle in them fountains.' It was when she lapsed into the Glasgow vernacular that Jennifer realised Bev was very drunk.

'You've been drinking.'

'I just had a wee drop of sherry to heat me up and now I'm going to buy another bottle of my favourite Walnut Brown.'

'Oh Bev, don't drink any more. Please don't. Especially on an empty stomach. Let's go for something to eat. You promised we would. I've got two pounds.'

'See him up therr.' Bev staggered to her feet and pointed upwards: 'he's cawed Nelson. An' this squerr is cawed after him. Some victory or other he hud. See me, ah'm no ignorant. Ah know a thing or three.'

'Yes, but come on and get something to eat. It'll make you feel better.'

'Better? Better?' Her drunken good cheer suddenly drained away. 'I'll never feel better.'

'You must have made some money if you're able to buy drink.'

'My mammy was a decent respectable woman,' Bev sighed. 'She hadn't any money but she had her pride. What have I got, hen?'

With an effort, she brightened up.

'Come on. We'll find a chippy and treat ourselves.'

And so they did. Bev still insisted on buying her bottle. They ate their fish and chip suppers sitting in a deep doorway in Shaftesbury Avenue. They hoped to stay there all night. However, an unshaven man wearing a long coat tied with string arrived to claim the doorway just as they were settling down. He gave them both such a kick to shift them that Jennifer gasped with pain. She struggled up clutching her backpack. Bev jumped up too but shouted at the man – once they were both at a safe distance,

'We might have knew it was your skipper. It still has your putrid stink about it.'

There was certainly the most vile stench off the man, a mixture of urine and faeces. He made a rude sign at them before skippering down.

They must have walked for miles after that. Jennifer felt like fainting from fatigue. Conversation had long since become too exhausting and they were trudging along the dark streets in silence when suddenly Bev spotted the derelict site.

'That'll do us,' she said, dragging Jennifer along by the arm. 'Hallelujah, there's even a fire.' Jennifer had begun to lag behind. She felt as if she was moving in a dream and was ready to sink down anywhere. Still, she murmured apprehensively, 'There's a whole lot of men there.'

'They're alkies and winos by the look of them. They won't do us any harm.'

'How do you know that?'

'Listen, hen, I've been there myself. See if Marlon Brando had come to me and said, "You can have me or a bottle", so help me, I would have taken the bottle.'

Jennifer managed a weak smile.

'You're kidding me.'

'No, honestly, hen. There's no romances among alkies. They're just a crowd of drunks sharing a bottle. The bottle's the be-all and end-all of your life when you're like that. I'm telling you the bottle I've got is our passport to a warm skipper and an even warmer welcome.'

And so it was. Bev shared her bottle generously around. As a result they were given a place nearest the fire and treated, and toasted, as if they were a cross between friends and members of the royal family.

Jennifer sank into a deep sleep to the slurred sounds of 'It's a long way to Tipperary, it's a long way to go . . .'

She awoke chilled and shivering. It was as if her hip-bones had broken out of her skin. Every bone in her body ached and she could hardly move. It took her ages, moaning out loud, to ease herself into a sitting position.

The fire had disintegrated into a heap of ash. Bodies were

bulky shadows in the cold, grey light. Jennifer's luminous watch told her it was in the early hours of the morning.

Somebody groaned. 'Anybody got a bottle?'

A few grunts and mumbles indicated by their tone that there were no bottles. Jennifer had never seen such pathetic dregs of humanity. Unshaven, unwashed, poorly clad, some of them weren't wearing enough to protect them against the weather. Others were bulky with layers of assorted clothes. There was something frightening too about the dark sunken eyes and the way hands like claws violently trembled once the bodies attached to them began to stir.

Jennifer shook Bev awake.

'Christ,' Bev groaned, 'I could kill for a drink. Got any money left?'

'No. Not a penny.'

'Shit. I'll have to find some cash pretty quick or I'll die of thirst.'

'Haven't you any money left yourself?'

Bev began searching through her trouser pockets and then her plastic bags. In one of the bags she found fifty pence.

'That won't get me a bottle.'

'I was thinking of tea. A hot cup of tea will make us both feel better. Come on, Bev. Let's see if we can find a place. Anyway,' she lowered her voice, 'I'm bursting to go to the lavatory.'

'Och, OK. Give me a hand up. At least a cup of tea'll keep us going until the punters start appearing. Although they're usually in such a hurry to catch the bus or the train or the underground to their work, we'll be lucky if we make anything for hours.'

They reached Euston Station eventually. No other place was open as far as they could see. They went to the Ladies first, used the lavatory, had a wash and brushed their hair. It was a worry having to part with money at the turnstile but it was worth it. They re-emerged feeling almost human again. Then the cup of tea they shared thawed them out and made Jennifer feel at least a bit more able to face another day.

Just as she and Bev were wandering across the concourse, Jennifer caught sight of a familiar figure. There was no mistaking that curly head, that odd mixture of clothes. It was Bessie Alexander, Daisy's mum.

'Oh my God,' Jennifer wailed.

'What's up?'

'That woman over there. She mustn't see me.'

'Come on.' Bev grabbed her hand and pulled her towards the nearest platform.

'What if she comes down here? There's nowhere to hide.'

There were no trains waiting. Not even many people. They would stick out like the proverbial sore thumb.

'If she's going for the Glasgow train, she won't get it on this platform.'

They stood for a while until they heard the tannoy announce the train to Glasgow. Jennifer began to cry.

XXVI

BESSIE WAS KEPT waiting so long at the hospital she thought she'd never see Glasgow again. Gregory was already on his way back to Scotland, so she was on her own. She doubted if she'd ever see Gregory again.

At first when she'd felt her ribs crack, she'd gritted her teeth. It wasn't easy when Gregory was bouncing up and down on top of her, not to mention distracting her with conversation. But then there came one bounce too many and she just opened her mouth wide and screamed. The scream reverberated, ricocheted, filled to bursting point, it seemed, every corner of the hotel. One thing was certain: there was nothing wrong with her lungs.

That was when Gregory really lost his dignity. He fell off her, scrambled to his feet, grabbed at his trousers and did such a funny dance in his haste to get into them that she would have laughed had she not been in such pain.

'What the hell . . .?' he was gasping.

She was gasping too. But it was with the struggle to try to sit up. She couldn't do it.

'My chest. I can't move. Gregory, help me up.'

He did so but she felt his help was only to hasten his flight. At the same time as hauling her up, he was struggling into his shirt.

'My God,' he wailed, 'a heart attack!'

If it had been Peter, he would have complained, 'Trust you to take a heart attack at a time like this.' She suspected Gregory was thinking the same thing.

'No. It's my ribs. I think they're broken.' She stood up, clutching at her naked bosom and peering down as if expecting the dreadful sight of a rib-bone sticking out.

'Get your clothes on before somebody comes,' Gregory hissed at her. 'The whole place must have heard you.'

'I can hardly breathe, never mind move. How can I get my clothes on?'

'Here, I'll help you.'

He tried to fasten her into her bra and just in time caught another scream in the palm of his hand. 'It's all right,' he said. 'If we just get out of here, I'll take you for medical attention.' He abandoned the bra and managed to ease her into her loose top and trousers before there was an urgent knocking.

'Are you all right, Mrs Seymour?' a muffled voice asked through the door.

'Yes.' Her voice sounded pathetic.

'I'll open the dor,' Gregory whispered. 'You show yourself.'

Yelping with every move, she reached the door. Gregory swung it open and stood stiffly out of sight behind it, as if he was glued to the wall.

She tried to smile at the security man and members of the hotel staff who were congregated outside.

'I'm sorry to have caused any alarm. I fell and hurt my chest. I think I'll need to go to hospital. Would you please phone for a taxi?'

Gregory packed up there and then and carried his overnight bag with great dignity to the taxi along with her own. He said he would never forget the humiliation of settling the bill at the desk and having to suffer the barely concealed hilarity in the staff's eyes on the way out.

He could not, he assured Bessie, go back there that night, or ever again. They all knew how she must have come by her injury. He could see it in their faces. And they thought it was his fault.

'Damn it,' she managed. 'It *was* your fault.'

He looked pained but he did say, 'I'm sorry, Bessie. Are you all right?'

'All right?' She meant to laugh sarcastically but it was as much as she could do to try to hold herself together while she struggled to breathe. Even talking became out of the question.

Gallantly he waited with her in Casualty, but after two long hours she managed to say, 'You go on home, Gregory. They're obviously going to keep me in overnight. There's nothing more you can do.'

'I don't like leaving you like this.'

'I'll be fine. Honestly. On you go. There's no point in you hanging around all night.'

'Well, if you're absolutely sure.'

'Yes, I'm absolutely sure.'

'Very well.' He gave her one of the rail tickets, dropped a kiss on her brow and repeated, 'I feel awful leaving you like this. I'm so sorry.'

She nodded in recognition of the fact. Then he backed away and disappeared.

Well, she thought, so much for romance. That's the last I'll see of him. At least in the capacity of a lover. She didn't feel sad. On the contrary, she had a hysterical urge to laugh but daren't. At the same time she was embarrassed. Guilty too, of course. Actually she didn't know why she wanted to laugh because it wasn't in the least funny. It was terrible. Disastrous. A complete humiliation.

As it turned out she was in the hospital the whole night. Most of the night anyway. But not in a bed. On a stretcher. She was, after an absolute *age*, examined and gave another of her award-winning screams. Then she was X-rayed, after another lifetime of waiting. Then they bound her up. Or kind of half bound her up with a stretch bandage which flattened one boob and allowed the other complete freedom. She looked very odd once they got her top back on. Another taxi took her to Euston Station in order to catch the early morning train. She had to carry her overnight bag awkwardly under one arm before she managed to plead with a railway worker to put her out of her agony and he kindly carried her bag the rest of the way to the train. She would never forget that journey home as long as she lived. Every movement of the train nearly made her faint, and to manoeuvre out of her seat to go to the toilet was an impossibility. It was amazing how one needed to use chest muscles to get up and down. She'd never realised that before.

The painkillers she'd been given helped, but not much. Back in the Central Station in Glasgow, another railwayman helped her with her bag and half lifted her into a taxi. Then there were the stairs to the flat to negotiate. The taxi man was kind too. As well as carrying her bag, he took hold of her arm and supported her as she slowly eased her way upwards, one step at a time. He even rang the doorbell to save her raking through her handbag for the keys.

'What's up with your face?' Peter asked as soon as she shuffled into the sitting room. 'I thought you weren't coming back until tomorrow morning.' He and Granda were watching television and Peter had only half an eye on her.

'I fell,' she said, 'and broke my ribs.'

'Trust you,' Peter said, 'to do a stupid thing like that.'

'I'm going to bed.'

'Put the kettle on first. We haven't had our tea yet.' His whole attention had returned to the television.

The bloody selfishness of them. Sod them and their tea! Oh, if only she could be shot of them. If only she had some money and somewhere to go – she'd go.

'Make your own tea,' she said and wept cautiously, for fear of hurting her chest, all the way to the bathroom. In bed she had to sit propped up with pillows the whole night. She couldn't get up in the morning other than to make an excruciating journey to the bathroom and back. Peter gave her a cup of tea in bed before he went to work and Daisy promised to make the meal when she came home from school. Bessie sat listening in a mixture of mental and physical agonies as Granda shuffled and crashed about the house having a terrible argument with President Nixon.

This is your life, Bessie thought. This is your life. Anger blew up to her head and she escaped in spirit to the loft where she slashed colour on to canvas. Peter was quite indulgent – for a couple of days. It was almost as if he enjoyed being in charge, having her helpless. Daisy didn't make the meal, when it came to it.

'I'm sorry, Mum,' she said, 'I just haven't time. Nigel is coming for me an hour earlier than we'd arranged . . .'

There was a long story then about Nigel and why there had been a change of plan.

'Well, if you could just make me a cup of tea, Daisy.'

Daisy had very quickly done so. Practically flung it at her in her rush to get on with the urgent business of putting on the glamour for Nigel. She'd favoured Bessie with a quick kiss though before she'd disappeared.

Silence again. In the silence, Bessie tried to think how she could escape. What could she do? Where could she go? How could she get the money to live? How could she find the courage? Granda was now chatting with his brother Bert who'd died five years ago. He was telling Bert he was going to get married to Mary McLellan. They were arranging a stag night now. After a while Granda opened the bedroom door.

'Oh there you are,' he said. 'All ready and waiting.'

'Go away, Granda,' she managed. 'And shut the door. I'm not well.'

'My bonny wee bride.'

He came hirpling gleefully towards her bed.

Oh my God! He was trying to get in beside her. She let out a belter of a scream. Really let it rip. It was quite amazing. Lungs like drums she had. Nothing else about her was powerful. On the contrary, she was worryingly weak, physically and morally.

Granda got the fright of his life. He jerked about like something out of a silent film.

'Eh? What? What's up, Bessie? What's all the racket? Was that you?'

'Just get out, Granda. Get out. Go back to your room. I'm not well, can't you see?'

'All right. There's no need to bring the house down. I only wanted to know when I was going to get my tea. I've been sitting through there for days without a bite to eat.'

'Peter'll be in soon. He'll make you something to eat. Now will you please *go*.'

He went away muttering to himself. The scream had hurt her ribcage and she took another painkiller. It made her feel sleepy and she was glad.

After a couple of days of unusual care and attention, the novelty for Peter wore off. It was about time she was up and around, he said. She'd be going as stiff as a poker, and that wouldn't do her any good. Then it was, 'Are you still in bed?'

The tea and scrambled eggs on toast was reduced to tea and toast. Then the toast disappeared and she only received a cup of tea. Even this was handed over with a grudge. Eventually she had to get up and creep about the house doing what she could. Slowly she healed. At least her ribs did. However, her period came heavier than ever. This time it never stopped. From one month to the next it just went on drawing her life's blood from her. The doctor gave her more Valium. He had always said everything was 'just her nerves', and this was no exception. He never even examined her. Somehow she still managed to hang on to her painting, shutting herself up in the loft long after everyone was in bed, the spotlights illuminating the cam-ceiled cave.

At one point she phoned the Samaritans and had to hang up because she recognised a Quaker voice on the line. She leaned her head helplessly down on the phone. She was beyond weeping. Then one day she returned to the doctor's house – he had a room in his house he used as a surgery – feeling as if she was going to die and ready to go down on her knees and plead with him to do something, anything, to help her. She discovered he'd gone on holiday. As soon as she returned home, she checked how much money she had, then phoned another doctor and made a private appointment. This doctor told her she had a tumour and must be admitted immediately to hospital for a hysterectomy. Peter took the news quietly. She didn't care what he or anybody was thinking, but she could imagine he wouldn't be feeling very pleased. She seemed to be making a habit of neglecting him. Although he did appear worried. He helped her to pack, carried her case and drove her to the hospital.

In the hospital they had to 'build her up' for a couple of days before she was fit enough to be operated on.

Peter came to visit every day and sat anxiously watching her. She even began to feel sorry for him. Only she had more important things to think about.

Out came not only her womb but her ovaries. She had been a right mess, the surgeon said. But she would be all right now.

All right? Her hormones, her nerves, her mind, her emotions were in absolute turmoil and chaos. She felt no longer a woman. She felt she had lost her femininity. She felt . . . oh, she felt . . . so utterly bereft. The last dregs of her self-esteem had gone.

XXVII

BERNARD SAW THE woman come on to the lot and hover in the wings, watching Eve and the boys performing. He thought she must be one of the make-up artists or one of the females from the costume department. None of Hudson's men approached her and this seemed to confirm she was legit. Nevertheless, he kept his eye on her.

The scene finished and Eve and the boys were walking across towards the exit when the woman suddenly shot forward and flung herself around Dave's neck.

Bernard, who was nearest, beat the other security guys to it. He hauled the woman off and, with a jerk of the head, indicated that the boys should continue on their way.

The woman was struggling and babbling out a whole lot of nonsense.

'Calm down,' Bernard snapped. 'Dave's gone and you'd better be on your way too.'

'Let go of me, you big ape!' the woman spat at him. 'Who are you to come between those who are joined in holy matrimony? Let no man put asunder, the Good Lord said.'

Christ, Bernard thought, another nutter. This time a religious one. Always the worst.

He propelled her outside.

'Dave isn't married. And the next time you come anywhere near him, I'll have you arrested.'

'The Good Book says . . .'

'Or better still, I'll have you chucked into a madhouse where you belong. Now bugger off and don't come back.'

He shoved her towards one of Hudson's uniformed guards who dragged her, yelling and protesting, towards the nearest gate.

Later he was glad that Eve had arranged to join the boys and their friend for a drink at the bungalow. He wanted to check the layout of the Beverly Hills Hotel and the bungalow where the boys were staying.

The Pink Palace, as the hotel was nicknamed, was an unusually shaped place with its stucco walls painted salmon pink. Flanked by tall palm trees and other lush greenery, it looked more striking than the hills rearing up behind it. In the Beverly Hills garden there were ten luxurious bungalows, long buildings with low tiled roofs, large windows and rooms big enough to hold a grand piano.

He walked around the place and had a word with the security men already there. Then the hung about for a while, outside in the garden and inside the house. All the time, in the background, was the tinkling sound of laughter and talk rising to endless crescendos. This was the boring part of the job, waiting, and for hours on end. It gave him too much opportunity to think.

At last he heard Eve calling goodnight to the boys and he escorted her out of the bungalow and into the waiting limo. All was quiet and still, except for a gentle rustle in the bushes and slight nodding of the high palms. When they arrived back at the Beverly Wilshire, it was to discover that the man who had been pestering Eve had got himself arrested. Not knowing that Eve wasn't there, he'd turned up with a gun and tried to shoot a path to her room. Sean had eventually managed to disarm him.

Bernard froze at the thought, yet he couldn't help being proud of his nephew. Sean was proving to be a first-class operator despite being the youngest in the firm. He had a good physique, hard and muscular without being hefty. No doubt he would attract many a pretty girl before long. Probably already had. He had been worried at first about Sean perhaps being more vulnerable than Sally. But not a bit of it. Even now after only a few weeks, Sean was as tough as they come. Those soulful brown eyes were deceptive.

'Good work,' he told Sean. 'Disarming anyone isn't an easy thing to do.'

Sean grinned.

'Praise, Bernard?' The twins had dropped the 'Uncle' since joining the firm. 'Are you sure you're feeling all right?'

Cheeky young devil.

After that night they had peace from the male nutter but the woman was reported to be hanging about the bungalow. She was the one who gave all the headaches for the rest of the stay in Hollywood. Dave was inundated with phone calls, letters and gifts. This woman lived in fantasy land and really believed she was married to the musician. It was really beginning to get to Dave, who was obviously relieved when they boarded the plane for home. They left busy LA with its skyscrapers that looked as if they were made of glass. They flashed in the sun during the day. At night they sparkled like huge beacons crowding together and vying with each other in height.

'I'll be glad to see my girlfriend again – somebody sane and normal,' Dave told Bernard. 'We plan a quiet wedding soon after I get back.'

'Quiet?' Bernard said. 'You'll be lucky.'

'It's all arranged. The minister's going to marry us in Mary's flat. There'll be just the two of us and a couple of witnesses. We didn't want a lot of fuss and publicity. Mary's six months pregnant.'

'Right. Congratulations then, I hope it all goes well.'

He was glad to be back in Britain himself. He liked America, especially New York. He'd been to the Big Apple several times and found it more vibrantly alive than Hollywood. But it was always good to come home. Glasgow was still his number one favourite city. More for the people than for anything else. And of course having been born and brought up in the place, that's where his roots were.

If and when he married, Helen would, he hoped, sell her flat and come to live in Glasgow. He'd buy a nice place for her with a big garden for the children and an indoor gym where they could all work out. Helen wasn't enthusiastic about anything as strenuous as karate. Yoga was more her line. But the children were keen. He'd already bought them karate suits and taken them to the local karate club. Many a laugh they'd had sparring together. Helen would feign anger and say,

'Bernard, will you behave yourself. You're getting them too excited.' Or, 'Bernard, stop it, somebody's going to get hurt.'

The children would complain that she was being a spoilsport. 'We're enjoying ourselves, Mum,' they'd say.

He'd bought each of the kids a couple of T-shirts: one that sported an American football logo and one with Beverly Hills emblazoned across it.

He'd bought Helen a more expensive gift from one of the posh shops on Hollywood's famous Rodeo Drive. She always said he shouldn't bring anything back but he enjoyed giving presents to her and the kids. Usually he bought something for Sean and Sally too but now of course they could buy things for themselves. He still bought a present for their young sister, Maureen, and for their mother and father and grandmother. He hoped his gifts to Caroline, Michael and Martha would act as peace offerings. They had not been happy, to say the least, about Sean and Sally coming to the States with him.

As a last-minute impulse he bought Jennifer a couple of T-shirts as well. Before he got a chance to deliver them to her, however, before he'd even had the chance to go out to the cottage, Michael phoned him at the office.

'Bernard?'

'Michael! I was meaning to go out to the cottage tonight after I tie up a few loose ends here. Did the twins not tell you?'

'Yes, but I thought you'd better know about this straight away.'

'About what?'

'Robert Anderson has been here.'

'Robert Anderson?' Bernard echoed in surprise. 'I haven't heard from Robert in years.'

'Did you see his daughter before you left?'

'Jennifer? Yes, why?'

'She's gone missing.'

Bernard absorbed this information in silence for a moment. Then he said, 'Surely he doesn't believe . . .'

'His ex-wife does, I think. At least it was her who told him that you'd been with Jennifer. Had her up at some hotel . . .'

'That woman's a bloody menace. I bumped into Jennifer at

the Who Dunnits concert. She and her friend – Daisy Alexander – are fans and I arranged for them to meet the boys and get their autographs. I wasn't even there in the hotel when they met the group. I got a girl in the office to fix it.'

'I just thought I'd better warn you, Bernard. The poor guy has been all over the place. I know how he must feel.'

'I do as well,' Bernard said. 'Jennifer's a nice kid. I'll do what I can to help. Robert moved to Bearsden after he remarried, didn't he?'

'Yes, he left me his address and phone number in case I heard anything.'

'I think I must have it somewhere but give it to me just in case.'

Bernard jotted down the number.

'OK. Thanks, Michael. I'll get in touch with him right away.'

After he replaced the receiver, Bernard sat staring at it for a few minutes. Concern for Jennifer fought with fury at Andrina. He battled for control of his feelings until he was able to dial Robert's number and speak with a calm voice.

'Robert? Bernard O'Maley here. I've just heard about Jennifer. Michael phoned. First of all, let me assure you that I have had nothing whatsoever to do with her disappearance. I'm as fond of Jennifer as I am of my own niece. I'm shocked and concerned and I want to help as much as I can.'

There was a pause. Then Robert said quietly, 'Thanks, Bernard. I didn't believe that her disappearance was anything to do with you. I'll be grateful for any help you can give me.'

'When did she go missing?'

'Just after you left for the States, apparently. I was abroad on holiday and didn't find out until I returned. God, Bernard, it's been well over a month now. Anything could have happened to her. I'm worried out of my skull.'

'Can we meet? I'll need a list of everyone she knows – friends at school, at any clubs, people who live around her home area, etcetera. I'll get on to it immediately. I'm not a detective, of course, but my work experience and contacts should help.'

'Andrina would know more about her friends.' Robert was

fighting for control. 'I haven't been keeping in touch with her as much as I should. I feel as guilty as hell.' He cleared his throat. 'I lost touch with the neighbours in Monteith Row years ago. Would you go and speak to Andrina?'

'Leave it with me. Leave everything with me, Robert. I'll make it my first priority, I promise you.'

'Anything could have happened to her,' Robert repeated. 'It doesn't bear thinking about.'

'I've got your address,' Bernard said. 'I'll be in touch.'

XXVIII

BESSIE FELT SO weak after the operation she had to lie down for a rest every afternoon. Or every afternoon that she got the chance. She began to seriously wonder if it would be possible to slip something into Granda's tea. She'd mentioned this to Daisy once and added – 'Something lethal!' Daisy had giggled, knowing that she didn't mean it. It was true that she was only joking when she said the lethal bit. However, if she thought she could have successfully managed it, she would have slipped him one of her tranquillisers. Granda always refused any medication. 'Strong as a horse,' he was fond of boasting. And she'd say, 'Aye well, one of these days, I'm going to call in the vet and have you put down, Granda.'

Granda laughed, knowing she didn't meant that either. 'I'll see you out,' he said.

She was beginning to believe him. Some days she felt she was floating away. Almost 'beyond the veil'. She'd once heard that expression at a Catholic funeral and thought it very appropriate.

One day, after a terrible night with Granda when he'd nearly set his room on fire, she'd meant to make herself a cup of tea but found herself hanging on to the kitchen table, unable to reach, far less fill, the kettle. She crumpled to the floor. She didn't faint. She just lay there, stretched out on the linoleum, absolutely at the end of her tether. It was then she said to God – and meant it with all her heart, mind and soul – *I can't cope any more. I'm just going to leave everything to You.*

Then the strangest, most wonderful thing happened. It only lasted a few seconds but she experienced the most exquisite sensation. At the same time she was suffused with light. She lay on the cold kitchen linoleum for a minute or two afterwards absorbing the miracle of it. She still felt weak. Nothing in her life had changed. Peter was snoring in one bedroom. Even his snoring had a resentful, grumbling tone. Daisy was sleeping in youthful contentment in another. She daren't think what Granda was up to in his room. But a jewel of happiness was now tucked away in her secret heart and it was giving her hope. She had not been having a one-way conversation with God. He had been listening.

Oh, many a time after that, she tried to explain the experience in other ways. It had been caused by her suddenly relaxing. Then of course she often thought, 'Why would God want to get in touch with me anyway?' Yet, all the time, she clung to the memory of how she'd felt and especially the sensation of being suffused with light. Quaker writings often referred to 'the light'. *Advices and Queries* ended with something that one of the northern Friends had written in 1656:

'Dearly beloved Friends, these things we do not lay upon you as a rule or form to walk by, but that all, with the measure of light which is pure and holy, may be guided; and so in the light walking and abiding, these things may be fulfilled in the spirit, not from the letter, for the letter killeth, but the spirit giveth life.'

Why me? she kept thinking in genuine humility. Even when she read in *Christian Faith and Practice*: 'In the Light, everyone should have something to offer', she couldn't imagine what she could have of the slightest value to offer, in or out of the Light.

After a while she thought of her painting, then blushed at her temerity. Where had that got her, or anybody? Except a disastrous trip to London to break the Seventh Commandment.

She hadn't been back to the gallery since then. Nor had Gregory been in touch with her. She hadn't been fit enough to climb the stairs to the attic to work but as soon as she regained enough energy, she hauled herself up the rickety ladder to savour the smell of paint and feel in touch with herself again. But now there were even more distractions than usual.

There was the distress about Jennifer's disappearance and first

Jennifer's daddy coming asking about her and then that Bernard O'Maley person. They still hadn't found her.

Then her own father died. He and her mother had been very close. Her poor mother was inconsolable. There was a big funeral in the Church of Jesus in Bearsden. Her sister Moira had seen to all the arrangements. It was a sad Christmas. Usually it was her mother who had the family for a jolly Christmas dinner in Bearsden, but this year a very subdued Mrs McVinney and Moira had come to her. Nevertheless, her mother had gone to the trouble of cooking and bringing along a turkey. It just needed to be heated up. Granda had been comparatively *compos mentis*, so all in all it hadn't been too bad. She'd managed.

Then Granda had taken ill. Peter had tried his usual blinkered trick of dismissing the true situation with, 'It's only his age,' but she knew Granda better than he did, and Granda was in pain.

'Peter, I'm getting the doctor whether you like it or not,' she told him.

It turned out to be a strangulated bowel and Granda was carted off on a stretcher to the hospital. As the ambulancemen were carrying him out, he turned to her and said in one of his few lucid moments, 'You'll be glad to see the back of me, Bessie.'

'No, no, Granda.' She put a big effort into trying to sound genuine. 'And I'll be in to visit you in the hospital just as soon as I can. Take care now.'

Peter of course, better late than never, was making a great fuss of Granda. He insisted he was the one to go with the old man in the ambulance. 'You stay and make the tea,' he told her.

Granda died the next day. Bessie had arrived at the afternoon visiting hour and was told that he'd just 'slipped quietly away'. She reckoned it was the only quiet thing Granda had ever done since she'd known him.

Peter sobbed broken-heartedly at the funeral. She really felt sorry for him. But he refused to be consoled. Instead he turned bitterly on her because she was unable to shed a tear.

'Even Daisy wept for Granda – but you? Oh, not you. I've never been able to understand you.'

Well, that was true anyway. She felt sad. Sad for Peter and sad for Granda. Sad because she had no tears left. In her secret heart though a spark of gladness burned. She would have more free time to paint. She could go up to her studio now with no interfering cries of 'Bessie, Bessie, where's my tea?' Or 'Bessie, I couldn't get to the bathroom in time.' 'Bessie . . . Bessie . . .'

The day after the funeral, when she was alone in the house and actually, unbelievably, free from any worries or interruptions, she went up to the loft. She sat in front of her easel and allowed the sweet joy of freedom to course through her veins. She was still sitting there hours later when Peter and Daisy returned home. As if in a dream she heard them moving about downstairs. Eventually Peter's head appeared through the open trapdoor.

'What do you think you're playing at? What about our tea?'

'Just coming,' she replied automatically.

Later her mother arrived. Her mother had never been one to visit her. Perhaps once or twice a year at the most.

'You know you're always welcome to come out to see us in Bearsden,' she always used to say. Now, feeling lost and lonely without her partner, she began popping in to see Bessie more and more often. Morning, noon and night, in fact.

'Moira works shifts,' she explained, 'and then she has her own life to lead.'

Why is it that no one thinks I should have a life of my own? Bessie thought, but she didn't say anything. Her mother was so obviously lonely and missing her father. And it was true that Moira worked shifts at the library and was out a lot.

'Since your father died,' her mother explained, 'I can't bear to be alone. I just can't bear it.'

Then, who would have thought it, Moira of the prim manner and horn-rimmed spectacles, met a man, no oil painting himself, became engaged to him within a few months, and announced they were planning to emigrate to Canada.

'We want to take Mother with us, of course,' she assured Bessie. But Bessie knew (and she suspected that Moira also knew) that her mother was far too old to tear up her roots and travel thousands of miles to live in Canada. Even though everyone kept assuring her that Vancouver was a beautiful city.

'No, no,' her mother said. 'I was born here and I'll die here and be laid to rest beside my husband.'

Peter then suggested – *Peter* of all people – that she should sell her house in Bearsden and come and live with them in the flat.

'You could have Granda's old room. We would do it up for you and make it any way you fancied.'

Bessie could hardly believe her ears. He had just come out with this plan to her mother without ever discussing it with her. He'd never once hinted . . . She was so overwhelmed with hatred for him she could have died of it.

Later he'd told her in private, 'Your mother'll pay her way and the extra will help you with the housekeeping.' He meant help *him* financially, Bessie thought. He knew. He must have known that she was just beginning to feel the benefit of being without Granda in the house. She was beginning to regain some energy. The anxiety and fear that had so often taken away her ability to sleep, or to relax, had gone. It was so wonderful. It was a kind of happiness. She thanked God for it. She'd been getting on so well with her painting. There was such peace and quiet while Peter was at work during the day and Daisy was at school.

'Oh Peter,' her mother had put her arm around him and kissed him. 'How kind of you, dear. You'll never know how I appreciate this. I'd feel so happy and safe with you and Bessie. And of course it would be wonderful seeing my lovely grand-daughter every day.' Then she'd turned to Bessie and added, 'But wouldn't it be a bit much for you, dear? I wouldn't want to be a worry or a burden to you.'

What could she say except 'Of course you wouldn't be a burden, Mother.' This was, after all, her mother, who was more entitled to be looked after by her than Granda.

It's not that I mind. I know it's right that after giving birth to me and bringing me up, she should be looked after in her old age by one of her daughters. And if she won't go with Moira and Moira won't stay here, then it's up to me. It's only fair. I see that. But oh, I've used up so much energy and patience and everything else on Granda. I don't think I've anything left for her.

But what could she say? Her mother was so grateful, so excited, so happy at the prospect of moving in.

So, there you are. OK, God. Che sarà sarà.

XXIX

'PLEASE TRY TO stop drinking, Bev. You're ruining your looks and your health.'

'Aw, shut up.'

'Maybe if we saved up enough, we could get train tickets and go home. We'd be all right if we stuck together. Think of it, Bev. We could go back to Glasgow if we could get enough money together.'

'Then what? Eh? Do you think Glasgow DHSS is going to be any different than down here? So what do you fancy, eh? Sleeping in Kelvington Park or Glasgow Green? Oops! Couldn't do either, could we? Glasgow Green is too near your fuckin' Fisher. And Kelvingrove Park is too near Gus the Gunman. You look surprised, hen. Didn't I tell you Gus had a gun?'

'But why would he want to harm you now? It's ages since you've been away.'

'He used to frighten me with it. He was evil, that man. He tormented me with that gun. Just for a change from knocking me about. Just for laughs. It depended on the mood he happened to be in. I never knew. Sometimes he could even be Mr Charming. I never could find out where he kept the gun. If I had, I would have shot him with it.'

'Oh Bev . . .'

'Think I'm kidding, hen? Well, I'm not. I used to dream of shooting that man while he slept. To be free of fear, that's what I prayed for. Oh aye, I used to pray. Please God help me, I used to pray. But He never did, hen. I had to bloody well help myself. Anyway, you that's suddenly got the idea of going home. Where's home for us? Have you asked yourself that? Where's home? *What's* home?'

There was silence for a long minute. Then Jennifer said, 'Home for me was with my granny. I didn't actually live with her but I always felt more at home at her place when I went to visit her. She's in hospital.'

Jennifer had an overwhelming longing to find out how her granny was keeping.

'I think I'll phone.'

'Home?'

'No, the hospital. They seemed to think she'd be kept there for ages. So Granny's neighbour told me.'

Bev shrugged, then took a swig from her bottle.

'You do what you like, hen, and I'll do what I like. OK?'

'They couldn't trace the call, could they?'

'Shouldn't think so.'

'Anyway, I was thinking, Bev. We're both old enough now by law – well Scottish law anyway, I don't know about English – to get married. That surely means we must be legally entitled to leave home.'

Bev laughed.

'I've been over the age of consent for a long time. So we haven't broken any laws? That's a relief!'

'What I mean is, no one can force us to go back to live at home. Can they?'

'I don't know. You're the clever dick.'

'So if we stick together and protect one another – just as we've done here – we'll be all right.'

'Well, hen, you might be all right. You can tell old Fisher to fuck off. What do you plan to do with Gus if he turns up? Frighten him away by wagging your finger at him?'

'We could report him to the police if he came near you but I honestly can't see him turning up, Bev. Not after all this time. A man like that. He's sure to have found someone else to bully by now. Oh Bev, just think – to be back in Glasgow again.'

'You're dreaming. Even if we managed the fare – look at us. We're a couple of dirty tramps. Bag ladies. Not even ladies. I'm an alkie.'

'No, you're not,' Jennifer protested. 'Oh Bev, you're not.'

'You keep telling me I've a drink problem. That's just a polite way of putting it.'

'You're not an alcoholic. I didn't mean that.'

Bev sighed. 'You're not *just* a dreamer any more. You're a restless dreamer. While I'm in such an honest mood – you could make it. But not me. I've got nobody. You've got your daddy and your granny. Oh, I know you've told me your daddy puts his precious Laura first. But Laura or no Laura what do you bet your daddy would still help you. And your granny's probably OK by now.'

'Bev, you've got me.'

'We're not joined at the hip, hen.' She lit a cigarette. 'Aye. It's time you went back. You're a lot tougher now than you were when I first met you. You could tell that guy to fuck off, all right. And your daddy would help you to get cleaned up and get a job. And once you had a job, you could maybe get a wee house of your own.'

'Now *you're* dreaming.'

'Aye, but it's a dream that could come true for you. I was just being selfish before. You wouldn't need to sleep rough back home. You go for it. I'll help you with your fare.'

'I couldn't leave you.'

She looked at Bev's pinched face, and the dark shadows under eyes that were still as blue as the sky. Her good bone structure proved that she had once been a really fine-looking woman. Once she had fair hair. Now her hair, like her skin, had dulled. But she wasn't really a tramp, or a bag lady. She tried to keep herself clean. They both did. They tried to have a wash every day. Either in a station lavatory or in a fountain or a pond in one of the parks, or in Trafalgar Square. It wasn't easy to wash and dry clothes but they usually managed that too. At least they tried to keep their panties clean.

To wash and dry their jerseys and trousers wasn't possible. Neither of them had a change of trousers and Bev's jersey was big and long and a terrible problem to dry. She did try to wash it once but even when she held it in front of the hand dryer in the lavatory for ages, it was no use. They were both thrown out and Bev had to put the jersey back on, soaking wet. She hadn't a shirt to wear underneath. At least Jennifer had that.

Scottish reticence and an inborn shyness prevented Jennifer from displaying much outward affection for Bev. Certainly she could never have said out loud that she loved her. But she did. Now she said, 'You're my best friend. I'm not going to leave you here on your own.'

'I'm touched,' Bev said sarcastically, but Jennifer could tell by the way Bev averted her eyes and the nervous tic on one side of her face that she really was moved. They were sitting in the small park area in the middle of Russell Square. The trees were bare and they could see the huge Russell Hotel across the road. In there would be comfortable beds, wonderful bathrooms, dining rooms with everything you could wish to eat and drink. They liked to sit and imagine what it would be like to stay there. It was another world. There were so many places like it in the vast metropolis of London. Hotels, restaurants, theatres all mobbed with well-dressed, well-fed people, enjoying the good things in life. Especially at night, the whole place lit up and sparkled with lights and life.

A different world.

The world that she and Bev belonged to was dark and cold, hard and dangerous. Back streets, derelict buildings, shop doorways. The police moved them on, of course, long before the shops were due to open. They were forced to keep constantly trudging about, as much to prevent seizing up with the cold as anything else. Sometimes Jennifer was sure she'd die of it. Now, at Christmas, all they needed was snow to finish them off. Maybe it was the time of year that was making her feel especially homesick. She imagined George Square in Glasgow all lit up with fairy lights, and people singing Christmas carols in front of the City Chambers. Then at New Year it would be such a happy, friendly crowd milling about, singing and dancing and wishing each other a Happy New Year.

Her granny always made a spicy Christmas pudding at Christmas and fruit cake and shortbread at New Year.

Jennifer sighed.

'I tell you what,' Bev said, 'you phone your granny. If you haven't enough for the phone, I can help you out. I've nearly a pound . . .'

'But we haven't had anything to eat yet . . .'

'Never mind that just now. We'll be OK. The Salvation Army won't let us starve at Christmas. We'll find out where they dole out their Christmas grub. No, you phone the hospital and see how your gran is. They can do wonderful things with stroke patients now. She'll maybe be able to speak to you herself. If you can't speak to her, phone your daddy.'

'We won't have enough for both calls.'

'Well then, why don't you ask for a reversed charge call. When you phone your daddy's number, I bet he'll be so glad to hear from you he'll be delighted to pay.'

Jennifer felt apprehensive as she and Bev started searching for the nearest phone. And worried.

'But Bev, I told you. I can't leave you. If I go back to Glasgow, you'll have to come with me.'

'OK. OK. We'll work something out. But first, just make the phone call, will you?'

They sorted out enough coins between them to phone the hospital. No chance of a reverse charge call there. Eventually Jennifer got through and asked, first of all, if they would tell her which ward Mrs Sophie McPherson was in. She was asked to wait.

'She'll have been discharged by this time. She'll be back home,' Jennifer said to Bev. 'I should have tried her house first.'

Then a woman's voice on the phone asked, 'Are you a relative?'

'Yes, I'm Jennifer Anderson, her granddaughter.'

'I'm sorry, Miss Anderson. Your grandmother died three days ago.'

Jennifer replaced the receiver, then stood staring at it. Her eyes slowly filled with tears that spilled fitfully down her cheeks.

Bev said, 'What's up?'

'She's dead.'

'I'm sorry, hen. Och never mind.' She put her arm round Jennifer and pulled her to her. 'Have a wee swig out of my bottle.'

XXX

ANDRINA LIT UP a cigarette and blew smoke towards Bernard. She hated him for coming back into her life, disrupting it. It couldn't just be a coincidence that he had turned up and immediately afterwards Jennifer had suddenly disappeared. He must have had something to do with it. Even if it was just to unsettle Jennifer. Like he's unsettling me now, she thought.

She wished Paul was there. She tried to avoid Bernard's eyes because when she looked at him, she wanted him right there and then. He knew it too. His eyes had that deep dark sexual awareness. She could drown in it.

He was remembering, as she was remembering, and his eyes were telling her that he wanted her too. But he kept asking questions about Jennifer.

'I told you, she didn't know any of the neighbours,' she repeated, unable to resist sliding him a smouldering sidelong glance. 'Any more than just to say hello or good evening. She always kept herself to herself. You shouldn't have been pestering them.'

'Pestering them? They were only too pleased to help.'

'But they couldn't help, could they?'

'You never know. Little things mount up and begin to make a picture. I've been to the school as well.'

She tutted.

'What on earth will everybody think?'

'Does it matter?'

'Well, you know what people are like.'

'I know what you're like.'

She inhaled deeply on her cigarette.

'Oh?'

'Still worried about protecting your respectable scandal-free image. Still as randy as a bitch on heat.'

'How dare you speak to me like that! You who seduced me when I was only a girl.'

'Come off it, Andrina.' He continued coolly: 'can you give me the address of that friend of hers – Daisy somebody. I'd like to talk to her next.'

Andrina was visibly trembling as she got up, went over to the writing bureau and scribbled something on to a piece of paper.

He took his time reading it. It was only a few words. She knew he was lingering near to her just to torment her. No other man she'd ever known exuded the powerful sexuality that he did. Before she could do or say anything, he had left the sitting room and was strolling across the hall towards the front door with that subtle self-confident swagger of his. Then, without even turning to say goodbye, he was gone.

Oh, how she hated him for what he could do to her. Her whole body throbbed with passion. She went over to the drinks cabinet and poured herself a large vodka. Alcohol was something she was normally careful about. It was too easy to put on weight at her age. In the days when she'd known Bernard she'd thoughtlessly indulged in everything that aroused the senses. He had fed her with Belgian chocolates, champagne, caviare, strawberries and cream. She'd been carried away by dreamy, sensuous music.

He hadn't changed. She had known him so well years ago, and she knew him still. As she sat drinking the vodka, and inhaling deeply at her cigarette, her mind drifted back over the passionate hours she'd spent with him. She recalled his big, tanned, muscular body. Oh, how beautiful he had been.

She leaned back in her chair and stretched luxuriously pas-sion melting away the hatred. How lucky she was to have had such an experience. It was something beautiful and special, a God-given gift to be treasured in secret between them. And he had promised to come back, to keep her informed about how his investigations were progressing. She would be ready for him next time, dressed in the erotic way she knew he liked.

Andrina awoke the Sunday after Bernard's visit, her blood

still hot with need. As soon as Paul awakened, she caressed him into arousal and they had the best sex they'd ever enjoyed together.

Now she felt sated with pleasure, fulfilled, satisfied with her world. Even thoughts of Jennifer lost their anxious edge. Jennifer would be all right. She would be enjoying herself somewhere on her own. She always had been a loner, always hanging back, never wanting to join her and Paul in anything. Jennifer *must* be all right. Even the hospitals had been checked. She was not ill. She'd been involved in no accident. She *knew* Jennifer was perfectly all right.

When Paul got up and made a pot of tea and brought a tray back to the bed Andrina murmured, 'Darling, put on our Gregorian chant tape. I feel so wonderful. I feel our love this Sunday morning has almost been a religious experience.'

Paul enthusiastically agreed. 'Yes, if we'd had time I would have loved to go to morning service. I really feel in the right mood.'

She smiled and walked her fingers up his arm.

'So do I, darling.'

They lay in each other's arms and listened to the spiritual music and felt uplifted. Andrina thought it wonderful. She felt their relationship blessed, purified. Soon, they would be married. Paul had, at last, asked his wife for a divorce. He hoped to get a 'quickie' as he called it and they'd be married as soon as possible after the final papers came through.

It hadn't been easy for him these last few days. His wife hadn't taken it at all well and his children had been difficult too. Young people could be so selfish. Poor Paul. She was sorry for him and glad that she had been able, this morning, to soothe away any doubts or anxieties.

They lay listening to the music and felt in complete harmony.

She was sorry when they had to get up and get dressed but she tried to make the rest of the day a really memorable and happy one for him. She wished he hadn't to go back to Edinburgh later that evening but he still had many things to attend to, loose ends to tie up at home. Soon, however, they would start looking around for a house in Glasgow so that they would have a home of their very own to move into as soon as they were married.

Everything was working out perfectly. She sang in the choir and gazed at Paul as she sang. She could see the admiration and pride in his eyes as he gazed back at her.

She wasn't even afraid of Bernard coming back. People like Bernard had their uses. There was a wicked side to them but from such wickedness could come good. She knew this now, and the knowledge gave her a deep satisfaction.

She sang going about her household chores. She'd long since given up her job and was content to look after the house and concentrate on making tasty dishes for Paul to enjoy.

'You're a wonderful cook,' he told her with an appreciative sigh after relishing one of her meals. 'And a perfect housewife. You keep this flat like a new pin. You're even good at sex. How lucky can any man get?'

She blew him a kiss, wondering dreamily as she did so when Bernard O'Maley would return.

XXXI

'BUT . . . I SAW her only yesterday. She was perfectly all right.' Andrina's stricken gaze clung to the nursing sister in disbelief.

'Your mother was never perfectly all right, dear,' Sister Gilchrist gently corrected. 'She'd suffered a serious stroke.'

'But I thought . . .'

'Drink your tea. Is there anyone I can phone to come and collect you? You shouldn't be driving when you're in such a state.'

Dazedly Andrina shook her head.

'There's no one.'

The words had an ominous ring. They brought fear. Paul was in Edinburgh with his wife and family. He'd warned her never to phone or in any way contact him when he was there. Things were at a very delicate stage in his divorce negotiations. It would take very little to make his wife turn nasty. She could withdraw her cooperation just out of spite. Paul had so many anxieties at work as well as at home they always overwhelmed any problems of her own.

'Your fiancé?' Sister suggested. She'd met Paul on a few occasions when he'd accompanied her to the hospital.

'He's away at the moment.'

'A friend, then?'

With a gust of thankfulness, Andrina remembered Bessie.

'Oh yes, my friend Mrs Alexander. She'll come.'

'Give me her number. I'll phone her while you drink your tea. Then I must do my rounds. Will you be all right waiting here?'

'Of course. You've been very kind.'

Left alone in the Sister's office, Andrina sat with a mercifully blank mind. Automatically she sipped at the hot sweet liquid. Her usually straight-backed graceful figure had shrunk. She was like a rubber doll from which most of the air had seeped away. That was how Bessie found her.

'Andrina, I'm so sorry.' Bessie hurried over and put her arms around her. 'Come on, I'll take you home.'

'I don't know if I could drive . . .'

'Of course not. I've got a taxi waiting outside.'

Firmly supporting her, Bessie led her friend away.

Once in the Monteith Row flat, despite Andrina's protests of not being hungry, she made an omelette, some toast and a pot of tea.

'You'll feel better if you eat something. And don't worry, I'll stay with you tonight.'

Andrina's lips trembled.

'Thank you, Bessie.'

'You'd do the same for me.'

'You knew Mummy, didn't you?'

Bessie nodded.

'A most unusual and interesting woman.'

'Yes, she was very highly thought of in Bearsden. She worked hard for the church. Even before she went to live in Bearsden she was always busy helping somebody.' Andrina cast a tragic gaze across at Bessie. 'I'm afraid I let her down. I wish I hadn't.'

Bessie tutted.

'Now, don't you go blaming yourself for anything. I admired your mother very much but she had impossibly high standards. Nobody could have lived up to them.'

'I did try.'

'Of course you did. She ought to have been very proud of you.'

Andrina gave a half-heartbroken, half-sarcastic laugh.

'Proud of me? If only you knew.'

'I know you're not only a beautiful, talented woman, you've a good, kind heart as well.'

'Oh, Bessie.' Andrina stretched out her arms like a child. 'What would I do without you?'

Bessie gave her a comforting hug, then said, 'Come on, drink your tea. We've a lot to arrange. Everybody will have to be notified for a start. Sophie was a very popular and respected woman in her community and in the church. A great many people will want to attend her funeral.'

'Oh dear, I don't even want to think of such a thing. It's too awful.'

'It's best to keep busy. I'll help you.'

There had been a time – a lifetime ago, it seemed now – when she and Bernard had actually looked forward to her mother's funeral. Surely they must have been joking? She had been perfectly serious when she'd told Bernard that she'd never marry him while her mother was still alive. She had been far too terrified of the scandal. She knew her mother would disown her if she discovered her daughter having anything to do with Bernard O'Maley. And that, of course, was eventually what happened.

But long before Sophie had found out about her affair with Bernard, they'd discussed what Andrina would wear at the funeral. Bernard promised to buy her the best and most expensive outfit in town. She saw herself in a glamorous wide-brimmed hat – of shining Italian straw perhaps. And high-heeled shoes.

'Have you anything black to wear?' Bessie asked as if reading her mind. 'I personally don't think it's important but your mother was a stickler for doing the conventional thing, wasn't she? I think you should wear it as a mark of respect.'

'Poor Mother,' Andrina said, 'she'd never rest peacefully if I turned up in scarlet or white. I'll buy something tomorrow.'

Sophie McPherson, she put in the newspaper notice. Dearly beloved mother of Andrina Anderson.

'I did love her, you know,' she told Bessie.

'Of course you did,' Bessie assured her. 'And she loved you in her own way.'

Andrina felt a terrible anxiety to believe the words.

'She loved my father but I never once saw her kiss him or even take his arm. She didn't seem able to show love or affection.'

'Poor Sophie. All shut into herself like that. I once tried to kiss her goodbye after an especially enjoyable visit. She was so hospitable. But she shrank back as if she was terrified of any display of affection. I think she must have been hurt and betrayed in the past so much that she was never able to get over it and trust anyone again.'

'You're probably right. She was painfully neurotic. Never at peace for a moment.'

'Well, she's at peace now, Andrina.'

Andrina nodded.

'I must give her a funeral that she'd be proud of. She was terribly proud as well, you know. Yes, I'll do the funeral tea. I won't let her down in that.'

'Oh, Andrina, that's far too much for you to do at such a time. Get a caterer to come in. Or better still, book a meal at a hotel.'

'No, you said it was best to keep busy, Bessie, and you're right. I want to do this for my mother.'

Bessie hesitated then reluctantly gave in.

'If you feel you must.'

It was the saving of Andrina. Plans for the funeral filled her mind to the exclusion of everything else. She was determined that every detail of the service and of the funeral tea afterwards should be perfect. It was as if it was her last chance to please her mother.

Everything was indeed perfect. The coffin was the best that money could buy. There never had been such a profusion of flowers. The undertakers were suitably dignified. The line of cars slowly following the hearse were gleaming black Daimlers. A host of solemn, well-dressed mourners paid their last respects.

Andrina looked lovely standing beside the coffin in the church as she sang her mother's favourite hymn. Then in a clear voice she gave a moving eulogy.

Sounds of sobbing echoed through the church.

'Your mother was always so proud of you, Andrina,' people said afterwards. 'And rightly so.'

They complimented her on the meal too. Throughout the whole day she kept her head held high. She was gracious and attentive to everyone. It was only after the mourners had left and she was alone with Bessie again that cracks showed in her dignified composure.

'Did I do all right, Bessie?'

'You were wonderful.'

'She always liked me to sing in the church.'

'You sang beautifully, Andrina. You really did. It was extremely moving. What you said too. No wonder so many people couldn't hold back their tears. You were so very genuine in your praise of her. And so loving.'

'I tried my very best,' Andrina said. Then added wistfully, 'I always did.'

XXXII

JENNIFER DIDN'T KNOW what she would have done without Bev. Her grief would have been too much to bear on her own. Bev made her talk about her feelings. They shared their memories – Jennifer's memories and love for her granny and Bev's memories and love for her ma, as she called her mother. Huddled together in shop doorways they'd stare out at the dark night and talk, half to each other and half to themselves.

Bev said,

'My ma was battered as well, you know. Funny that, eh? Me shacking up with the same kind of bastard as she did. You'd have thought I'd have had more sense after seeing what happened to her. Living through it with her. But it's not a matter of sense, is it? I mean you believe the bastards, you trust them, you fall for them and once they've got you . . .' She shook her head. 'Then, after every time it happens, they tell you how sorry they are. Oh, they can be so bloody convincing. They swear it'll never happen again . . .' She lit a cigarette and puffed at it for a few seconds before she was able to go on.

'I'd heard it all before. My da was the very same with my ma. My poor ma. I wish I'd been able to help her. But you get hell of a mixed up inside. I mean, I loved my da as well, you see. And I kept believing him just like my ma did. But oh, my poor ma.'

Jennifer didn't say anything. Didn't even look round. They both stared ahead, the bond of sympathy so strong between them it was almost tangible.

Eventually Jennifer managed to speak.

'You and your ma loved each other, despite everything. All right, you both had weaknesses and made mistakes but they were only in trusting and loving too much. Or maybe in trusting and loving the wrong people too much. But you and your ma loved each other, that's something to be happy and glad about. When I was a very young child, I loved my mother but I don't think I ever really trusted her. Then the love withered away. My granny became the only person I could depend on. She always wanted me. Always took my side. Was always there for me.' Jennifer struggled to control her voice. 'I loved her for that. For her loyalty. For the feeling of security she gave me. She could be quite fierce, you know. She once fought off a murderer. It was in all the papers at the time. I always felt she'd protect me against anything. Even my mother. Yet, my mother is so beautiful, so charming, that everyone likes her, especially the people in the church . . .'

Her voice acquired a bitter, sarcastic note.

'She sings in the choir, would you believe. Sometimes, when I watched her and listened to her, I used to think — maybe it's me. Maybe I'm just jealous of her because she's so beautiful and likeable and I'm neither of those things. But then I'd remember that my granny knew her better than anybody. My granny could see through her and that made an extra strong bond between my granny and me. It was like a secret we shared. Now she's gone and there's only me and I feel so vulnerable, so unsafe, so outnumbered. Who is there to believe me now?'

'There's me,' Bev said.

'Oh, but if you met her, you'd think I was just being stupid, Bev. You'd be on her side. Once you saw her . . .'

'Aw, shut up. Don't insult me. You accuse me of being too trusting. Well, it's time some of that rubbed off on you. Surely to God you can have a wee bit of faith in me. And I could say much the same to you as far as your granny is concerned. You loved her and she loved you. That's something you should be glad about and grateful for. And to hell with your selfish, randy sod of a mother.'

'I suppose you're right.'

'You still want to go back to Glasgow, don't you?'

'I suppose so.'

'Never mind "suppose so". Do you or don't you?'

'Yes, I do.'

'OK. We'll both go back.'

'And to hell with Gus McCabe?'

'To hell with Gus McCabe. From tomorrow we work everywhere from morning till night – bus queues, theatre queues, everything that moves, we ask for money. Then we'll sit outside Euston Station with a bit of cardboard saying "Please help us to get home to Scotland". That should do the trick.'

For the first time Jennifer turned round.

'Oh Bev, I hope so. Oh, wouldn't it be wonderful to see Glasgow again? London's all right for Londoners and tourists with plenty of money. But Glasgow's home.'

Bev burst into song,

'We belong to Glasgow, dear old Glasgow town . . .'

Jennifer giggled.

'You always manage to cheer me up.'

'Aye. Right. That's my good deed done for today. Now, belt up and let me get some sleep.'

Jennifer settled down as best she could on the piece of cardboard she now carried around under her arm. It did very little to cushion her bones against the hard ground but at least it absorbed some of the cold. She still felt chilled to the marrow, though. They would only sleep, if they slept at all, for a short time. Then, to prevent themselves dying of hypothermia like so many other homeless people, they would get up and start walking about. Only the other day they'd stumbled across the dead body of an old man. He'd literally frozen to death. That night Jennifer felt she was going to freeze to death too. The only thing that kept her hanging on was the thought of returning to her native city. Bev had once said, 'Where's home? *What's* home?' but they both knew in their hearts that 'home' was Glasgow.

Eventually, near to tears with the misery of her blood turning to ice, Jennifer groaned out loud,'Bev, I can't bear another minute of this. I'll have to get up.'

'Aye, OK hen.' Bev struggled into a sitting position. 'Here, do you remember in front of the Central Station – you know, in Gordon Street?'

'What about it?'

'There's gratings – something to do with the Central Hotel

– hot air belts up from there all the time – all night long, I've heard.'

'Gosh, what a marvellous skipper.'

'Aye, that's where we'll be able to thaw out.'

Jennifer laughed.

'Not tonight we won't.'

'Soon though. Now that we've made up our mind.'

They staggered stiffly to their feet.

'My God, I could kill for a drink.'

Jennifer tutted, 'You're always saying that.'

'Well, it's true.'

'Something's just occurred to me.'

'What?'

Shoulders hunched forward, they slowly began to plod along the dark, deserted street.

'We don't need to worry about being recognised in Glasgow. My skin looks a different colour. I'm not sure if it's weather-beaten or ingrained dirt. A bit of both, I suppose. And my hair's like rat's tails. Cutting it, especially my fringe, with nail scissors hasn't improved how I look.'

'You're not actually dressed like a Paris model either, hen.'

'You needn't talk. Bev, the bag lady.'

'Aye, OK, OK. Our nearest and dearest won't recognise us.'

'Nearest and dearest – that's a laugh!'

By the time the city came to life and they could start begging, Jennifer wanted to sink down on to the pavement, hard or not, and just huddle there, not doing anything. She felt exhausted and ill. Bev looked as if she felt the same.

Rain swirled around the two friends as they stood outside the tube station entrance at Tottenham Court Road. Soaked to the skin they trailed along to Oxford Street and hung around Oxford Circus for a while. After that they made their way back to Great Russell Street and stood outside the British Museum. From there they found themselves wandering through Russell Square, then Gordon Square, automatically drawn towards Euston. There they sat huddled together on the pavement outside the station with the piece of cardboard propped up in front of them. They had tried begging within the shelter of the station but the police had chucked them out.

They sat with heads sunk into their chests, Bev too exhausted to hold her head up, Jennifer too ashamed.

'Please help us to get home to Scotland' was written on the cardboard and Jennifer repeated the words in her head for hours like a mantra.

At last, grudgingly, they used some of the money they'd collected to buy a cup of tea and a pizza which they shared between them. Jennifer hadn't wanted to touch a penny but Bev said, 'Look, hen, we're going to pass out if we don't get something. Then some rotten sod'll steal our dosh. And I don't know about you but I'm dying for a pee.'

'I've been in agony for hours. I wouldn't be surprised if I've wet my pants,' Jennifer confessed.

'Well, come on, you silly cow. Let's treat ourselves to a pee.'

Afterwards, when they were washing their face and hands in the gloriously hot water in the station Ladies, Bev said, 'I've seen the day when I'd try to be quiet and dainty having a pee. All worried in case anyone heard me, if I was out visiting somebody and using their lavvy. Now I sound like a horse and I don't care a damn. It's just such a bloody relief.'

Jennifer laughed despite the misery of the rain-sodden clothes sticking to her body and making her teeth chatter.

'I know what you mean.'

The tea and the pizza helped and they were able to face returning outside.

'Tea's OK,' Bev sighed, 'but, oh, I . . .'

'Don't say it,' Jennifer interrupted fiercely. 'Don't even think about it. We need every penny to get back home. Just keep thinking about Glasgow.'

'Aye, OK, OK.'

After dark they worked theatre land. From Shaftesbury Avenue to St Martin's Lane. From Haymarket to the Strand. Among the glamour and the glitter, the beautiful expensively dressed people and the sparkling lights, Jennifer and Bev looked and felt like waifs from another planet. Often they separated and met up again at pre-arranged times and places. Each time Jennifer was in an agony of suspense in case Bev had spent any money.

'Think of the Central Hotel,' she kept saying to a dripping Bev. 'Think of that grating, that lovely hot skipper.'

'Aye, OK hen.' Bev wiped away the rivers of rain from her face with the end of her jersey. The jersey was half hidden by a black bin bag stolen from a stationer's shop piled up with rubbish that had been left out for the refuse collectors. After emptying out the rubbish, Bev had torn a hole in the plastic bag and stuck her head through it and she'd fixed Jennifer up with the same makeshift rain cape. The only trouble was they had been soaked to the skin before they'd managed to find this protection.

'Better late than never,' Bev said. 'And it suits you no end. Now if we can just get a couple of smaller white bags for our heads, that'll complete the outfit. Black and white – very smart, eh?'

Jennifer managed a chittering laugh but she was almost weeping. They still hadn't enough money. As they trudged about looking for a safe skipper, Glasgow faded far away and became no more than a dream.

XXXIII

WHEN BESSIE'S MOTHER had said she couldn't bear to be alone, she'd meant it. She followed Bessie about, was at her heels the whole day, brown eyes anxious, sparse dry frizz of hair neglected. Bessie wondered if grief had gone to the old woman's head, knocked her completely off balance emotionally. Mrs McVinney was full of fear. Bessie discovered she not only locked her bedroom door but jammed a chair under the door handle every night.

She delayed going to her bedroom for as long as possible. The television was kept on until all hours. Then, through the bedroom wall, Bessie could hear her mother's radio. It went on the whole night. Talks, music, game shows, quizzes, news from everywhere from Moscow to Timbuktu, America to China, Africa to the Netherlands, Scandinavian countries to the Holy Land. Bessie didn't know about her mother but felt she was becoming an expert in world affairs. She'd tackled her mother about it.

'Mother, why on earth do you keep your radio on all night?'

'It's company for me, dear. I hope you don't mind. I'll try and turn it down a bit if it bothers you but I'm getting a bit deaf, you see . . .'

'But you've got Peter and Daisy and me for company. We're here all night just through the wall.'

'I know, dear, but your father was always with me in our bedroom. It was where we were closest . . .' Her cheeks, dried and wrinkled like old parchment, suffused with colour. 'Not that I mean in a – you know – that kind of way. We were soul mates, your daddy and I. God joined us and I look forward to the day when He'll join us together again.'

Bessie tried to tell herself that it wouldn't last for ever. It didn't last for ever with Granda. It had only felt like it.

And it felt like it again.

The only time she could escape from her mother was on Sunday mornings at Meeting for Worship. Her mother had always been shocked at Bessie having anything to do with Quakers.

Bessie didn't bother explaining or defending any more. She was too grateful to get away on her own from the flat and enjoy a bit of peace and quiet.

Please help me to be patient and loving with my mother. You know she's a good, kind woman and a good Christian. She deserves to be cherished and looked after in her old age. I want to look after her and make her feel happy and secure and cherished. I don't mind You looking into my heart, because that's truly what's there. Nevertheless there are times when I feel I could kill her. Remember I felt like that about Granda too? I'm getting depressed with myself but what can I do? That's what I feel.

She tried to believe that somehow God would work everything out for the best. But it wasn't easy. Her mother would reprimand Bessie for her choice of women's magazines. The old-established *People's Friend* became the only magazine that met with approval. Arts publications with their nude or modern paintings were definitely out.

'You ought to be ashamed of yourself, Bessie,' was the sad murmur. Pictures were taken down off walls; Peter helped with much gleeful enthusiasm.

'I've never liked these monstrosities.'

Peter and her mother became like the terrible twins, ganging up against her.

Bessie began to catch them whispering together in corners. They would stop when she entered the room. She believed they were speaking about her, hatching some plot against her, even. Then she worried about becoming paranoid. A couple of times, she'd lost her temper with her mother. A dreadful, undreamed-of occurrence that brought tears to her mother's eyes and outrage from Peter.

She hadn't shouted or anything. It was just that she had allowed her irritation to get the better of her. But then, her mother managed to climb up to the loft one day when Bessie was out at the shops. She'd tidied the place. More than that – to use her own words – 'I've given it a really good spring clean, dear.'

It was too much.

'Hells bells!' Bessie yelled. 'Is there no place on earth I can call my own? No place where I can have my privacy? You'd no bloody right to set foot in my studio, far less interfere with anything.'

Her mother had drooped away, quietly weeping, to her room, which was even more terrible. Bessie had to apologise, of course, but it was through clenched teeth. She was genuinely sorry to have hurt the old woman, who had obviously thought she was doing a good turn. But Bessie still fumed in secret. There was a fire raging inside her.

'How could you do that to a poor old woman?' Peter sounded truly shocked. 'It's you who are selfish. *And* cruel into the bargain. And to your own mother!'

'All right. All right. I've said I'm sorry,' she told him.

In the end she not only couldn't say anything, she couldn't do anything.

When she did get herself moving, she got into such muddles. The house began to look like a tip. Her mother tried to do things to help but somehow only made everything worse, and when she spoke helpfully over Bessie's shoulder in the supermarket she nearly blew what was left of her mind.

I'm sorry. I'm not having any more of this. Hell or no hell, I've had enough.

After that, she either didn't get up in the morning, or she sat in a corner of the kitchen, withdrawn into a silent world of her own. What was the use? was the most frequent echo in a mind gone dull and totally lethargic. What was the use?

Her mother eventually called in the doctor. Surprise, surprise. Anti-depressant tablets. Drugs. The simple answer to unasked questions.

But there you are.

'Take your medicine, dear,' her mother urged. 'And that will make everything all right.'

'No, it won't, Mother.'

'But the doctor said . . .'

'What does he know or care about me?'

'Oh, now, Bessie, don't be silly, dear. The doctor knows best.'

'I'm exhausted. I'm tired out of my mind. I've nursed my father-in-law for years. For years, Mother. You don't know what that means, do you? You've never had to do it, you see. Your mother and father died in a nursing home. Father died in a hospital.'

Her mother withdrew from her, hurt, worried, frightened.

She's reading my mind. She's getting the message. I'm sorry but I just cannot help it.

No more was said that day but the next day her mother quietly announced, 'I've decided that I'll go into a retirement home. There's a very nice one in Bearsden and all my friends are in the district. They'll be able to visit me.'

Bessie brightened with hope.

'And you'll be able to visit them, Mother. And of course you won't be on your own. There'll be plenty of company for you there.'

Then she felt guilty and struggled to douse the light in her eyes.

'Of course, we'll miss you, Mother.'

'What are you talking about?' Peter recovered from his first wave of shock. 'Your mother's not going into any old folks' home. What a disgrace. What a showing-up that would be. There's plenty of room for your mother here. There's no reason for her to leave, and as far as I'm concerned, she's perfectly welcome to stay.'

Bessie stared at him, his tight mean mouth, his bulging eyes, his white bald head.

'Do you know something, Peter? I hate you. I really do hate you.'

Her mother became agitated to the point of tears.

'Oh dear, I don't want to cause any trouble or ill-feeling between you. I'm really sorry I came, Bessie. I didn't mean any harm.'

'I know, Mother, and I'm sorry too. It's just as I said. I'm so tired.'

Her mother got up and came over and kissed her.

'I can see that now, dear. Now, don't you worry. Everything's going to be all right.'

Then she disappeared to her room.

Within a few days she'd arranged to go into a private nursing home owned by the Church of Jesus. Bessie went with her and could sense, even see, the nervous beating of her mother's heart. She's afraid, but she's doing this for me, Bessie thought. And she remembered with anguish the thankfulness in her mother's eyes when she'd first been shown into the bedroom in the flat: 'I'll be safe and happy here for the rest of my life. Thank you for taking me in, Bessie. It's very kind of you, dear.'

The old woman lasted barely two months in the home. Bessie visited her every afternoon until one day – one beautiful sunny day – she'd gone to Bearsden in the morning instead. That afternoon she'd been invited to tea by Andrina McPherson. She'd bumped into Andrina in town and been struck again by the woman's beauty.

'I'd love to paint you,' she'd said and Andrina had been flattered and intrigued. She had taken her sketchpad to the house in Monteith Row and after a delicious tea, Andrina had posed for her. How happy they'd both been. Bessie had never felt so happy in years.

Then she'd had a phone message from Daisy.

'Mummy, the matron of the home says you're to go there immediately.'

Andrina had kindly driven her to Bearsden in her car.

She had run down the corridor towards her mother's room only to be stopped by a sad-faced nurse outside the door. The expression on the nurse's face said enough.

'No, no.' Bessie shook her head.

'I'm afraid so,' the nurse murmured. 'We found that she'd passed away when we went to see why she didn't come through to the dining room for her normal cup of tea.'

'No. Oh no.' Her mother had died alone. 'Oh, poor Mother.'

She had gone straight back home and shut herself up in the loft. Not even bothering with a brush, she smeared paint over the canvas with her hands, smacking it on. Mixing it with her tears.

XXXIV

BERNARD STARED AT the photograph of Jennifer that Robert had given him. Straight, nut-brown hair, a fringe reaching her eyebrows, earnest grey eyes, a wide sensitive mouth, a faint freckling over the bridge of her nose and cheeks. She was fifteen when the photo had been taken and she looked twelve. When he'd last seen her in the flesh, she must have been sixteen, nearly seventeen, and she still had a vulnerable, childlike appearance. He tried to imagine what she'd look like now at seventeen, going on eighteen. That is, if she was still alive. He hadn't said to Robert but he knew that many youngsters, especially women, either ended up in prostitution or as victims of malnutrition, hypothermia or murder. London was the place most runaways made for. He'd thought this from the start but he'd made a thorough check of Glasgow's homeless and down-and-outs just in case. The irony was Jennifer didn't need to be short of a few pounds – at least after she was twenty-one. Sophie had ordered in her will that the Bearsden house had to be sold and the proceeds and any other money put into a trust fund for Jennifer.

The girl could of course have found a job and a place to live, but he doubted it. He'd checked every agency in London. Nobody had her name on their books. He felt sorry for Robert. Guilty too for the way he'd betrayed him in the past by sleeping with his wife. How Robert had managed to forgive him, he didn't know. He would have committed murder in the same circumstances. Of course, when Robert found out, it had killed their friendship. Now they were slowly picking up the old threads again. They'd met for a drink several times and he'd been out to Robert's home in Bearsden. He also dropped into the karate club now and again to give Robert a hand with the lads, and to do a bit of sparring. A new PE teacher had joined the club and was more or less taking over from Robert. Guy Nolan was young, keen and aggressively fit.

It was true that Robert had visibly aged in the past few months.

'The chances are she's perfectly OK,' Bernard said. 'She'll have used a different name, got herself a job and a place to stay and be living the kind of life she wants to live.'

'But surely you would have come across her by now.'

'Not if she's using a false name, and London's a big place, remember. But I haven't given up hope. I'll find her. I promise you. It makes it more difficult if she's using a false name, that's all.'

'Bernard, I appreciate all the trouble you've gone to. You've enough to do seeing to your own work. You can't have much time to yourself, much of a life for yourself, with all this and the security jobs you've been doing.'

Bernard shrugged.

'I suppose you could say my job is my life. Funnily enough, I've had to do another bit of detective work.'

'Oh yes, I think you told me. That woman who's been pestering one of the Page Boys. You would have thought she'd have given up long ago.'

'Nutters like that never give up. They're obsessive, and their obsessions get worse, not better. She got worse of course when she discovered that Dave was married and had a child.'

'Oh well, I suppose she can't do much harm from America.'

'She's kept in touch by sending him filthy, disgusting pack-ages.' Bernard shook his head. 'She's a good looking woman too. You'd never think that her head was full of worms. Anyway, the last stuff had English postmarks so she's over here. And now she's sending death threats to Dave's wife and child.'

'The quicker she's found then, the better.'

'Aye. The police are on to it and I've been doubling up enquiries with those I'm making about Jennifer. I've also had to put twenty-four-hour guards on Dave and his family. They've been going through hell because of this crazy female. Dave wants me to be with his wife and kid and I occasionally take a turn with them but I can't be there all the time.'

Robert supported his head in his hands for a moment or two.

'I feel terrible imposing on you so much, Bernard. Even if you'd accept payment . . .'

'Forget it. As I told you, while I'm on the phone or out and about trying to trace this crazy woman, I'm doubling up with enquiries about Jennifer. I think I've got a good lead on the woman so I'm off to London again tomorrow. Dave has to be there in a couple of days for a concert. This woman is in London so while Dave's there, I'll be stepping up security all round.'

'The more I think of London, Bernard, any hope I have seeps away. I can't see how anyone can be found there.'

'Missing people are being found all the time, Robert. Especially homeless kids. They've favourite haunts – railway stations during the day, shop doorways at night . . .'

'Oh God.'

'There's also agencies and religious groups and hostels, remember.'

'Jennifer hasn't turned up at any of these places so far.'

'I'm just as obsessional as that crazy woman. When I put my mind to something, I never give up. I'll find that woman, and I'll find Jennifer, believe me. And it's not just me on the job. You've met my nephew, Sean, haven't you?'

Robert nodded.

'Good looks obviously run in your family, Bernard. He'll break a few hearts, that one.'

'He's not just a pretty face. He's a first-class operator and he's on the forefront of both cases. He's travelling with me to London tomorrow.'

Bernard was glad that his brother Michael had become more relaxed in his attitude to Sean being part of the firm. Indeed he showed pride in his son when Bernard praised the lad's expertise at the job. He tried to be fair and give Sally equal praise. There was no doubt in his mind though that of the two, Sean was the one in whom he had the most faith. Sally was good, but more impulsive and aggressive. Sean was an operator after his own heart. Without needing to be told, he put into practice Bernard's own ethics and beliefs. Sean gave everybody he had to deal with – even the worst drunks or gangsters – a certain modicum of calm respect. The priority of his security firm was to avoid trouble, so he and Sean spoke to the gangsters as if they were businessmen because that was how they regarded themselves. All of his men kept the peace in pubs and clubs, prevented punters or fans from getting hurt at gatherings, indoors or out of doors, and prevented harm to any individual principal.

Sean could keep that peace in exactly the way Bernard did himself. There was an aura of strength about him, an air of quiet authority. He, like Bernard, gave respect, and was respected in return.

Bernard had already decided to give him a few more years, and then make him a partner in the firm. He would have perfect confidence in Sean as a partner right now. The lad was still so young, however, only twenty years of age. Perhaps on his twenty-first birthday: a partnership because, despite his youth, he was one of the best in the business.

Robert asked, 'Have you kept in touch with Bessie Alexander? Her daughter might still get a letter or some sort of communication.'

'She seems to be having her own problems at the moment. I called up there the other day. Her daughter's getting married – a shotgun affair. Apparently the father's none too pleased about it. But don't worry. Either Sean or I will keep checking with them.'

'I feel I should be doing more.'

'You're a teacher, Robert. You've got enough responsibility with that. I keep telling you,' he grinned at the older man, 'leave everything to the experts.'

Robert smiled wanly in return.

Bernard rose, hitching his shoulders and buttoning the jacket of his Giorgio Armani suit.

'I've another call to make. I'd better get going.'

They had been having a drink in a pub in West Nile Street. Now Robert got to his feet, shabby in comparison in his old tweed jacket with its leather elbow patches.

'I'd better make a move and get home. Laura will have dinner waiting for me.'

'Can I give you a lift?'

'No, I've parked the car round the corner.'

'Still that old banger?'

'Not the old banger you remember.'

'Another old banger?'

'How did you guess?'

They parted laughing. Bernard drove off in his Porsche and gave Robert a wave as the teacher was easing his lanky body into an ancient Cortina.

The 'other call' he'd to make was to Robert's ex-wife. Andrina had phoned the office and left a message for him to come to Monteith Row that evening. He hadn't mentioned this to Robert in case Robert thought it was good news about Jennifer. Bernard didn't believe that it was. He had still to make up his mind what to do about Andrina. He knew she had wanted him from that first visit he'd made to the house enquiring about Jennifer.

He could bet his last dollar that this was the reason she'd asked him to call tonight. She really was begging for it.

XXXV

*W*HAT IS IT about this place? Are there people-magnets stuck to it or something? First Granda comes to live here. Then Mother. Now Daisy's husband has moved in. Soon there'll be a baby as well.

Peter's been telling me I'm useless, hopeless and helpless for so long, it's got to me. I keep telling myself that it's not true but I can't quite convince myself any more.

I've painted so much – the loft is stacked with canvases but I've only ever sold a few and they were mostly to friends and relatives just doing me a kindness, I'm sure.

I haven't a penny in the bank. So how could I buy a place of my own? Or pay a rent if there was a place to rent? Peter wouldn't part with a penny to help me to survive. So how could I even get anything to eat? What if I was lonely? What if I became fearful like Mother? I hope the fact that Mother left what money she had to the Church of Jesus secured her a place in heaven. But it didn't help me much, did it?

But I keep thinking – damn it, I am going to get out of here! I am going to survive.

Then the other day, I went into a café. There were newspapers on a shelf near the table where I was sitting. I picked one up and began leafing through it just to waste some time. Anything to delay going back to old sour face and the awful grind of my life. It was while I was sipping my tea and trying not to weep and turning the pages of this newspaper that my eye caught a 'flats to let' column. It consisted mostly of furnished flats at ridiculously high rents. Then I noticed an unfurnished place at an astonishingly reasonable rent.

Now, maybe I'm wrong, but I took this as a sign from You. You were throwing me a lifeline. If that's true, I thank You most sincerely. Oh, I thank You from the bottom of my heart.

I went straight to the factor. I got a viewing time. Oh, it's such a lovely place. I had to supply references and I managed to get a couple of really good ones.

You'll probably know this already. I'm sure You must have organised the whole thing. But anyway, I got the flat.

I've got a place to go to. Imagine!

I haven't told a soul except You.

I'm so excited, so happy, so sad, so afraid. But thank You. Thank You. Oh, thank You, God.

XXXVI

IT WAS JUST as he thought. She was waiting for him, posing for him exactly as she'd done long ago. The outside door was ajar. That was the first confirmation. He knew she would be waiting in the bedroom. He entered the hall and shut the door behind him. Sure enough, there she sat on the edge of the bed, dressed in a low-cut black top that displayed generous cleavage. Her skirt was slashed up to her thigh. Her black-stockinged legs were crossed and he could see the lace tops of her stockings and above them, the soft white flesh.

She was even wearing, as she so often used to, a wide-brimmed hat and she was gazing at him, smouldering-eyed, from underneath its brim.

He went over to her and slid his hand up her leg and into her groin, at the same time pushing her back on to the bed. He caught her look of surprise. In the past they had played so many leisurely games. He had enjoyed her with his eyes as she had paraded about the room for him. She had performed a slow striptease like a professional. He had kissed her from the soles of her feet to the top of her head. He had covered her in rose petals. He had licked champagne from her most intimate parts. He had been both gentle and passionate.

This time it was fast. Afterwards she sounded dazed, confused.

'I suppose . . . it's been so long, Bernard darling. I don't blame you for being impatient. But remember how wonderful it used to be? We took our time. We were real gourmets . . .'

'Yes,' he said. 'But I loved you then.'

There was silence for a long minute as the words sank in. Then she said in a small, tight voice,

'Get out.'

'Sure.' He got up from the bed and zipped up his fly. 'I'm off to London tomorrow. I don't suppose you're interested or you would have asked me, but as well as other business, I'm following up a few leads I hope might help me track down Jennifer. I'm as certain as I can be she's in London.'

'You always were a bastard. Time has obviously done nothing to improve you.'

'That's my Andrina. You never could see past your fanny.'

'Get out. And don't ever come back here again.'

'I'm on my way.' He turned at the door, winked at her and said, 'Thanks.'

The bedside clock she flung at him bounced noisily off the door. He left the flat smiling to himself. Yet he couldn't deny the deep sadness in him. He had loved her, and for so many years. No way though was he going to allow her to use him again and not only that, but to ruin his relationships with other women.

She was a witch, and a bitch, and he had been a fool to have loved her so much and for so long.

It was for Robert's sake and for Jennifer's, not Andrina's, that he would continue to look for the girl. God knows what would have happened to her by now, if she was still alive. Prostitution, probably. Some pimp would have his claws in her. One problem Robert hadn't thought of – Jennifer was of a legal age to do what she wanted. Even if Bernard did find her, he couldn't force her to return with him to Glasgow. It would have to be done by persuasion.

Eve Page and the Page Boys were booked into the Hilton but weren't due to arrive for a couple of days. Meantime he and Sean checked the hotel's security and then both went out to do their first day's foot-slogging detective work.

Bernard opted for the railway stations, the underground stations and outside theatres and cinemas and main tourist areas like Trafalgar Square.

Sean was to explore the streets along by the river. They both had a picture of Jennifer and they planned to show it to every prostitute, dosser, wino and homeless person they came across.

By late afternoon, Bernard was beginning to feel it was a hopeless task. He hadn't even stopped for anything to eat since breakfast and, despite his physical fitness, he was feeling tired. It was a hot summer's day and he was wearing a suit. It was part of his policy that he and his men always looked smart and well turned out at all times.

He longed for a beer and wished now he had stopped for one at Euston. He'd already been to all the other stations and the surrounding streets without success. Now he cut through Russell Square on his way to Oxford Street and Shaftesbury Avenue via the British Museum. Begging was one way home-less people survived and he reckoned where there were lots of tourists, there would be beggars. He decided to give his feet a few minutes to cool off on one of the seats in the tree-lined grassy area of the square. It was then that his heart took an unexpected leap of joy. There, on one of the benches, sat two females. One was a disreputable-looking blonde. The other, hardly recognisable in her neglected state, was Jennifer. He had an excellent, well-trained memory for detail and there was no mistaking that waif-like figure and that way she had of gazing apprehensively upwards. At the moment, she was blinking up through the too-long straggly ends of her fringe. She wasn't looking in his direction. Neither of them had noticed him. They were both gazing as if in a dream at the huge Russell Hotel towering up over the trees.

He approached them carefully and soundlessly. Then once in front of them, blocking their view, he said gently,

'Hello, Jennifer.'

Silence. Then the blonde turned to Jennifer and asked incredulously, 'Is that your daddy?'

Jennifer shook her head.

'The fucker then?'

Another shake of the head.

'It's Bernard. He's a bodyguard.'

'Wow!' the blonde gasped. 'He can guard my body any time.'

Bernard sat down on the bench beside Jennifer.

'Your daddy's sick with worry about you.'

'He's got Laura. I find it hard to believe he's all that bothered about me. Especially after all this time.'

'He's never stopped looking for you and worrying about

you. I volunteered to help. One of my men and I have been searching everywhere for you.'

'I notice you've never mentioned my mother.'

'I'm sure she's been worried too. But I can tell you this, Jennifer, your father's a broken man. He's aged before my eyes with worry about you.'

'I'm sorry,' Jennifer said in a small voice. 'I didn't mean to hurt him.'

'All he wants is for you to come home.'

'I can't.'

'How do you mean, you can't?'

Bev interrupted then.

'We haven't any dosh for the fare for a start.'

'Oh, don't worry about that.' Bernard still addressed Jennifer. 'I'll pay for your ticket back to Glasgow.'

Jennifer said,

'It's not just the money.'

'What then?'

'No way am I ever going back to Monteith Row or anywhere near my mother and that creep of a man she sleeps with.'

'OK. We'll find you somewhere else.'

'Not at Daddy's love nest either.'

'OK. We'll find you someplace else, I said. *I'll* find you someplace else.'

'And another thing,' Jennifer said, 'I don't go anywhere without Bev. I don't know what I would have done without her. She's from Glasgow as well and she wants to go home. Don't you, Bev?'

She turned to the other woman, who nodded enthusiastically. Bernard hesitated, groaning inside. There were limits. However, he managed in the end, for Robert's sake – he owed him, after all – to capitulate.

'Aye, OK. Bev as well. Now, I'm on another job down here, so I can't get back to Glasgow for a few days.' He brought out his wallet. 'I'll give you enough money to get cleaned up first of all. For God's sake, get your hair done. You don't want to give Robert another shock seeing you in this state. I'll also give you the fare home. No, on second thoughts, I'll go and get your tickets. Will you promise to stay here until I get back? I'll pick up a taxi. I won't be long.'

He replaced the wallet without giving them any money. 'When I get back, I'll give you the tickets and the money to get yourselves a make-over. OK?'

Both women nodded, flushed now, obviously excited. It was pathetic. They stank to high heavens.

He winked at them before leaving.

'Stay cool.'

XXXVII

'WHAT DO YOU mean – you've got a flat?' Peter was outraged.

She hadn't dared tell him until everything was signed, sealed and delivered. She'd received a generous cheque from a couple for whom she'd painted a picture of their son. With that cheque she'd paid a couple of months' rent in advance. She'd already secretly moved a suitcase and all her canvases out of the house. She hadn't meant to tell Peter in front of Daisy and Nigel, but there never seemed to be the opportunity to be on their own. Even in their bedroom, by the time she'd cleared up and got through every night, he was snoring.

'Will I make you a cup of tea, Mummy?' Daisy sounded apprehensive and childish.

Nigel said nothing, just stared owl-like at her through his thick spectacles, obviously dumbfounded.

'I've got a flat and I'm leaving here and going to start a new life on my own.'

'Don't be stupid.' Peter dismissed the mere idea.

She struggled to keep calm.

'I mean I'm leaving you, Peter.'

'What do you mean – you're leaving me?'

'Our marriage has been over for years.'

'You're mad,' Peter said. 'You've gone right off your head.'

Certainly she had developed one hell of a headache.

'I've already taken one suitcase over to the flat, and everything from the loft. I've a holdall ready for me to collect from the hall cupboard. And that's it.'

Peter had gone a sickly grey.

'You're not taking one item out of my house. Everything in

this house belongs to me. I've worked hard all my life for everything in this house.'

'I don't want anything from this house, Peter. Apart from my paints and canvases which I'm quite sure you don't want anything to do with, all I'm taking is my clothes and some personal gifts. Things that my mother and father gave me, for instance.'

Her mother had once given her a lovely patchwork quilt that she'd sewn herself. Her and Father had decided to buy one of these electric overblankets and they didn't need the quilt any more. Then there was the mug nine-year-old Daisy had given her on her birthday. On it were painted the words 'To the best mum in the world'. She had always treasured that.

She'd called to see the bank manager, and what a traumatic experience that had been. However, she had managed to convince him that she had earned a fair sum at her painting and her prospects of earning much more were very good indeed. She felt guilty about that. She hadn't felt in the least confident about her earning capacity. So desperate was she, however, to get a loan to buy a bed to sleep on and a chair to sit on and perhaps even a table for the new flat, she put on a performance of a confident, professional woman that deserved an Oscar.

She was given just enough to buy the bare essentials including a kettle, a couple of pots and pans, and enough linoleum with which to cover the floors.

'But Mummy, you can't,' Daisy wailed, tearful now. 'What's going to happen to us? What's going to happen to me?'

'Darling, I'm not moving to another planet. And you're a married woman now, don't forget. I wasn't much older than you when I was expecting and I had Granda and Peter to look after, as well as seeing to myself.'

'But you can't,' Daisy repeated. 'What about my career? I can't look after a baby when I'm at university. I'll have to have an abortion.'

'Of course you won't. Find out if they have a crèche or nursery facilities. I'm sure lots of other students have had to cope with the same problem. Ask around. Get professional advice. Now, I really must go. I've written my address down on this piece of paper. I'm not on the phone yet but I hope to get one put in as soon as possible.'

There was a stunned silence as she walked from the room out to the hall to collect her bag. There would be plenty of taxis cruising around and she planned to hail one as soon as she got downstairs and out of the building.

'Mummy!' Daisy ran after her and caught her at the outside door. Daisy, such a sweet baby with a downy head, suckling at her breast. Daisy, toddling, then bumping down and holding out plump outstretched hands to be picked up.

'Don't leave me, Mummy. I'm sorry if I've upset you in any way. I didn't mean to.'

Nigel and Peter appeared behind her.

Peter said, 'How can you be so selfish?'

That did it! She shouted at them.

'Selfish? *Me?* I've kept this house spotless. I've made your meals. I've been a bloody cleaner, laundry maid, nurse, every damned thing. *And* I've managed to paint as well. What the hell have any of you done?'

Peter was the first to recover from the initial shock.

'You've gone off your head. I always knew . . .'

'You know nothing, especially about me. You've been too wrapped up in your mean-minded, whining self.'

'You shouldn't talk to Daddy like that,' Daisy sobbed.

Bessie turned on her.

'I'll talk any fuckin' way I like!'

'Oh!' they all cried out in shocked unison.

'And as for you,' Bessie went on, 'you've done nothing with your life. You expect life to do everything for you. And me to be your skivvy into the bargain. You're completely irresponsible. You thought nothing about having this baby except I'd take it off your hands. Well, tough luck. This time you'll have to take responsibility for your own actions. I've had it up to here with the lot of you.'

She got out, struggling breathlessly with the heavy bag, down the stairs, and out on to the street. A taxi came by, and she clambered into it.

Her heart and head were still thumping with anger as the

taxi weaved its way through the traffic from the south side of the city to the West End.

It was the side of town where the university and the BBC were situated and it was peopled with lots of young students and television people. The flat was in a red sandstone building in Botanic Crescent.

A low road ran off Queen Margaret Drive, where the BBC was situated, and alongside the leavy, tree-lined Botanic Gardens. Arching up to the right of this road, and separated by a grassy belt and more trees, was the Crescent. First of all there were large three-storeyed terrace houses, one of which housed the BBC Club. Then there were four-storeyed red sandstone buildings with big bay windows and gardens in front. Her flat was one up. She paid off the taxi and lugged her bag through the tiled close and up the stairs.

Key in the door, door opened, step inside, shut door behind her.

She'd done it!

She dumped the case down and began wandering through the flat. It was far too big for anyone on their own. A hall big enough to have a party in. A huge kitchen. A bathroom big enough to live in. A large bay-windowed sitting room of ballroom proportions, looking on to the trees of the Crescent and the Botanic Gardens beyond. Two bedrooms. A large dining room. The dining room, facing the front and bright with sunlight, could be her studio.

Everything was so big, so empty, so quiet. She felt faint.

'Courage, Bessie,' she told herself firmly.

Her voice echoed through the cavern of silence.

XXXVIII

WHAT BLISS! AT Bernard's expense they'd had a shower at the station and a shampoo and blow-dry at the hairdresser's. Then Bernard booked them into a small but comfortable hotel. They'd washed their clothes and luxuriously soaked themselves in a hot bath. He had told them he'd contact them again in a couple of days. Meantime they were just to relax and enjoy a rest and some good grub.

'He's a gentleman and a scholar,' Bev said. 'Sexy with it as well, eh?'

'I suppose he is,' Jennifer giggled.

'No suppose about it, hen.'

'He's old enough to be our father.'

'Not mine, hen. Anyway I wouldn't care if he was old enough to be my grandfather. I'd still say he was gorgeous.'

'I've always like him. Not in that way,' Jennifer added hastily. 'I used to call him "Uncle".'

'Oh aye. Was he another of your mammy's boyfriends?'

'Oh no, I don't think so. Bernard was a friend of my father. He must still be, judging by the way he was talking about him.'

'I suppose you're right. Anyway, what a bit of luck! I was beginning to think we'd never make it.'

Jennifer could have said – what with you drinking the money each time we managed to gather some together. But she held her tongue. She couldn't blame Bev for drowning her sorrows. Now though, they had a real chance to make a fresh start. It was wonderful.

'Do you know,' Jennifer admitted, 'I'd begun to feel I wasn't part of the human race. Just some garbage for people either to ignore or push out of their way.'

'How do you think I've felt? I've been on the streets for

longer than you. And I was alone at first. God, that was no joke. Terrified out of my wits, I was.'

'I don't know how you survived.'

'Och we're all tougher than we think, hen.'

They enjoyed a delicious dinner, then stretched luxuriously out on the two single beds in the room and watched television.

'This is the life,' Bev said. 'Our sexy pal can take as long as he likes. I'd be perfectly happy to stay here for a week or two, never mind a day or two.'

Jennifer snuggled further into the duvet.

'Me too. Still, I suppose it'll be good to see Glasgow again.'

'It's not going anywhere.'

'I'll feel safer there. It's not so big and I know my way around. And Fisher had better not try to come near me again. I'll tell him where to go.'

Bev laughed.

'That's my girl. You tell him to fuck off.'

'No way am I going back to live with my mother ever again.' Jennifer's voice grew loud with emotion.

'OK. OK. Nobody's saying you have to go back to her.'

'I don't want to live with my father and Laura either.'

'Don't worry. You won't.'

'As long as we stick together. Even if it means sleeping rough in Glasgow, I don't care.'

'Well, I do, hen. I'm getting too old for skippering. It's not too bad in summer. But with another winter coming up . . .'

'Right enough. It doesn't bear thinking about. But surely in Glasgow, somebody will help us.'

'When are you going to phone your da? You promised Bernard.'

'Tomorrow, when I feel better.'

'You should have let him phone like he wanted to.'

'I just want to get myself together first.'

'Aye, aye, OK. Now will you shut up. I'm trying to watch the telly.'

Jennifer was quiet after that, drifting in and out of warm and comfortable sleep. On the edge of her consciousness, however, tiny worries and apprehensions still niggled. Bernard wasn't going to keep them in this hotel or any other hotel for ever. Once they got back to Glasgow, he'd deliver her to her father and that would be that as far as he was concerned. He had enough to do even now without bothering about her. A crisis had arisen with one of the Page Boys. Or rather, with his child. Some mad woman had kidnapped Dave's baby. Bernard had left immediately he'd had the call on his mobile phone. But he'd reminded her once again by calling over his shoulder:

'Phone Robert right now, Jennifer. Tell him you're OK. Tell him you'll be home in a couple of days.'

'Yes, all right,' she'd replied.

But she hadn't been able to bring herself to phone. In trying to analyse why she was putting off contacting her father, she came to the conclusion that the tough shell she'd grown around her in order to survive these past months would suddenly shatter at the sound of his voice. She'd be a little girl again and the horror of all she'd gone through since she'd last seen him would completely overcome her.

But perhaps tomorrow, after a decent sleep – she felt as if she'd never had a decent sleep for years – she would feel better, stronger, able to cope. It was one thing being able to cope physically, of course. She'd discovered, like Bev, that she was tougher than she looked or what she'd always thought she was. If someone had told her that she'd survive icy winter nights in draughty shop doorways, or desolate days trudging, chittering ankle deep in snow, or being soaked to the skin with no hope of getting dry, she wouldn't have believed them.

Emotionally it was a different matter. She'd toughened up a bit. At least on the surface. She didn't believe she'd go into such a panic if faced with Paul Fisher again. To some degree, however, she was still at the mercy of her emotions. Strangely enough, even more so now that there was a chance of getting back to a more comfortable and civilised way of life. She wanted to take that chance, longed for it. No way did she want to go back on the streets again, in London or in Glasgow or anywhere else.

Neither she nor Bev wanted even to put a foot out of the hotel. It was as if it might disappear if they left it and their food and shelter there evaporate into a dream like all their other dreams. They wandered about inside, admiring every corner of the place. They sank into the comfortable chairs in the lounge. They felt like queens being served in the dining room with its pristine white table cover and sparkling cutlery.

They appreciated, savoured, every moment and every moment was sheer joy. The second night when they settled down in bed to watch television, Jennifer said, 'Just think of all the poor folk out there just now trying to find a decent skipper.'

'Aw shut up. Don't spoil things.'

'I wasn't trying to spoil things. I was just being thankful that we're not one of them any more.'

'Aye, well, don't count your chickens, as they say. Don't tempt fate.'

'How do you mean?'

'You know what I mean, hen.'

Jennifer fell silent. Eventually she said,

'Daddy'll see us all right.'

'Oh aye? Your daddy's a man of money and influence, is he? He can buy us a flat? Or get the council to give us one? I thought you told me he was just a poorly paid teacher in some rough school.'

'Well, yes, but . . .'

'Stop kidding yourself.'

'Do you know anybody?'

'Oh aye, Gus McCabe. A very influential man. Owns a big flat in Byres Road. Plenty room for us there. Two punchbags. He would just love that.'

'I meant on the council.' Jennifer sighed. 'I wish my grandfather was alive – as well as my granny. Grandfather was a senior magistrate at one time. He would have been Lord Provost if his health hadn't failed.'

'Too bad.'

Suddenly they were both diverted by a news item on the television. It was about the Page Boy kidnapping, as it was called. The police had arrested a woman and the baby was safely back with its parents.

'That means our sexy pal's off the hook. What do you bet

he'll be here at the crack of dawn to pick us up and shove us on the first train going up north.'

'Isn't he coming with us?' Jennifer queried anxiously. 'I thought he was.'

Bev shrugged.

'Don't know, hen. We'll just have to wait and see.'

As it turned out, Bernard couldn't come with them. He saw them on to the train and waved them off with the promise he'd see them as soon as he could in Glasgow. He thought Jennifer had contacted Robert and took it for granted they'd be met by him in Glasgow.

Once the train sped off, Bev said, 'You're crazy, lying to him like that. What's the idea?'

'I didn't actually lie to him.'

'You let him think that you'd phoned your da and everything was OK. Why, for God's sake?'

Jennifer's face screwed up with anxiety.

'I just want to take one step at a time. I just want to get back to Glasgow first.'

'OK. OK. It's your funeral.'

XXXIX

WHEN BESSIE SHUT the sitting-room door, the outside door reverberated as if someone was trying to get in. Often there was a creaking of floorboards, probably from the flat above but it sounded as if someone was walking into Bessie's hall. The bedroom at the back was near the well of the stairs and voices or footsteps of anyone going up or down the stairs made sudden, hollow sounds that startled her. The bathroom door squeaked. So did the kitchen door. A rushing, hissing sound seemed to go on for ever before dying away into the walls. She couldn't fathom or trace it. Eventually she realised it was one of the neighbours who'd flushed the toilet. She peered timidly out from behind her curtains and tried to assess whether or not she was in friendly territory.

She longed for a friend, someone to speak to. She went to Meeting on Sunday morning, but kept her head down except when it came to the time to smile and shake hands with everyone. She escaped before the tea and biscuits and chat, however. What could she say to these good people?

'Oh by the way, I've changed my address. I've walked out on my husband and pregnant daughter.'

She couldn't be bothered cooking. It seemed such a waste of time just for herself. She opened a tin of soup for lunch and ate a packet of crisps. She had several cups of tea during the afternoon and then for what she had begun to call dinner at home, she had a slice of bread and jam, and a cup of coffee.

Back in the Shawlands Cross flat, they'd changed from the old Scottish custom of 'high tea' and now had 'dinner' each evening. This had been Daisy's idea. Daisy was all for 'moving with the times'. And having 'proper civilised eating habits'.

Bessie wondered how civilised the family eating habits were

since she'd left. She somehow couldn't imagine Daisy, or Peter or Nigel making the three-course family meals plus coffee that she had been cooking every night. And of course they wouldn't go out for a meal. Peter was so mean he'd always refused to even buy her a cup of tea outside.

'We've plenty of tea at home,' he'd say. It wouldn't matter if she was collapsing with fatigue or her tongue was hanging out with thirst. No tea or food in a restaurant and that was that.

Her anxiety about Daisy not getting enough nourishment grew to panic proportions. She'd never forgive herself if Daisy became malnourished and the baby suffered. She didn't really believe that Daisy would get an abortion. Several times she'd gone out and hung about outside a phone box. At last she'd dialled the flat. There was no reply. She worried about that as well. It was dinner time. They were always in at dinner time. She couldn't bear the worry and suspense a moment longer. She jumped on a bus to take her over to Shawlands Cross. Once she tracked Daisy down, she would stress to her the importance of eating well. After all, the poor girl was still very young and it was her first pregnancy. She could be upset about her mother deserting her in her time of need, could be pining and unhappy and generally neglecting herself. By the time Bessie had reached Shawlands Cross, she was in a state of near collapse with worry and agitation. She hurried from the bus but before she had a chance to run across the road to the flat, she had to stop at the lights because they'd changed to red. As she stood along with a crowd of other people waiting for the return of the 'green man' Bessie's eye was caught by a group of people tucking into fish suppers at the window table in Jaconalli's chippy. Obviously, Daisy, Nigel and Peter were not being starved of nourishment after all. It didn't look as if Daisy was pregnant either. She was wearing her skin-tight dress, the one she said she could not get into only a few weeks ago.

Bessie caught a bus back to the West End.

Botanic Crescent was still and quiet except for a faint babble of voices as she passed the BBC Club. The cool tiled close and stone stairs leading to her flat were empty and alien. The hollow sound of the door opening and shutting echoed in her heart as well as every room. She hurried into the kitchen to switch on her transistor. She was truly glad of the radio. It was company. She wasn't used to being on her own in such silence. She had never been on her own in her life. There had been her mother and father and Moira in her first home. Even old Towzer had been company. Then after her marriage, there had been constant company from the word go. To think she'd always longed to be on her own for a bit of peace and quiet. Freedom! she'd always thought. Oh, for freedom.

Now, look at her. With an effort she pulled herself together. Anger helped. Bloody hell! *Fancy them wolfing away at fish and chips!*

Her fingers itched to paint. She felt feverish with the need to work. Tomorrow she would start another painting of Andrina Anderson. This time she would do the painting for herself. The first one had been a present for Andrina. The poor woman's daughter had disappeared and she was being very brave about it. She had also been kind and sympathetic when Bessie's mother had died. It was because of that that Bessie had not only given her the painting as a present but had made the portrait less than completely honest. In a way it was the same as she'd done for the couple whose son she'd painted. She had been trying to be kind and please the recipient. That was why of course neither painting had pleased herself. The one of Andrina had especially niggled at her and left her feeling frustrated and unfulfilled.

She had made a good copy of Andrina's beauty. But a photograph could have done that. There were other things about the woman that intrigued her as an artist. She liked Andrina. She was charming and talented. Her mother had obviously passed on her cookery and baking skills to her daughter: Bessie had enjoyed more than one delicious tea at Andrina's flat and it cheered her up to think of visiting there again. She resolved to phone Andrina the very next day and arrange a visit. She was sure Andrina would agree to more sittings. She had enjoyed posing. Not only that, but she happily chatted all the time while Bessie painted. She didn't expect any verbal response, didn't even seem to notice the one-sidedness of the conversation. Bessie was sure she did notice the untidiness and, by Andrina's standards, lack of material comforts when she visited Bessie's flat. However, Andrina was too polite to say anything about that. Instead, she pressed invitations on Bessie to come to the Monteith Row flat.

Bessie found her a complex kind of person and she had become quite obsessed about how she could convey this on canvas. She wanted to be with Andrina again, to study her again. The more she thought along work lines, the less lonely and afraid she felt. She began to recognise and become familiar with the sounds of the place. Indeed, instead of being fearful in the house, she began to feel safe.

Much of the echoing noise, especially of her own footsteps, was caused by the bare linoleum or bare floorboards. But she had another worry. Her money was fast running out. She would enjoy having tea at Andrina's for more reasons than the quality of the home baking. Bessie was fast becoming just plain hungry.

The date with Andrina was for a few days hence. Meantime, the problem of the lack of money loomed large. Bessie was forced to seek out the nearest office of the Department of Health and Social Security. She had never set foot in such a place before and found it a painfully humiliating experience. The only thing that saved it from being a total disaster was her artist's eye. She had a small sketchpad in her handbag – something she never moved without – and she passed the time by surreptitiously sketching the different characters around her.

There were lantern-jawed men with hunched shoulders and loose, shabby clothes. There were harassed women, old before their time, nursing babies and shouting at older children who were racing about and causing a disturbance.

'Do you want me to get flung out, you wee bastards?' was one woman's desperate cry. Another woman, miserably hunched and weeping, was explaining to another woman how she'd acquired her terrible black eye. Her companion's face was creased with sympathy and she kept shaking her head and tutting.

The air was heavy with hopelessness, anxiety and despair, the décor a seedy and depressing dark brown. Everyone had been dehumanised by being given a number. When your number was called, you went over to the counter where you were forced to answer the most intimate questions and discuss your most private business in full hearing of the person on either side of you at the counter. Not to mention the waiting folk sitting behind you.

Bessie tried to hang on to some pride and dignity. She was honest about her circumstances. She also told them that she was an artist, and was just having a temporary lull in her earnings. Perhaps this was slightly more hopeful than honest. However, the word 'artist' seemed to have a bit of magic attached to it. At least for the lady behind the counter who was dealing with Bessie's case. After filling in a few forms, Bessie was told that she would receive a cheque, and a book for future payments that she could collect every week at the local post office. She was even treated with a modicum of respect and quite a nice smile.

The cheque, or indeed the payments, didn't amount to much as far as electricity, gas and any other bills were concerned but at least she had been given time to get herself organised, to try to establish an income. The DHSS had thrown her a lifeline, God bless them.

Jubilant, she hurried straight from the DHSS office to the nearest fish and chip shop and bought a fish supper. Then she returned to the flat and sat cross-legged on the floor of her studio, eating the fish and chips out of their newspaper wrapping.

The room was large and square. Two long windows framed the empty fireplace, flooding the room with cool, clear light. The floorboards were already taking on the traditional studio look with flecks of paint splashed here and there. A particularly large yellow smear showed where Bessie had inadvertently stood on a tube of cadmium yellow. On the far wall stacks of canvases awaited her attention. Her easel took pride of place in the centre of the room like some primitive altar. A stool beside it held her palette and jars of oil and turps. Discarded brushes were scattered among the paint-soaked rags around the base of the easel.

The huge canvas on the easel dominated the room. Stark images of industrial might, wheels and cogs, crushing humanity, alleviated only by the central images of rebellious figures locked in mortal combat with the nightmare of rampant industrialisation.

She felt great satisfaction gazing at those rebellious figures. And the fish and chips were absolutely delicious.

XL

Oh GLASGOW! THE train clanking over the bridge. The River Clyde sparkling underneath. Central Station. Not too big like Euston. Familiar. Manageable. Scottish accents all around. Bouncy bustle and friendly smiles.

Oh Glasgow!

Jennifer and Bev stood dazed and smiling at nothing in particular and everything in general. They couldn't believe they'd actually made it.

Finally Bev said, 'Now what, hen?'

The smile faded from Jennifer's face.

'I suppose I'd better phone Daddy.'

'About time too. If you'd phoned in London when you were supposed to, he would have been here meeting you.'

'I know. I know. I just wanted to be safely here first. I suppose I didn't want to risk anything going wrong.'

'Aye, OK daftie. You're here now.'

They found a phone box and crowded close together into it, fussing about getting the right money between them. Jennifer dialled the Bearsden number. As soon as she heard Robert's voice she began to weep as she'd known she would. Impossible to contain her grief.

'Daddy.'

'Oh Jennifer, darling. Where are you?'

'The Central Station. Uncle Bernard bought our tickets.'

'Don't move from there,' Robert said. 'I'll be with you as fast as my car can take me.'

'Thanks, Daddy.'

She hung up and let the sobs racket out.

'Will you shut up?' Bev shouted. 'What the hell are you

bawling about? The time for that was when we were nearly freezing to death in some rotten skipper, not now.'

'I know.'

They squeezed out of the phone box and Jennifer wiped her eyes as best she could on the back of her sleeve.

'Now look at you,' Bev groaned. 'You were like a tramp before in those old rags. Now your face is a mess as well.'

'At least we're a lot cleaner now,' Jennifer managed.

After a minute or two's silence Bev said, 'Look, hen, this is your chance. Don't mess it up with trying to tag me along. I'll be OK.'

'You shut up. Do you really think I'm going to walk away from you now?'

'You don't owe me anything.'

'What?' Jennifer shouted incredulously. 'I owe you everything. I'd be dead or worse if it hadn't been for you. I'll never desert you, Bev. Never.'

'Don't talk rot. A thousand things could change between now and never.'

'I won't change.'

'Aye, OK, OK.'

They stood in silence after that, Bev clutching her two plastic bags and Jennifer clinging on to her backpack.

'There he is,' said Jennifer at last. And she began to weep again.

'What's up with you, you silly wee cow?' Bev muttered irritably. 'Smile for the man. Look pleased to see him, for Christ's sake.'

The sight of the thin, gaunt-faced anxious-eyed man with hair more grey than brown running towards her about broke Jennifer's heart. She loved him and regretted, more than words could ever express, having caused him pain. She fell into his arms and she could feel his tears mingling with her own. Eventually he let her go and dried both their faces with his handkerchief. He was leading her away when she suddenly remembered Bev. The tragic look in the older woman's eyes when she turned back made Jennifer feel ashamed.

'Wait a minute, Daddy. I want you to meet my best friend,

Bev. I wouldn't have survived this past year if it hadn't been for her.'

Robert put out his hand.

'Bev, I'm very pleased to meet you and I thank you for anything you've done to help my daughter.'

'Think nothing of it, pal.' Bev had quickly recovered her usual cheeky manner.

'Can I give you a lift anywhere?' Robert asked politely.

Jennifer said, 'Daddy, she's nowhere to go. Nor have I, for that matter. I'm sorry but I don't want to stay either with you or with Mummy. All I know at the moment is that Bev and I must stick together.'

Robert studied them both for a moment. Jennifer remembered that serious, thoughtful look so well. Then he said, 'We've obviously a lot to talk about and things to sort out. Meantime Bev is very welcome to come with you to Bearsden. You look as if you both need a good meal. Let's start with that.'

'Thanks, Daddy.'

They didn't speak much in the car. Except Robert said, 'It's maybe not the right time to tell you this, darling, but because we're going to Bearsden and we'll be passing her house and you might want to . . .'

'It's all right,' Jennifer said quietly. 'I know. I phoned the hospital.'

'Right.'

Another silence. Then:

'What part of Glasgow do you come from, Bev?'

'Anderson originally. But I've been around a bit.'

'Any family?'

'Not a bleeding one.'

Jennifer nudged her. She didn't want her friend to make a bad impression. The sight of Bearsden, however, overawed them into silence. Even Jennifer had become so used to the rough and seedy side of existence that she had forgotten what suburban good life could look like.

Along the wide, undulating street known as the Switchback with its leafy trees and pretty bungalows. Then on to Canniesburn Toll and Drymen Road. More mature trees. Big villas now set back in large, well-clipped lawns. Past 'the village', the row of shops, and the terrace where Sophie had lived. Then along a bit and across the road, Laura's bungalow. Jennifer saw Laura watching for them from the sitting-room window.

The car stopped. Laura disappeared then reappeared at the front door.

'Do come in. Are you all right, Jennifer?'

'Yes, thank you.'

'And who is this?'

'Bev, my best friend.'

'Hello, Bev.'

Bev nodded but kept unusually quiet.

'I've some nice homemade soup heating up and I've a steak pie in the oven. I'm just seeing to some chips. You go into this bedroom and dump your belongings, girls, and tidy up if you like. There's a bathroom *en suite*. Then come through to the kitchen and we'll eat. Robert, you open a can of peas while I see to the chips.'

Left alone in the bedroom, Bev whispered, 'Very posh. Bathroom *en suite*! Do you think it'll be OK if I have a pee?'

'Of course. Don't be silly, Bev!'

Jennifer was tidying her hair at the dressing-table mirror when Bev reappeared, tugging up her jeans.

'Have you seen it in there? A coloured suite and all sorts of bottles of God knows all what perfumery stuff. And, would you believe it, there's a doll with a knitted dress and underneath the dress is a spare toilet roll. The place is carpeted as well. This is the life, eh?'

'I'm not staying here.'

'You're daft.'

'You don't understand. I've nothing against Daddy or Laura but they're so happy together, I've always felt I don't belong. An intruder. I found you can feel more lonely being a goose-berry than you can on your own.'

'Oh, aren't you the sensitive one! Well hen, I'm not that fussy. As far as I'm concerned, this is a lot better than what we've been used to. And they're welcome to their lovey-dovey bit.'

'It's not just for my own sake. I don't want to spoil things for them. And this is their bedroom, by the way. The spare room hasn't got an *en suite*.'

'Oh, is that not terrible. I'm going to complain about that, so I am.'

They went through to the kitchen, giggling secretly together but once in the room, they were once more quiet and uncertain.

Robert said, 'Come on now, don't be shy. Sit down at the table. Make yourselves at home.'

They sat, heads lowered, only tentatively glancing up now and again when they were spoken to.

'Is Bernard still down there?' Robert asked.

Jennifer nodded in between taking mouthfuls of soup. 'I think he's coming back to Glasgow tomorrow.'

'I'll never be able to thank him enough for finding you.'

'He's been very kind to us,' Jennifer said. 'Saw us on to the train and everything.'

'After you have your meal, you must phone your mother. She'll be so glad to hear from you.'

'I'm not staying with her either. Has she got married to that Fisher man?'

'As far as I know, the divorce isn't through yet. Anyway, she's still at Monteith Row.'

'Nothing's changed then.'

'Surely you can at least phone her, Jennifer, and let her know you're all right.'

Jennifer shrugged.

'If you say so.'

He was trying to palm her off on to her mother. Just as he'd always done from the day he'd married Laura. But her mother wouldn't want her either. Especially not with Bev.

No, nothing had changed. Suddenly she felt as if the soup was choking her.

XLI

BESSIE HAD SOME difficulty in trying to explain to Andrina that this painting was going to be different from the original one that Andrina had prominently and proudly displayed on her sitting-room wall.

'It's not really meant to be you,' she lied. 'It's more like how a writer uses a model from real life as a trigger for a fictional character he wants to create.'

She hadn't wanted Andrina to see it and did succeed in preventing her from having even a glimpse while she was working on the picture. It would have seriously inhibited her if Andrina had made any comments, good or bad.

Once it was done, it was done. She didn't care what Andrina said then. At the same time, she had no desire to hurt or upset the woman. To paint this picture was something she felt she just had to do. And she'd done it. That was all. She did feel the better for having done it, though. Indeed she gazed on the finished product with a kind of reverence. In a way, she felt like this about all her paintings. She never really believed she could do it and when she did manage it, she always thanked God most sincerely for the miracle.

Andrina had stolen a peek at it before she could remove the canvas.

She'd stared at the barely recognisable picture with its red and green tones instead of flesh colours. Bessie quailed inside, expecting an outburst of fury and insulted as well as hurt feelings. But not a bit of it.

'Gosh!' Andrina laughed. 'I see what you mean now about just needing a trigger like writers do in creating fictional characters. That's not me at all.'

Side by side with Andrina, Bessie gazed at the picture. It

showed passion. Yet there were other layers, like shadows, overlapping each other, cooling into a blank distance. What the critics were later to call 'chiaroscuro'.

'You're not angry?'

'Of course not.' Andrina shrugged. 'As I said, it's nothing like me. You've made something up. To be honest though, Bessie, I can't say I like it. It's not very *nice*, is it?'

'I don't think of my paintings as being nice or not nice.'

'Anyway, I'm glad you're not expecting me to hang that on my wall.'

Bessie wrapped the canvas and packed it away. Her visit to Andrina's house finished with a delicious lunch and Andrina chatting away quite the thing. The painting was never mentioned again. Andrina seemed to have quite a talent for not thinking about anything she didn't want to, or that she sensed to be unpleasant. She hadn't mentioned her daughter for ages. Although to give credit where credit was due, when Bessie asked if there was any news of Jennifer, Andrina said, 'I pray every night that she is safe and well and that one day she'll return.'

It made Bessie feel guilty and ashamed.

More often than not, she completely forgot to say her prayers. Actually she never knew what to say. Or, as often as not, she said so much she fell asleep in the middle of her long list:

Please, have mercy on everyone who is in pain either at home or in hospitals. Be with them. Comfort them.

Please have mercy on anyone who has suffered a bereavement. Comfort them and give them strength.

Please be company to the lonely.

Please stop men fighting and warring with one another. Help them to have patience and to understand each other's point of view. Help them to feel for each other.

Please help and protect little children. Keep them safe from harm.

Even when she hadn't fallen fast asleep before she came to her more personal requests, she seldom had the temerity to request anything. She preferred to keep reminding herself of how lucky she was. Now she really was experiencing freedom. Sometimes she danced around the house hugging herself in thankfulness and joy at the extent of her good fortune. This was her space. She could be alone if she wished. She could sketch and paint for as often and for as long as she liked. She could go out and come in whenever she liked. There was no one to question or criticise her. She could even invite whoever she liked to the house. Andrina had been several times but only after a formal invitation. Andrina liked everything to be correct and well organised. There could be no squatting on the floor by the fire with a mug of tea and a sandwich when she came to call.

'I always like to behave properly, Bessie.'

Most of her neighbours, Bessie had discovered, were out at work during the day and were usually too busy catching up with tasks in the house, or too tired, to socialise. They were very pleasant people, though. At least the ones she'd met so far. And what a bit of a luck! She'd got chatting to an awfully nice woman in the Botanic Gardens. Bridie O'Maley. She was there with her family. Innumerable children were running wild all over the place while Bridie sat plump and bespectacled, calm as you like, enjoying an ice-cream cone.

'O'Maley?' Bessie echoed. 'You're not by any chance related to Bernard O'Maley?'

'My brother-in-law. I'm married to Frank, the youngest of the family.'

'The one that writes the television plays?'

'That's him.'

'Gosh, they're great. I always used to enjoy them. I haven't a television set at the moment but I hope to get one again soon.'

'You know Bernard then?'

'He called up at my old house over in the south side a few times asking about Jennifer. Did you know Jennifer?'

Bridie shook her head.

'I don't think so.'

'She's the daughter of a friend of mine. She ran away from home. She's been missing for ages and Bernard was trying to help find her.'

'You hear about an awful lot of folk going missing these days. Especially young folk. It's a worry.'

Bridie had invited her back for a cup of tea. Sh

two closes along the Crescent. Bessie had a lovely time and invited Bridie to come to her place.

Then, as if she hadn't been lucky enough to have found a new friend, Bessie sold the Andrina picture for an enormous sum. She'd taken it to Gregory's gallery in the hope he might raise some much-needed cash for it. She hadn't seen him for ages although he had phoned after she'd returned from London to check that she had got home safely. He'd been impressed with the painting. Or so he said. Anyway, he told her to leave it with him. Next thing she knew, some American millionaire who had a famous art gallery in the States had commissioned six paintings. It had made the newspapers and Bessie had become a bit of a celebrity overnight. It wouldn't last, of course, but it was exciting. Especially when the millionaire had started asking to see all of her work.

Now unexpectedly she had enough money to buy the flat. Once that had been done, she'd paid the gas and electricity bills, and had the phone put in. She carpeted the bedroom and bought some furniture, curtains, and a television. Then she stocked up on paints and canvases and a new easel. In the end she'd spent practically every penny on the strength of the American's cheque. But oh, what fun she had. What joy! She kept walking round and round the flat with hands clasped under her chin hardly daring to believe her good fortune. She had everything, every room exactly as she liked it now. The colours, the textures – a delight to the eye. Back at the Shawlands Cross flat, most things, she realised now, had been to Peter's taste.

Bessie looked into the hallway and thought of the stark contrast to her previous lifestyle. Gone were the swirling brown and orange carpets and beige walls with their minute flower patterns. She sighed with mingled relief and pleasure as she cast her eyes again around the varnished floorboards that gave the hall a clean, open look. The only furniture was an old kitchen table with two drawers that she'd placed at the end wall. She'd painted the table a pale Mediterranean blue. On it, apart from the phone, was a tall, narrow purple ceramic vase that she had turned into a light. Beside it was a large white plaster bust she had rescued from a skip outside the art school and subsequently repaired.

The walls were a very pale bluish lilac and instead of paintings or prints, she had hung a couple of outrageously bright ethnic rugs.

The whole flat was like heaven on earth and in it she had precious freedom, freedom of mind, freedom of spirit. No responsibilities.

She relaxed in the sitting room in a soft pool of light, reading. The large room was warmly dark with only a few of the variety of lamps illuminated. They cast orange glows and huge shadows across the walls and on to the high ceiling. The wall opposite the old Victorian fireplace was covered in a disparate collection of paintings, some of which she'd worked on even before her marriage. Huge landscapes, small sombre etchings, bright splashes of colour, all depending on the mood she'd been in at the time. Above the fireplace she had placed a huge antique wooden-framed mirror so that the paintings seemed to surround her, encompass her with their colour and textures. Her shadow mingled with the rest making her feel part of her room, her home.

No sooner had she begun to appreciate her peace, her freedom, than on to her doorstep arrived unexpected visitors.

One of them she recognised immediately as Jennifer. The child had obviously suffered something terrible. Her face was so drawn, so pinched and unhappy. An older woman, equally pathetic, stood close to Jennifer on the doormat. Behind them was a worried-looking man that Bessie remembered as Jennifer's father.

'Oh Jennifer.' Bessie clutched the girl to her and gave her an affectionate hug. 'Come away in, dear. It's so wonderful to see you're all right.'

As it turned out, Jennifer couldn't stay either with her father or her mother. They'd been given Bessie's new address by Daisy, and they'd come to appeal to Bessie to give Jennifer and her friend shelter.

'I'd pay for their keep until they get fixed up with a job,' Robert said. 'And find a place of their own. It would only be a temporary arrangement.'

Bessie closed her eyes. But she could still see the tragic appeal in the faces of Jennifer and her friend. How could she turn them away?

So there you are.

You're doing it again, God.

XLII

'FORGET IT,' BERNARD said. 'I was working down in London anyway.'

'No, I'll never be able to do that, Bernard. By the looks of her, you got her just in time. She looked half-dead.'

'You should have seen the state she was in when I first found her. At least she'd had a clean-up and been fed and rested before she arrived back here.'

'You must at least allow me to pay you for the hotel and train tickets.'

'Listen, Robert, I employ a hundred or more men now. I get business from all over the world. I'm not short of a bob or two, believe me.'

'But that doesn't mean . . .'

'Forget it, I said.'

'At least let me buy you another drink.'

'OK. OK.'

Robert went over to the bar and in a few minutes came back carrying two pints of beer. He knew that Bernard seldom drank spirits, didn't drink much at all in fact. Bernard liked to keep his wits about him. It was part of his job.

'What do you make of that Bev woman?' Robert asked after he'd settled down at the corner table opposite Bernard. It was early evening and the pub was as dim and hushed as a church. Only another couple of men stood over at the bar drinking and talking confidentially. The seats and benches at the few other tables by the wall where Bernard and Robert sat were unoccupied.

'A right wee hairy.'

Anxiety tightened over Robert's eyes.

'A prostitute, do you think?'

Bernard shrugged.

'Maybe not. Anyway, don't worry. I don't think Jennifer has been on the streets in that sense. In fact, I'm sure she hasn't.' He firmed his voice in an effort to banish Robert's anxiety. 'On the contrary, I believe Bev's been protecting Jennifer. The tart with the heart.' He tried to keep the sarcasm from his voice but didn't succeed. Bev was obviously on to a good thing sticking to Jennifer. Not only had she had a free ride to Glasgow, she now had a good billet. Robert had been telling him about fixing both females up in a flat in the West End.

'How did Bessie take it?' He went back to the subject now. 'Surely she didn't welcome Bev with open arms. Let's face it, Robert, that female doesn't exactly look as if she belongs there. She looks like a wee alkie to me. I'm not complaining – as I told you, the money means nothing to me – but the drink bill at the hotel suggested she'd downed enough to sink an Irish navvy. Jennifer doesn't drink, does she?'

'No. She wouldn't even take a sherry or a glass of wine with the meal when I took her home that first day.'

'So what's happening with Bev?'

'I don't know. There's bound to be problems and it's not fair on Bessie. The first problem is that Jennifer is sticking to Bev like glue. She won't move a step without her. How is she going to get a job or any place else decent to live or make any friends of her own age with somebody like that as a hanger-on?'

'Big problem,' Bernard said.

Robert sighed.

'Enough about my problems. How did that business with Dave work out?'

'Oh, I had a few leads that paid off. I tracked the woman down to a restaurant where she was working as a waitress. I'd picked up some clues from her letters about the place – a nickname it had and something she mentioned about some other famous guys who went there. This was supposed to make Dave jealous. A right nutter she was.' Bernard shook his head. 'Beautiful, though. You'd never guess to look at her. Anyway, I told the police about the letters and where she was and they picked her up. Belongs to a wealthy and influential family in the States, would you believe. She'll probably be deported back to LA. She knew me from that time I was over in Hollywood with Eve and the boys. I had a letter from her the other day threatening to kill me.'

'My God, Bernard.'

Bernard grinned.

'I can live with that. It's not the first death threat I've had. In my job you get used to it.'

'And I've always believed teaching was the most stressful of jobs.'

'Well, put it this way, Robert, I wouldn't change places with you. I couldn't cope with your kind of stress. I'd murder some of the ungrateful wee bastards you have to deal with, day in day out.'

'I haven't regretted a moment of teaching. But I must confess recently I've been feeling more like sixty-six than fifty-six.'

'Now that you know Jennifer's OK, you'll be fine.'

'But is she? That's what's worrying me.'

'Bessie seems a decent motherly kind of woman. She'll look after her and make sure she's OK.'

'She's a bit odd though, don't you think?'

'You mean with all this art business? I wouldn't hold that against her. From what I've heard she's heading for the big time. They're planning an exhibition of all her latest work and because there's been a hype of publicity and that old American guy is paying such a high price for the paintings, she's a bit worried about security. She phoned my office. I probably won't be there but I've promised to send one of my men. Sean can go along.'

'That's your nephew?'

'Yeah. A great kid. He'll take over once I give up and I'll be sure of the business being in capable hands.'

Robert hesitated, then said, 'By the way, you know that Andrina's been friendly with Bessie?'

'I knew Andrina was the model for one of the paintings the American bought. It's a real corker. Makes you think, doesn't it? You'll have seen it, I suppose.'

'Yes. Amazing, isn't it? I see something different in it every time I look at it. You mentioned earlier that nobody would guess by looking at that nutter what she was like inside. The same applies to Bessie, don't you think? That's one of the reasons I said about her being a bit odd.'

'But the thing that's inside Bessie is talent, Robert. There's nothing sinister, nothing to worry about in that.'

'Oh I know. I've just got into the habit of worrying about everything these days.'

'You must be neglecting your karate.'

'Too true.'

'Well, there's your answer. Get back to a good training routine. Do regular work-outs. Get the old deep breathing going. But who am I to tell you? You're the guy who taught me everything I know.'

Robert laughed.

'Not quite, Bernard. But you're right about getting back to my old routine. That's the answer.'

Bernard glanced at his watch.

'I'm going through to Edinburgh tonight. I think I've mentioned Helen and the kids.'

Robert smiled.

'A few times. It sounds serious.'

'Yeah. There's only one thing wrong with her.'

'And what's that?'

'She's from Edinburgh.'

Robert laughed.

'The Far East? Terrible!'

'I've told her – she'll have to forget that and become a Glaswegian.'

'Quite right.'

'She's thinking about it. I'm going to insist on an answer tonight.'

'Good for you. I wish you luck.'

'She's got great kids.'

'You a family man? It takes a bit of imagination, that one, Bernard.'

'I'm going to give it my best shot.'

'Seriously, Bernard, if how you've been to Jennifer is anything to go by, you'll do all right.'

'Thanks.' He rose to his feet. 'I'll let you know how it goes.'

'I'll stay and finish my beer. Here's to you!' Robert raised his glass in Bernard's direction before the big man strolled away and disappeared out on to West Nile Street.

XLIII

IT WAS DRIVING Bessie mad the way Jennifer kept trying to keep the place clean and tidy. Bev didn't seem to care. But, damn it, *she* cared when Jennifer even came into the room she used as a studio and began trying to tidy and clean it up. She knew that Jennifer didn't mean any harm and was truly trying to be helpful. Nevertheless, if Jennifer came into the studio once more, especially while she was working on a painting, and started picking things up, she'd scream.

'I *like* everything covered in paint,' Bessie insisted. '*I* like to be covered in paint.'

'Oh, Bessie.' Jennifer laughed and gave her an affectionate hug. Bessie hadn't so far dared to say so, but as far as being houseproud was concerned, Jennifer was a bit like Andrina. Bessie could see the pained expression on Andrina's face at the sight of Bessie's chaotic living conditions. She also noticed the fastidious way Andrina had removed newspapers, bits of paint rag, pairs of tights and other sundries from any chair before sitting down on it. But Andrina never said anything, never complained or criticised. Jennifer never complained either but she had tutted a bit when Bev spilled face powder on the spare room carpet.

'Damn it all,' Bessie said, 'it's *my* carpet.'

The drink stains were a different matter, however. That indicated a different kind of problem. A problem suffered by Bev.

'Bev, you've been drinking all my booze,' Bessie accused.

'OK, OK,' Bev admitted. 'I had a wee refreshment. Is that such a big crime?'

'It was more than a wee refreshment, as you so euphemistically call it.'

'Oh my,' Bev turned to Jennifer, 'she's blinding us with the big words now.'

Jennifer said, 'She shouldn't have spilled any of the stuff on the carpet, Bessie, but don't worry, I'll clean it up.'

'You've got a drink problem, Bev,' Bessie repeated.

Bev rolled her eyes.

'Here we go again.'

'Well, haven't you?'

Jennifer answer for her friend.

'Maybe she has a wee problem, Bessie. It started, you see, when her boyfriends battered her about and now she can't seem to stop. At least not for any length of time.'

'All right,' Bessie said, 'now that we know what's up, we can try to do something about it. For a start I'll make sure I don't have any drink in the house. It wouldn't be right of me to put temptation in your way.'

'Gee, thanks a bunch.' Bev's mouth twisted with sarcasm, but Bessie said, 'No thanks needed, Bev. We all have our problems and weaknesses. Now, let's think. What else could we do? Counselling? A doctor could maybe advise about that. Or how about Alcoholics Anonymous? They're supposed to be really supportive and understanding.'

'Forget it!' Bev began to look panicky. 'You're not going to put me into any strait-jacket.'

'Strait-jacket? Of course nobody's going to put you into any strait-jacket, Bev.'

Jennifer was also beginning to appear tense.

'I think it was more just a figure of speech, Bessie. She's been battered about and in and out of hospitals so much, and all sorts of people there kept doing all sorts of things to her. She just can't cope any more. She's had enough of people trying to help her.'

Bessie's heart melted towards Bev. She knew how it felt not to be able to cope.

'I'm sorry, Bev, if I've blundered in with two left feet and said all the wrong things. I seem to have a knack for it.'

Bev shrugged.

'I shouldn't have nicked your booze.'

'Oh, you didn't *nick* it. You and Jennifer are my guests here and very welcome to share everything I have. It's more just a case of manners, I suppose, of asking first. I sound like a schoolmarm now,' she groaned. 'Just ignore me, girls. Or, I tell you what, let's make a bargain. I'll put up with your faults, if you'll put up with mine. That way we can all stay good friends. OK?'

'Aye OK. But I feel you've got the worst of the bargain, hen.'

Jennifer said, 'Once Bev starts work she'll be all right. It's been a worry not being able to get a job.'

'Back to the old waitressing,' Bev said. 'I'm quite looking forward to it. We used to get some good laughs.'

'Hard work though – on your feet all the time,' Bessie said, secretly glad that after tomorrow, because Bev had found a job at last, she would be out of the house all day.

No harm to the poor woman. But it's awful difficult for me even to think about work while she's forever hovering about me with a fag in her mouth, peering over my shoulder, laughing and making rude comments about my painting. She's a poor soul, I know that. But she's keeping me back from my work.

Jennifer was having more difficulty in finding a job although she had the better education of the two. Eventually, her father suggested she go to Jordanhill College and take a teacher training course. Jennifer hadn't been very sure at first. She'd asked Bessie.

'Do you think I'd be any good with children?'

'You've been good with Bev.'

'Bev isn't a child.'

'Surely it's the qualities of kindness and understanding that matter. That's what you've shown with Bev. And look how good you've been babysitting for Bridie O'Maley's lot.'

'I suppose you're right.' Jennifer laughed. 'If I can survive the O'Maley crowd, I can survive anything. But little did I ever think I'd follow in my father's footsteps.'

'You couldn't have a better role model as far as I can see. He's a good man.'

'I know. I'm glad he's so happy with Laura.' Anxiety tightened over her face.

'I hope you understand why I didn't want to go and live

with them, Bessie. I know it would have been so much easier for you if I had.'

Too true, Bessie thought, and immediately felt guilty. 'I told you right from the beginning that you were welcome and I meant it,' she said.

'I couldn't go to Monteith Row either. I'd rather have died than gone back to live with my mother.'

Bessie kept silent. Andrina wasn't perfect – who was? But surely she wasn't *that* bad. The way Jennifer talked, anyone would think her mother was a monster.

Jennifer went on in a slightly bitter tone, 'I know you like my mother. She can be so charming.'

'Well, we've just got to take people as we find them, Jennifer, and Andrina's never done me any harm. In fact, if anything, she's been kind to me. You always sound so bitter about her. Don't you believe she was really pleased to see you again and to know you were safe and well? I do.'

Jennifer shrugged.

'I suppose so.'

'And she is your mother.'

'She gave birth to me – yes.'

'And brought you up.'

'That's what you think.' The bitterness had returned. 'In between her fancy men, maybe.'

Bessie sighed.

'I see. Your mother is so beautiful, and so sexy. I suppose men have always pursued her. Maybe that puts her in much the same category as Bev.'

'What?' Jennifer screeched in disbelief.

'Not in looks,' Bessie hastily tried to explain. 'But I was just wondering if your mother had an addiction like Bev has an addiction and she has to struggle with temptation just as much as Bev has. Only it's a different addiction and a different temptation, that's all. If you see what I mean.'

She wasn't sure what she meant herself. She hadn't had time to think it through.

Jennifer was silent. She too seemed to be trying to think things through. Eventually she murmured, 'I never thought of it like that.'

Another silence. Then, 'Have you met her latest?'

'Paul Fisher?' Bessie said.

'What did you think of him? Be honest, Bessie.'

Bessie hesitated, then said, 'I wouldn't trust him as far as I could throw him. But your mother thinks the world of him and she's the one who's going to marry him.'

'He can be very charming. Especially to my mother.'

'But . . .?' Bessie prompted.

'In confidence?'

'Of course.'

'He was always trying to come on to me. You know, things he'd say, touching me accidentally on purpose, just generally being a pest. At the same time, I knew he hated me. He believed I was trying to put my mother off him and I suppose he was right about that. Then he tried to have sex with me. That's why I ran away. That's what he wanted all the time, I suppose – to get rid of me. Frighten me completely out of the picture. And he succeeded.'

'Oh dear . . .' Bessie, lost for words, pulled Jennifer to her and cradled her in her arms. Jennifer began to weep against Bessie's chest.

'She didn't believe me.'

'There, there,' Bessie repeated, as she patted and nursed Jennifer. 'There, there.'

XLIV

JENNIFER HAD STIFFENED away from her mother's embrace the first time she'd come to see her at Bessie's. Bessie had done her best to keep the conversation going during the visit. Even Bev had kept trying to break the ice, but Jennifer had remained sullen and silent. At least she had been spared having to face Paul Fisher, because her mother had come on her own. Andrina and Bessie had become friends. Bessie seemed to be able to make friends with all sorts of unlikely folk. Bessie liked people. She'd recently even tried to make excuses for Fisher. Although Bessie had denied this.

'I thought you said you wouldn't trust him as far as you could throw him.'

'I wouldn't. And I'm a bit worried about how much your mother trusts him. There's an immature, naïve bit about Andrina.'

'Oh, that'll be right,' Jennifer scoffed. 'She's the most self-centred, selfish woman imaginable. She cares about no one but herself and her own gratification. It's just her nature, Bessie.'

'It's strange,' Bessie looked thoughtful, 'how patterns can repeat themselves. Your mother had an awful childhood. She felt neglected and unloved, just like you do. Maybe that explains why she seems to love herself so much. It's her way of compensating, and feeling more secure. Maybe the sex thing has something of that in it too. I know she's physically a very sexy person. There's no denying that. All the same . . .'

'Bessie,' Jennifer interrupted, 'will you leave the psychology to the psychologists. You know nothing about it. You especially haven't a clue about my mother.'

'Oh, I don't know. We've had some long talks, Andrina and I.'

'*She's* talked a lot, you mean.'

'Well, even so. I did learn about what kind of childhood she had.'

'My granny was one of the kindest, most loving people in the world. I wouldn't believe a word against her. If my mother has told you my granny was cruel and unloving to her, she's a liar.'

'No, no, dear. Your mother was terribly upset when Sophie died. But none of us are perfect, Jennifer. You'll have to learn to stop seeing things in black and white. I'm sure your granny was one of the kindest and most loving people in the world just as you say. She certainly was kind and loving to you. But you mustn't close your eyes to the fact that she disowned Andrina, didn't speak to her own daughter for years.'

'With good reason. I loved my granny and I'm not going to sit here and allow you to try to stop me loving her.'

'God forbid!' Bessie cried out. 'There isn't enough love in the world. No, no, real love is surely being able to love people *despite* their faults. Knowing their faults, understanding them, and *still* loving them. Loving the *person*, not the faults. I think we should always try to separate the two. Oh, please don't think I'm trying to *stop* you loving anybody, Jennifer. Especially Sophie, who was always so good to you. I'm putting my two big feet in it again. I'm sorry. It's just that I keep thinking how we all seem to be victims of victims.'

'My mother a victim? That's a laugh. As far as I can see, she's always done all right for herself, thank you very much.'

Bessie sighed.

'Maybe you're right. Anyway, who am I to dole out advice? A right old mess I've made of any relationships I've ever had.'

Jennifer couldn't help laughing at that, but her conversations with Bessie made her think. Thoughts kept hovering about the edges of her mind, making her feel – not exactly worried – but uncomfortable.

The next time Andrina came to tea she at least spoke to her and was somewhat taken aback by the eager gratitude in Andrina's manner as a result. Of course, it probably stemmed from guilt. Her mother had felt guilty and now she imagined she was being let off the hook. All was forgiven, the beautiful

Andrina was thinking. Well, it wasn't. At the same time, Jennifer was surprised at the idea of her mother feeling guilty. She'd never thought her mother had ever felt anything at all. At least as far as she was concerned.

Andrina began to include her in her confidences with Bessie and her appeals for advice and, it seemed for reassurance.

'We've been going together for ages now – Paul and I – and I know he's doing his best to get a divorce but honestly, sometimes I think all this legal business is going to go on for ever. Now he tells me his wife is contesting it and that means the divorce will take years before it can go through. We've had to postpone buying a house. I've never wanted him to set me up in a house in his name. Not until we were safely married. I mean, what if something went wrong and he walked out on me? At least I've got a place of my own at the moment.'

'Have you met his wife?' Jennifer asked.

Andrina shook her head.

'I've wanted us all to talk things over face to face but Paul would never hear of it. His wife suffers from arthritis, poor soul, and it's understandable that he doesn't want to upset her. But as I keep telling him, I've no intention of upsetting her. We might even get on very well together. We might become good friends.'

'I hardly think so,' Jennifer said.

'It can happen,' her mother said in such a knowing manner that Jennifer took it that it actually had happened to her mother before.

After Andrina had gone, she said to Bessie, 'Would you believe it?'

'What?' Bessie had begun to wash the dishes. Bev would soon be home with her feet killing her and much in need of a cup of tea and something to eat.

'Imagining she could be best friends with his wife.'

Bessie shook her head over the soapsuds.

'That's what I meant about her being a bit naïve. Poor Andrina. She sounded worried, didn't she? I can't help wondering what that man's up to.'

'I wouldn't be a bit surprised if she's done it before.'

'What?'

'Managed to be friendly with the wife of her current lover.'

'More like wishful thinking. She wants what she wants without any bad feeling. Could you dry, dear, and put the dishes back on the table. Bev'll be in soon.'

'All right. It's a bit pathetic in a way.'

'What is?'

'Being so conceited and so blinkered.'

'She has something to be conceited about. If I looked like that, I'd be awful pleased with myself.'

'There's not a thing wrong with your looks, Bessie.'

Bessie laughed as she dried her hands on her apron. 'You must be joking.'

'For a woman your age,' Jennifer said, gazing at her earnestly, 'you haven't any wrinkles worth speaking about . . .'

'No, don't let's speak about my wrinkles.'

'. . . And you've such thick curly hair. But best of all, you've got a *caring* face . . .'

'Careworn, you mean. Hurry up with these dishes, Jennifer. You accuse Andrina of talking too much! Now, what did I tell you – there's Bev at the door. And this is her pay day so we'd better keep our fingers crossed.'

'I'll answer it.'

The moment she opened the door, Jennifer's heart sank along with her spirits. She'd been so caught up with thoughts about Andrina, she'd forgotten it was Bev's pay day. Usually she went to meet her and managed to prevent her going to the nearest pub. Today, she had put her mother first and now, seeing Bev, smelling the reek of alcohol from her, she was overcome with regret.

'Sorry hen,' Bev said, walking unsteadily into the hall. 'I just went in for a wee refreshment because we'd been run off our feet all day. Just a wee pick-me-up, you understand . . .'

'If you could just keep it to one or even two drinks, Bev.'

'Aye, aye. That's all I meant it to be.'

'Well then . . .' Jennifer followed the small, skinny, busty figure into the kitchen.

'You've got us now and this nice home. You don't have any sorrows to drown now and nothing to escape from.'

'OK. OK.' Bev addressed Bessie. 'Your turn.'

'I never said a word.' Bessie was putting cutlery on to the kitchen table. 'Sit yourself down. You've had a long day. You must be tired.'

'Saint Bessie,' Bev sneered. 'Always ready with a helping hand.'

Jennifer tutted and cast an anxious, apologetic glance towards Bessie. 'Now, Bev, there's no cause to take anything out on Bessie,' she said. And then to Bessie: 'She didn't mean anything. It's the drink. It always makes her a bit sarky.'

'I don't care what she calls me. I've more urgent and important things to worry about. Like the exhibition.'

'Oh yes, when is it?'

'It opens a week today. There's been a whole lot about it in the papers already. All that publicity makes me nervous. And Lester Morgan commissioning all my work like that. Did I tell you he's got a huge gallery in the States? It all seems like a dream. Or a miracle or something. I can't believe it. Can't take it in yet.'

'What are you going to wear, hen?' Bev asked. 'You'll be the celebrity. You'll have to look special.'

'Oh, don't start that again. I'd a hard enough time with Andrina. She wants to take me shopping on Monday.'

'Wear a skirt, for God's sake. Or a dress. You can't slop into the limelight in your old trousers. Especially stained ones like those you've got on.'

'It's not that I don't like skirts and dresses. I do and I've nice long ones, but they always make me look like a walking wigwam.'

Bev and Jennifer laughed at this image, and Jennifer said, 'You always put yourself down, Bessie. There's nothing wrong with your figure. You just don't make the most of yourself.'

'Aye, hen, this might be your big chance in more ways than one.'

Bev made an unsteady path to the nearest chair and thumped down on to it.

'There'll be a few handsome men there, as well as your old millionaire. I'll bet one of them's bound to fall for you if you put on the glamour. Jennifer, hen, give us a pull off with these shoes. They're stuck to my bloody feet.'

'Me put on the glamour?' Bessie laughed. 'I'm no Andrina. Anyway, she'll be the belle of the ball, not me.'

'You haven't invited her!' Bev and Jennifer cried out in unison.

'Well, I couldn't very well say she couldn't come, could I?'

'Oh, Bessie,' Jennifer groaned, 'she'll spoil your big day.'

'Oh well,' Bev said, 'I wasn't going to come in case *I* spoiled it. But if she's going to be there – what the hell!'

XLV

AFTER TRYING ON everything she had in her wardrobe including the new outfit she'd been persuaded to buy in Frasers, Bessie ended up in a pair of denim trousers and a loose denim shirt.

Jennifer and Bev had capitulated in good grace, saying, 'Och well, I suppose she might as well be herself. And at least the trousers aren't covered in paint.'

They dressed themselves down, instinctively not wanting in any way to outshine Bessie at the 'big do'. They had both been looking forward to 'dolling themselves up', as Bev had put it, and it was a terrible wrench to abandon their smart outfits. Jennifer opted instead for a pair of denims and a open-necked checked shirt. With a sigh, Bev donned the plain black skirt and white blouse she wore at work, only indulging in a strand of pearls and a pair of high-heeled shoes. She sprayed perfume all over herself to cover any smell of food that might have clung to her waitressing clothes.

On the way to the gallery in the taxi, Bessie seemed to shrink smaller and smaller.

'This is terrible. I need to go to the bathroom again.'

'Bessie, forget it,' Bev told her. 'It's just nerves. Enjoy yourself. This is your big day. You've done it, hen. You've made it.'

'I haven't done anything different from what I've always done.'

'You've never hit the headlines like this before, have you?' Jennifer said.

'It's that Lester Morgan.' Bessie fidgeted with agitation. 'Americans have to do everything in such a big way. He couldn't just buy one painting, take it back to the States and quietly hang it in his gallery. Now he's gone and taken pneumonia or bronchitis or something and won't be there tonight. That sounds awful. Of course I'm sorry for the poor man but what with one thing and another, I just know the night's going to be a total disaster.'

'Come on, hen,' Bev scoffed. 'You were tickled pink before.'

'And pleased and excited,' Jennifer added.

'Of course you were, hen. I'm telling you, it's just last-minute nerves. Like brides have before their wedding.'

'For pity's sake don't remind me of my wedding,' Bessie wailed. 'That's liable to make me suicidal.'

Bev and Jennifer giggled.

'Never mind, hen, once you're there you'll be OK. You'll have a great time. Just think of all the different kinds of folk that'll be there and the ideas you'll get for more pictures.'

That cheered Bessie. But not altogether.

'It's just I'm terrified about people not liking my pictures. It's like being naked, you see. My paintings are such an intimate part of me somehow. People can feel, or think, or say, what they like about them. But not when I'm *there!*'

She became agitated again.

'I'm dying to go to the bathroom. I'm going to disgrace myself, I know it!'

'There'll be a toilet in the gallery,' Jennifer put an arm around Bessie's shoulders. 'You'll be able to go there, don't worry.'

Bessie nodded, tense and white-faced.

'Anyway,' Bev scoffed, 'what are you blethering about folk not liking your pictures? Why do you think there's been all this fuss? Why do you think the American guy wants to show off your pictures here, there and everywhere? Especially that one you did of Andrina. Why do you think everyone wanted this exhibition?'

'It's the stand-up one that's worrying me more than any of the others.'

Bev and Jennifer had christened the Andrina portrait 'Stand up the real Andrina!' And even Bessie now referred to it by that name.

'They'll love them, all of them.' Jennifer gave Bessie's shoulders a reassuring squeeze. 'And they'll love you.'

The gallery in Sauchiehall Street was huge and spacious. A chrome and wooden stairway led the eye up to the mezzanine floor where some of the smaller exhibits were on display. The full-length windows at street level were draped with swaths of natural muslin, giving a soft light without shadow. The uncluttered floor of polished pine stretched from wall to wall with only one or two chrome and leather chairs to break the surface. Small track spotlights focused on Bessie's progressively larger canvases. It was as if, with her freedom, her canvases mirrored her spiritual development and confidence. Cameramen and reporters were crowding round someone over near the 'stand-up' painting.

'What the . . .?' Bev said. The three of them had entered the gallery unnoticed. Everyone's back was to them. All eyes were straining to see the centre of attention.

'It's her.' Jennifer could hardly speak for fury. 'I knew it! She just has to be in the limelight.'

Bev was also enraged.

'The fuckin' cow – look at her as well – dressed to kill. By God, I'll kill her when I get my hands on her.'

'Oh please,' Bessie whispered, 'don't cause any trouble, girls. I'd rather keep in the background, honestly.'

'Don't be daft. Who's she to steal your thunder?'

'Well, she was the model for the painting.'

'She's so . . . so stupid, so egotistical.' Jennifer was stuttering with anger. 'She doesn't see what the picture's saying about her. She doesn't see what everyone else sees. She's just making a fool of herself.'

'Oh dear, poor thing. I hope the papers don't print anything that'll hurt or upset her. She doesn't mean any harm?'

'What?' Bev spluttered. 'Look at her. She's not caring a fig about you. She's evil.'

'Oh no.' Bessie was appalled. 'Oh no, you mustn't even think such a thing. Andrina is *not* evil. She's more like a thoughtless child. A child needing constant attention.'

Bev and Jennifer groaned, then Bev said, 'Well, hen, you may be daft but I'm not. She's not going to get away with this. You're not going to stand here like an accident looking for somewhere to happen and nobody paying a blind bit of notice.'

Suddenly, and to Bessie's horror, Bev loudened her voice into an absolute roar, 'Here she is at last, folks! The star of the show you've all been waiting for. The Glasgow girl – the genius that everyone in this city is rightly proud of.'

'Oh God!' Bessie groaned.

Bev and Jennifer began to clap and cheer and the crowd of people, including the reporters and photographers, moved towards them.

Then Andrina came sashaying towards Bessie, but Bev and Jennifer were too quick for her. They wriggled through the crowd and caught her, linked arms with her and turned her in the opposite direction.

'What are you doing?' Andrina's expression seesawed between astonishment and annoyance.

They let go of her in front of a waitress carrying a tray of glasses full of champagne.

Jennifer said, 'We just wanted to make sure you got a drink. We wanted to be the first to toast you.'

'Oh, I had a drink, darling. I must have put it down somewhere. I love champagne, don't you?'

Bev said, 'Never drink anything else. Oops!' She had lifted a glass from the tray and bumped into Andrina, splashing the champagne all down Andrina's glamorous outfit.

'Oh sorry, hen. Here, let me mop it up for you . . .'

'Leave it alone. You'll only make it worse. Oh, I'm absolutely soaked.' Andrina's voice broke. 'I don't know why, but I'm sure you did that on purpose.'

'What?' Bev's eyes widened. 'Now what reason could I possibly have for doing such a thing? No, no, hen, it was just a wee accident and I'm really sorry, so I am.'

'I'll have to go home and change now.'

'Oh, is that not a terrible shame,' Bev sympathised.

'Do you want me to come with you, Mummy?' Jennifer asked.

'No thank you, dear. That's kind of you but I'll just get a taxi. I'll be all right.'

'I'd slip out of the back door if I were you,' Bev advised. 'You don't want anyone to see you like that. You look as if you'd peed yourself.'

'Oh!' Andrina gasped in distress.

'Are you sure you don't need me to come with you?' Jennifer repeated.

'No, no, dear. You stay and enjoy yourself. Give me a ring tomorrow and let me know how things went.'

When she'd hurried away, Jennifer said, 'I feel awful.'

'Why? It got rid of her, didn't it?'

'I know but I can't help feeling sorry for her.'

'What? A few minutes ago you were furious.'

'I know. She is terrible, right enough.'

'And she had to go.'

'Yes, you're right. She would have completely spoiled everything for Bessie.'

'I know how you feel, though,' said Bev. 'She's that bloody likeable with it!'

They began to giggle and the champagne they swooped on and began to drink did nothing to quell their hilarity.

'Here, would you look at that,' Bev nudged Jennifer.

'What?'

'That gorgeous man over there.'

'He looks like security. Remember Bernard told Bessie that he couldn't come tonight but he would be sending his nephew, Sean.'

'He looks as if he's more interested in guarding Bessie then the pictures. Look at the way he's staring at her.'

'Maybe Bernard has told him to act as Bessie's bodyguard.'

'Och away, this is Glasgow, hen, not Chicago. Here, look at her looking at him now.'

Jennifer rolled her eyes.

'For goodness sake, Bev. You've a one-track mind. Bessie's old enough to be his mother.'

'Maybe so. But I detect some of the old animal attraction there.'

'That's just you. There's no maybes about it. She *is* old enough to be his mother.'

'OK. OK.' Bev held up her hands. 'It's all in my dirty one-track mind.'

XLVI

FOR A FEW minutes Andrina was distraught. She couldn't get away from the gallery quick enough. She couldn't bear anyone to see her in any way less than perfect. Perfectly demure when she attended church. Perfectly glamorous when she went anywhere else. Perfectly sexy when she was having a sexual encounter. She had always been as meticulous about her clothes and her personal appearance as she was about her house.

After she had arrived safely home from the gallery, she was tempted to change and go to the casino to see Paul. Then she thought it might look a bit odd. He knew how much she had been looking forward to spending the evening at the exhibition. She could go back to the gallery but it might look strange turning up wearing a different outfit. She calmed down once she was safely back at Monteith Row and had taken off the stained garment. She slipped into a frilly satin négligé and stared at herself in the long mirror in the bedroom. Suddenly she felt lonely. Unhappiness that seemed out of all proportion to the evening's events frightened her. She struggled to quell her foolish fears. Apart from the accident, she had enjoyed the evening. It had been absolutely lovely being photographed and admired by everyone. It made her think that she ought to have been an actress or a model. One of the photographers had, in fact, asked if she had ever been a model. She'd laughingly replied, 'No, never' and he's said, 'You pose like a professional.'

The whole episode had been delightful. Indeed, she couldn't remember ever having enjoyed herself so much in her whole life. Not only did she feel famous, she *was* famous. She had only come to realise this as she posed beneath Bessie's painting.

It had been a pity that Bev had spoiled such a gloriously happy time. Thinking of Bev brought back the unhappiness.

She was sure the woman had spilled the drink over her on purpose. Yet why should Bev do such a thing? She had never done anything nasty to Bev. Even though she secretly thought the woman was not a proper friend and companion for Jennifer, she'd still been as kind and as charming as she could to her. She hadn't once interfered with the friendship, never said one word against Bev. She hardly dared face the thought, because it was so bewildering, so hurtful – but Bev didn't seem to like her.

She tried to tell herself that it didn't matter whether Bev liked her or not. Why should she care? But she did. She couldn't bear anyone not to like her. Standing in front of the mirror in her bedroom, she faced this indisputable fact. She blamed it on her mother. All these years, from babyhood up until the day her mother died, she'd suffered from her mother's dislike. First, Sophie's downright, cruel neglect. Then her active dislike. She'd never been able to please her mother, no matter how hard she'd tried.

And oh, how she'd tried. A lump of regret and sadness swelled up in her throat. She'd never understood her mother's behaviour any more than she understood Bev's. For years her mother, her own mother, had refused even to speak to her. She'd hated Sophie for that and all the other cruelties and neglect. Yet at the same time, she had loved her. In this vulnerable moment, gazing helplessly at herself, she realised this. And she deeply regretted never being able to please her, no matter how she tried.

Her mother had never recognised any good about her at all. Never. She never saw that Andrina was a loving and demonstrative person. Or that she was a good cook and housewife. Or that she looked good. Nothing. Often she still longed to appeal to her mother. Why were you like that to me? What harm did I ever do to you?

It took a terrible effort to pull herself together. She was just being silly. She was making a mountain out of a molehill. Bev was such a clumsy person and the way she tottered about on those ridiculously high heels, it wasn't surprising that she'd stumbled and spilled the drink. Of course it was an accident.

She decided to have a leisurely bath. She had face pack as

well and tried out the new eye-pads that she'd treated herself to. Her eyes were her best feature, everyone said so, and she took great care of them.

Afterwards, she put on fresh make-up in readiness for Paul's arrival. During the few days – or rather nights – he stayed with her, she kept her make-up on in bed. She was always eager to look her best for him. This night she took particular care, perfuming her body, painting her toenails, applying several coats of mascara to her long lashes. They didn't always have sex because working so late as he did, he was sometimes too tired. Tonight, she not only wanted but needed him to make love to her, to hold her in his arms, to tell her how beautiful and desirable she was. Unfortunately, as it turned out, Paul had had such a stressful time at the casino, he wasn't even interested in hearing about the lovely evening she'd had at the gallery. He was full of talk, as he undressed and came to bed, of someone who had been cheating the system and losing him a terrible amount of money. She listened dutifully and sympathetically. Tomorrow, over 'brunch' – Paul always slept late – he would feel better and she would get the chance to tell him about her triumph.

In the morning she slipped out of bed, put on fresh make-up and dressed. Then, as usual, she went out for the morning papers before cooking Paul's favourite mixed grill. He enjoyed relaxing at the kitchen table reading the papers, while she busied herself at the cooker. He looked very handsome in his pale blue shirt and navy suit. The dark colour of the suit made his slicked-back fair hair all the more striking. Like her, Paul took a pride in his appearance. As he always said, 'I've a reputation to keep up. And of course I'm in a glamorous occupation. Appearances are important.'

'One or two eggs, darling?' she asked, smiling round at him. To her surprise, he glowered angrily back at her.

'Have you read this?'

'What?'

'What they've written about you in all the papers.'

Her heart began to flutter apprehensively.

'No, I thought I'd enjoy a good read after breakfast.'

'You'll not enjoy this. If you do, you're an even bigger fool than they're making you out to be.'

'What?' Her heart was pounding now and she felt faint. 'I don't know what you're talking about. The journalists and photographers were all terribly nice. One of them even said – '

'For God's sake, Andrina. Why didn't you tell me you were the model for the picture in the exhibition?'

'But . . . but it wasn't really me, you see. Bessie said it was an act of creativity like writers create fiction characters. They often get inspiration, an idea from real life, but . . .'

'She got an idea of you all right. Christ, I don't know how I'll be able to face them in the casino, or my wife and family.' His voice grew louder and he crashed up from the table. 'Why the hell did you need to blabber about me? You stupid cow, you had no right to mention my name.'

She put her hand on the cooker to steady herself.

'All I said was that you were my fiancé and you had the best casino in Scotland. Darling, I said nothing but good about you. I'm proud of you and I wanted them all to know . . .'

'Well, I'm bloody well not proud of you. And you're not my fuckin' fiancée. I'm a married man. I'll have to go through to Edinburgh right now and see if I can't straighten out this mess. I'll probably have to contact the press as well. I'll have to think what's best to do.'

What mess? I don't understand.'

'You've made a right fool of yourself, you idiot. But you're not going to get away with making me look a fool as well. You're not going to drop me in it.'

Andrina had begun to weep.

'In what? I don't understand.'

'Oh, stop saying that. Just read the bloody papers. I don't suppose you'll even understand what they're saying, but I'm not waiting to find out.'

She watched in disbelief as he stormed from the kitchen. After a few minutes, she heard the front door bang. It was a long time before she could move. Only the smell of burning brought her back to life and she hastily switched off the cooker and rescued the burning frying pan. By the time she had doused the flames and got the crisis under control, it was as much as she could do to stumble over to the table and collapse on to a chair. Too terrified now to look at the papers, she waited until she had enough strength in her legs, then she got up and made herself a strong pot of tea. Her hand trembled so much as she poured out a cupful that some of it splashed into the saucer. Heedlessly, she drank from the cup, keeping her eyes averted from the papers.

They lay on the table, lethal bullets waiting to pierce her heart.

XLVII

BESSIE GROANED.

'This is terrible, absolutely terrible. How could they?'

Bev lit a cigarette and relaxed back on one of the kitchen chairs. 'It wasn't the journalists. It was her, the silly cow. Serves her right.'

'Even if she's read the papers,' Jennifer said, 'she might not understand what they're getting at.'

'Come on, Hen,' Bev scoffed, 'she can't be that daft.'

Bessie rubbed at her hair in distress, giving it an even wilder appearance than usual.

'I lied. I more or less told her it wasn't her. I said an artist often works like a writer. You get an idea or a stimulus from real life, then create something new out of it.'

'Well, that's perfectly true,' Jennifer soothed her.

'Don't let's kid ourselves,' Bessie said. 'That painting was my interpretation of Andrina.'

'What about the other one she's got on her wall? That was your interpretation too.'

Bev said, 'You just told the truth as you saw it, hen. And the guys from the papers have obviously seen it as well – helped by the blind conceit of the woman posing under the picture and rabbiting on about herself and her precious fiancé.' She flicked at one of the papers. 'According to this, a happily married guy with three of a family.'

'I wish I'd never painted the awful thing now. I feel really terrible. Poor Andrina!'

'I suppose I'd better phone,' Jennifer said. 'I did promise.'

'I don't know how I'll ever be able to face her again,' Bessie said, making Bev cry out, 'Will you shut up and stop being so daft. You've done nothing wrong. All you've done is paint a bloody picture.'

Jennifer agreed.

'Yes, Bessie, if artists had to worry all the time about what people thought and what effect their work might have, they'd never do anything, would they!'

Jennifer rang Andrina's number.

'Is that you, Mummy?' she said. She was taken aback by the quavery, fearful voice at the other end of the phone. After a moment or two she replaced the receiver and turned to the others.

'She burst into tears and then hung up.'

'I should go and see her.' Bessie nursed her head in her hands. 'Apologise. I don't know.'

Bev stubbed out her cigarette. 'Well, I do. You're not moving from here. You go if you like,' she added to Jennifer.

Jennifer nodded.

'I suppose I'd better.'

Bessie burst into tears. 'Some Quaker I am.'

'God!' Bev groaned. 'Now she's bringing religion into it!'

'Well, it says in *Advices and Queries* that we should value that of God in everybody and we should not make use of another person "through selfish desire".'

'OK. OK.' Bev turned to Jennifer. 'While you are out, hen, get some sackcloth and ashes for Bessie.'

That brought a faint smile to Bessie's face and she dried her eyes. 'Sorry,' she said. 'On you go, Jennifer.'

On the way to Monteith Row in the taxi, Jennifer felt tense and emotionally confused. She was completely on Bessie's side and agreed with Bev that what had happened with the newspapers was all Andrina's silly fault. She had called the tune and now she was paying the piper. At the same time she couldn't help feeling sorry for her mother. Especially when she remembered the bewildered voice on the phone. Andrina had sounded like a frightened child.

Once at Monteith Row, Jennifer hurried up the stairs and rang the bell of the flat. There was no reply. She knocked loudly on the door, still no response. She tried calling through the letterbox.

'Mummy, it's me. Open the door. It's all right. I'm on my own.'

Eventually the door opened a crack and Andrina's face, swollen and blotchy with tears, peered apprehensively out.

'It's all right,' Jennifer repeated. 'It's only me.'

The door opened wide and Andrina stretched out her arms. 'Oh Jennifer . . .'

Jennifer patted her mother as she led her back into the kitchen.

'How could they do that?' Andrina sobbed. 'How could Bessie do that? I love Bessie.'

'And she loves you. She's terribly upset at all that nonsense in the papers. But you know what journalists are like.'

'No. No, I don't. I don't know what anyone's like any more.'

'It's a nine-days' wonder. No, not even that. Mummy. What's news today is history tomorrow. You'll see, by tomorrow, they'll be on to something else and somebody else.'

'Bessie told me that that picture . . .'

'I know what Bessie told you and it was the truth. The trouble is, once something is in the public domain, everybody's free to find their own truth in it. Their own interpretation, or whatever.'

As Andrina accepted Jennifer's handkerchief and mopped at her face Jennifer added, 'I'll make us both a good strong cup of tea, will I?'

'Thank you, dear. You're very kind. Forgive me for being so upset. It's not just the newspapers. Paul's left me.' Tears welled up again and she hastily wiped at them with the handkerchief. 'He called me such awful names. I didn't think . . . I mean, how could he speak to me like that? And how could he desert me just when . . .' She stuffed the handkerchief against her mouth and fought for control.

Jennifer plugged in the kettle and set out two cups and saucers. Both women were silent until the tea was made and poured.

'Nothing would surprise me about him. Not after the way he treated me. But you didn't believe me, did you?'

'Oh Jennifer, I'm so sorry. I honestly didn't think . . . I mean, I loved him, you see . . .'

243

'But you didn't love me.'

'Oh darling, I did. I do. Oh please forgive me.' She began to sob uncontrollably and Jennifer said,

'I can't do that, Mummy. Not when I think of all I suffered after I left here. And I couldn't stay. I was too afraid.'

'I tried to find you. I really did try.'

'What good would it have done – if you had found me?'

'And then I thought you must be all right. I really convinced myself that you must be all right.'

'I can believe that.'

'I never meant you to suffer. I can't bear to think I made you suffer.' Andrina's voice had acquired a note of hysteria and her eyes stretched wide with distress. 'I'd rather die. I wish I was dead.'

'For goodness sake,' Jennifer groaned. And then, realising that Andrina might be in danger of actually doing something reckless or foolish, she asked, 'Would you like me to come and stay with you for a few days?'

'Oh darling, would you?'

'Just for a few days.'

'Oh, Jennifer, thank you. I feel so devastated.'

'You'll be all right. Drink your tea. Then wash your face and put on fresh make-up. I'll have to go and tell Bessie and Bev, and collect some things.'

She worried all the way back to Botanic Crescent. Part of her pitied her mother and wanted to be with her to look after her. Another part of her wanted no such thing. Far better, and happier, to continue living with Bessie and Bev, without taking on more responsibilities. She had enough to cope with trying to keep Bessie's place clean and tidy and Bev on the straight and narrow. For a few minutes in Andrina's kitchen, she'd wrestled with the idea of bringing Bev over to Monteith Row. However, she couldn't, try as she did, see such an arrangement working out. Bev would be far too much for Andrina. Anyway, no way would Bev be persuaded to live under the same roof as her.

'What?' Bev screeched when she heard the news. 'Have you gone out of your tiny mind? You can't stand the woman any more than I can.'

'I wouldn't have considered moving in even for a few days if Fisher had been there. But he's left her, apparently.'

'There'll be another Fisher in no time, what do you bet?' Jennifer sighed.

'Oh, I suppose so. That's why I made it clear it was only a temporary arrangement.'

'And don't think for a minute,' Bev said, 'that I'm going with you – temporary or not. But it won't be temporary. Wait till you see. Once she's got you there – that'll be it. And then what'll I do?'

'You can stay on here. Can't she, Bessie?'

Bessie had been sitting listening.

'Of course!' She made an effort to look sincere. 'Of course you can, Bev.'

'Aye. OK hen. Thanks.'

'When are you going?' Bessie asked Jennifer.

'As soon as I pack my things. I promised I'd be right back.' Then, seeing the expression on Bev's face, she hastily added, 'It won't make any difference to us. I'll still see you every day, Bev. After all, it's only twenty minutes or so from here.'

Bev shrugged. 'As I've told you before, we're not joined at the hip.'

'I know. But I don't want anything to come between us or spoil our friendship. I couldn't bear that.'

'You're breaking my heart. Away back to Monteith Row, for God's sake. I've got my work to go to.'

When Bessie saw Jennifer to the door Jennifer said, 'I hope I'm doing the right thing, Bessie.'

'She is your mother.'

'Today it felt as if it was the other way around.'

'You've had to learn to survive in very hard and dangerous circumstances, Jennifer. She hasn't.'

'Maybe it's time she did learn to fend for herself.'

'She needs you, Jennifer. I think you're doing the right thing.'

Jennifer kissed Bessie.

'You will keep an eye on Bev, won't you?'

'Don't worry.'

Jennifer raised her voice.

'That's me away, Bev.'

'Aye. OK. What do you want me to do? Tell the Provost to put all the flags at half mast?'

'Cheerio, then.'

Bev bawled back, 'Just go, for God's sake!'

XLVIII

SOMETIMES THINGS HAPPENED all at once – good and bad – and Bessie's life became confused. It was good that Jennifer had been reconciled with her mother. Bad that she had now to cope with Bev on her own. Well, not bad exactly. Bev wasn't bad. She just had a drink problem. It got worse after Jennifer left. She came in drunk and it wasn't even pay night. And when Bev was drunk, she could be very difficult indeed. If Jennifer could see that beige carpet in the spare room now!

And added to the confusion was what had happened in connection with the young security man who'd been at the exhibition. Sean O'Malcy was Bernard's nephew. At the exhibition, despite all the people crowding around her asking questions and taking photographs and praising her pictures, she became aware of Sean's eyes on her. He had such a steady, thoughtful gaze. She'd thought – what a nice-looking young man. His stare had made her feel somewhat uncomfortable but she'd told herself that security men were like that. It was their job to be observant. Bernard had watchful eyes but his were different – hard, suspicious. Sean's eyes were a deep liquid brown that seemed to melt into every secret corner of her being. She felt herself begin to blush and become flustered. It was a struggle to bring her wayward feelings under control. He had come up to her afterwards and asked how she was getting home.

'I don't know. A taxi, I suppose. I came in a taxi.'

Her heart was swelling and interfering with her breathing. Especially when he smiled at her and offered to give her a lift home in his car. It wasn't a soft smile. His lips drew tightly back to show strong white teeth. She was tempted to abandon

Jennifer and Bev to their own devices. Steady on, Bessie, she chided herself. What on earth are you thinking about?'

'Thank you, Sean. But there's my two friends who lodge with me. Jennifer and Bev.'

'There's room for them too.'

'Fine, then.'

He had told her to sit in the front beside him while Bev and Jennifer chattered together in the back seat. They were both drunk. All that champagne! That must be why I'm feeling so strange, Bessie thought. She'd had a few glasses of champagne herself. The thought relaxed her and she was able to smile at Sean in the darkness of the car and talk naturally to him. He was such a nice boy and with such startling good looks. He wasn't as big and brawny as his uncle. Maybe just over six feet tall, long-legged, broad-shouldered and narrow-hipped, and obviously very fit. She could imagine his rock-hard muscles. Even the muscles on his face were hard and taut, so that when he smiled, his cheeks tightened back into an indentation on each side, harder than dimples. Only his eyes seemed different. If the eyes were the window of the soul, there seemed strange enigmatic depths to Sean. His dark stare haunted her long after she'd gone to bed that night. She tossed restlessly about, desperately trying to banish him from her mind. But his stare refused to go away, penetrated deep inside her.

The next day she got up early, made herself a strong cup of tea, told herself not to be daft, and busied herself preparing breakfast for Bev and Jennifer. Then, of course, they'd read the morning papers and everything was banished from her mind, except thoughts of Andrina. Helped by Jennifer and by her own capacity for self-deception, Andrina had to all intents and purposes completely recovered from her original distress. Despite the fact that she could be selfish and egotistical, she was also an affectionate woman and readily forgave Bessie for any pain and embarrassment she might have caused.

'I know it wasn't your fault, Bessie,' she said after they'd warmly embraced. 'It was these awful newspapermen. Anything for a lurid or sensational story. They're so ignorant too.

They got it all wrong. They obviously know nothing about art.'

By this time Sean had called at the house several times. The exhibition was to go on tour and as well as keeping her up to date on how things were going while it was still in Glasgow, he discussed arrangements for moving the paintings during the tour and exactly where each venue would be. She knew in her secret heart that he didn't need to do this. She had been kept informed of everything by Lester Morgan's lawyer. Lester had been flown home in his private plane. His doctors thought he'd stand a better chance of a complete recovery back in Williamsburgh.

However, Sean was such a nice young man and just trying to be helpful. It would be unkind to put him off. So she kept telling herself. But she couldn't help wondering if there was more to it than that. Just in case, by some unlikely chance, there *was* more to it, she tried to do the right thing and discourage him. She dropped her age laughingly into the conversation whenever she could although it felt like plunging a dagger into her heart. She knew he was barely twenty and she was double that age. She also managed to divulge that she was a Quaker. That was usually a right turn-off.

However, Sean said, 'Bessie, I don't care a damn what age you are. Or if you're a bloody Hottentot. So will you forget it!'

'How can I forget it? It's a fact. And it's important.'

'Not to me.'

She felt on dangerous unknown territory. Surely it *couldn't* be that he was romantically interested in her? No. Of course not. Silly woman.

Bev and Jennifer had begun to tease her about him and Andrina was becoming intrigued.

'He seems to have a crush on you, Bessie,' she said.

Bev gloated. 'Didn't I tell you, Jennifer? And she feels the same about him, you mark my words.'

'I'm dying to meet him,' Andrina said. 'You must introduce me to him, Bessie.'

Bev blew smoke from her cigarette in Andrina's direction. 'Over my dead body,' she said.

'Why not?' Andrina's eyes widened innocently.

'Because I'm not going to allow you to spoil Bessie's fun.'

Bessie tutted and fussed about, pouring more tea for everybody.

'You're daft, the lot of you. I'm old enough to be his mother.'

'So?' Bev raised a brow. 'Grab the chance with both hands, hen. It might be your last chance of having a wee fling.'

'Do you like him, Bessie?' Andrina asked.

Bessie cursed herself for blushing, and the hot tea didn't help.

'Of course I like him. He's a nice boy.'

Bev laughed.

'He looks all man to me, hen.'

'Be sensible, Bev. Even if I did fancy him – *which I don't* – I'm too old.'

Andrina cried out: 'Old? You're not old, Bessie. You're two years younger than me!'

Jennifer had begun to look anxious and uncertain.

'You don't really . . . I mean, even if he did . . . you wouldn't . . .'

Bessie sighed.

'Don't worry, Jennifer. Apart from anything else, I'd never have the self-confidence to have a love affair with anyone, far less a handsome young man. Sean could get anyone and I'm sure in his job he meets lots of glamorous young women. Why should he feel in any way romantic about me?'

'Yes, it'll be your painting,' Jennifer said. 'Some people go overboard for any kind of talent. Guys go overboard for women like Eve Page and she's no chicken. If she couldn't sing and was just an ordinary housewife, they wouldn't even look at her.'

'Thanks, Jennifer,' Bessie said with an unusual note of sarcasm in her voice.

'I'm only thinking of your own good. What you need, Bessie, is a nice older man who loves you for yourself and will look after you in your old age.'

'You're cheering me up no end.'

'I just don't want you to get hurt, Bessie. You're not very sophisticated or streetwise, are you?'

'No, I suppose not.'

Andrina looked dreamy.

'I wouldn't mind a younger man.'

'Oh, shut up, Mummy.'

'Really, Jennifer, your manners have deteriorated terribly since you've been away.'

Bev laughed.

'She wasn't away at a finishing school in Switzerland, hen. She was living rough.'

'Well,' Andrina looked huffy now, 'you'll never get any man to admire you for any reason unless you smarten yourself up and learn how to behave properly.'

Jennifer rolled her eyes. She didn't say anything then but as soon as her mother had swanned off to the bathroom, she remarked to Bev and Bessie, 'Could you beat that? I'll certainly never learn how to behave properly from her.'

'I don't like to hear you talk like that about your mother,' Bessie said. 'It means a lot to her to do everything properly. Look at the way she sets her tea-table when Bev and I go over there. I know you enjoy all her wonderful cooking. And I'm sure you appreciate her beautifully folded napkins and the fine bone china and silver tea service. I always marvel at the trouble she goes to cutting all the crusts off every sandwich . . .'

'For goodness sake, Bessie, you know fine what I meant. Anyway, I *have* somebody who admires me. At least I think he does. I hope he does. I certainly admire him.'

Bessie was happily surprised.

'Really? Who is he? When did this happen?'

Bev also leaned forward with interest.

'Here, you're a dark horse. I'm supposed to be your best pal. I thought we didn't have any secrets from each other.'

'I haven't seen either you or Bessie for over two weeks, remember. I've had so much to do with getting everything organised for Jordanhill. It was through that I met him, in a way. I'd gone over to see Daddy and get his advice about a couple of things and Freddie was there.'

'Freddie?' Bev and Bessie exchanged glances. Then Bev said, 'And who is this Freddie when he's at home?'

'He's a teacher, like Daddy. He started his teaching career in fact at Daddy's school. But now he's in Bearsden Academy. He teaches French and German. He's terribly clever.'

'What the hell does he see in you then?' Bev asked. Jennifer knew Bev didn't mean to be offensive, so she just shrugged.

'I don't know. But he insisted on taking me home that first night and then he asked me to go to the opera with him. He got tickets. It was great. I'd never been to an opera before. We've been out several times now and we've chatted on the phone. I really do like him.'

'Like who?' Andrina wanted to know as she returned to the kitchen.

Jennifer blushed.

'Oh, just somebody I've met.'

'You've got a boyfriend?'

'You don't need to sound so astonished, Mummy. I'm not a freak or anything.'

'You're a lovely girl, Jennifer,' Bessie said.

'No, I'm not that either, Bessie. Anybody with a freckly face and hair like mine is no raving beauty.'

Andrina said, 'If you hadn't that awful fringe, dear. And there are creams and things to cover up freckles – even to get rid of them, I've heard. I'll take you tomorrow to my hairdresser and beautician – don't worry, I'll pay for everything . . .'

'No thanks, Mummy. If Freddie doesn't like me for myself, than I don't want him. It wouldn't be me all tarted up. Anyway, I'd feel naked without my fringe.'

Bessie sighed.

'You're quite right, Jennifer. For better or for worse, it's always best to be yourself.'

She was thinking of Bessie Alexander, not Jennifer Anderson, and accepting that as far as she was concerned. It would be for worse.

XLIX

'TELL ME, DARLING, what's he like? Why have you never brought him home to meet me?'

'Actually, you have met him, Mummy.'

'I don't think so, dear.'

'Yes, years ago. Freddie told me. He remembers. At his cousin's house. His cousin Jane. Uncle Bernard's ex-wife. You know Jane.'

'Of course I know Jane.' She thought for a minute. 'I vaguely remember a Freddie. But that's ages ago. You'd only be a child then. He was a grown man.'

'I wasn't going out with him then.'

Andrina's eyes went vague as she tried to work things out.

'He had just started as a teacher at Robert's school, I think. That would make him at least a man in his twenties. So he must be in his thirties now.'

'So?'

Andrina lit a cigarette.

'I think he was the one your daddy had problems with. Now, what was it again . . . I wish I'd paid more attention at the time. Your daddy went on so much about his school and his colleagues and his pupils – honestly, he could talk about nothing else. I stopped listening eventually. It became so boring. He just lived for that school. I expect he's still the same but the woman he's married to now is a teacher, so I suppose that'll be her pet subject too.'

'I guess I'd better not talk shop then once I get a job.'

'Oh, I'm sure you'll not be like that, dear.' She didn't look at all sure and she added. 'I hope you won't. All the same, you seem to be following in your father's footsteps. First the profession and now the partner.'

Jennifer laughed.

'Mummy, Freddie and I aren't married. We're just good friends.'

'I don't understand that.'

'What?'

'Going out with a man so much and still being just good friends.'

'Mummy, you're hopeless. Sex isn't the be-all and end-all of life. Or relationships.'

'It's a very powerful physical and emotional need.'

'Not for me.'

'Now you're getting me worried. It's not natural to be like that.'

Jennifer felt a pang of bitterness and was tempted to bring up her experience with Fisher. Although she'd got over the trauma of his attack, deep down it still affected her, made her shrink within herself for protection. She felt angry too, angry that her mother had let her down so badly. But Andrina had been pathetically eager to make up for that. With difficulty Jennifer pushed Fisher to the back of her mind.

'There's no need to worry,' she told Andrina coolly. 'I'm in no hurry, that's all. I want to concentrate on my career for a while before getting serious with anyone.'

'Yes, of course, you've plenty of time. And I don't want to lose you just yet. You're happy here with me, aren't you?'

'I suppose so,' Jennifer admitted. 'But I must try to visit Bessie and Bev more often. I feel guilty about Bev.'

'Darling, you're not her keeper and she is a mature woman.'

'Well, she's older than me. I don't know so much about being mature.'

'You often talk about being streetwise, Jennifer. Don't you think she is as well? More so even than you?'

'All the same, underneath that tough exterior, there's another Bev. I suppose all of us have different layers. We're not all what we seem on the surface.'

'Anyway, to get back to Freddie. Whether I've already met him or not, why don't you bring him here for dinner one evening?'

'I'll see. I'll maybe mention it to him when I see him tonight.'

'I hope he cooks you a decent meal and doesn't just open lots of tins.'

Jennifer didn't care if he bought fish suppers from the local chippy, she just enjoyed Freddie's company, talking to him, listening to him. She was also looking forward to seeing his flat.

It turned out to be a very respectable place up a tiled close in Roxburgh Street in the West End. He ushered her eagerly into a spacious hall and then through to a large kitchen where he poured her a sherry while he added the final touches to the meal.

In the dining room, romantically lit by candles, she smiled across the table at him.

'You make me feel ashamed.'

'Ashamed? How do I manage to do that? It's certainly not my intention.'

'You're such a good cook. I can't cook at all. My mother's the one in our house for producing wonderful meals.'

'It just needs a bit of practice, that's all. And a helping hand from Marks & Spencer's food department.'

'Ah, so that's your secret.'

'I worry about you, Jennifer.'

'Because I can't cook?'

'No. Because you're training to be a teacher.'

'What's wrong with that?'

He sighed.

'When I remember how I was when I was at your stage . . .'

'You were at university before you started teaching, weren't you?'

'Yes and so full of airy-fairy notions and high ideals. I soon got that knocked out of me, I can tell you. Teaching is for the tough.'

'Oh, come now . . .'

'No, I mean it.'

'Not every teacher is a karate black belt like Daddy, surely.'

'No, but it helps. Apart from being able to defend yourself, it gives you self-confidence and that gives you an aura of strength and authority. If you're not tough physically, you've got to be strong in spirit.'

'Defend yourself?' she laughed. 'Against what?'

'Seriously, Jennifer, you must try to get into some place like Bearsden Academy.'

'So that you can keep an eye on me?'

'I mean any school in a respectable neighbourhood. As compared with where Robert teaches.'

'As far as I can gather, Daddy likes his school and he has a good relationship with his pupils.'

'You're not your father, Jennifer. You look so fragile and waif-like. They'll make mincemeat out of you.'

Jennifer laughed.

'Oh Freddie, you can't always judge by appearances. I'm tougher than I look. If I can survive on the streets of London, I can survive in a Glasgow school. As a matter of fact, I think I'd like the challenge of a tougher school. I'd feel I was doing something worthwhile if I managed to help some of the more deprived children. Daddy tells me a lot of them have slept rough so I'd be off to a good start understanding how they feel.'

'OK, maybe because of your experience you'll be better able to cope than I was when I began teaching. I certainly hope so. But another thing, just because I teach in Bearsden doesn't mean I'm not doing a worthwhile job. I believe I am, and I believe the children in respectable districts are just as much entitled to attention and consideration as anyone else. Their schools should be given just as much funding as the schools in tougher districts.'

'Sounds fair enough to me.' Jennifer cocked her head to one side and studied Freddie's earnest, bespectacled face. 'Do you like teaching?'

Freddie took a long time in answering.

'I still get discouraged and frustrated, but more by the powers above than by the children.'

'I take it you don't mean God.'

'Just the gods in the Education Department and the government.' He shook his head. 'All the red tape and paperwork. I see the day coming when we'll be so snowed under by all that, we won't have time to teach at all. But as far as the actual teaching is concerned – yes, I do like it. And I don't regret going into it, despite my horrific experience at Sinnieglen. Robert deserves a medal for sticking it out there for all these years.' He smiled. 'Maybe where I went wrong was in not taking up karate.'

'You seem to have done all right without it.'

'I work out in the gym for an hour or two each week and I have the occasional swim. But there's so much paperwork to do at home I don't get much time for sport. Or any kind of leisure activity . . .'

His smile always warmed her. It was so kind and shy and boyish.

'I'm glad you came, Jennifer. I enjoy your company so much.'

'Come on,' Jennifer said, 'I'll help you with the dishes.' She got up and started gathering up the dirty plates. Freddie came across to her and said, 'Leave that just now.' He sounded quite masterful, not a bit shy. 'I can't kiss you if you hold a stack of plates between us.'

She felt a flutter of nerves that edged near claustrophobia.

'I don't want to leave you with all the debris. It wouldn't be fair,' she said.

He took the plates from her and put them back on the table. Then he took off his glasses. His eyes looked loving, and tender, if a bit short-sighted. He didn't seem to notice her shrinking back. Then he kissed her so gently and held her so comfortably, she managed to relax a little.

'Of course,' he said, 'if you do go to Sinnieglen, Robert could always keep an eye on you. But I'd still feel better if you were safely beside me in Bearsden Academy.'

She couldn't help laughing then. In fact, she felt so relaxed and so safe in his arms, she even told him about Andrina's dinner invitation.

L

BESSIE KEPT LOOKING at her watch, then at the clock. Then she went to peer anxiously out of the front room window. It was now two o'clock in the morning and Bev hadn't come home. She was on one of her drinking bouts but even so, she usually came staggering and falling up the stairs by midnight. Once the pubs were shut, she made straight for Botanic Crescent. Well, straight wasn't too apt a word. She took the whole width of the pavement and often the road as well. Sometimes she slurred out a song coming up the stairs and this had caused a complaint to be raised by one of the neighbours. Bessie had apologised on Bev's behalf and promised it wouldn't happen again. The noise, she meant. She knew it was no use promising that Bev wouldn't get drunk and incapable again. She spoke to Bev about it of course. Many times. Bev was always very reasonable when she was sober.

'Aye, OK hen. I'll not do it again. I've no right to cause you so much trouble and worry. You're a good soul, so you are. I don't know how you put up with me. If you'd any sense in your head, hen, you'd chuck me out.'

That was true. They both knew it. They also both knew that Bessie, being Bessie, couldn't throw her out on to the street. Especially now that Bev had lost her job.

'I wasn't drunk,' Bev had assured Bessie. 'I'd just had a couple but the boss smelt it on my breath. I was that upset, hen, I went right out and had a bucketful – right there and then.'

Bessie didn't know what to do for the best. She had commissions for work and wanted peace and quiet to get on with it. She'd had several phone calls from Lester Morgan, who planned to return to Britain soon and had been thinking of renting a separate studio and hiding there from Bev so that she could get on with her painting. At the same time, she couldn't help asking herself what was most important in the end – a human being and a good friend, or some tubes of paint and a piece of canvas. Bev was a good friend. To mention but one friendly act out of many, when Bessie had gone down with the flu, Bev had nursed her, couldn't do enough for her. During that time, she'd never touched one drop of alcohol.

'Oh Bev,' Bessie had said afterwards, 'you're so good to your friends. Why are you so bad to yourself?'

'The booze, you mean?' Bev shrugged. 'I don't know, hen. Sometimes I think I was born with this weakness in me.'

'It's half the battle if you can admit it's a weakness, a problem. That's what I've heard. The next step is to get help, Bev. Professional help.'

'I'm past believing that anyone can give me a magic cure.'

'I'm not saying there's a magic cure, but surely you'd get advice . . .'

'Once when they put me in hospital, I was in for a month. They told me I was a compulsive drinker. They gave me loads of vitamins. I felt the better of having that rest and all them vitamins. But, the first day I got out, I bought a bottle of sherry and that was me again. Nothing's any use, hen, believe me. You see, I don't take the drink. It takes me.'

'But you can keep off it. You've proved that. You can keep off it for weeks, sometimes a couple of months at a time. If you could just resist that first drink, Bev.'

'I know, I know. And I will try.'

Bessie wasn't sure if it was the right thing to do but she had started meeting Bev at her work on pay night, as Jennifer used to. That worked for a while but then Bev started drinking on other nights. To prevent the stair-singing being repeated, Bessie usually watched for her coming home and immediately she saw her staggering up the Crescent, she raced down and linked arms with her and whispered to her to keep quiet. Bev always whispered back in a giggly sort of way and, supported by Bessie, tiptoed as best she could up the stairs and into the flat.

But tonight there had been no sign of her. Bessie couldn't understand it. As far as she knew, Bev hadn't any money. Worry and anxiety gave her a splitting headache but she couldn't relax to sleep even after she'd taken a tablet. She wondered about telephoning the police but hesitated in case it might get Bev into trouble. On the other hand, the police might think it was none of their business if a grown woman was a few hours late in coming home. Exhausted, Bessie had fallen asleep in an armchair near the window. She awoke stiff and unrested. After checking her watch she got up and hurried to Bev's room. Bev wasn't there and her bed had not been slept in.

Now what am I supposed to do?

A small secret voice deep inside her whispered that she was glad to be free of the problem of Bev. She had gone, hopefully for good. She would, if her previous history was anything to go by, be sleeping rough. With any luck, Bev had returned to the other world of the homeless.

Bessie felt ashamed of the voice.

OK. OK. I know perfectly well what I'm supposed to do.

At last she left the house to go and look for Bev. She had put off the task for as long as she could by having a hot bath to loosen her aching bones. She was too old to be sleeping in chairs. Then she had three cups of tea and a bowl of cornflakes. She had to force the cornflakes down because she wasn't really hungry.

She wandered about the West End first of all. She combed every inch of the Botanic Gardens. Once she'd found Bev dead to the world in one of the glasshouses. Bev had said later, 'I just went in to have a wee look at all the tropical plants and trees and the heat in there knocked me out. It was like a bloody oven.'

This time there was no sign of her in the Gardens or the glasshouses. No sign of her in any of the streets or doorways of the west side of the city. At the end of the afternoon, Bessie returned to the house to have something to eat and a rest. She'd only had a cup of tea and a cheese sandwich in a café at lunchtime. After sitting with her feet up for half an hour, she heated the remains of a steak pie and forced herself to eat it along with some tinned peas. Now she felt sick with worry. She tried to watch *Coronation Street* on television, but that didn't help. It was now pitch dark outside. Bessie debated with herself whether or not she should postpone a further search until morning. After all, it was a very cold night. It was the cold that reminded her. Jennifer and Bev had once spoken about the gratings outside the Central Hotel in Gordon Street.

'If ever we're needing another skipper,' they had joked – or so Bessie had thought at the time – 'it's over these gratings in Gordon Street.'

Bessie flung on a warm cape and hurried from the house. She was rather fond of capes and had treated herself to two. One was actually a poncho and it had been the primitive colours that had attracted her. She now wore the other, a dramatic red cape with a long stole that she flung over her shoulder to make the warm nest over her ears and chin. She felt glad of its protection. An icy wind was hissing through the trees in the Crescent and Bessie was thankful that she was wearing her high boots over her trousers.

There was a long queue for the taxis outside the Central. A London train must have come in. Bessie skirted the queue and saw over beside the wall, the group of winos and down-and-outs crouched over the gratings. Much to her disappointment, there was no sign of Bev. Plucking up courage, she approached the group and, addressing the only female present, asked if she knew somebody called Bev and described her friend. The woman looked like the absolute dregs of humanity. Her skin was as coarse as old leather, her eyes sunken and inflamed, her teeth brown stumps. Her head and body were covered in a hotchpotch of shawls and scarves and a man's long raincoat tied in the middle with string. She stank with a mixture of alcohol and Bessie daren't think what else.

'I might have seen her. I've an awful memory, hen. It's the cold that does it. If I had the price of a bottle of whisky to warm me up, it might help.'

Bessie hesitated, then took the plunge.

'Here.' She gave the woman some money. 'Now tell me about Bev. Where is she?'

The woman looked positively gleeful. Bessie thought she was going to do a dance.

'The wee blondie? Skippered down in London? Then came back to do a bit of waitressing? Aye, she was here and we had a rare chat. Nice lassie. She shared a bottle with me. A real stoater, it was. By Christ, it was a lot better than the jake I'd been drinking before she came.'

'Where is she?' Bessie was getting desperate.

'I think you might find her by the Anderson bus station, hen.'

'Thank you.'

Rather than wait in the queue at the taxi rank, Bessie began to half walk, half run in the direction of the Anderson bus station. By the time she was nearing it, she was out of puff and had to slow down. Every now and again, in fact, she'd to stop to get her breath back. It was during one of these times that she noticed a car slowing down alongside her. The driver rolled down his window and beckoned her over. For an eager, hopeful, crazy moment, she thought the word had got around about her search for Bev and this was someone who had information to help her. She hurried, smiling gratefully, over to the man. But before she could ask him anything about Bev, he said, 'How much?'

She'd always had a slow-working mind, especially when it came to thinking the worst. So she just stared at the man in bewilderment for a few moments.

'Look,' the man said, 'you're not getting into the car until you name your price.'

The penny dropped, as the saying goes. And Bessie went. She ran as fast as her legs could carry her until, seeing a cruising taxi, she hailed it and sat shivering in the darkness as the cab skimmed through the city streets.

It was only when she was safely in her own home that she burst into tears of distress. Even there, she jerked with fright when she heard the doorbell ring. So upset was she, she nearly didn't answer it. The ring was repeated several times and finally she went to the door and close to it in an anxious voice asked 'Who is it?'

'It's me, Sean. I said I'd try to call up tonight, remember?'

She hadn't, with all the worry about Bev. Hastily trying to dry her eyes on the sleeve of her blouse, she opened the door.

'Bessie, what's wrong?' Sean came in and immediately took her into his arms. That set her off into another paroxysm of sobbing. Being in his arms, held tightly against his hard body, completely unnerved her.

She babbled out what had happened.

'Bessie, darling,' he said, 'what am I going to do with you?'

LI

*W*HAT ARE YOU *trying to do? Test me or something? I keep failing, so what's the point? Humiliation? All right, You're really going for the jackpot now. Sean loves me. And I love him. Oh, I do, You know I do. I love everything about him. I love his perfect body. It's so beautiful. I love to watch him. He has the grace of a tiger, smooth, effortless, powerful. I love his deep rich voice, his dark eyes. I love his hard, tight smile.*

He held me in his arms and I felt I belonged there. Oh, you don't need to tell me. I know only too well that I don't. He kissed my tears away and I became breathless with a mixture of passion and panic.

He kissed my mouth and I felt hungry for him yet oh so ashamed of myself.

The awful thing is, you see, the outward shell of me is getting older but inside, I'm as young as I ever was. I'm still the wee girl I was at home in Bearsden. As well as being that wee girl from Bearsden, I'm still the same foolish teenager. I was always concerned about the small size of my boobs. Well, here I am in my forties and still worried about my bust measurement. Granted I have more around there than I used to, but still not enough to give me as sexy a cleavage as Andrina. Except when I wear my new Wonderbra. What a find! When I look at myself in the mirror, I'm full of admiration. And yes, I'm looking at myself an awful lot these days. I know that there's no future in any relationship with Sean. At the same time, I'm nearly killing myself in my efforts to try to look as attractive as possible for him. After these ghastly aerobics classes, I literally stagger home. I'll have to give them up. Talk about murder!

I bought myself one of these electric things that are attached to the wall and from it goes a band round your waist or your hips and vibrates like mad. I staggered away from that as well. I felt every part of me, including my head, vibrating for hours afterwards.

Talking of heads reminds me of my yoga classes. I stood on my head there. Murder that was as well. And oh, the torture of not eating chocolates. I seem to be a chocaholic. I never realised it before. If I take one I have to guzzle the lot. Now I really know the struggle Bev has and how she must feel. I suppose it's the same with any addiction.

I still don't know what to do about Bev, by the way. I think she's into prostitution. She denies it. Although she admits she doesn't know any more what she does when she's drunk. She told me she woke up and found herself lying in bed beside this strange man in a filthy room in some slum or other. She was so ashamed she vowed she'd never touch a drop of booze again. That's when she came back to me. She was in an awful state, poor soul. She'd escaped in such a hurry she hadn't even stopped to look for her bra and knickers. Horrible, she said the man on the bed looked and still snoring like a pig when she left.

So Bev and I are both struggling with our addictions. Absolute torture, it is. I'm getting now that, apart from Sean, I think about nothing else except chocolates. I know it sounds ridiculous. But there you are.

And what's it all for? To make myself look younger and slimmer and more desirable. Remember how I worried about Gregory seeing me naked? Now I'm agonising about Sean seeing me.

But wait a minute, what is all this? What am I thinking of?

No, it must stop. To be perfectly accurate, it hasn't started. Not the sex part anyway. Although Sean wants it to. Bev says he's besotted with me. I can hardly credit it but he does act like somebody who is very much in love. He sends me red roses. That's never happened to me in my life before. He tells me I'm beautiful. That's a first as well. He says I'm so different from anyone else he's ever known. I'm so talented, he says. Jennifer keeps saying that's what's at the root of it. Poor Jennifer is obviously afraid that I'll turn out like her mother and start having a string of affairs. Apparently Andrina even tried to flirt with Freddie Hancock, Jennifer's boyfriend. There was a big bust-up over that. Not that Freddie had responded or encouraged Andrina or anything, Jennifer said. She blamed everything on her mother.

So why do I go on with all this charade of exercising and dieting and spending a fortune on beauty parlours? I've become a sucker for creams and potions and pills that claim to cure wrinkles and bags under the eyes and generally reverse the ageing process.

Sean tells me he loves me just as I am. I want to believe him. I do believe him.

He says I'm every inch a woman. He says I've such good bone structure and such a good clear smooth skin. He had me looking in the mirror the other day. He actually stood beside me and said, Look at yourself. Look at your lively hair. I had to laugh at that. Lively hair! Look at your sweet face. Look at your shapely, womanly body. Shapely, womanly body! I like that. And do you know, as I looked at myself, I began to think — well, I really don't look so bad for a woman of my age.

You glow, he said. I liked that too. I knew where the glow comes from, of course. It's the love I have for him lighting up my body, my skin, my eyes, my life.

Just now and again, only occasionally, very tentatively, I wonder if, after all, it could be possible for Sean and I to have an affair. Oh, I don't mean anything serious or permanent. Nothing will change the difference in our ages. But I'm a free agent and so is he. Would it be so bad to give physical expression to our love? Just for a little while?

LII

IN ONE WAY at least it had been a relief to leave Bessie's flat. Jennifer loved Bessie dearly and she realised that Bessie had the right to live how she liked. However, it was a source of some exasperation how untidy Bessie was and how she got paint over everything. Maybe it was because Jennifer had been brought up in Andrina's immaculate flat that made her yearn for cleanliness and order. She had certainly yearned for a home like that during her nightmare on the streets. She had also been accustomed to seeing her mother always so perfectly turned out and kept being shocked by Bessie's dishevelled state. Bessie often wiped her paint-stained hands on her clothes and it didn't make a bit of difference if she didn't happen to be wearing one of the smocks that Jennifer had persuaded her to buy. Bessie just wiped her hands on whatever she happened to be wearing. When she got paint on her hair, she looked like a human rainbow.

'Bessie!' Jennifer would repeat patiently, 'why don't you use your paint rag?'

But Bessie was always losing paint rags.

On the other hand, it had become increasingly difficult to be civil to Andrina after the dinner party for Freddie. She ought to have known, of course. Actually she had known. She'd said to Freddie days beforehand, 'My mother's a very attractive woman.'

'Yes, I remember,' Freddie said. 'Once seen, never forgotten.'

'She's sex mad as well.'

'Really?' Freddie laughed. 'Well, that's interesting. I'm beginning to look forward to this dinner.'

'It's not funny.'

'Why the worried face? You don't think . . . She's not really likely to make a play for me, surely?'

'Would you like to take a bet on it?'

'You can't mean it, Jennifer. Apart from anything else, she knows you and I are serious, doesn't she?'

'Oh yes. I've told her often enough. But believe me, that won't make one bit of difference to my mother.'

'Darling, forgive me for laughing but honestly, you've no need to worry. I'd prefer you to your mother any day. You're the one I love and want to marry, not your mother. I don't care if she does a striptease or goes down on her knees and pleads with me to go to bed with her — it's not on. I can't see it happening, though. I think maybe you're overestimating my charisma.'

As it turned out, her mother hadn't actually done a striptease but she'd done just about everything else. Jennifer had never been so embarrassed in her life. Andrina had worn a low-cut blouse and a long skirt with a slit up one side almost to her hip. She'd had her hair done and her face beautifully made up. She'd cooked a meal more fit for a king than a schoolteacher. She'd even produced a bottle of champagne. And an expensive box of Belgian chocolates. Freddie had been overcome with it all. Or so it seemed to Jennifer at the time. The intensity of his appreciation had been only too obvious. He not only praised the meal to the highest heavens, he praised Andrina.

She blossomed and thrived on every word. She fluttered her lashes and smiled her shy sideways smile at him. She leaned over him as she plied him with more champagne and showed far too much bosom. She gazed up at him with round starry eyes as he said goodbye and told him she'd enjoyed his company *so* much.

Jennifer had been furious.

'But . . . but . . . I don't understand, dear.' Andrina had looked genuinely taken aback. 'I thought everything went perfectly. I thought you'd be pleased. I tried so hard.'

'Yes, you did, didn't you?'

'Well, then, what's wrong? Why are you angry with me?'

Later Jennifer had to concede that what Bessie said was probably true. Andrina couldn't help it. It was just the way she was. All the same, it was very hard to bear. It was, in fact, bloody infuriating. The quicker she was married and living permanently in Freddie's flat the better. She was living more there than in Monteith Row as it was.

The flat needed redecorating and once they decided that the date for the wedding was to be sooner than later, they set to with a will to transform the place. She hardly took time to go and buy her white dress. Her mother was getting her outfit made and was always darting off to the dressmaker's and enthusing about the lovely material and the perfect fit.

Jennifer did see to the invitations. Her mother hadn't wanted her to invite Bernard but she'd insisted. Apart from the argument about Bernard, Andrina was in seventh heaven organising everything, although she did take a lot of persuading to accept Jennifer's wish that Bessie and Bev had to be her matrons of honour, and the O'Maley children bridesmaids and pages. However, she eventually got together with Bridie and they agreed that the girls should wear pale blue dresses with tartan sashes. The pages, Andrina enthused, would look wonderful in tartan trousers and waistcoats.

She had kept voicing her worries about the O'Maley young people.

'These O'Maley children are a bit wild, don't you think, dear? Do you think they'll be able to behave properly?'

She wasn't too concerned about Bessie. 'I'll see that she wears something pretty,' she said. And: 'Are you sure Bev will remain sober long enough to walk up the aisle with you?' she worried.

'They'll all be fine.' Impatiently Jennifer brushed aside all her mother's criticisms. She was looking forward to moving into a home of her very own far more than the wedding. Her home *and* Freddie's, of course. She could hardly wait. Freddie was her best friend as well as her lover. They went walking in Botanic Gardens arm in arm, chatting all the time. They went shopping together. He was looking forward to the actual wedding more than she was.

'All that lovely grub your mother's providing! I can't wait.'

'Oh, I see,' Jennifer said, half in fun. 'My mother is the big attraction of the wedding day, not me.'

269

'Oh sure.' Freddie gently pulled her into his arms. 'And why do you think I'm marrying you? Because you've a mother who's a good cook?'

She rested her head against his chest.

'You won't ever let her come between us, will you?'

'Darling, how could I? I admire you. I adore you. What's more, I'd trust you with my life. Forgive me for saying this, darling, but I wouldn't trust your mother one inch – not as far as any kind of relationship is concerned.'

'I suppose she's a bit pathetic, really,' Jennifer conceded.

'I've more mature pupils in Bearsden Academy.'

'What do you bet she'll try her best to outshine me on my wedding day?'

'Do you care?'

Jennifer thought for a moment.

'Not really. As long as we're happy. Oh Freddie, the flat's lovely now, isn't it?'

'I can't wait to carry you over the threshold.'

She laughed.

'I've been over the threshold on my own two feet a hundred times already.'

Although it was a white wedding, it was to be a quiet affair. There weren't many relations on either side. As far as friends were concerned, the O'Maley brothers, their wives and families were invited. A few schoolteacher friends of Freddie, and Bessie and Bev. That was about all. Except, of course, Daisy and her husband, Nigel. Jennifer had invited them for Bessie's sake in the hope it would result in a reconciliation.

Jennifer had hesitated about inviting Sean O'Maley because, as she said to Bev, 'I'm worried about Bessie becoming too fond of him and then getting hurt.'

'You can't invite all the other O'Maleys including his mum and dad and his Uncle Bernard, and not him. Don't be daft.'

Jennifer sighed.

'I think the world of Bessie – I hope she knows what she's doing.'

'If she wants to risk getting hurt, that's her decision. Anyway, I think she can handle it.'

'All right. I'll send him an invitation with the rest. Or at least my mother will. She's in her element just now. She's even doing all the catering, you know. She's already got her freezer and Bessie's stacked with goodies.'

'Of course I know it,' Bev groaned. 'I'm dying to get my teeth into some of that stuff she's cooked, but it's as much as my life's worth to touch it.'

'I'm pleasantly surprised at Bessie's interest in getting a new outfit for herself.'

'Oh yes?' Bev laughed. 'Let me tell you our Bessie is a reformed character. After every painting session, she has a bath and washes her hair and changes her clothes just in case . . .'

'Just in case what?'

'Just in case Sean arrives on the doorstep unexpectedly, of course.'

'Poor Bessie.'

'Poor Bessie nothing! She's got a gorgeous young boyfriend. What's poor about that?'

'It's terrible. I wonder if I should talk to her,' Jennifer murmured half to herself.

'Don't you dare!' Bev said. 'Just you concentrate on your own man. It's "poor Bev" you should be saying. I'm the only one who hasn't got a man.'

'If you could just keep off the drink, Bev. It's ruining your looks.'

'I'll do my best to keep sober at your wedding anyway, hen. I've treated myself to a dress and coat. I won't let you down, don't worry. I wonder what our Andrina is going to wear. She's promised to get a wee suit made. Have you seen it yet?'

'No, I haven't been over to Monteith Row for ages. I can hardly bear to leave Freddie for a minute. Oh Bev, he's so good to me. I enjoy his company so much. He makes me feel good about myself too. I know I'm not beautiful like Mummy but he makes me feel beautiful.'

'How is she, by the way?'

'Oh, she's busy getting everything ready for the reception and she's quite happy for me to keep out of her way. I'm going over to Daddy's place a couple of days before the wedding to relax and of course Daddy will bring me to the church and give me away.'

'I wonder what Bernard's new wife is like. That was a quiet affair. Bridie told me that even his brothers weren't there. It was just at a registry office and Sean and Sally as witnesses.'

'Oh well, the whole O'Maley family can have a get-together at my wedding. Except the Tony one. I've never met him. He's always away on tour with his band. I think Bridie said he's based in Liverpool now. Bridie says I'm better not knowing him. He's pretty awful, apparently. She says her husband, Frank, is definitely the best of the bunch.'

'Well, she would. I thought Sean's dad was very nice. But that old mother-in-law of Michael's spoiled Bridie's party, remember that night?'

Jennifer laughed.

'I know. I wasn't going to invite her but Bridie said Michael wouldn't leave her out there in the cottage by herself. He's awful good to her. So I thought – och, why not? So they're all coming. A good job the house at Monteith Row has big rooms.'

'Here,' Bev said, 'something's just occurred to me. I'd better warn Bessie.'

'About her and Sean, you mean? Oh, for goodness sake, yes. If his mother and father notice anything between them, they'll not be exactly pleased, will they?'

'No, not exactly. Not that it's any of their business. But we don't want any trouble or ill-feeling on your wedding day, hen.'

LIII

BESSIE HAD TO put her foot down when a drunken Bev brought a man to the house.

'Don't look so bloody shocked,' Bev sneered. 'You bring your man in so why shouldn't I?'

Bessie ignored Bev and addressed the man, who was perfectly sober and obviously just a punter Bev had picked up.

'This is my home. Bev only lodges here. Would you please leave.'

The man shrugged and left without saying anything. Bev was furious. She staggered after Bessie into the kitchen.

'What do you think you're playing at? Who do you think you are – Saint Bessie? You lost me a couple of tenners there.'

'So you *are* on the game?'

'Never you mind what I'm on. I pay my keep, don't I? I can't get a regular job. How am I supposed to live?'

'You've had several jobs and lost them through drink. And don't try to shift the blame on to me for charging you for your keep. You pay me a mere pittance, Bev, and you know it. Even if you were my sister and we were sharing a home, you'd have to pay your share.'

'OK. OK. I'm paying my share. But where I get the money is my business.'

'Not when you start bringing men home and using this place as a brothel. Apart from anything else, that man could have turned nasty.'

She made a pot of coffee and set out cups. 'Here, drink this and try to sober up.'

'I don't want your bloody coffee. That's all I ever get from you. Coffee and lectures. Lectures and coffee.'

'Just get it down, Bev. We'll talk some more when you're sober.'

'Get it down yourself.' Suddenly she grabbed the cup of coffee and flung it at Bessie. Bessie cried out as the boiling hot liquid splashed her neck and soaked into her jersey. Hastily she pulled the jersey off and tossed it aside before dashing to the sink and splashing herself with cold water.

'You're not my bloody sister, or my mother, or my anything,' Bev slurred. 'You're nothing but a pain in the arse. I'm going out for a drink.'

'The pubs are shut. Go through to your bed.'

'Who said anything about pubs?' She waggled a finger. 'I know places and I know people.

'I know places and I know people,' she mumbled again. She got up, knocking her chair over, and made for the door. Bessie watched helplessly as she disappeared out to the hall. Then there was a thud and when Bessie went out Bev was lying unconscious near the front door. It took all her strength to drag her into the bedroom and haul her up on to the bed. It wasn't that Bev was a big heavy woman. Far from it: she seemed to have been getting smaller and more emaciated-looking recently. Nevertheless, Bessie wasn't a big woman either and she certainly wasn't muscular or strong. After struggling to undress Bev, and covering her with the duvet, Bessie felt over-strained and exhausted. It wasn't the first time she'd had to put Bev to bed, but bringing the man to the house was really too much. Something had to be done. But what? She'd read somewhere that nobody can help alcoholics. They have to hit rock bottom before they can help themselves and that's the only thing that works. It was beginning to look as if by providing shelter and supportive friendship, she was only postponing the day when Bev would be forced to do something permanent to help herself. Bev couldn't be frogmarched to AA. Bev couldn't be forced to do anything.

Yet, how could she abandon Bev? How could she put her out on the streets? She couldn't be so cruel. Nor could she live with the guilt of such action. Then other thoughts began itching at her mind. Thoughts she didn't want to face.

Perhaps this was a case of having to be cruel to be kind.

Perhaps she was just too afraid of the guilt she would feel. For the rest of the night she struggled to try and think things through and find out what was right, and what was the best thing to do for Bev's sake. She knew in her heart that she should put Bev out to find her own salvation. She had tried everything else.

The next day, as usual, Bev didn't remember a thing about what happened. Sitting at breakfast together, Bev was chatting away quite the thing. She'd been a bit bleary-eyed and confused at first but after she'd had a couple of mugs of tea and she'd been persuaded to eat some cereal, she became her usual chirpy self. Eventually she said, 'What's that red mark on your neck, hen?'

'You threw a boiling hot cup of coffee at me last night. I was lucky I was wearing a thick jersey or it might have been worse.'

There was silence for a long minute. When she was sober, Bev never argued about what she'd done when she was drunk. She always took Bessie's word for it.

'I'm awful sorry, hen. You're the last person I'd want to hurt. You know that. I swear to you. I'll never touch another drop of alcohol as long as I live.'

'Oh, Bev, how many times have you said that?'

'This time I mean it. I definitely mean it.'

'Another thing – last night you brought a man back here.'

Bev looked evasive.

'I'd clicked, had I? About time I had a boyfriend.'

'This was a punter, Bev. Now, I must make this absolutely clear. I can't have you using this place for prostitution.'

'Oh God . . .' Bev put her hand to her eyes. 'I'm sorry, hen. It won't happen again. I promise you. That'll never happen again.'

It was then that Bessie knew she should have said – No, it won't happen again because I want you to pack up and leave here right now. But she couldn't. Instead she said,

'If you'd just avoid taking that first drink, Bev.'

'I told you, hen. I'll never touch another drop.'

'Not even at Jennifer's wedding?'

'Especially not at Jennifer's wedding. You and Jennifer are

my best mates. The last thing I want to do is spoil the wedding for either of you. I know how you're looking forward to it as well. Then she added half to herself, 'I'll just keep thinking it's for your sake and Jennifer's sake . . .'

'For your own sake, Bev. It's for your own sake.'

'Aye, OK, hen.'

'And never mind thinking it's for the rest of your life. Just concentrate on today. It's just one day you're to worry about. Every morning when you get up, tell yourself – I've only to make sure I don't take that first drink *today*.'

'All I have to do,' Bev sighed. 'If only it was as easy as that.'

'What's the alternative? Think of that. Think of what you're doing to yourself.'

'It's what I'm doing to you, hen, that's what worries me. I'm so sorry.'

'That was yesterday. Today is what we must concentrate on.'

Bev nodded. 'Is Sean coming today?' she asked.

'I'm not sure. It depends if he's working in Glasgow or further afield.'

'Don't worry. If he does come, I'll keep out of your way.'

'You don't need to do that. We don't go to bed or anything.' Bev raised a brow.

'Why not? You're obviously crazy about each other.'

'You know why not.'

'Bessie, age doesn't matter these days.'

'Well, it should. He could get a young woman. Why should he lumber himself with me?'

'Because you're a lovely person and because he loves you.'

'Oh Bev, what am I going to do?'

'You're going to go to bed with him for a start and enjoy a bit of real loving. Don't you want to?'

'Of course I want to.'

'Well then. You talk to me about living just for the day. Why don't you take your own advice? Just think of today. Enjoy it and to hell with tomorrow.'

Bessie laughed as she got up and started clearing the table.

'That wasn't exactly the advice I gave you.'

Bev got up then.

'Leave these. I'll wash up. Along you go to your studio. I'll come through in a wee while and see how you're getting on.'

Bessie's smile still clung to her face but she was suddenly knotted with frustration and exasperation. This couldn't go on. She could stand everything else except interference and lack of freedom to work in peace. To have Bev filling the studio with cigarette smoke and cheeky chatter made it impossible to work.

No, something would definitely have to be done.

LIV

' "SHALL I COMPARE thee to a Summer's day?
     Thou art more lovely and more temperate." '

'I didn't know you read Shakespeare.' Bessie struggled to appear casual as she made a pot of coffee.

Sean was lounging back in a chair watching her.

'I remember that sonnet from school.'

'You said the lines beautifully.'

'I meant them. You are lovely.'

'Oh Sean . . .'

'And I love you.'

'I keep telling you, you mustn't talk like that.'

'And you love me. You do, don't you?'

She couldn't lie to him.

'Yes, I do.'

'Well then . . .'

'It's because I love you that I don't think we should take our relationship any further. We're loving friends just now. That means you've no serious commitment to me. You're free to meet a younger woman, somebody a lot more suitable.'

'We've already gone over all this. I don't want a younger woman. I just want you. Bessie, Bessie, how many times must I tell you? There's nobody like you in the whole world. You're beautiful, you're gentle, you're talented, you're loving, you're caring and far too generous for your own good. I want to look after you.'

She stood helplessly gazing at him, the coffee pot forgotten in her hand. He came over to her, took it from her and put it on the table. Then he gathered her into his arms.

'Bessie, my dearest love. You mean more to me than anything or anyone else in the world.'

He had said all this before in letters. Everywhere he went he sent her the most beautiful love letters. She had them hidden away in her dressing-table drawer. Every night before she went to bed she read and re-read every one. Some of them started – 'Beloved'. Others 'Dearest' or 'My Dearest Love' or 'My Lovely Girl'.

Girl! She could have wept at that. Oh, to be a girl again for him. She remembered her girlhood and realised now that she had been lovely then. Fair haired, with grey-blue eyes, a clear, smooth skin and a slim figure. She'd told Sean this with sadness and regret in her voice and he'd said,

'But darling, you're still the same girl – in looks as well as in everything else.'

How kind he was. How she wished what he said was true. Perhaps she did look that lovely girl to him because looking at her through the eyes of love he was unable to see clearly or to think realistically. But oh, how wonderful it was to be in his arms, to be made to feel safe, and loved, and beautiful! As she surrendered to his kiss, she allowed herself to be transported to that other rose-tinted world. She allowed herself to believe in it, to savour it, to treasure it. Just for tonight.

He carried her through to the bedroom and, unable to face the harsh reality of the light, she pleaded with him not to switch it on. Even so, she clutched her arms across her body in case, by some grey shadow of the moon flitting through the window, he might see her scars and imperfections.

Gently he prised aside her arms and kissed every part of her until she relaxed and was able to stroke him and kiss him in return. He kept telling her how beautiful she was –

When all the time he was the beautiful one.

As she sank deeper and deeper into physical rapture, even as she allowed waves of it to completely engulf her, the certainty remained that what was happening was wrong. She was only enjoying a few moments of love. It was a self-indulgence; a selfish act from which no good could come.

Just this once, she kept telling herself. She told him how much she loved him. His smooth dark hair, his dark, thoughtful eyes, his hard taut features. The steely sinews of his neck, his powerful chest and arms. His firm, flat abdomen and narrow hips, his long strong legs. She kissed and caressed every part of him.

They were in a daze afterwards. Forgetting the coffee, forgetting that Bev had come in and was singing to herself in the kitchen, they said goodnight. They didn't even arrange when they'd see each other again.

'Well then,' Bev said when she joined her in the kitchen. 'So you've taken the plunge at last. How was it, eh? Wonderful, I'll bet. Your eyes are shining, hen.'

Bessie flopped down on to the nearest chair.

'Have I gone mad or something?' she asked.

'Mad with happiness, by the looks of you. I'm hell of a jealous. Fancy landing a gorgeous guy like that.'

'Why is my life always so complicated and difficult, I wonder.'

'Here, hen, I only wish my life could have a complication like him.'

'Nothing ever turns out as I expect.'

'Stop moaning, for God's sake. Just think yourself damned lucky.'

Bessie took a deep breath.

'Yes, I suppose things could be worse.'

'A lot worse. Well?'

'Well what?'

'Haven't you noticed anything about me?'

'Oh Bev, you haven't had a drink.' Bessie went over and hugged her friend. 'Good for you.'

'Do you know where I was earlier on?'

'Where?'

'The reading room of the Mitchell Library, of all places. I wanted peace and quiet to think but I couldn't go to the park in case I met some of my drinking pals and was tempted. So I sat in the Mitchell Library leafing through newspapers and magazines, and thinking. I'm forty and what have I done with my life? I haven't even any weans. You've been lucky, Bessie. You've been married and you've got a daughter and one of these days you'll have grandchildren.'

'I'm not so sure about the grandchildren,' Bessie sighed. 'Daisy's been pregnant to Nigel already and she had an abortion. She doesn't want any children, she says. As far as marriage is concerned, I wasted over twenty years of my life tied to the wrong man.'

'At least you've done something now. You've made your mark, hen. People know your name and respect it. And now you *have* got the right man.'

'Oh Bev, I love him.'

'I know you do, hen. And he loves you.'

'It's so wonderful. I still can't believe it. It's like something I've dreamed up.'

'Believe it, hen, and be happy.'

Bessie nodded.

'Yes, I should treasure every moment and be thankful, shouldn't I?'

'Well, I would if I were you. By God, just give me the chance of a decent, loving fella . . .'

'Your chance will come, Bev. Maybe you'll meet somebody nice at the wedding.'

'I doubt it. As far as I can gather, most of the guys invited to the do are married.'

'You never know, maybe some of Freddie's schoolteacher friends. Anyway, there'll be other times and other places.'

'Does Jennifer know you've turned veggie? Or Andrina? I suppose she's the one who'd better know.'

'I still eat fish. But yes, I did mention it to Andrina. And it'll be OK. She's going to make a broccoli quiche and a lentil dish. I can't remember what she called it.'

'Sounds horrible.'

'No, you'd be surprised. I really enjoy vegetarian dishes now and they make me feel so much better. I've lost a bit of weight as well.'

'That's not with what you eat, hen. That's all this mad exercising you do. A treadmill! What next?'

'It was in a sale at the sports shop.'

'You're getting to be a bloody masochist. That exercise bike was bad enough but weights, and that vibrating thing, and now this . . . I know why you're doing it, hen, but you've no need to be pushing yourself so much. He'd love you anyway. He loves you for yourself. I'm sure he'll have told you that.'

He had, of course. But the self-image that she'd held or been conditioned to hold for so many years couldn't be so easily ignored or changed. Her past was stirred up when Peter called unexpectedly. She had been enjoying Satchmo singing 'What a Wonderful World' on her record player and he'd really put a damper on it. He'd come to ask her, not to return 'home' exactly, but to get together again. On his terms, of course. All would be forgiven. He would sell his flat and come to live with her in the West End. She would be allowed to continue with her painting as long as she kept it to regular hours – say two hours a day while he was at work. She must forget about it though, switch off, the moment she stepped out of her studio.

He'd give her a little more housekeeping money, he assured her magnanimously. Things would be much easier for her than they used to be, he promised.

Of course, he said, the place would have to be kept a lot better than this. He wasn't used to living like a tramp or a gypsy. In disgust he looked round the untidy sitting room with its coloured bean bags and piles of magazines, books, records and tapes strewn around on the floor. Not to mention its trailing greenery. Somehow her plants always got out of hand and spread upwards, outwards and sideways in riotous profusion. She even had a large nude painting on the wall but Peter tried to avoid looking at that.

She stared at him. She thought of all the years he'd whittled away at her self-confidence and she could have wept.

'Peter,' she said as calmly as she could, 'I want a divorce.'

He stared at her in amazement.

'What do you mean, you want a divorce?'

'Ask my lawyer,' she said, getting up and beckoning him towards the door.

'You've showed yourself in your true colours here.' His voice betrayed a quiver of disappointment. 'This place is like a tip. I take a pride in myself and my home. You obviously have no idea what pride and decency mean.'

'Goodbye, Peter.'

'Divorce or not, you'll not get a penny out of me.'

She suddenly saw him as a pathetic old man, and felt sorry for him.

'I don't want anything from you. Nothing at all.'

They were in the hall now and she was praying to be free of him, never to see his sour, misery-laden face again. Yet, at the same time, sorry for his wasted years as well as her own. Maybe with someone more like himself, someone more conventional, he could have been a different and happier man. She wanted to say that she was sorry but knew it was no use.

'Goodbye,' she repeated firmly and closed the door.

LV

SEEING PETER AGAIN and talking to him – or rather listening to him – had made Bessie appreciate her new life all the more. Leaving Peter had been a rebirth. She had started to find her true self from the day she'd walked out of his house.

In galleries and museums she took pleasure in touching things, feeling the curves of statues, the texture of tapestries. She walked down Byres Road at midnight and soaked up the buzz of lights and cars going by, and the noise of people enjoying themselves. She often worked by spotlight until one in the morning. Then because she had been so absorbed, she'd forget what time it was. She'd go out to the shops and wonder why they were all shut. Then she'd laugh at herself. Life was good. She felt herself open up like a flower in the sun. Her life with Peter seemed like a bad dream now.

Peter had always made her out to be stupid but he had taken her for a right fool if he thought she didn't know the real reason he'd called at her flat. She had established herself as not only a good painter but a painter who could make money. It was the money that had attracted Peter, the money he wanted, not her.

Sean wanted her for herself. She knew that from the honest, the sensitive as well as the passionate way he treated her. She knew by the patient way he kept building up her self-confidence. She would become agitated and reluctant to allow him to keep the light on while they made love. She would try to cover herself up and hide her nakedness. She would plead with him, 'Don't look, please don't.' He would gently take the covers away and say, 'For goodness sake, you're fine. You're lovely. Why should you be so embarrassed? I like you for what you are. I find you attractive the way you are.'

'I just can't see myself as attractive.'

'What do I see, Bessie? I'll tell you. I see a person who is slim, has a good figure. A delightful person who has blonde bubbly hair. You're a bit older than me, but you look lovely. Yes, OK, if I want to be picky, you've got small flaws here and there. You're not perfect but who is? But Bessie, believe me, you are an attractive person.'

When he was away from Glasgow on a job, he wrote to her as often as he could. The first thing he did when he returned to the city was come and see her. Each time was like the first time. Seeing each other, speaking to each other, making love, was always an unbelievable delight, a magic journey of discovery. She was still shy but gradually she began to think – Yes, Sean is right, I don't look so bad. But more important than how she looked was how Sean made her believe she, as a person, was *worthwhile*. She *mattered*. She was worthwhile as a person *in her own right*.

It was incredible. Deep down she began to really believe it. 'You look great,' he enthused. And her shoulders went back. And her head balanced with easy dignity on a straight back.

She went to Meeting and just sat feeling grateful for being given the gift of love. Yet afraid to pray in case God would remind her that she was doing wrong. Yet could loving, and being loved, be wrong? She wanted to ask somebody's advice but didn't know who or how. After Meeting finished she wanted to cling on to someone's hand and say, Please help me and advise me. Instead she just shook hands and smiled around. And said nothing.

Then Sean asked her to marry him as soon as her divorce came through. He wanted to leave his parents' cottage and get a place of his own. He wanted her to sell the Botanic Crescent flat, and come to live with him as his wife.

Oh, if only she could. Oh, heaven on earth. She asked him if they couldn't just go on as they were – taking one day at a time, just living for the day. He said 'no'. He loved her and wanted her as his wife. He wanted to start planning for their future.

What future?

She timidly, apprehensively, turned an inward eye to God.

Please help me.

It was all she dared to say.

To Sean she pleaded, 'Let's leave any discussion about our future until after Jennifer's wedding. My mind's full of all the excitement and preparations for that just now.' Reluctantly he agreed. She discovered, however, that he'd been forced to say something to his family. They'd questioned him about his frequent visits to Botanic Crescent until eventually he'd admitted that he not only loved Bessie, but had asked her to marry him. They were horrified, as Bessie had known they would be. Bernard had promptly sent him on a job to London but Sean told her not to worry, he'd be back in plenty of time for Jennifer's wedding.

Then, of course, Bernard no doubt had been asked to visit her and sort things out, because he knew her better than Sean's parents and he'd been to her flat before.

She knew the moment she saw his big body framed in her doorway that he'd come about her relationship with Sean. She allowed him to push past her and stride through to the kitchen. Heart in mouth, she followed him. He turned on her with hard, angry eyes.

'What the hell do you think you're playing at?'

'If you're referring to my relationship with Sean, I think that's my business.'

'The hell it is! He's only a boy. His mother and father want something better for him than this. He deserves something better than this. They blame me, of course, for sending him on the job at your bloody exhibition. I blame myself. But it's the last thing any of us would have thought might happen.'

'We love each other.'

'Aw, don't give me that shit. He doesn't know what love is. He's had no experience of love, or life, or anything. OK, as an older woman, you can give him a bit of experience, but that's all. Even that has a touch of obscenity about it. You're the same as his mother – fair, fat and forty.'

She flushed and fought to hold back her tears.

'Would you please leave?'

'OK. I'll go but I'm warning you, Bessie. You're not going to be allowed to ruin Sean's life.'

After he'd gone and she was left standing in the empty silence of the kitchen, the tears came. She felt as if, unexpectedly, her life had collapsed about her like a pack of cards.

By the time Bev came back from visiting Freddie's flat where she'd been helping him and Jennifer to paper their hall, Bessie was quietly composed. She was sitting drinking a cup of tea when Bev entered the kitchen.

'Oh good, is that tea on the go, hen. I could do with a cup. The love-birds had me working like a slave over in Roxburgh Street. I was up and down that ladder like a bloody yo-yo.' She poured herself a cup of tea and sat down opposite Bessie at the table. It was then that she noticed Bessie's red-rimmed eyes.

'Have you been crying?'

'You could say that.'

'What's up, hen? What's happened?'

Bessie took a deep breath.

'Oh, nothing that I didn't expect.'

'How do you mean?'

'His family found out and are on the warpath.'

'Aw to hell with them!'

'Bernard arrived as their spokesman.'

'Christ, I know he can be a great guy but I've always said I wouldn't like to cross him. I can just imagine what it must have been like, but don't let him or any of them get you down and spoil things between you and Sean.'

Bessie nodded, then took another mouthful of tea.

'Sean and I are going to talk things over after the wedding.'

'God, they'll all be at the wedding!'

'I know. I wish they hadn't known until afterwards. It's going to be awkward. To put it mildly.'

'For God's sake, remember it's supposed to be Jennifer's happy day. Try not to cause any trouble and spoil things for her.'

That brought Bessie to life.

'What?' she cried out angrily. 'Me cause trouble for Jennifer? That's the last thing I want to do. If there's going to be any trouble, it certainly won't be caused by me.'

You're a fine one to talk, she thought, but managed, with great difficulty, to hold her tongue.

LVI

ANDRINA KEPT CHANGING her mind about what to wear at the wedding. She had shown a book of patterns and sample materials to Bessie, and Bessie had suggested one of the soft pastel florals. Bessie also suggested a suit or a long-sleeved jacket over a dress.

'For pity's sake, Andrina, whatever you do, don't go showing too much leg or bosom. You'll just embarrass Jennifer.'

'What does Jennifer know about style, Bessie? Anyway, she's so enamoured and completely carried away with that flat she's hardly taken any interest in what she's going to wear herself. Honestly, the way she goes on about that place!'

'Oh well, after being homeless and living in the awful conditions she did, I suppose it's sheer heaven having a place of her own. Let her enjoy it.'

'Of course! You know me, I'd never dream of interfering. No, I'm letting her go her own way. But honestly, Bessie, I shudder to think what kind of wedding she would have if it wasn't for me. Something like Bernard's latest, I suppose. Did you hear that he didn't even have his brothers there? And heaven knows what kind of meal they had.'

'Bernard was here the other day.'

Andrina looked intrigued.

'Really?'

'Trying to warn me off Sean.'

'What a cheek! It's none of his business. I hope you told him so.'

'Yes, I did. But of course, it's understandable in a way. Sean is his nephew.'

'That doesn't mean to say he can run Sean's life. Or yours. Fancy him, of all people, telling you or anyone who they should or shouldn't have sex with. He'd have sex with anything that moved.'

Bessie laughed.

'Oh Andrina . . .'

'It's true. My mother always said he was an animal and she was right.'

'Now, you don't mean that.'

'I do. I hate him.'

'You're just saying that. I can't imagine you hating anyone. But I appreciate your loyalty.'

'He probably fancies you himself and he's jealous of Sean having you.'

Bessie laughed again.

'Don't be daft.' Then she became serious again. 'No, I knew it would happen when any of Sean's family got to know about us. It's the age difference. Of course, I hadn't been prepared for a confrontation with Bernard. Sean will be furious when he finds out. I won't tell him, especially what Bernard said.'

'What did he say?'

'He suggested it was a kind of incestuous thing. He more or less said I was a carbon copy of Sean's mother. Fair, fat and forty, he said.'

'Oh, how awful.' She rushed over and hugged Bessie. 'How cruel and how untrue. You're nothing like Caroline O'Maley. And you're certainly not fat, Bessie. Oh, I do hate him. I do!'

'It's all right. I've got over it. Don't say anything about this to Jennifer. She thinks the world of him and we don't want to upset her when she's so happy just now. Promise me?'

'Yes, all right. But he makes me so mad. Arrogant bastard.'

'Andrina!' Bessie was amused rather than shocked.

'I know I'm not usually a swearing woman. But he'd make anyone forget their good manners.'

'Just calm down. I have. By the way, to change the subject, I hope that's the last lot of stuff you've brought today. My freezer can't take any more. And don't forget, everything in there has to be carted back to your place nearer the time. When, exactly?'

'The day before should do. I'll get Freddie or Robert to bring everything over in the car.'

'Are you sure you're going to manage everything, Andrina?'

'Of course, dear. I've catered for far bigger parties than this. My goodness, this is nothing – just a few people in comparison with the parties I used to have when I was married to Robert. You didn't know me then, of course. I remember our house-warming party. The place was absolutely packed and overflowing and I'd baked and prepared everything myself.' She smiled proudly. 'And that was without the help of your freezer. It's all down to being well organised. And enjoying it, of course. I enjoy cooking and baking and being a good hostess.'

Bessie studied her beautiful face with interest.

'Won't you feel any embarrassment with Robert and his wife being there?'

'Huh!' Andrina tossed her head. 'Why should I feel embarrassment? I feel nothing for him.'

'That's all right then.'

'I'm going to enjoy the whole occasion enormously.' She lowered her voice confidentially. 'She's a grumpy schoolmarm type, I believe.'

'Here, you'll never guess the other visitor I had.'

'Who, dear?'

'My millionaire. Well, he's not mine exactly. But you know who I mean. He's had a spell of convalescence back home in Williamsburgh and now he's come over again to arrange for the packing and shipping of my paintings. They've been exhibited all over Britain. And he wanted to see what I've been working on.'

'Absolutely everyone knows your name. I'm very proud to have you as my friend.'

'Oh, for goodness sake, don't be daft. I think *he* must be daft to spend so much money on my pictures. And to want to buy everything I paint doesn't strike me as being all that sensible either. I don't like being inhibited in any way and I told him – '

'What's he like?' Andrina interrupted.

'Tall. Almost as tall as Bernard, I'd say. And well made like him. But with a shock of snowy white hair and a white moustache.'

'Is he going to be around for a while?'

'A few weeks. I've invited him to dinner. I'm going to cook him a really nice meal. I feel I owe him. He's been so kind.'

'Why don't you ask him to the wedding?'

'He's never even met Jennifer. Or Freddie. He'd not know anyone there.'

'He'd know you. I expect, to a man like that, it would be quite a novelty — a homely Glasgow wedding. He'd jump at the chance.'

'But it's not up to me to invite people to Jennifer's wedding. It's up to Jennifer.'

'And to me, Bessie. I'll put an invitation card in the post for him today as soon as I get back home.'

Bessie shook her head.

'Andrina!'

'Oh, why not? He'll enjoy it. You know he will. And, as you say, he's been so good to you — paying you all that money . . .'

'Yes, all right, all right. But we'd better check with Jennifer first.'

When Bessie did mention it to Jennifer, Jennifer was delighted.

'What a wonderful idea, Bessie. Yes, definitely, you must invite him. Maybe something will come of it yet.'

'Come of what?'

Although she knew what.

'You and what's his name — Lester Morgan.'

Jennifer had always been worried about the idea of her and Sean.

'Jennifer, I've no romantic designs whatsoever on Lester Morgan.'

'I bet he fancies you. Think of it, Bessie. You'd be set up for life. No more money worries.'

'I haven't any money worries.'

'I wish I'd enough money to afford to stop working,' Andrina sighed. She'd had to go back to work part-time and vowed she'd give it up at the drop of a hat if she could.

'I'd never do that,' Bessie said. 'My painting is part of me. It *is* me. I'd die without it.'

Dreamily, Andrina closed her eyes.

'If I came into lots of money, I'd go on a world cruise. Wear lovely clothes. Dine at the captain's table. Meet handsome Italian lovers.'

'Yes, I'm sure you would,' Bessie said.

After Andrina left, Bev came in. She'd managed to get another waitressing job, this time in a small private club in a lane off Argyle Street.

Bessie noticed her friend was unusually subdued. 'Are you all right?' she asked.

Bev hesitated and then said, 'A man I used to know came into the club tonight.'

'An old flame?'

'I lived with him for a while. He used to batter me about. Threaten me with a gun sometimes.'

'Oh Bev! He didn't try anything tonight, did he?'

'Gus McCabe, his name is. He can be such a charmer when he likes, and he liked tonight. Apologised for how he'd been before. Made a whole lot of excuses. Complimented me too. Said how good I looked, etcetera. Offered to buy me a drink.'

'Oh, you didn't, Bev . . .'

'No, I didn't. But I felt like one, I can tell you.'

'Thank God you're all right.'

'Kept insisting on seeing me again. Taking me out for a meal. He wanted to be good to me to make up for everything, he said. You should have seen the smart suit he was wearing. And he'd one of those crombie coats. He always looked the gentleman, that man.'

'Oh Bev, don't listen to him. Don't go out with him. That kind never changes. He'd do the same to you again.'

'Don't worry, hen. I don't want anything to do with him. I hope to God he doesn't come back. I'm frightened of him, so I am.'

LVII

'I'D BE DELIGHTED to go to Jennifer's wedding,' Lester said. Bessie had served him a meal in the kitchen: Marks & Spencer's steak pie, potatoes and mixed veg. She'd made a Scotch trifle with lashings of sherry for pudding. He was obviously a man who relished his food. He sat with a big white napkin tucked into his collar and demolished every crumb she put before him. Afterwards he thumped his wide girth and said,

'By God, that was good!'

'I'm glad you enjoyed it,' Bessie said, rising. 'Come on through to the sitting room with your coffee.'

He rose too.

'I'll help you wash the dishes first.'

'Oh, let them wait.' Bessie dismissed the dishes with an airy wave of her hand. 'I sometimes let them pile up for a couple of days. I've far more interesting things to think about.'

'It's time you had a dishwasher, Bessie. I'll send you one for Christmas.'

She laughed.

'Don't you dare! You've done more than enough for me already.'

He followed her through to the other room, coughing loudly and thumping a fist against his chest.

'What have I done?' he asked. 'Except to have the good luck to discover a wonderfully original talent.'

'Are you all right?' Bessie asked. 'You've still got a terrible cough.'

'I'm fine. Fit as a fiddle.'

'Can you find a seat? Just put those books on to the floor.

I seem to collect so many books these days I can't find enough places to put them.'

'Why is that? Couldn't you afford books before?'

'Well, I suppose that was part of it. But even if I got books out of the library it caused a terrible fuss. Of course there was time, or rather the lack of it. I nursed my father-in-law for years. Day and night.'

'By the sound of it, it was a miracle you managed to paint.'

'I suppose it was. Looking back it certainly seems like that. I'd made a studio up in the loft and I used to shut myself up there whenever I could. Usually when my husband was in so that he could keep an eye on his father. I suppose it was a bit selfish of me.'

'Nonsense. Why shouldn't he take a turn with the old guy?'

'You're a widower, aren't you, Lester?'

'Yes. My wife died of cancer several years ago.'

'Oh, I'm sorry.'

'It was a blessed relief in the end. For her, I mean. I wanted to hang on to Alice as long as possible but she was in pain.' He shook his head. 'I miss her still. We had a good marriage.' He made an obvious effort to brighten. 'Now,' he said and took a deep swig of his coffee, 'I want to see the rest of your work. I can't wait a moment longer.'

'Oh, relax and have another cup of coffee. There's plenty of time to look at my paintings.'

'No, I insist.' He got up. 'Right now. Lead me to them.'

'You're an awful man,' she said. 'Where do you get all your energy?' He was seventy if he was a day but with a fresh complexion and a luxurious bush of hair.

'Enthusiasm, Bessie. Enthusiasm. And my love of all things beautiful. You must come out for a visit, Bessie. I've got a houseful of antiques and beautiful *objets d'art*. You'd love them too. And I could introduce you to so many interesting people. Painters, sculptors, writers.'

'Sounds wonderful.'

'Come back with me next month.'

'Can I take a rain check, as they say in your country. I've rather a lot on my mind just now, Lester. What with the wedding and everything. My friend Bev and I have to be Jennifer's matrons of honour.'

He looked puzzled and she laughed.

'That's the term used for a woman too old to be called a bridesmaid. That's what I think, anyway.'

'You're not too old for anything, Bessie,' he said gallantly.

His attention was caught by the canvases stacked around the studio and the large one propped on the easel. He went into mounting raptures of delight as he examined each one in turn.

'Bessie, Bessie, what a treasure trove. What a find! I'm going to have a wonderful exhibition of all your work over in the States. Oh, you must come. You must be there for the opening.'

Bessie felt overwhelmed, even slightly embarrassed by the extent of his excitement. She couldn't help thinking – surely they couldn't be *that* good. Her success in the art world still didn't seem quite real to her.

'I'll let you know nearer the time if I can manage.'

Lester was like a child with new toys. She could hardly drag him away from the studio. At first she said it was too cold and was making him cough, but he ignored that. It came to the point when she had to be almost rude.

'It's getting awful late, Lester, and my friend Bev will be in soon. She works nights in a club in town and she's so exhausted and footsore when she gets in, I usually run a hot bath for her and make her a cup of Horlicks.'

'Oh sure, sure. I've taken up far too much of your time. I'd better shoot off.'

'No, I've enjoyed your company. I really have, Lester. Do come again. You'll always be welcome. But I'll see you at the wedding anyway.'

'I'm really looking forward to that, Bessie. It's kind of your friend to include me.'

He gave her a bear hug before waving her goodbye and clattering down the stairs.

Bessie smiled to herself and shook her head as she shut the door and returned to the kitchen. Next time I see him, she thought, I must remember to ask what vitamins he takes. Surely there must be some magic potion he swallowed to give him such energy.

Yet he was probably right when he said his secret was enthusiasm. It was amazing what effect the power of the mind and the emotions could have on the body. Hadn't she been transformed by her love for Sean? She looked an entirely different person from the bent, careworn woman who had been married to Peter. Thinking of Sean and her love for him, she cleared the kitchen table and washed the dishes, singing happily.

Maybe Sean would like to come with her to the American exhibition. She began running Bev's bath, adding the herbal bath salts that always helped her friend's aching feet. She usually had the bath timed just right for Bev's arrival and Bev would immediately sink gratefully into it. Then they'd have a cup of Horlicks together. Horlicks helped Bev to sleep. These past few nights she had been unusually tense and anxious. Every night Bessie prayed that Bev would not be tempted to start drinking alcohol again to help her relax. Bessie knew all the excuses for Bev's bouts of drinking. This time of course there was the genuine fear of Gus McCabe.

She went to the front-room window and peered anxiously down the Crescent for Bev's small figure clipping along in her high-heeled shoes. The Crescent was deserted, the only sound the creak and rustle of the trees in the wind. Then she heard the throb-throb of a taxi as it approached the close. It stopped and Bev emerged and hurried inside the building. Bessie was waiting with the door open when she arrived.

'Are you all right?' Bessie asked as she locked up for the night.

'I'm all right now.'

Bev was trying to light a cigarette with a violently shaking hand. She dropped her handbag and its contents spilled noisily out on to the hall floor. At that Bev burst into tears.

'Don't worry,' Bessie said. 'Away through and get your bath. I'll see to this. Then we can talk.'

'Do you believe in fate, Bessie?'

'I believe in God. And I believe we should take responsibility for our own lives.'

'A lot of bloody good that is to me.' Bev's mouth twisted with bitterness. 'Or your – something of God or good in everyone. There's people that are just plain evil, Bessie, and I know better than you about that.'

LVIII

'OH SEAN.'

'Just until I find a place for us both.'

'Darling, I don't mind you staying here. You could stay here for ever as far as I'm concerned. I mean, if we were getting married, it would be silly to give up this lovely flat. Far more sensible for you to just move in here.'

'There's no "ifs" about it. We *are* going to get married.'

'It's just I didn't want to rush into things. We'd agreed to wait until after Jennifer's wedding to talk about us.'

'That was before Mother and Father and Bernard started trying to lay down the law. I'm not a child. How dare they try to interfere in my life. And worse, how dare they speak about you as they did? I couldn't stay there another minute, Bessie.'

He gave her one of his clinched smiles. 'Good job I didn't. I set upon Bernard and my father separated us just in time. Bernard's not your run-of-the-mill older guy. He'd probably have made mincemeat of me.'

'Oh Sean. I'm so sorry there's been all this trouble with your family.'

'Forget it. It's high time I left home for good anyway. Now, can I move in with you now or are you going to throw me out? It's make-up-your-mind time.'

'All right. But what we arranged still stands. There's nothing permanent until we talk everything through after the wedding's out of the way.'

'OK. OK. But if you ask me, it would be better if you gave this wedding a miss. Can you imagine what the atmosphere's going to be like? I don't care a damn but you seem so concerned about everything being perfect for Jennifer. I just can't see how it can be in the circumstances.'

'Oh dear.' Bessie's face creased with worry. 'But I can't just not go. Jennifer would be so hurt. She regards Bev and me as her best friends. We've to be her matrons of honour. And don't you dare laugh.'

'I'm not laughing, darling.' He pulled her into his arms and snuggled kisses into her neck. 'Of course, if you're a matron of honour, you must do your duty.'

'You *are* laughing!'

'Let's just be happy together and to hell with everybody else. We'll go and we'll enjoy ourselves. I hear the bride's mother is a wonderful cook.'

'Yes. That's another thing. I couldn't let Andrina down either. She's bound to need a helping hand. The reception's far too much for her to do all on her own.'

'OK. OK. I said we'll go. And we'll dance, shall we? Like this?' He grabbed her by the waist, lifted her off her feet and whisked her round and round. She screamed and laughed in protest.

'Stop it, you idiot! You're making me dizzy.'

As usual she was amazed at his easy strength. She often sensed a joy about him, a kind of celebration of his physical strength and fitness. Or maybe it was just a joyous celebration of youth. She felt saddened by the thought, but it was only a sadness for herself.

He had put her down when suddenly there was a noisy scrabbling at the front door. Somebody was in a panic to get the key in the lock. Then they recognised Bev's voice.

'Bessie!'

In a few rapid strides Sean made it to the door first. Bev fell into his arms and then reached for Bessie.

'I'm sorry, hen. I didn't mean to cause you any trouble but I was frightened he was following me. He tried to stop me in the lane when I came out the club, but I got away and then – '

'Who?' Sean interrupted as he took a quick look outside at the empty stairway. 'Describe him. I can have a word with him. I'll guarantee he won't bother you again.'

Bessie was already leading Bev through to the kitchen. Sean strode after them.

'Bev, did you hear me?'

'Yes, but he'll be well away now and anyway, I don't want to cause you any trouble, Sean. He's a right nutter, this guy.'

'I've dealt with nutters before.'

Bessie had gone pale with anxiety.

'Darling, let's just leave it to the police. Bev has told me about this man. He owns a gun.'

'I've dealt with gunmen before.'

'Oh darling, please. I couldn't bear to think of you in any danger.'

He smiled then.

'Bessie, it's my job.'

'I know, but I still can't bear to think about it.'

Bev dried her eyes and tried to sound calm.

'You can phone for the police if you like. Or I can call at the local station tomorrow morning. But it'll be his word against mine. I know this guy. I've been through this before. He's a respectable businessman from a good family and he can charm the birds off the trees. The police won't want anything to do with it. Anyway, they can't be there to protect me every night when I come out of my work, or anywhere else I am in the dark.'

'OK, Bev. We'll leave it for now,' Sean said, but he winked over at Bessie. 'Just you try to relax. Take a hot milky drink and a tablet to make you sleep.'

Bessie made her the drink and gave her the tablet before tucking her up in bed.

'You're going to be all right, Bev,' she soothed her.

'Aye, OK, hen.'

Back in the kitchen, Bessie looked at Sean.

'Do you not think I ought to have phoned the police?'

'She's probably right. It would be her word against his. What proof has she? She hasn't a mark on her.'

'It's awful to let him get away with frightening her like that and with what she's told me about what happened in the past with him, it won't stop at just frightening her.'

'He won't get away with it. I know that club. It's on

Bernard's books. Bernard's got most of the clubs and pubs in Glasgow sewn up. I'm going to work there tomorrow. Just for the one night, if I'm lucky.'

'Oh Sean.'

'Don't worry. You can come with me if you like. We can have a nice meal and relax and listen to the music. There'll be no problem. Just keep clear of Bev. Let her go out on her own.'

'But surely it would be better if I stuck close to Bev and came out arm in arm with her . . .'

'You can't be there to protect her every night, Bessie, any more than I or the police can. You just do as I tell you.'

He tried to make her laugh again. He danced with her. He tickled her. He tried to take all her clothes off in the kitchen. She did laugh and allow herself to be chased protesting through to the bedroom. But even as they made tender and passionate and dazzling love, her deep apprehension remained.

Bev was all apologies next day and made a determined effort to be cheery and brave.

'Sorry I went over the top last night. It was just he stirred up such awful memories. I don't think he'll try anything again. I could report him to the club and he'd lose his membership.'

'Is that the Hole in the Wall club?'

'Yes, do you know it, Sean?' Bev asked. 'It's very nice. Small and terribly select. No bouncers needed or anything like that.'

'Oh no,' Sean corrected, 'there's always a man checking the place and on call from the owner's other club along Argyle Street, the Clock Tower. I had to go from the Clock Tower to the Hole in the Wall once. It was just a member who'd downed one whisky too many. He was making a bit of a nuisance of himself and I persuaded him to leave in peace. Normally it's one of the quietest clubs in Glasgow.'

Bev sighed.

'I know. I was happy to get any job but especially happy to get one in that place. I felt so safe.'

Sean patted her hand.

'And you will be safe, love.'

'Oh aye,' Bev cheeked back, 'you going to turn into a fairy and wave your magic wand or something?'

'You'd be surprised what magic I can perform.'

Bessie felt so sick with worry she couldn't eat any breakfast. 'Sean wants to take me to the club for a meal tonight but you said it was a private members-only place, didn't you, Bev?'

'Oh yes, it's all these well-heeled businessmen and their wives who go. You'll not get in unless you've a special membership card. The door's always kept locked and it's only your card that can open it from the outside. It's one of these electronic things.'

Bessie felt relieved but only for a moment because Sean said, 'I know the manager. One phone call and we're in. Don't worry.'

'Are you doing this to try to nail Gus McCabe?' Bev asked him.

'Ah, so that's his name, is it?'

Sean was perfectly relaxed and smiling, lounging back on the kitchen chair, his long legs stretched out under the table.

'Oh here.' Bev looked worried now. 'Keep clear of him, for God's sake. I'd never forgive myself if you got hurt, Sean. I know how much you mean to Bessie. Oh please. I'd go back to that man rather than have anything bad happen to spoil things between you and Bessie.'

'My dear wee Bev,' Sean said, 'I'm not going to allow anything bad to happen to any of us.'

Bessie went over to the cooker, fetched the coffee pot and refilled their cups. She looked perfectly calm but inside she was repeating like a mantra,

Please, keep Sean safe. Oh please.

LIX

THE ENTRANCE HALL of the club had an air of money. It was in the crystal chandelier, the tall Chinese vase and Persian carpet. It was in the heavy oak-panelled walls of the entrance and the door of the 'Ladies Rest Room'. Inside the rest room was a crystal vase of fresh flowers. Padded coat hangers hung ready on the brass rod in the cupboard where ladies could safely leave their coats. Two deep-cushioned armchairs awaited any lady who wished to have a rest. Gold taps glistened at the washbasins, along with piles of soft handtowels. No noisy hand dryers or rough paper towels here.

Bessie hung up her cloak then examined herself in the long mirror. It was on occasions like this, when she was out with Sean, that she worried most acutely about their age difference. She lived in fear of someone mistaking her for Sean's mother. Yet as she looked at herself, she was soothed by the memory of Sean's words: 'You're beautiful. You're a worthwhile, beautiful person.' She rubbed a powder puff over her face and added a little rouge to her cheeks. There was nothing she could do about her hair. After she rejoined Sean in the entrance hall, they went through to the restaurant bar area. In one corner a man was playing lazy, sentimental music on a baby grand piano. In another there was a bar with four high stools fronting it. A couple of men were drinking and quietly talking there. Sean led Bessie over to one of the half-dozen or so tables and settled her into a chair. It was late and only one other couple was eating a meal.

'Very nice,' Bessie said, indicating the pristine white linen table-cover and napkin, and the sparkling glasses and cutlery. She had another look at the gold-framed paintings that had caught her eye when they'd first come in. 'There must be a high membership subscription for this place.'

'There's three bedrooms upstairs and a room through there with comfortable chairs and plenty of magazines and news-papers.'

Just then Bev approached them, ordering-pad and pencil at the ready. She was looking very smart in her black dress, white lace collar and apron. Her blonde hair was tied back in a white lace ribbon. She smiled.

'What are you having, folks?'

Bessie studied the menu.

'It's a bit late for me to be eating dinner. I think I'd better skip the starter. I'll have the poached Highland salmon with the lemon and lime butter sauce.'

Sean ordered Aberdeen Angus braised steak with wild mush-room and forester sauce. Then they watched Bev trip away to the nether regions of the kitchen.

'She looks quite perky again,' Sean remarked. 'She's made a quick recovery.'

'You can never tell with Bev. But she is spunky, right enough. She always seems to bounce back. As long as she doesn't start drinking again. That's what worries me.'

The food was delicious and after the coffee, Sean said, 'Come on, let's have a dance before the pianist quits for the night.'

Bessie was embarrassed.

'This isn't a dance hall. Sit down, for goodness sake.'

Sean laughed and pulled her up from her chair.

'There's enough room over by the piano for a few turns. Come on. What are you afraid of?'

It occurred to her that if she'd been sweet seventeen she would have eagerly melted into his arms and danced all night, and not have cared who saw them. However, there was no one else left in the room but themselves and the pianist, so she smiled at Sean and allowed him to take her into his arms. The pianist was playing and singing softly, 'A kiss is just a kiss, a sigh is just a sigh . . . as time goes by'. It made her feel sad and she clung to Sean and pressed her cheek as well as her body against his. She wished she could merge completely with him

– become one with him so that time would never matter any more.

'I love you,' she told him.

'And I love you, darling.' After a few minutes, he said, 'It's nearly the time Bev said she would be leaving.'

'Oh Sean . . .'

'You go to the Ladies' Room and collect your cloak. I'll meet you in the entrance hall.'

He left her standing by the piano and before she could say anything, or call to him, he'd disappeared. She murmured a quick thank you to the pianist before hurrying out to the hall. Sean was nowhere to be seen. Hastily she collected her cloak but had only waited for a moment or two when she heard a cry from outside. She rushed to open the door and peer out into the gloom of the lane. In the amber light over the doorway of the club, she saw Bev struggling with a man. Before she could move, another figure shot out of the darkness and felled the man with one blow. Immediately Bessie recognised Sean's tall, sinewy figure. She rushed and put her arm around Bev as Sean hauled the man to his feet, then doubled him up with another punch to the lower abdomen. The man sank to his knees clutching himself and groaning in agony. Sean jerked him up again and pushed his face close to the man's.

'Listen! If you go anywhere near Bev again – anywhere near her – you'll have me to reckon with, and I won't let you off so lightly next time. I know your name, I know where you work. I know where you live. Remember that.'

He flung the man to the ground and turned to Bev and Bessie, who were still clutching each other, rigid with shock.

'Come on, girls. Time to go home.'

He linked arms with them and dragged them away to where he'd parked his car. Bessie marvelled at how calm and relaxed he looked as he drove home. His arms hung loose, his hands rested easily on the wheel. He joked with Bev.

Afterwards, Bessie said 'You amaze me.'

'I'm *that* good at making love?'

They were lying in bed together and she gave him a friendly punch.

'Don't be so conceited. I was talking about earlier. It didn't seem to bother you in the slightest.'

'Oh that!'

'I was so worried. I couldn't bear anything to happen to you.'

'Darling, my job is to prevent trouble and when I can't prevent it, deal with it as quickly as possible. I'm dealing with situations like that all the time. Well, not *all* the time. There's quite a lot of variety in the job. That's what makes it so interesting.'

'I admire you so much, Sean.'

He put a finger against her lips.

'I *will* begin to sound conceited if you keep going on like that.'

'I was only joking. You're far from being conceited. Not like Bernard. No doubt he's got plenty to be conceited about. But he's very arrogant and self-assured, isn't he?'

'Bernard's a great guy. OK, I was mad at him for how he tried to break us up but he meant well and he'll come round in the end when he sees how happy we are together. He's always been good to me and the rest of the family and wanted the best for us. He's a real cool operator. You should see him in action.'

'You obviously admire him.'

'Yes, I do. But I still would never allow him to say a word against you.'

She snuggled down gratefully but as usual his hard muscular body reminded her of his youth and vigour and she felt a pang of − she was not sure what − regret, fear, sadness. To soothe away her uncertain emotions and concentrate only on love, she began to stroke his body, and kiss it. He responded with loving caresses until they were both overcome by a wild torrent of passion.

'I love you.' The words were repeated over and over again to each other and Bessie felt the emotion so genuinely and so strongly, she believed that, if necessary, she would die for him. That was one belief she had not the slightest doubt about whatsoever.

What did she matter compared with this loving, courageous, beautiful man?

The next day he had to go to a job in Edinburgh and he was up and dressed before she was awake. Normally, anxiety awoke her first so that she could slip out of bed, put on some make-up, tidy her hair and be presentable for him. This morning, however, he wakened her with a kiss and her breakfast on a tray along with a single red rose in a small vase.

'Here's the morning paper as well. I'll have to go. I'll see you tomorrow.'

'You can't manage back tonight?'

'No, it's an overnight bodyguarding job. After I see the guy safely off tomorrow afternoon, I'll come straight back here.'

She nodded then raised her face for his kiss. She felt like weeping with anxiety for his safety but managed to smile and say, 'Take care.'

'Of course. Do you think I want to miss the wedding on Saturday?'

Then he had gone.

Courage, Bessie, she told herself firmly. Then she settled back to enjoy the luxury of breakfast in bed and to read the newspaper at her leisure. It was wonderful to be treated so well, to be loved and cherished and looked after. Oh how she savoured it.

Thank you. Thank you.

LX

SEAN CAME BACK early from Edinburgh and insisted on taking her shopping.

'Shopping?' Bessie laughed. 'What on earth for?'

'Something I want you to wear at the wedding.'

'But darling, I've already bought that velvet trouser suit.'

It was in a deep royal blue, almost navy, and she loved the richness of the colour and the soft feel of the velvet. She was always taking another admiring look at it in the wardrobe. There was also a white blouse to wear with it. It had a frill at the neck, and cuffs that frilled out from each sleeve. 'I thought you liked it.'

'I do, except for one thing. I think you should wear a skirt instead of trousers.'

'There was a skirt to go with the jacket but I thought the trousers would be more suitable for me.'

'Why?'

She shrugged.

'My legs aren't as good as I'd like them to be. Trousers hide them.'

'Bessie, there isn't a thing wrong with your legs.'

She saw the tightening of his mouth and the slight hardening of his eyes and she felt afraid. Not that he would strike her or anything so dramatic. But she feared a lessening of his love.

She forced a laugh.

'All right, a skirt it shall be.'

He insisted on buying her a dress as well. It had a nipped-in waist and softly flared skirt and she was amazed at her reflection when she tried it on. Sean stood beside her at the bedroom mirror.

'Now,' he said, 'what is wrong with that figure and those

legs? If you can't see how attractive you look, there's something wrong with your eyes.'

She had to admit, at least to herself, that she did look good. Indeed she didn't look much older than Sean – if at all. She realised that her flushed cheeks, her eyes that sparkled with a kind of wonder, were all due to love, but, yes – her figure did look neat and her legs shapely. Even her ankles appeared slim in the high-heeled shoes Sean had persuaded her to buy. She had promised to wear them at the wedding.

'Meantime,' Sean said, 'we're going to christen the dress. I'm taking you out tonight for dinner.'

They decided to go for a drink first and then eat in a hotel near the Campsie hills.

Once out of the city Sean stopped the car, and hand in hand they enjoyed a walk. She took off her shoes and carried them in her free hand. At one point she teased him by running away from him. He caught up with her and they fell laughing on to the velvety soft grass. She was breathless from running and the kisses he showered her with.

'How do you fancy making love al fresco?' he said.

'Don't you dare!' Secretly she felt panic-stricken. 'Just you contain yourself until tonight when we're in bed.'

He laughed at her. 'Contain myself? I haven't heard that one before.'

It was an expression her mother had used when she was extolling her to be patient.

'Well,' Bessie's voice held a note of apology as well as embarrassment, 'I can't help thinking how near we are to the cottage where your folks live. I'd die if any of them happened to pass by and see us.'

'I've just had a thought,' Sean said. 'Why don't we call in now on our way to the hotel. We've plenty of time before dinner. I've booked a table for half-past seven.'

'Call in?' Bessie's eyes widened with shock. 'Why?'

'Well, I think it would be better to break the ice by meeting them before the wedding, instead of at it. Don't you? If we weren't going to be at the wedding it would be different. You wouldn't need to meet them at all if you didn't want to. But as things stand . . .'

She was silent for a moment. She had been worried about a confrontation at the wedding. Although she was determined to be as inoffensive and as friendly as possible and not allow anything to spoil Jennifer's day. Nevertheless . . .

'All right, darling,' she murmured uncertainly. 'Maybe it would be for the best.'

He kissed her.

'They won't eat you. I won't let them.'

She nodded, too worried now to speak.

It turned out that only Sean's father, Michael, and Martha, Sean's grandmother, were at home. Michael was restrained but polite. He made them tea and set the table with cakes and scones and strawberry jam. He seemed a caring kind of man, judging by how kind he was to his mother-in-law. He helped her out of her cushioned easy chair by the fire to a seat at the table and tucked cushions at her back. Then he made sure she had what she wanted to eat before attending to Sean and herself. His conversation was limited to offering them more tea and cakes or commenting on the weather. Martha, however, was not so circumspect.

'Well,' she suddenly announced, staring in Bessie's direction. 'I can understand now what he sees in you. You don't look like a woman in her forties. All the same there's no getting away from the fact that that's what you are.'

Sean said, 'What does age matter?'

'It matters a hell of a lot to me,' Martha bawled at him indignantly. 'I used to be a fine-looking middle-aged woman once and now look at me!'

'A likely story,' Michael said. 'I've known you for years and you've never looked any better.'

'You shut your ugly face!' Martha said. 'One thing's for sure, you never won any beauty contests.'

Bessie felt quite upset at the way the conversation was going but Sean seemed used to it – indeed they all did. Both Michael and Sean laughed and Martha continued to tuck into her scone and strawberry jam with obvious enjoyment.

Back in the car, Sean said,

'They're always like that but in actual fact, although they'd never admit it, they're very fond of one another. It's a pity my mother and my sisters weren't in. I'm sure they would have loved you, Bessie. But of course I might have known they'd be in Glasgow shopping for things for the wedding. And they'll probably make a night of it and have a meal there as well. Mother's been back and forth several times trying to get something for Gran but Gran keeps giving the thumbs down. At the same time she refuses to go with Mother to the shops.'

'I don't suppose she's able. It's a wonder she's managing to the wedding.'

'Oh, my father takes her everywhere in a wheelchair. She'll be there all right. Especially when she knows there's going to be a good feed. The old girl enjoys her grub. Father liked you, by the way. I could tell.'

Bessie wasn't so certain but her heart warmed to Sean for trying to reassure her.

They were too early for dinner so they passed the time by having a drink at the bar. There was only a young couple there and they'd set the jukebox to play a Shirley Bassey number. They were dancing to it in the non-touching way that young people had, as if they were in a dream of their own, dancing on their own. Sean and Bessie got up to dance but Sean held Bessie close in his arms.

Afterwards, in a dream of love, Sean took her hand and led her into the small, dimly lit dining room.

'You look especially beautiful tonight,' he told her.

She nearly replied it was only because in the shady room with only the soft candlelight, he couldn't see her faults. But she managed to swallow back this comment. She knew Sean didn't like her to put herself down. He had shown her, made her keenly aware, that it was only a habit, something she must now learn to discard.

She felt good. She felt beautiful. And oh, she didn't want to leave him now.

LXI

IT WAS THURSDAY and Jennifer was on her way to Bearsden to stay until the wedding. She decided to call in at Bridie O'Maley's house and check that the bridesmaids and pages hadn't caught measles or chickenpox or anything awful, and also to make sure that their clothes were ready. A plump bespectacled Bridie happily assured her that all was well and every one of them, including Frank and herself, were looking forward to the wedding with great excitement.

The only worrying note had been when Frank appeared from his writing room to join them for a cup of coffee. He was a tall man like his brothers but in every other way except his height, he wasn't like them at all. Lanky and awkward-looking with long floppy hair and a thin sensitive face, he was dressed casually in faded denims and an open-necked denim shirt.

'All set for the wedding, Jennifer?'

Her face lit up.

'Oh yes. Wait till you see our flat. We've got it exactly as we want it now. You must come to our housewarming party.'

'Great.' Frank raised his coffee cup. 'Cheers. Here's wishing you every happiness in it. I hope first of all the wedding goes well. You've made a brave mix there.'

'How do you mean?' Jennifer was taken aback and Bridie hastily cut in:

'Frank, for goodness sake, get back to your room. What's the idea coming out at this time in the morning? You usually stay out of my way until lunchtime at the earliest.'

He rolled his eyes and said to Jennifer, 'She'd lock me in there all day if I let her. A right slave-driver she is these days.'

'Well, we need every penny he can earn,' Bridie explained.

'The price of children's clothes and shoes — especially shoes — it's just terrible.'

'But what did you mean,' Jennifer persisted, 'about a brave mix?'

Frank hesitated, then said, 'As far as I'm concerned, Bessie can spend the rest of her life with Sean and the best of luck to them. Unfortunately the rest of the family, especially Bernard, isn't so enthusiastic about the affair.'

'Oh that!' Jennifer said. 'I agree with Bernard and his family, as it happens. I think Bessie is being very foolish. Not that I've anything against Sean. He's very nice but far too young for Bessie. It can't last and I don't want her to get hurt.'

'As far as I can see,' Frank said, 'they love each other.'

'Yes, I know. Or at least they're in love. It's a different thing, don't you think? And it doesn't last.'

Frank looked thoughtful.

'Well, it's an interesting idea to pursue — the different kinds of love and whether or not . . .'

'You've set him off again!' Bridie interrupted, laughing and shaking her head. 'The next thing we know he'll have a play about a love affair between an older woman and a young man.'

'Well,' Frank said, 'it would make a good story. And especially with all the family conflict it triggers off.' He was beginning to look intrigued. His eyes were filling with a glow and a hint of a smile that betrayed anticipation hovered about his mouth. 'It could even lead to violence if . . .'

'For goodness sake,' Bridie shouted, 'would you shut up and get back to your room, Frank!'

'All right. All right.' Frank rose from his chair. 'I'm going.' Already he had a faraway look. He wandered off, cup in hand, and disappeared back into his writing room.

Jennifer said, 'I thought that if the family met Bessie and Bessie met them — Sean's mum and dad I mean — they'd get on famously together and Bessie would come round to their point of view and . . .' She began to look a bit concerned. 'Maybe I haven't thought about it enough. But Bessie gets on so well with everybody and everybody likes her, I just thought . . .'

'Of course,' Bridie patted her hand. 'It'll all work out fine, you'll see. I'm sorry about Frank. He's always putting his foot in it. He's away in another world half the time. You've seen what he's like. Don't let him worry you. I don't.'

Nevertheless Jennifer couldn't help feeling a niggle of anxiety. She decided she might as well pay Bessie a visit. After all, she was only a couple of closes along the Crescent and Bessie might be offended if she just passed by without calling in to at least say hello.

Bessie was delighted to see her and rushed to put the kettle on.

'No, honestly,' Jennifer stopped her, 'I couldn't drink any more coffee just now. I've just had a cup with Bridie.'

'Are you sure?'

'Yes. I just didn't want to pass your door.'

'I'm so pleased to see you. Have you been out to Bearsden?'

'I'm on my way. Daddy collected my case and dress and everything yesterday. He wanted to collect me and take me over then as well but I'd one or two things still to do to the house.'

'It must be like a wee palace by now. You're only five minutes or so down the road but you might as well have been miles away for all any of us have seen of you lately.'

'I know, but once the wedding's over and Freddie and I come back from our honeymoon, you must come to the housewarming party.'

'And Sean?' Bessie queried.

'Oh, is that still on?'

'Jennifer, you know perfectly well how Sean and I feel about each other. He's coming with me to the wedding.'

'I was just wondering...' Jennifer hesitated and avoided Bessie's eyes. 'I mean, do you think that's wise... In the circumstances, I mean...'

'You invited him.'

'Mummy invited him. It was Bernard I insisted who must have an invitation. I was just thinking about you, Bessie. Sean's mother and father are quite understandably concerned about your relationship with Sean. I mean, you told me yourself.'

'I promise you, Jennifer, I'll be as nice to them as I possibly can.'

'But it's how they might be to you . . .'

'Oh, don't worry about that. I'm just going to concentrate on being a matron of honour you'll be proud of. It'll be a happy day, you'll see. Everyone will *want* to make it a happy day for you.'

Jennifer kissed her. 'As long as you're going to be all right,' she said.

'Your mother has bullied me into getting a new outfit. But I dug my heels in and refused to buy the matronly dress and coat she picked out. I've bought a dark royal blue velvet suit and a white frilly blouse to go with it. Very feminine, Sean says. I'd got trousers at first but he made me get a skirt instead.'

'That sounds nice, Bessie . . .' Then she added, somewhat uncertainly, 'And not too young.'

'If you like I'll try it on now to make sure it meets with your approval.' Bessie's tone held amusement.

'No, no. I'm sure you'll look fine.'

'And I haven't been near a tube of paint recently so you've no need to worry on that score.'

'Where's Sean just now?'

'Through in Edinburgh.' She sighed. 'Bernard keeps sending him on jobs away from Glasgow. I'm just hoping Bernard doesn't find any work abroad for Sean to do. If there's any kind of security job comes up in Australia, you can be sure Sean will be the one Bernard will pick to go.'

Jennifer thought that would be a good idea and the best thing that could happen but she refrained from saying so. Instead she changed the subject.

'The buffet supper Mummy has planned sounds wonderful. Freddie's really looking forward to it.'

'I'm going over on Friday night to help her get things organised.'

'That's kind of you, Bessie. Now, I'd better get over to Bearsden. Both Daddy and Freddie have insisted that I stop working in the house and just pamper myself until the wedding. Laura's made appointments for me in the local hairdresser and beauty salon. She's really kind. I'm so glad Daddy's got somebody nice this time. Mummy's all right in her own way,' she added hastily, 'but you know what I mean.'

Bessie laughed.

'Yes, I know what you mean, dear.' She went to the door with Jennifer. 'I'll see you at the wedding then?'

Jennifer smiled and waved goodbye. Going down the stairs she thought – yes, her mother *was* all right. She had her faults and weaknesses but then, who hadn't? Bessie had proved she was far from perfect. It was really very foolish and self-indulgent of her to be taking over Sean's life the way she was. But knowing Bessie, it wouldn't be a conscious selfishness. Her love for Sean was blinding her to what she was doing.

Then she remembered Bernard. If anyone could sort people out, and avoid trouble, he could.

LXII

ANDRINA WAS BLISSFULLY happy. The buffet was all organised. She'd written out a menu for her own benefit. The house was sparkling. She'd polished every corner. Her kitchen was large and had a dining area which had once been a bed-recess. A table in there would hold all the puddings. The Scotch trifle made with lashings of sherry wine was decorated with cherries and looked beautiful in her large crystal bowl. Then there were *crèmes brûlées*, strawberry gâteaux, fresh fruit salad, lemon torte and a chocolate mountain of profiteroles. And of course jelly for the children. All around the kitchen she'd spread platters of roast beef, fresh salmon decorated with cucumber, broccoli quiche, lentil bake, prawn, apple and celery salad, cold poached supreme of chicken set in a Chablis sauce with a lattice of leek and aspic jelly, and of course, green salad. In the sitting room there would be coffee, *petits fours* and chocolate mints. Bottles of white wine would be suitably chilled in the fridge and red wine would await uncorked at room temperature.

Andrina was looking forward to the event. She imagined how she would swan around making sure everyone enjoyed themselves. The occasion would be not just a great success, but a triumph. But there was even more to it than that. It was a smack in the eye for Paul Fisher. Although of course he wouldn't be there to see it. He'd never set foot in the flat since the day he'd been so insulting to her and walked out of her life. It was for good in every sense, she realised now. Clearly he had never appreciated her. She was well rid of him. Now she was extremely excited about Lester Morgan being at the wedding. So far she hadn't met him. She had meant to pop over to Bessie's on the evening he had been there to dinner.

318

Bessie was not the world's best cook and she'd prepared a wonderful pudding to take over to help Bessie out. Unfortunately, Freddie had arrived to collect Jennifer's case. He had been so flattering about her cooking that she felt she had to offer him supper, and he just stayed and stayed. It would have been so interesting to meet Lester before the wedding, more or less on her own, and she was disappointed she didn't manage it. But she was too polite, too good a hostess, to hasten Freddie away. Lester sounded very nice, as well as being a millionaire. It was the millionaire part that thrilled Andrina the most. Already she had been transported in her dreams, whisked off to America to live a life of luxury and to be pampered and adored as Lester's wife. She dreamed of furnishing a huge house in elegant Williamsburgh, of lying out on the patio sunbathing and sipping tall glasses of iced tea. She dreamed of queening it as a hostess to all the important people of the district and in the art world. She saw herself arm in arm with Lester and him gazing proudly down at her as they strolled into the theatre or to other large houses where they had been invited to dinner. It was a bit difficult to see him clearly in her mind's eye because she had not yet met him. But the description Bessie had given her was enough to create a picture. It was just a little hazy, that's all. It was her enjoyment of being his wife that mattered, the thrill of all the luxury, the petting and pampering. The sex.

In bed at night she vividly imagined them making love. It seemed ages since she'd been with a man and she longed with every passionate fibre of her being for a man to love her, caress her, penetrate her. So intense and vivid were her imaginings and such was the fever of her need that she gave herself an orgasm. Even in sleep she dreamed of being happily married to Lester. By the next day she felt convinced that not only did she already know him, but their impending marriage was a fact. She was singing about the house in seventh heaven. She had always known that she was meant for better things. She could hardly believe that she'd once been tied to a boring, poverty-stricken schoolteacher. Or that she'd once been foolish enough to fall in love with a bully of a man who was still the same coarse, foul-mouthed bouncer in pubs and clubs that he'd always been.

When Bessie arrived with Sean and the food that had been stored in Bessie's freezer, she had become so carried away with thoughts of her happy future that she almost told them about it. But they were full of talk about Jennifer's wedding.

Now Bessie was saying,

'Bridie was telling me that Frank was putting his foot in it and worrying Jennifer.'

'Worry her? How could he worry her?'

'Apparently he thought you'd made a brave mix of guests.'

Andrina shrugged.

'If he meant Robert and Bernard, I couldn't care less. I'll be perfectly charming to both of them, I can assure you.'

Sean gave her one of his hard dimpled smiles. She noticed how strong and white his teeth were. When he smiled he'd almost a predatory look. It reminded her of Bernard in a way. Although it was Bernard's eyes that made him look wicked.

'I think,' he said, 'Frank was meaning how my family would act to Bessie. And that might cause an atmosphere.'

'Oh!' Andrina felt herself flush. She'd forgotten that neither Bessie nor Sean would know about her affair with Bernard. 'Of course. That's what I meant too. I'll see that everyone mixes well and there's a lovely friendly atmosphere. My parties have always been a great success and this one will be no exception, I assure you.'

'Do you want me to stay overnight?' Bessie asked. 'And give you a hand in the morning?'

'No, no, dear. Just help me unpack these things and lay one or two items out to defrost. That roll of meat, for instance, will take absolutely ages. It's as hard as a rock.'

'It's far too much work for you, Andrina. I'll come back for an hour or two tomorrow. Even if it's just to wash dishes and hoover the place.'

'Oh, all right, dear. That would be a help.'

She gave them tea and dainty sandwiches and fairy cakes after they'd unpacked everything and put some of the things in the fridge and others out on platters. She longed for them to go away again. Not because she didn't like them. Indeed she was very fond of them both. But the secret loving way they kept looking at each other and the way Sean often held Bessie's hand or put his arm around her shoulders made Andrina feel lonely. She needed to get back to Lester. Visions of him and their happy future together obsessed her the whole night, and the next morning.

'Are you all right?' Bessie asked eventually. They were having a cup of tea before Bessie went home to dress. 'You're awful quiet. You're not losing Jennifer, you know. You're not losing a daughter, as they say, you're gaining a son.'

'What? Oh yes. No, I'm fine.'

'Well,' Bessie finished her tea, 'I'd better be off. Sean will be back soon and we're picking Lester up at his hotel.'

'I must have a bath with my new bath salts. They have a gorgeous perfume. And I'll take my time and have my make-up and hair just perfect.'

Bessie laughed.

'I'm sure you will. I'd better rush. I'll pick up a taxi outside.'

'Oh, will I phone for one for you? Or do you want me to drive you home?'

'No, no, not at all. There's always plenty of taxis cruising about. You just relax now and enjoy your bath.'

They kissed, and when Bessie had gone, Andrina danced along the hall, round and round, making her skirt swirl out. She never wore trousers – she had such shapely legs, it would be a pity to hide them.

She sprinkled a generous amount of bath salts into the steaming water, undressed, climbed in and lay back with eyes closed.

It was while she was carefully applying her mascara that she remembered her mother. How shocked she would have been to see her now.

She sighed. It was surprising that Sophie had ever managed to conceive. Was it because of her unnatural attitude to sex that her mother hated the child that was the result of that conception?

Andrina leaned forward, chin cupped in hands, and gazed at herself in the mirror. Her mother had hated her. She could face that now. But still she could not understand why. She felt overwhelmingly sad about the coldness she could still feel emanating towards her from Sophie, even from beyond the grave. Probably the lack of love from her mother was the reason she'd turned to Bernard with such passion and appreciation. She could even face the fact of her love for Bernard now. If it hadn't been for her mother, she would have married him. Looking back she realised that Bernard had loved her too. She could have wept. It was only with a determined effort that she managed to banish her mother from her thoughts. She raised her chin and pulled back her shoulders.

She was a beautiful, loving and lovable woman. And this was her happy day. This was the first day of the rest of her life.

She donned her ivory satin underwear. Then the off-the-shoulder ivory two-piece slithered on. She perched the wide-brimmed ivory straw hat on to her glossy crown of auburn hair. Finally her high-heeled ivory shoes complemented her dainty feet and shapely legs. A choker of pearls, high against her creamy throat, made an elegant finishing touch. She stared with satisfaction at her shining reflection in the long mirror. She gave a happy twirl.

With adrenalin pulsing through her veins and almost making her float through the air, she set off to stun everyone in the company, especially Lester Morgan.

LXIII

JENNIFER WAS SO excited that she had become confused, uncertain, even apprehensive. Before, she'd been so busy with working in the house, she had not had any time to think. She hadn't realised how tired she'd become; it wasn't until she'd arrived at Laura's house in Bearsden that the exhaustion hit her. Far from making her feel better, loafing about with nothing to do made her lethargic and depressed. Laura and Robert were out at work during the day. At least on the Thursday and Friday, and it was then that Jennifer sat in the quiet bungalow with time to think.

It occurred to her for the first time that Freddie was quite a few years older than her. She was still only a young girl. She had all her life before her. She was about to start her teacher training course at Jordanhill College. She got on well with Freddie, of course. Who wouldn't? They were good friends. But was that a good enough reason to get married? Was she more in love with Freddie's house than with Freddie? Her mind shuddered back to the nightmare of being homeless and struggling to survive on the streets. No way could she ever risk going through such a scenario again. She longed for the permanent safety of the flat in Roxburgh Street. Did she long for the permanence of Freddie?

Laura had persuaded her to go and have her hair done, plus a manicure and a face make-up on the Saturday. Really nervous to the point of visible agitation by this time, she'd cried out, 'I like my hair long and straight, and I like my fringe. I don't want it changed. It wouldn't be me. I don't want a whole lot of make-up on to try and hide my freckles either. That's the way I am.'

'No one's wanting to change you, darling,' Laura said. 'It'll be a nice treat for you to have your hair shampooed and your make-up and nails done, that's all. You'll be able to relax in the salon and then just come back here and put on your dress and veil.'

It was a white cotton dress with a high Victorian-type stand-up collar edged with a little pleated frill and leg of mutton sleeves. A simple coronet of flowers topped her veil and she was to carry a posy of matching flowers.

She'd gone to the hairdressing and beauty salon, but with bad grace. She felt in what her mother would call 'one of her moods'. She stared with a mixture of gloom and despair at her reflection in the hairdresser's mirror. A freckly-faced wee girl, that's all she was. What on earth was she getting herself into? She didn't want to get tied down in marriage or anything else. She even began to think of her rootless time in London as a sort of freedom.

How could she cope with studying at college, cleaning and cooking and running a house, and looking after a man? Panic set in. She couldn't do it. She suddenly felt childish. She wanted her mother. She longed for her, and needed her as she had longed for her and needed her when she had been a small child. Then she remembered with terrible sadness that her mother had never been there for her when she was a small child. Andrina had always been obsessed with Andrina, and Andrina's needs and problems.

Jennifer could have wept then as she stared at her reflection, and later when she looked into the long mirror in Laura's house. Never before had she felt such desolation and loneliness. Her life stared back at her. Somehow she'd always been either at the mercy of other people or of circumstances.

'You look lovely,' her father said. 'I'm proud of you.'

He didn't know her any more than her mother did. He knew what he wanted, though. He wanted his safe, happy life with Laura. He *liked* being tied down. She doubted if he'd ever experienced true aloneness. Even as a small child she'd felt alone in spirit. Her father had been totally committed to caring about other children, children he called 'deprived'. He had been too busy to notice that she was being neglected and deprived. Oh, not of material things. Andrina had never failed to dress her like a little lady. But always, Jennifer felt, the priority of their love and understanding, as well as their time, had been for other people.

On her way back from the hairdresser's, she passed her granny's house and her sadness deepened a hundredfold. There was nothing for her here now. Once she was twenty-one, she would get the money her granny had left her and she could buy a flat, start a new life in Edinburgh or anywhere.

Yet here she was, doing nothing in her mounting agitation and confusion, as her father and Laura led her from the house. Her vision was blurred by her veil. Her hearing was all but blotted out by the panicky thumping of her heart. She didn't want to hurt Freddie. She didn't want to hurt or embarrass anybody, or to let them down – even her mother. Andrina had gone to so much trouble to organise a wonderful reception.

But oh, the whole thing made her feel sick at heart. She kept asking herself what she was doing and why. The only assurance and comfort she could find as the bridal car sped towards her mother's branch of the Church of Jesus in Rose Street in town was the fact that she could still say no. When the minister asked if she'd take this man to be her wedded husband, she'd say 'No!'

And she'd say no because when it came down to it, she was afraid that one day she'd suffer the same hurt from him that she'd suffered from her parents, especially her mother, the one person she'd once imagined most close to her, and whom she'd most trusted. No, she didn't want to be in that situation ever again. She'd rather be on her own. Safely withdrawn into herself, uncommunicative, uncommitted.

Before she realised it, she was at the church. The car had stopped and her father was helping her out. She was allowing him to arrange her veil and tuck her arm through his.

The organ music of 'Here Comes the Bride' was filling the church. Everyone was standing and looking round at her. Then she saw Freddie. He too was looking round at her. *Her* Freddie. The man in whose arms she'd already lain in the silent darkness of the bedroom in Roxburgh Street. The man who'd already promised to love and cherish and look after her and who had already kept that promise. She was not afraid of him. A smile came like a warm light to her face and with it, a glow of happiness. Freddie wasn't just her best friend. She loved him. And she knew, by the warm light in his eyes, he loved her too. The strength of that love gave her courage. She suddenly felt lucky. She would never need to be alone again. With Freddie by her side, she could cope with her mother, she could tackle anything.

The ceremony progressed and she said 'I do' with total conviction and great joy in her heart.

Then they were officially man and wife.

'This,' she told him as they left the church arm in arm, 'is the happiest day of my life.'

'Mine too,' Freddie said, squeezing her arm. 'Definitely mine too.'

Into the car now, she and Freddie with eyes only for each other. Eventually, however, Freddie said,

'I'm starving. I'm looking forward to the reception, aren't you?'

LXIV

'COULD YOU BEAT it?' Bev cried out. 'I could kill that woman! Cheerfully kill her.'

They were on the way to the reception in Monteith Row in Sean's car.

'It was a bit much, right enough,' Bessie agreed.

'A bit much? A bit *much*? The woman wore white at her daughter's wedding.'

'Ivory,' Bessie corrected mildly.

'White, ivory, what's the difference? Her and that big hat as well. She tried to outshine the bride, steal all Jennifer's limelight, spoil her own daughter's big day.'

Sean intervened.

'Oh, I doubt if it spoiled anything for Jennifer and Freddie. They're so wrapped up in each other they wouldn't even notice Andrina.'

'Everyone else did, though. You couldn't miss the woman. And Jennifer and Freddie certainly won't be able to miss her at the reception. She'll be swanning about showing off all the food she's made. I've a good mind to spill some more champagne.'

'Don't you dare,' Bessie warned.

'Never in my whole life have I ever known such a blindly selfish, egotistical woman.'

'Will you calm down and forget about Andrina. Just try to enjoy the rest of the day for Jennifer's sake.'

'Aye, OK, OK. But it's not going to be easy.'

It's not going to be easy for any of us, Bessie thought. She wasn't particularly looking forward to spending several hours in close proximity with Sean's family. Frank and Bridie were her neighbours and friends, but his parents, and his sister, his grandmother and Bernard were a different matter. She'd seen them in the church. She and Bev and Sean had been sitting in a different pew from the rest of the family and she didn't have the chance to speak to them. They had stared at her with undisguised hostility. Her heart quailed at being confined in the same room as them at Andrina's house.

Courage, Bessie, she kept thinking. The cars drew up one after the other in Monteith Row and everybody piled out and climbed the stairs. The children, noisy and jumping about with energy; the adults polite and restrained. Once in the house, and all crowded into the kitchen, she was introduced to Sean's mother and Bernard's wife, Helen. Helen was elegant in a honey-coloured two-piece and had some warmth in her manner, unlike Bernard, and his brother's wife. Old Martha was eagerly instructing Michael about what food to bring her from the mouth-watering spread. She was a mountain in brown silk topped with a hat decorated with artificial yellow roses.

Andrina, now without the cartwheel hat to hide the shining glory of her ruby-coloured hair, was bright-eyed and bushy-tailed and urging everyone to collect plates and napkins and enjoy the buffet. At one point, while Bessie was trying to ignore the black looks aimed towards her and was attempting to swallow down some salad, Sean's mother, resplendent in an apricot Crimplene dress and pearls, approached, plate in hand.

'I'd like a word with you – from one mother to another.'

In desperation, Bessie looked around for Sean, but his back was to her. He was laughing and talking with Jennifer and Freddie at the other side of the room. Jennifer looked like an excited little girl in her white cotton dress with its Victorian-style high frilled neckline. Freddie had a protective arm around her.

'You're a mother yourself,' Caroline went on, 'and as a mother you must know how I feel. Every mother wants the best for her children . . .'

She had obviously decided to hammer home the mother theme. Bessie groaned inside.

'As a mother, you must know what it's like to worry about your children's future. You want them to be happy and to have a family of their own one day. It's the natural way of things, don't you think?' She paused for a reaction but Bessie was already beginning to feel depressed and it took her a long minute to get up enough energy to speak.

'I understand how you must be feeling.'

'Well, why are you doing this to me? But most important of all, why are you trying to ruin Sean's life?'

'I'm not trying got ruin Sean's life. I love him.'

'Love him? You don't love him. You don't know what love is.'

'How can you say that? You know nothing about me.'

'I know you didn't stick with the man you promised to love and cherish until death do you part. You walked out on your husband.'

'You don't know the circumstances.'

'I know my circumstances. My husband's an alcoholic. I went through hell with him while he was drinking. There were times when he'd spent all his wages on drink and me and the children had nothing to eat. But I stuck by him. I did what I believed to be right for him. *That's* love.'

The Quaker William Penn had once said, 'Never marry but for love . . .' She had not loved Peter, that had been the problem. But oh, she truly loved Sean.

'What's between Sean and me is different altogether from the relationship I had with my husband.'

'Oh, that's quite obvious. Sean's only a boy, for a start. That's your daughter over there, isn't it?'

Bessie nodded.

'She's not much younger than Sean, is she?'

Bessie gazed helplessly over at her daughter. Daisy was even more like her Aunt Moira now than she'd been as a child. The same severe hairstyle, the same hornrimmed glasses. Her husband Nigel suited her perfectly. He was a right old-fashioned-looking berk as well. Bessie immediately felt ashamed of harbouring such uncharitable thoughts and, catching her daughter's eye at that moment, she smiled warmly across at her.

I'm glad, I really am, that Daisy and Nigel are well suited and happy together. And I'm glad, truly glad, that they both seem to get on so well with Peter.

Caroline said,

'She's married a man a few years older than her, hasn't she? And that's as it should be. And, God willing, she and her husband will be blessed with a family one day. And that's how it should be. That's right and natural. You're denying Sean the natural right to be a father as well as everything else.'

'I really don't think,' Bessie said in desperation, 'that all this is any of your business.'

'What?' Caroline gasped incredulously. 'I'm his mother. I carried him in my womb. I watched him grow up. I've loved him and taken care of him for all the years of his childhood. And you can stand there and say what happens to him is none of my business? My own flesh and blood?'

'Sean's not a child any longer. He's a man and how he lives his life is his own business. And how I live my life is my business.'

'Oh really?' Caroline raised a brow. 'I thought you were a religious woman.'

Bessie flushed.

'I'm a Quaker, if that's what you mean.'

'And how, tell me, can you square your present behaviour with your religious beliefs?'

She couldn't. All she could say was, 'We love each other. I can't see how, by loving someone, I'm doing anything wrong.'

'Oh, can't you? Well, if you profess to be a true Christian, I think you should look at the situation and your feelings for Sean again. No doubt it's most enjoyable and flattering to be having a romantic relationship with a handsome, virile man so much younger than yourself. But is it the right thing for Sean? He'll still be in his prime when you're an old woman. Is that the future you want for him? Looking after an old woman?'

Memories of the horrors of nursing Granda flooded Bessie's mind. She felt sick to her very soul.

'Will you excuse me?' she said very politely. 'There are other people I'd like to talk to.'

She moved away with as much dignity as she could draw around herself. She strolled across the room between the crush of children, eyes blurred, not knowing where to go. Bridie was intent on catching one of the children who was hugging a bowl of strawberry jelly to himself and dodging about. 'Frank,' she was crying out, 'get that bowl off him! Other folk want a share of that jelly.'

Bessie smiled at them in passing. *Please don't let me cry.*

Sean was still deep in conversation with Jennifer and Freddie. Three young people having a good time together. She couldn't see Bev anywhere, Andrina was over in the corner smiling and fluttering her eyelashes up at Lester Morgan. They were obviously having a good time too.

Bessie joined Andrina and Lester. Smiling, she said to Andrina, 'The food is delicious.'

Lester agreed enthusiastically.

'I was just telling Andrina what a talented woman she is. That's a talent too – creating such a wonderful meal, *and* being such a charming hostess.'

'Oh absolutely.' Bessie struggled to keep the bright smile on her face. 'I always enjoy coming to visit Andrina. The only thing is I eat so much I put on pounds of weight.'

Lester threw back his head and gave a resounding laugh.

'I was just telling the lady that I'd be as heavy as a prize bull if I came here very often.'

Andrina gazed starry-eyed up at him.

'You can come here as often as you wish, Lester. I admire a man who can appreciate good food.'

'I appreciate all the food and the beautiful things in life, honey. Good food, beautiful women. And believe me, I've seen a few beautiful women in my time, but none that can hold a candle to you.'

Andrina flushed and gave him one of her shy, sideways smiles. 'Oh Lester,' she said in her softest, sexiest, most inviting of voices.

Bessie felt extraneous. She moved away without either of them noticing. She slipped out of the ripple of noise in the kitchen into quietness of the hall. She tried the bathroom door, hoping to find solace in isolation. It was locked. Unexpectedly the tears spilled over as she turned away.

'Darling.' Sean strode towards her and pulled her into his arms. 'What has she been saying? When I asked Gran if she'd seen you, she said Mother had been talking to you.'

Bessie felt ashamed of her lack of control but she couldn't speak, couldn't stop the tears.

Sean's eyes glittered with anger.

'How dare anyone upset you like this. Wait there.'

He strode back into the kitchen before Bessie could put out a hand to stop him. She was in a panic of distress now. Hastily she tried to dry her tears. Her feet faltered towards the kitchen but she didn't feel composed enough to face anyone, far less intervene between Sean and his mother. She turned into the sitting room. At first she thought she was alone with her chaotic thoughts, then she noticed Bev sitting over in the corner, glass in hand.

'That's not alcohol, I hope.' Bessie was immediately jolted out of her own concerns.

'Don't start nagging at me and spoiling everything,' Bev said. 'I couldn't toast Jennifer's happiness in orange juice, for God's sake. I can't stomach the stuff anyway. Never could. What's up with your face? You look as if you need a drink.'

'Never mind about me. You're not just toasting Jennifer's happiness and you know it. You'd be through there beside her if you were, not sitting through here beside a bottle.'

'Aw shut up! Stop being such a wet blanket. Away through with your boyfriend where you belong, and think yourself lucky.'

'Don't try to kid me that you're happy, Bev. Drink doesn't make you happy.'

'Shut up, I said. What do you know about me? What do you know about anything?'

'Come on, Bev. I'll take you home.'

'Piss off. I've had enough of you. I'm going, but I'm going on my own. You stay with lover boy.'

'Bev, please . . .'

'Get your hands off me.' She grabbed the bottle and lurched for the door. Bessie hurried after her, and at the front door again tried to physically detain her friend. But suddenly Bev swung the bottle round and crashed it against Bessie's head. The bottle didn't break but Bessie, knocked back against the lintel of the door, felt as if her skull had been fractured. For a few minutes everything went black. When she came to she was sitting on the floor in a daze.

Blinking and taking a few deep breaths, she managed to pull herself back to her feet.

Far away, in the distance it seemed, were the happy sounds of a celebration. Clutching at the doorway, Bessie tried to steady herself.

LXV

THEY'D RETURNED HOME after the reception and been out again to cruise around in Sean's car searching for Bev.

'Look,' Sean said eventually. 'Enough's enough. Let it be, Bessie.' He swung the car towards home.

'Maybe if we had a walk through Glasgow Green. I was just thinking she might have gone straight from Andrina's into the Green.'

'We drove through there.'

'I know but maybe on foot we'd have a better chance . . .'

'No, Bessie. You've done all you could. It's time to call it a day. And I don't mean just for today either. It's time you left Bev to find her own salvation.'

'She wasn't even wearing her coat and it's a bitter, cold night.'

'Forget her, Bessie.'

'How can I forget her?'

'Try.' He stopped the car and helped her out. Then they climbed the stairs together arm in arm.

Once inside the flat, he helped her off with her cape.

'Cheer up, darling. It's supposed to be a happy day. Be happy for Jennifer. Be happy for us.'

'How can I be happy for us after causing a quarrel between you and your mother?'

'It wasn't a quarrel. I just told her quietly, but very firmly, that she must not interfere.'

He led her through to the sitting room and poured out a couple of glasses of whisky.

'Get this down you and you'll feel better. Remember you promised to set the date for our wedding after we'd been to Jennifer's.'

'I said we'd talk about us. But not tonight, Sean. Not with all this about Bev on my mind. Not to mention the bump on my head.'

'Don't remind me of that, Bessie. I could kill her for doing that to you. I wish you'd let me take you to a doctor.'

'No, I'll be OK after a good night's sleep. Tomorrow . . .'

'I'm off to London tomorrow.'

'But only for a couple of days. Sean, please, I just can't think about anything tonight.'

He put up his hands in good-humoured capitulation.

'OK. You win. We'll get everything fixed up as soon as I get back.'

She lay beside him in bed loving him for his consideration in not attempting to have sex with her when she was so tired and worried. Then loving him so much she wanted to give herself to him heart and soul and body. As if it were for the very last time. She turned to him and began kissing his dear face, his dark eyes, his strong taut features. Her lips moved into his neck and then lovingly over his firm body. He responded by showering her with tender kisses until their bodies and hearts and souls merged.

They fell asleep in each other's arms. In the morning, as usual, he gave her breakfast in bed.

'You spoil me,' she told him.

He dropped a kiss on her head.

'I love you.'

'I know. Being with you has been the happiest, most wonderful time in my life. I never knew before what it was like to be loved and cherished and looked after, as you've loved and cherished and looked after me. You've made me feel worthwhile.'

'You *are* worthwhile, darling.'

'Thank you, Sean.'

'Why the sad face then? We're only at the beginning of our relationship. We've years and years – the rest of our lives – to spend loving each other.'

She raised her face for his kiss.

'You'd better go, Sean. You'll miss your train.'

'OK. See you when I get back.'

'Yes. See you when you get back.'

His firm tread across the hall. The front door opened and shut. Then the empty silence of the house engulfed her. Absently she drank a cup of tea, then put the tray aside and lay back on the pillows. Her mind was lost in confusion. Her heart thumped with fear.

She got up eventually, dressed and went to Meeting. There she sat among Friends in the waiting silence. And gradually, in the peace, her spirit calmed. She waited for the tea and biscuits and friendly chat. She lingered, not wanting to leave the familiar sanctuary and not wanting to part with the others, longing to siphon off some of their courage and spiritual strength. Yet all the time knowing that it was not from them or from anyone that courage and strength must come. She slipped away on her own at last. She walked through the park, hoping yet without hope of finding Bev. *Please have mercy on Bev and keep her from harm.* She took the bus over to see Andrina but Andrina was not at home. She returned to Botanic Crescent and called in at Bridie's house rather than return to the solitude of her own.

Bridie's house was jolly and noisy and didn't give her any opportunity to think.

Frank called over the rabble, 'Sean's away until tomorrow then?'

'Yes, late tomorrow afternoon.'

'Why don't you come round to us for lunch, then? Come early. It'll pass your time and keep you from being lonely.'

'That's right,' Bridie agreed. 'I don't like to think of you in that big flat all by yourself. No word of Bev yet, I suppose?'

'No.' Bessie shook her head. 'Sean and I looked all over the place and no sign of her.'

'She's maybe gone back to London,' said Frank.

'I was wondering about that. There's a man here that she wants to keep clear of . . .' She sighed. 'But I don't know. Poor Bev. It doesn't bear thinking about. I wish I could have helped her.'

'Bessie,' Frank protested, 'nobody could have done more. I don't know anyone else who would have put up with her.'

'And after all,' Bridie cut in, 'she was nothing to you.' Then, seeing Bessie's look of surprise, she added, 'No relation, I mean. It wasn't as if she was your sister.'

Later that evening Andrina and Lester arrived at Bessie's flat. Andrina was bubbling over with happiness. Leaving Lester in the sitting room for a moment, she ran through to the kitchen on the pretext of helping Bessie to bring in the supper trolley. She wanted to have a private word.

'You'll never guess!' she whispered to Bessie.

'You slept with Lester last night and he was wonderful?'

'Yes, but not just that. He's asked me to go back to the States with him.'

'That was quick work.' She sounded sarcastic and she hadn't meant to be. She had slept with Peter the first time they'd been alone. She genuinely hoped Andrina would have better luck than she did afterwards.

'You've agreed?' she asked, but knowing that Andrina had jumped at the chance.

'Of course! We're crazy about each other. It was love at first sight, Bessie. Oh, I'm so happy.'

Bessie kissed her.

'I'm glad, Andrina. I really am.'

'You must come with us. You ought to be at the exhibition. Oh, think of all the fascinating people you'll meet, Bessie. Lester knows lots of artists and people you'd be interested in. Oh do come!'

Bessie smiled. 'Maybe I will. I'm very happy for you, Andrina.'

Next day Bridie wasn't so generous.

'Trust her,' she rolled her eyes, 'to get a rich old man with a bad cough. Next thing we know she'll be back, a wealthy widow queening over us all.'

Bessie shook her head.

'We don't even know if they're going to get married.'

'What do you bet?' Bridie said. 'She won't let him go, Bessie. She's landed him. Now all she has to do is haul him in.'

Bessie laughed.

'A willing victim, though.'

'Yes,' Frank agreed. 'Lester will go to the grave exhausted but after having enjoyed every last minute of his life.'

Bessie glanced at her watch.

'I'd better be going along and getting organised for Sean coming home. I haven't done a thing in the house, not even washed a dish, since before the wedding.'

Frank got up and saw her to the door along with Bridie. 'Oh, I'm sure Sean won't even notice the house. You're all he cares about,' he said.

The words echoed in Bessie's heart as she walked the short distance to her own flat.

Yes, he cares about me. And I care about him. I've been thinking and thinking about what is best for Sean. I know what would be best for me. It would be sheer joy for me to spend the rest of my life with him, to be loved and looked after by him.

That set me thinking. There is a purpose in everything. There was a purpose in me looking after Granda. I learned exactly what it was like.

I couldn't do that to Sean. He would look after me until the very end. I know that. But I couldn't submit him to such an ordeal.

I love him, you see. And I want him to have the very best in life. Not just for now but always.

I want him to fall in love again and with a young woman who can give him the love and loving children he deserves.

But oh, how can I find the courage?

But find it she must.

She'd never considered herself a religious woman. The bigotry of her mother's church upset her. She'd once gone to a service in a Baptist church and cringed with embarrassment when people kept sticking up their hands and yelling hallelujah. She'd more than once visited a Catholic church with Bridie and Frank and the ritual there had felt equally alien to her.

But she did believe in trying to understand the beliefs and the needs of others. To her the Quaker idea of 'that of God in everyone', whatever their God, was what she personally felt most at home with. Sometimes it was hard to find that small light in the darkness of herself or in others but it was something she felt was worth trying to find, and something always to be respected.

She struggled to find the light in her darkness now as she waited for Sean's return. By the time he arrived she had at least found enough strength to tell him that their relationship was over.

He was incredulous at first.

'Darling, you don't know what you're saying. We love each other.'

'Yes, I know. But one day you'll love someone else, Sean. You'll be happy again and you'll have a family and live a normal life.'

'A normal life? What are you talking about? The only normality I want is my life with you.'

'Sean, please try not to make it more difficult for me.'

'Are you trying to tell me you don't love me? Is that it?'

'Oh no. Oh no, Sean, never think that. I love you more than life itself and I'll always love you. It's because I love you that I'm letting you go.'

'Darling . . .'

He came towards her, arms outstretched, but she stopped him in his tracks by the sudden harshness of her tone.

'Just go! Take your overnight case. I'll pack and send the rest of your things out to the cottage tomorrow.'

'They've made you do this,' he cried out. 'They've been speaking to you again.' He was agitated now. His distress was twitching at his facial muscles, fevering his skin.

'Nobody has made me do anything, Sean. I have decided for myself. Now please walk out of here and don't come back.'

'Oh Bessie . . .'

She could see him fighting to contain his tears, struggling to be manly. But he was only a boy. She wanted to take him in her arms and comfort him, mingle her tears with his. Instead she turned away.

'Goodbye Sean.'

She went through to her studio and shut the door. She heard the silence in the rest of the house before the outside door clicked shut.

Only then did she allow the sound of her sobbing to escape.

She picked up her brushes. She didn't need a photograph of Sean in order to paint his portrait. The picture of him was etched for ever in her memory. Still weeping but with the greatest of care and concentration, she began putting paint on canvas. She had given him love. Now she was giving him a kind of immortality.

END

HOLD ME FOREVER
Margaret Thomson Davis

For Andrina McPherson, a teenager growing up in the Glasgow of the 1950s and 60s, Bernard O'Maley is exciting company, his stolen kisses an intoxicating glimpse of forbidden pleasure. Then her puritanical mother forbids their relationship because Bernard is too 'physical' and Andrina – having spent her young life craving her mother's approval – gives him up immediately.

But Bernard remains determined to make Andrina his wife. As he ruthlessly pursues the only woman he will ever love, Andrina is torn apart by her divided loyalties to her lover, her husband, her child, but above all else, to her mother . . .

Margaret Thomson Davis has crafted a spellbinding tale of obsessive passion and its far reaching consequences that will enthrall the reader to the very last page.

'She makes her characters spark with life'
THE GLASGOW HERALD

KISS ME NO MORE

Margaret Thomson Davis

She is hypnotic, misguided and beautiful, no one is immune to her, least of all Bernard O'Maley who has been in love for as long as he can remember . . .

But Andrina McPherson is married and her steadfast, likeable husband will not put up with her behaviour for ever – especially when another woman shows him a first glimpse of real happiness.

Caught between an obsessive need to please her puritanical mother, Sophie, and a desperate passion for the very man Sophie hates most, Andrina walks a tightrope between triumph and disaster changing everybody's lives as she does so.

'She makes her characters spark with life'
THE GLASGOW HERALD

'The stylish, well observed work of this born storyteller is a cut above the rest'
GLASGOW EVENING TIMES

ALL THAT GLITTERS
Catrin Collier

Once a callboy, Haydn Powell returns to his native Pontypridd as the summer season's star. It is his dream come true, but it soon sours when he finds his family divided. Seeking consolation in the theatre's free-living society, he is nevertheless drawn to Jane Jones, the usherette. Influenced by a different world, burdened by bitter secrets and haunted by poverty, Jane is all too aware of the forces waiting in the wings, ready to destroy the new life she has made.

It is a time of personal drama and national crisis. For Haydn's brother Eddie, a champion boxer with a violent temper both in and out of the ring. For Jenny Griffiths, Haydn's childhood sweetheart, who loves one brother but turns to another. And for the entire community, committed to another devastating war so soon after the first; a war which will change their lives forever.

All That Glitters is a superb follow-up to Catrin Collier's highly popular *Hearts of Gold*, *One Blue Moon* and *A Silver Lining*.

SUCH SWEET SORROW

Catrin Collier

Pontypridd 1939. War-time austerity, air raids, blackouts and tensions strain family and community loyalties to breaking point. Ignoring his sweetheart Tina Ronconi's pleas, William Powell volunteers for the Welsh Guards. It is as difficult for those left behind as for those who leave.

For William's sister, Diana, divided from her beloved Tony Ronconi by a secret, and Wyn Rees, ostracised for his homosexuality, in whom she confides. For Bethan, Laura and Alma who wave their husbands goodbye, maybe for the last time. For Jenny, abandoned the day after her wedding to Eddie Powell, who refuses even to answer her letters. And for a small group of English conchies conscripted to work in the pits, one of whom is fervently loved by young Gina Ronconi.

As war fever sets in, so the persecution of 'enemy aliens' begins, and even the Ronconis face internment. Then news comes that the Allies are retreating and the Welsh Guards are fighting a rearguard action at Dunkirk. Some will return, many will not – and even for those who do, life will never be the same again.

'A page-turner . . . a terrific read' **Susan Sallis**